Raves for the novels of

Maggie A̶

Pants on Fire

"A witty, smart debut."
—*Daily Mail*

"Fabulously glamorous . . . highly entertaining."
—*Heat*

"Wickedly funny and realistic . . . the perfect read for any girl who's ever wondered if the grass might be greener on the other side of the world."
—*OK!*

Mad About the Boy

"A bubbly concoction of bitchiness, humor, glamour, and eccentricity written with great verve and enthusiasm."
—*Sunday Mirror*

Titles by Maggie Alderson

HANDBAGS AND GLADRAGS

PANTS ON FIRE

Pants
on
Fire

MAGGIE ALDERSON

B
BERKLEY BOOKS, NEW YORK

THE BERKLEY PUBLISHING GROUP
Published by the Penguin Group
Penguin Group (USA) Inc.
375 Hudson Street, New York, New York 10014, USA
Penguin Group (Canada), 90 Eglinton Avenue East, Suite 700, Toronto, Ontario M4P 2Y3, Canada
(a division of Pearson Penguin Canada Inc.)
Penguin Books Ltd., 80 Strand, London WC2R 0RL, England
Penguin Group Ireland, 25 St. Stephen's Green, Dublin 2, Ireland (a division of Penguin Books Ltd.)
Penguin Group (Australia), 250 Camberwell Road, Camberwell, Victoria 3124, Australia
(a division of Pearson Australia Group Pty. Ltd.)
Penguin Books India Pvt. Ltd., 11 Community Centre, Panchsheel Park, New Delhi—110 017, India
Penguin Books (NZ), cnr Airborne and Rosedale Roads, Albany, Auckland 1310, New Zealand
(a division of Pearson New Zealand Ltd.)
Penguin Books (South Africa) (Pty.) Ltd., 24 Sturdee Avenue, Rosebank, Johannesburg 2196,
South Africa

Penguin Books Ltd., Registered Offices: 80 Strand, London WC2R 0RL, England

This is a work of fiction. Names, characters, places, and incidents either are the product of the author's imagination or are used fictitiously, and any resemblance to actual persons, living or dead, business establishments, events, or locales is entirely coincidental.

PRINTING HISTORY
Penguin Books Australia Ltd edition / 2000
Penguin Books Ltd edition / 2001
Berkley trade paperback edition / September 2005

Library of Congress Cataloging-in-Publication Data

Alderson, Maggie.
    Pants on fire / Maggie Alderson.—Berkley trade pbk. ed.
        p. cm.
    ISBN 0-425-20571-1
        1. British—Australia—Fiction. 2. Separation (Psychology)—Fiction. 3. Australia—Fiction.
I. Title.

PR6101.L44P36 2005
823'.92—dc22

                                                                        2005047824

PRINTED IN THE UNITED STATES OF AMERICA

10 9 8 7 6 5 4 3 2 1

In memory of
Douglas Alderson

acknowledgments

I wish to thank the following people without whom this book would not have been possible:

The very wonderful Julie Gibbs—a jewel among women. Fiona Daniels and Hannah Robson for assiduous editing and life support—one Skip, one Pom, two treasures. Debra Billson for another fab cover. And all the Penguins, especially Gabrielle Coyne, for being so delightful to work with. Valerie and Tim Olsen for lending me Bower Bird Cottage, a very special place where much of this book was written and the bower bird came to see me. My mother Peggy for not complaining too much about the amount of time I spent holed up in her study and my sister Mary for reading the result with her legal-eagle eye. Mia Freedman, Wendy Squires and Lisa Wilkinson for the hilarious year at *Cleo* and Paula Joye for keeping the flame. Josephine Fairley for being such a very good friend. My lady writer pals for advice and friendship: Jessica Adams, Kathy Lette and Karen Moline. And Helen Garner for precious words of encouragement. John Alexander for allowing me to leave the *Herald* on a long piece of elastic. Greg Hywood and Paul McGeough for allowing me to take more unpaid leave to finish this book. Everyone in Sydney who has ever invited me to a party—especially Deeta Colvin for four unforgettable Cointreau Balls. Spikey Carr for the gallery. And darling Popi, for being there. Smiling.

Kookaburra sits on the electric wire,
Jumping up and down with his pants on fire.

Children's rhyme, Australian

Chapter One

Of course an erect penis is all very well at the end of a party, rather to be desired generally, but it's not the first thing you expect to see when you enter the room. Yet there it was, in all its concupiscent glory, on the head of a man with a small goatee beard.

I'd been feeling a tad conspicuous in my own headgear coming along the road but, on seeing this creation, my two-foot halo of flamingo-pink feathers, cunningly fashioned out of three cheap feather boas, suddenly seemed a bit tame.

"Well, you certainly seem to be enjoying yourself," I said to Dickhead, leaning past him to refill my glass with champagne. I'd already drained the first one in the five paces between the waiter at the door and the drinks table in the corner of the large white room.

"Did you make it?" I asked him, taking a closer look at the lovingly painted papier-mâché.

He turned, giving me a very unsubtle once-over.

"You know somewhere you could buy one of these? Of course I made it."

"Clever old you. But why?"

"Become I come to this party every year. Which means that every Australia Day for the past twelve years, I've been in this room, wearing a stupid hat. I've always felt like a dickhead, so this year I thought I might as well look like one, too."

I nodded enthusiastically—this was my kind of conversation.

"So, following your argument, am I to take it that the guy over there wearing the Indian chief's headdress has always felt like one of the Village People and now he's decided to go public about it?"

"Loud and proud, baby. And that's the other reason I'm wearing a big fat dick on my head. Because that's what this party is really all about."

"Big fat dicks?"

"Yep. They might be talking about opera, or the government's new policy on unemployment benefits—which stinks, incidentally—but what every man in this room is really thinking about is cock."

"You included?"

"Oh yes. Especially me."

I hoped my face didn't fall too obviously. Not that I've got anything against gay men—in fact, you could probably describe me as a full-blown fag hag. I just didn't particularly want this bloke to be gay. He was very attractive in an odd way, despite the ghastly goatee, and he was funny. Even when he was being quite rude I couldn't help noticing he had beautiful green eyes, and I liked the way they creased up when he licked the paper on the joint he was rolling. And I liked the way he lit it, took a quick toke to flame it up and then held it to my lips.

"The only difference," he explained, as I sucked prettily, "is that I'm thinking about my own." With which he took the joint out of my mouth, clamped it between his teeth, winked and pushed his way back into the crowd, holding four glasses and a bottle of champagne.

"And if you want to continue this conversation," he said over his shoulder, "try the back bedroom."

"Otherwise known as the Persian room," said a voice from behind me.

I turned round to see a slim man, dressed entirely in black. He was about thirty-five, with dark skin, short black hair standing up straight like a brush, and one ironically raised eyebrow. You noticed the eyebrow particularly, because it stayed raised whatever the rest of his face was doing.

"Persian?" I said, picturing a lavishly tented parlour, with belly dancers and Nubians.

"Persian rugs. Drugs. Antony Maybury, how do you do?" He held out his hand.

"Georgia Abbott, lovely to meet you."

"Yes, I know, the famous Georgiana Abbott. I was wondering when I'd meet you. Good handshake. That looks like a real Pucci catsuit. Nice shoes."

"What? How kind, although I wouldn't say I was famous. How did—"

"Darling," he said, both eyebrows now working in turns. It was like watching a puppet show. "What you have to understand is that this is a very small town and you are new to it. You've moved here from London, an acme of world glamour, rivalled in our colonial imaginations only by New York. You have worked for European magazines, which we buy like slavering wretches at vastly inflated prices when the cover date is already three months old because we think they might let us in on all the interesting stuff that's happening over there in the fashionable hemisphere. We've seen your name in print, and I know for a fact that you have been to Naomi Campbell's house and have Karl Lagerfeld's home phone number. To us, you are famous."

He looked me straight in the eye, as he lit a very long cigarette with a very gold lighter. One eyebrow was still up there, which seemed quite an achievement with all the eyeballing and cigarette lighting that was going on.

"Blimey," I said.

"Well, enjoy it, because this may be a small town by world standards but it's a tough one. The knives are just as sharp here as they are on Fleet Street or wherever, and they are wielded by the most surprising people.

"And two other things." He counted them out on his fingers. "One: watch out for that Jasper O'Connor, he's as big a prick as he looks in that stupid hat; and two: you need to have manicures. Sydney is a nails town. You're a smart girl, you'll find out. In the meantime, if you'd like some more unsolicited advice, call me. This is my card. Goodbye."

With one last salute from his eyebrows, he picked up one empty glass and two full bottles of champagne and shouldered into the crowd.

Feeling slightly like I'd just been mugged, I looked down at the small card he'd given me, which said "Antony Maybury. Costumier," and automatically ran my finger over the type to see if it was engraved.

"Yes, it *is* braille," I heard him say, but when I looked up, he'd gone. And then I realised something else about Antony Maybury, costumier. He was the only person at the party not wearing a hat.

Even though it was just after four in the afternoon the place was already pumping, and the lavishness of the headgear made the room seem even more crowded than it was. The noise level was unbelievable, with shrieks of hilarious laughter and general yelling almost drowning out the DJ. There seemed to be all age groups here, from beautiful young creatures to middle-aged men and women, and they were all milling around, hopping from group to group and greeting each other with great hugs and cries of delight.

I had been invited to this fixture in Sydney's alternative social calendar just a few nights before, when I'd met its host, Danny Green, at a special preview of an exhibition at the Powerhouse Museum.

I wasn't aware I knew Danny until he bustled over to me, with three cameras around his neck, kissed me warmly on both cheeks, and pushed me together with two total strangers to take our picture. I had no idea why and it seemed rude to ask. He seemed very nice, whoever he was.

"Oh and Georgie," he'd said, after asking how to spell my name and ignoring my repeated corrections of "Georgia, not Georgie, Georgia." "You must come to my Australia Day party this weekend. Everyone comes—you'll love it. You can meet all of Sydney in one go. It's in my studio and the only rules are: wear a hat and bring a bottle. I lay on the tea. Everyone lays on top of everyone else."

He whooped with laughter and thrust an invitation at me, featuring a picture of him in a Mad Hatter's topper with a condom tucked into the band, holding a black poodle wearing the same.

"And the great thing is," he added, conspiratorially, "even though it's on a Sunday, everyone's got the Monday off, so we can get as trashed as we like."

When I got home that night I called the only person I felt I'd really got to know in the two weeks I'd been in Sydney, to find out if I should go or not.

Liinda Vidovic was the features writer at *Glow* magazine, where I worked. It's a monthly glossy aimed at eighteen- to twenty-six-year-old women and full of useful information about orgasms, lipstick with the precise anatomy of the male sexual organs. Following our advice, conscientious readers of *Glow* could learn to jog in high heels, lose weight through multiple orgasms, exercise their stomach muscles while delivering the perfect blow job and balance their cheque books while flirting with the boss (male or female, we advocate flirting with everyone, even dogs and inanimate objects).

When I came in as deputy editor, Liinda and I bonded on sight because we had the same Prada handbag. (I didn't find out until later that hers was a Bangkok fake.) I was also intrigued to find out that she'd changed her name from Linda to Liinda by deed poll, because it was more fortuitous in numerology, one of the many *ologies* which rule her life.

Bag aside, Liinda was also thrilled to meet me because she knew I'd arrived from London with a severely broken heart. Liinda loves emotional catastrophes more than anything. There's always the chance she might get a feature idea out of them. I was shaping up to be "If You Leave the Country, Will He Leave Your Heart?," which was definite coverline material. And coverlines are everything on a magazine like *Glow*. As the editor, Maxine Thane, is always telling us: "Coverlines are what sell magazines, girls. Not all the shit inside."

I did believe Liinda liked me—she had done my astrological chart within an hour of our meeting and announced with glee that we were destined to have an intense, supportive friendship punctuated with major dramas, because she is a triple Scorpio and I am a Gemini with Scorpio rising. But I was also aware of the coverline factor, although I couldn't really blame her—my romantic disaster was a gothic horror.

The man I had come to Australia to forget is called Rick (rhymes with . . .) Robinson. What can I tell you about him? He's the senior art director at a major London advertising agency. Very highly paid, very good looking (black hair, blue eyes, devastating smile, that kind of thing), very bright, very successful, very groovy. We'd been together for five years and were, in fact, "engaged" (a "hideously" bourgeois term, according to Rick). But it wasn't his impressive CV and vintage Mercedes convertible that attracted me—I really loved Rick. He was funny. He was thoughtful. He was an Exocet missile I bed.

And yes, it was too good to be true . . . I came home one evening ready for a cosy night in front of a video, but when I hit play on what I thought was *Roman Holiday,* I was treated instead to a home video of Rick strutting around naked, flexing a cane, while a melon-breasted hooker dressed as a schoolgirl lolled on our sofa. She wasn't wearing any knickers.

Rick had been surprised when I left him ("I didn't think you'd mind, George . . ."). So were my friends—he was rich, nice *and* good looking, was I crazy? I'd never felt saner. Although I felt slightly less sane two years later, when I was still single—and Rick was living with one of my erstwhile friends. I was lonely, I was horny and I bloody well missed him.

Then, one particularly gloomy London December day—the kind when the grey sky sits on your head like a tight hat—Tina, the Australian picture editor on *Kitty* magazine (where I was working at the time), came to my rescue. I was sitting in my office sobbing—as you do—because I had just opened *Country Life* to a page announcing the engagement of yet another dumb, bun-faced girl I'd been to school with (to the heir to a minor earldom).

"What you need," said Tina, understanding the situation in an instant, "is some sunshine and a good root." Then, after explaining what a "root" was, she told me she'd heard there was a job going back in Sydney on *Glow.* I stopped crying immediately. A little ray of sunlight lit up my brain. I already knew the mag and loved it. We had it airmailed over to the *Kitty* office every month, so we could rip off all their ideas. I'd love to work on *Glow,* I decided—and wasn't Sydney full of gorgeous men who looked like Mel Gibson, but taller?

I applied for the job straightaway, had a five-minute phone conversation with the editor and took it. The starting date was in one month's time. My friends thought I'd gone nuts again. But I knew exactly what I was doing—I'd read *A Town Like Alice,* I knew what happened to English gels who went to Australia. They met marvellous men with strong forearms who tipped their hats, saved your life and then took you off to live in a house surrounded by verandahs on a farm as big as Wales. I could hardly wait.

After two weeks in Sydney I hadn't met him yet, and I wondered if Danny Green's Australia Day party might be a good hunting ground. So I got on the phone to ask Liinda's opinion.

"Danny Green?" she said in her gravelly voice, the product of several daily packets of Marlboro and a fair helping of affectation. "Yes, I know him. He's a half-witted social photographer—you'll probably be in the *Sun-Herald* party pages, how embarrassing for you. Danny Green knows every junkie model, society hooker, ageing hack, corrupt magazine editor, actor-turned-waitress, bitter fashion designer, trust-fund bunny, coke-addicted stockbroker, anorexic hairdresser, closet queen, career bullshitter and bum bandit in town.

"He's famous for parties which I'm told resemble the last days of the court of Caligula. You're guaranteed to leave with your IQ three points lower than when you arrived. I'd rather walk naked through the David Jones cosmetics hall than go to one. You'll love it."

Looking round at the heaving mass of people, squealing and air-kissing each other under their hats, Liinda's assessment of the crowd seemed pretty accurate. And she was right, I did love it.

These posturing queens and chic, bitter women, all simultaneously smoking, drinking and shouting, clearly intent on embracing oblivion as soon as possible, were exactly my kind of people. Brittle, brilliant, pretentious, original, bitchy, hilarious, worn out, vicious, warm. Where fashion, art and the media collide, I thought. Home.

"What a lovely smile. You must be thinking about something you like." Standing next to me at the drinks table was a man who looked like something from a 1960s' Qantas travel poster. Dark blond hair, ridiculously white teeth, a perfectly judged sprinkling of freckles and blue eyes with regulation issue Aussie bloke crinkly edges, the whole package twinkling out from underneath a very battered and bent Akubra hat.

"Actually, I was thinking how much I like parties," I replied.

"Is that right? So do I. Wanna dance?"

Without waiting for a reply, or even a change of expression, he grabbed my hand and pulled me through the crowd to an area where people were throwing themselves around like lunatics. A lot of the men had their shirts off and their hands over their heads, all the better to show off their washboard stomachs and chunky upper arms.

"Billy Ryan," he shouted into my ear as he spun me into an accomplished rock and roll turn, seemingly oblivious to the fact that we were dancing to hardcore techno.

"Georgia . . ."

As he pushed me away into another spin I was able to get my first good look at him. In stark contrast to the rest of the crowd, who were clad in skin-tight T-shirts, lacy slip dresses, or general designer black, Billy Ryan was dressed in what I'd only recently found out were called moleskin pants, with riding boots and a blue and white striped shirt. It should have been dorky, but it suited him so well it didn't matter. In fact, he looked bloody gorgeous. He didn't seem the type who'd ask a girl in a pink Pucci catsuit to dance, but he did look like he might have a house with verandahs round it, so I wasn't arguing.

"It looks like quite a few horses have trodden on that hat," I said, as he whirled me into his arms and rocked me from side to side.

"They have. And quite a few cows."

"Are you a farmer?"

"Only at weekends."

"What do you do during the week?"

"I'm a stockbroker."

I took advantage of a two-hand double up-and-under to hide my grin. A good-looking broker who liked the country enough to have his own farm. This was the kind of man I'd been searching for. Someone like me, who loved the fast pace of the city but also needed to escape into nature. Someone who liked horses and gardens as well as dancing and parties. This was the man I had come to Australia to meet. A million miles from Mr. Advertising Genius and his taste for jail-bait. A man with solid values, good teeth and a sheepdog. Just perfect for a girl like Georgia.

By the time he pulled me into a waltz hold I was wondering where to get the towels embroidered. B&GR—a very nice monogram, good round letters. Georgiana Ryan, how do you do? I was considering names for our second son and worrying about where to send him to school when Billy stuck his tongue in my mouth. A real oral invasion. Squirmy and slimy, like a conger eel, not at all erotic.

"You're a great dancer," he said, while I gaped at him, speechless. "I'll find you later for another boogie," he added, kissing me again, this time on the cheek, and then he just left me, alone on the dance floor.

Still too stunned to say anything, I watched him go over to a tall, lean fellow, wearing the same kind of hat, who was standing by the wall. The tall guy shook Billy's hand enthusiastically and then they did some kind of primitive display of male bonding that involved a lot of back-slapping and grinning and head-shaking. I wished David Attenborough was around to do the commentary. Whatever they were up to, they both seemed to find something very amusing. I sincerely hoped it wasn't me and began to wonder whether coming to a party full of strangers had been such a good idea.

As they disappeared into the next room, still slapping and grinning, I caught sight of a familiar penis on the other side of the studio and made for it. I was just about to tap Jasper flirtatiously on the shoulder when I realised he was holding court to a group of about ten people crammed on an old sofa. I stood to one side to watch.

"Then Toohey comes into the room, like this . . ." Jasper crossed his eyes and trudged with bended knees, his teeth in the goofy position.

" 'I jus' wanna kiss ya, Raylene,' " he said in an exaggerated Australian accent. " 'I jus' wanna kiss ya. I won't do nothin' else, I promise, Raylene."

Then he stood up straight, stuck out his bum and chest and pouted. "So Raylene says, 'Well, you can kiss me, Toohey, but don't touch me hair.' "

His eyes blazing, arms waving around as he made his points, Jasper held his audience rapt.

". . . So that's the whole point," he continued. "Toohey is all of us. He's the quintessential Australian. When he can't tell Raylene he loves her, he is all of Australia—he's a kangaroo, he's a jackaroo, he's an Aboriginal kid playing with a stick, he's Olivia Newton-John, Kylie Minogue and Natalie Imbruglia on smack, he's a Mardi Gras queen with a sparkly jock-strap up his arse, he's a shark, a dingo, a traffic cop in tight pants, a Bondi lifesaver and a bent Kings Cross copper, he's John bloody Howard in drag, he's the Harbour Bridge, a Harry's pie, he's Ray Martin, John Laws and Molly Meldrum having a threesome . . ."

"But where does the Turkish bread come in?" asked a tiny woman in a severe black dress, wearing a fez.

"What Turkish bread?" said Jasper, annoyed at the interruption.

"The Turkish bread that has to feature in every short film for it to be shown in Tropfest this year."

"Oh, that. I haven't decided yet. Maybe Toohey will step on it and fall over . . ."

"Maybe he'll choke on it and we won't have to listen to his painful dialogue," said a voice from behind the sofa which I immediately recognised as Antony Maybury's.

"And whose camera are you using this year?" asked a man with a thin mouth and a thick moustache, wearing a Key West baseball cap. "Tony Abrovmo told me you didn't give his camera back for months last year and he wasn't going to lend it to you ever again."

"And haven't you already missed the deadline for this year's films?" said the fez woman.

As the crowd broke up into sniggering groups Jasper caught sight of me. "Hey Pinkie, there you are!" he cried, clearly glad of a distraction. "Come with me. I've got something to show you."

What is it with this party? I wondered, as he took my hand and dragged me off. People were either telling me what to do or physically assaulting me. I looked back to see some familiar eyebrows peeping over the back of the sofa. They did a quick one-two and disappeared again.

"I'm going to show you something you'll never forget, Pinkie," said Jasper, grinning broadly as he weaved through the crowd.

"You've already done that." I nodded in the direction of his penis hat.

"Oh, I'd forgotten I was wearing that," he said, taking it off and dumping it on the floor. "That's better, my brain's got some room. Come with me, little girl . . ."

He led me out the front door of the studio and up the main stairs of the building.

"We're not taking the lift for a reason," Jasper explained, beginning to puff after the second flight. "I want you to earn this. We'll just have a ciggie break here first, I think."

He leaned against the wall and lit up. I don't really smoke, but sometimes when I'm with someone who clearly adores it I can't resist trying it again in case it's nicer than I remember. So I helped myself from his packet and we smoked together in silence. It was horrible as usual. Every now and then Jasper looked at me, smiling and nodding as if we were sharing some great secret. I was beginning to wonder if he was actually mad, but after he'd ground both cigarette ends into the stairs with his boot heel he took my hand and we set off again.

Five more flights up we came to a door with a large padlock on it. Jasper pulled an enormous bunch of keys out of his jeans and opened it.

"I used to have a studio in this building. I kept this key because I always knew I'd need it one day. This is that day."

He threw the door open and we stepped out onto the roof.

Sydney Harbour was spread out below us, a map of shiny blue in the January sunshine. Curving over our heads was a clear dome the colour of skies I'd only ever seen on postcards. The water in the harbour sparkled like lurex. Yachts darted around like little white hankies and ferries chugged along purposefully. Everything looked choreographed. The view was unbroken right out to what I guessed were the Heads and the Pacific Ocean beyond. You could see all the way over to Taronga Zoo and to Manly in the distance.

"Wow," I said, for want of a better word. "We just don't have skies this big in England. Nothing is on this scale. Look at it."

"It's a pretty city, isn't it, Pinkie?" said Jasper. "Come round here."

From the other side of the roof we could see the entire skyline of the CBD, the Opera House, the Bridge, North Sydney and all the way to the Blue Mountains.

"Thank you, Jasper," I said. "This is incredible."

"Hey, Pinkie, how did you know my name? And what's yours, by the way? Not that I'm going to call you anything else but Pinkie until the day we die in each other's arms, but you might as well tell me for the record."

"Georgia. Georgiana Abbott."

"Georgie Abbott—you're the chick who's come over to work on *Glow*, right?"

I couldn't be bothered to correct him. Georgie, George, Ringo, whatever.

"So Georgie," he continued, "how do you like the bunch of tight-arsed neurotics you work with, then? Debbie Brent wouldn't know a decent photograph if it sprang up and gave her a pap smear, neither would that living skeleton Zoe Siegler, and Maxine Thane is tighter with a dollar than a nun's twat. Is that how you knew who I was? Did she tell you? Or was it that card-carrying psycho Liinda Vidovic? She boiled many bunnies lately?"

"Do you know everybody who works on *Glow*?" I asked him, appalled, but also intrigued.

"This is Sydney, Pinkie. Let's just say I know everybody."

I didn't know then quite how true that was.

After Jasper's outburst we just stood there for a while, gazing at the splendour around us, which I couldn't help feeling included him. Once he stopped trying to be clever—or basically, once he shut up, which was rarely—Jasper was really quite beautiful. He had dead-straight long black hair, which I'm a total sucker for, and a sensitive face with a delicate, refined mouth. He had a way of cocking his head to one side and looking up at you through narrowed eyes, which was very attractive.

The only thing marring Jasper's face—he even had nice skin—was that stupid little pubey beard. But with all my years of experience choosing cover shots from photographers' negs, before the model's zits had been digitally removed, I just narrowed my eyes and edited it out.

While I was sneaking covert looks at him, Jasper was having a moment of his own, spinning round slowly while gazing up at the sky, his arms spread out like wings. This gave me an excellent chance to observe him. Slim frame, built for speed rather than strength. Very long legs. Very long legs in bright pink trousers. Bright pink trousers and a double-breasted navy blazer with gold buttons. A pale pink button-down shirt. Hair slicked back and licking his collar. Aviator sunglasses with gold rims. Cuban heel boots. It was a kooky look. I liked it a lot.

"What are you doing?" I asked him.

"I'm trying to connect with the sky."

"Is it working?"

"I think I need another joint."

"And by the way, what are those trousers?"

He stopped suddenly and grinned at me, taking hold of the trouser legs and pulling them out to the side as if he was about to do a ballet-class curtsy.

"Golf pants. Like 'em?"

"I love them. They're nuts. And they go with my hat."

"Pinkie and Pink, you see? I took one look at that hat and thought, that Pinkie's for me."

I didn't comment. They can talk real pretty, these Aussie men, I thought. And they have quite the sparkliest eyes on earth.

But after Billy's uninvited oral assault I was still feeling a bit wary.

Jasper came over to the parapet, took out his cigarette papers and rolled another reefer, using only his left hand. I hadn't noticed he was left-handed before. He noticed me noticing.

"Ambidextrous," he said, twisting the end of the paper with his right hand and putting it between my lips. "Like Leonardo." With his left hand he flourished a Zippo lighter with an enormous flame and lit the tip. I took a hit and handed it back to him.

"Who are you, Jasper?" I asked. "What do you do? And why are you so horrible about the women I work with? Have you slept with all of them?"

"No, far worse. I've worked with all of them. I'm a fashion photographer. But one day I'm going to be a very famous film director and *Glow* magazine is going to beg me for an interview, which I will of course refuse."

"Can I be on your table at the Oscars?"

"You can come up and collect it with me."

After we finished the joint, Jasper insisted I try his routine of spinning round while looking at the sky.

"Whirligig, whirligig, Pinkie darling," he said, waltzing me in circles until I felt seriously dizzy. Then we went back to gazing at the view and I began to feel uncomfortably like he was looking for the right moment to kiss me. Glorious though the setting was, I really didn't feel like another mystery tongue sandwich, especially from someone who reminded me a little bit of Rick, so I suggested we should go back down to the party. I may have told some small fib about having abandoned a friend down there. Whatever I said, Jasper suddenly seemed to snap back to consciousness.

"The party, right, the party . . ." he said, resuming his nodding dog impersonation. "Yeah, friends, party, downstairs. We'd
better split, Pinkie. Well, it was good to share this with you. Perhaps I can show you some more incredible sights of Sydney before too long. This is my town, you know."

We caught the lift back down to the fourth floor. Outside the
door to the studio, where we could hear the party pounding,
Jasper stopped, gave me another of his head-on-the-side squinty
smiles and ran a finger gently over my cheek.

"It was fun, Pinkie. Catch you later, baby."

And then he disappeared into the studio, practically shutting
the door in my face. I pushed it open and squeezed back into the
crowd, which now seemed even bigger and noisier. The monot-
onous techno beats had been replaced with 70s disco and more
people were dancing. Others were piled on the sofas and arm-
chairs lined along the walls, locked in deep conversation.

After Jasper's brain-spinning dance I had no idea how long
we'd been upstairs, but I felt like the party had shifted a couple
of gears in that time. A passing waiter offered me a tray of
drinks and I took two glasses of water, downed them in quick
succession and put the empty glasses back on the tray.

Then I just stood there, realising that I didn't really know a
soul in the place. For the first time since I'd arrived at the party
I felt a bit self-conscious. And Jasper's joint was making me
super-aware of snatches of nearby conversation.

"You should have seen his face when she walked into the
room!" said a short red-faced man wearing a Madame de Pom-
padour wig to a tall thin woman wearing a bald wig.

"Well, I never thought he had any talent anyway," I over-
heard a middle-aged man in Playboy Bunny ears say to another
who was wearing a flowery ladies' swimming cap. "Just another
of Peter's pretty cocksuckers."

"But I thought that was his sister? So that's the mother? My God, the surgery! Who is her surgeon, do you know?"

"I heard he skimmed ten mill off the top and gave it back to them ready for the liquidators to move in . . ."

"No, she worked the flannel shoe back with the bias-cut georgette, it was so ug, we were all puking . . ."

"He paid someone to poison all those trees because they were blocking his view of the harbour . . ."

I stood there telling myself that none of these people were talking about me and trying to breathe deeply because I felt at any moment I could be violently ill. I tried to distract myself by looking at the whirling dancers—bad idea, too much whirling— I looked at the floor—no, too floory—at all the people—oh no, more conversation. Breathe. Breathe. Cigarette smoke, oh yuk. Pot smells, oh no! The music sounded terrifying. What was *in* that joint?

"I think you had better come with me."

Now I really was going nuts—this voice sounded like it was right in my ear. It was. Antony Maybury looked into my face with a serious expression, raised his left eyebrow and gestured with his right for me to follow him. I did. There was something about Antony that made me trust him, even in my brain-fuddled state. Unlike my other new male friends, he didn't grab my hand, but I followed easily in his slipstream along a corridor that ran past several rooms full of people, then round a corner and into another small room with nothing in it except big square cushions on the wooden floor. There were two picture windows framing a harbour view from a lower angle. Sparkly water. Yachts bobbing. Seagulls. The windows were open and a delicious breeze floated in. I pulled my pink feather hat off my head and practically fell onto the floor. I closed my eyes. The room went round and round. I groaned.

"Stay there, don't move," said Antony and left the room.

It was a great relief to be somewhere relatively quiet, and the breeze was heaven, but I still felt really awful. I kept having great flashes of insight, which would disappear as suddenly as they had come, leaving no trace. It was like trying to hold on to passing clouds and it had a strange effect on time. Each great thought seemed to last an aeon and then when they were gone, it was as if time had never existed. Most unsettling.

After what could have been two minutes, or several ice ages, Antony came back holding a huge bottle of Coca Cola, a glass with a slice of lime in it, a silver ice bucket, a flannel and a large dinner plate. He laid the cold, wet flannel on my forehead as he filled the glass with ice, then Coke, and handed it to me.

"You must drink this," he said. "It's the only thing that will make you feel better."

"What's wrong with me?"

"Supersonic hydroponic."

"What?"

"Marijuana. Pot. Mary Jane. Hemp. Weed. Grass. Ganga. Spliff. Silly cigarettes. Whatever you like to call it. But more so. Did you, by any chance, have a little smoko with Jasper O'Connor?"

"Well, yes, I did . . ." I was already on my second glass of Coke, which had suddenly become the most ambrosial drink the world had ever known. "I did have a few tiny tokes."

"Well, you've just had another Sydney lesson," said Antony, sitting down behind my head. "That wasn't a harmless little Portobello puff you just had. That was supersonic hydroponic Sydney weed, grown in water laced with all kinds of growth-promoting and mind-expanding chemicals. If you're not used to it, hydro pot can snake you out like a bad tab of acid. It can be very unpleasant."

"You're not kidding. I thought I was going bonkers. Do you

know, while you were gone, I thought of the most amazing thing to tell you about this party, but I . . . can't remember it . . ."

Antony threw back his head and laughed a very loud pantomime laugh.

"HA HA HA HA HA. Oh, that is classic hydro psychosis. You feel as though the meaning of the Rosetta Stone has been made clear to you, and only you, if you could just remember what it was. It's like being all sentient and having Alzheimer's simultaneously, isn't it. You poor little thing."

"But Jasper smoked most of the joint, and it was the second one I've seen him have. If I'd had that much I'd be in hospital."

"Jasper O'Connor is a famous pothead. He smoked pot all day, every day. People say marijuana is non-addictive. Jasper O'Connor and his like are proof that's total bullshit. He can't get out of bed in the morning without having a joint, and ensuring he has a constant supply, the stronger the better, is the main purpose of his life. Which is a shame, because he is a very talented photographer. Or he was. Pot is also the reason he makes pathetic short films, like the one he was describing earlier, and thinks they make Fellini look creatively constrained. It's also why he never meets the Tropfest deadline. He started out with a very good brain and he has fried it totally. I'd hate to see that happen to you."

Now on my third glass of Coke, I was starting to feel a little better and gradually became aware of a strange tapping noise just behind me. I turned around to see Antony leaning over the dinner plate, chopping up a small pile of white powder with a credit card. He made it into two neat lines, then got a fifty-dollar note out of his pocket, stuck it up his right nostril and lowered his nose to the plate.

"What on earth are you doing?"

"I'm having a line of coke." He sniffed loudly. And, putting his head back, sniffed again a few times. "Ooh, lovely. And another one, I think. Why not?" With a great snort he hoovered his way along the plate. Then he licked his forefinger, wiped it all around the plate and rubbed it along his gums.

"You were just telling me how bad pot is for you and you're doing *that*!"

"Each to his own, sweetheart. You just keep sucking on that kind of Coke in the bottle and I'll stick to this powdered version. Anyway, I didn't say there was anything wrong with drugs—I'm mad about them myself." And he roared with laughter again. "Now where did I hide that bottle of champagne I tucked away earlier?"

He got up and started throwing cushions around until he found the bottle and plunged it into the ice bucket.

I lay back on my cushion and closed my eyes. After four glasses of Coca Cola I was feeling much better. I could only just hear the *thump thump* of the music from the main studio and the occasional shriek. The harsh calls of unfamiliar birds and the arrhythmic clank of the halyards against steel masts on the yachts in Rushcutters Bay floated through the open window. I could feel the late afternoon sunlight warm across my face. . .

"Oh my GOD! I must close the blinds! You're getting sunlight on your face. UV hell."

It was Antony. He sprang up and let down the blinds with a crash. All the golden sunshine disappeared.

"What are you doing?" I asked him. "It was so nice before."

"That's another thing you don't know about. Sydney sun. Ultraviolet rays. Merciless. No ozone layer. You'll be a handbaghead within weeks if you put your dial anywhere near it. I never go to the beach and I wear Factor 30 every day on my face and hands. Even when it's raining. Have a look at the skin on Australian girls ten years younger than you. They have foreheads like Issey Miyake trousers." He shuddered.

"You live in Sydney and you don't go to the beach?" I shook my head. "No wonder you take drugs."

I had another glass of Coke. "This stuff really works. Thank you so much, Antony. It was good of you to come to my aid like that."

"It was my pleasure. You looked like you were about to vomit and it would have made such a mess of the dance floor. Have the great thoughts stopped?"

"Yes, thank you. It must be terribly tiresome being a genius if that's what it's like."

"Oh, ghastly. All the people I most admire had the most hideous lives. I think it's much better to be a cheerful under-achiever than be a Great Person and live a life of misery and wretchedness. Think of Coco Chanel. Came from nothing, basi-cally a whore. Nazi sympathiser. Died alone. Duchess of Wind-sor. Looked like a starved dog. Thought she was marrying the King and really married a closet queen. Died alone. Dorothy Parker. Misery. The bottle. Died alone. At least she had dogs. Frida Kahlo. Faithless husband. Knocked over by a bus. Died alone. Georgia O'Keefe. Never had children. Died alone."

"And she had the most appalling sun damage."

Now we both roared with laughter. The worst part of the hy-droponic heebie-jeebies had worn off and I was just left feeling relaxed and happy. I suspected my eyelids were drooping. I hoped it looked seductive rather than retarded.

"You *are* getting better," Antony said approvingly. "Now I know what would fix you up nicely."

He got a tiny plastic bag out of his trouser pocket and tapped a small pile of the white powder onto the plate.

"Oh Antony, I couldn't," I said. "I've never taken Class A drugs."

This prompted another of his laughing attacks. "Class A drugs. That is hilarious. Where on earth did you get that from?"

"Isn't that what they call them when they're totally addictive and completely illegal? I don't want to end up lying on the floor in a public lavatory. We had all those films about drugs at school and they always ended up in lavatories. It looked grisly."

"Darling, a little bit of hoochy coochy is not going to put you in a public lavatory—in fact a little tiny bit will make you feel ready to go dancing again. And you looked like you were having such a nice time with Billy Ryan before." His left eyebrow shot up.

I grinned at him. "You don't miss anything, do you?"

"I've always thought he was quite gorgeous in a National Socialist Party kind of way. Is he a good kisser?"

"Gruesome, actually. But he is a divine dancer. Totally in control."

Antony looked at me thoughtfully while his eyebrows did their thing. "Mmm. I bet he has strong hands from all the riding. And counting all that money."

"Oh," I said, raising one of my eyebrows in reply. "Does he ride?"

This set us both off laughing again and then, before I knew what was happening he'd put his finger in my mouth and was rubbing it along my gums. My mouth was filled with a very bitter taste. I swallowed.

"Yuk. Was that what I think it was?"

"Just a little something to get you back on the dance floor in the arms of your equestrian friend."

"Antony, really. You Class A-ed me when I wasn't expecting it and we haven't even been properly introduced. What appalling behaviour."

But I was smiling. My gums and the tip of my tongue had started to tingle and there was a strange fluttery feeling in my tummy. I could see Antony looking at me with increased eyebrow activity.

"Let's go," he said.

He picked up his champagne bottle and kicked the plate into a corner, while I took out my lipgloss, which I'd concealed in the band of my hat, and re-applied it in the reflective surface of the ice bucket. My face looked more interesting than usual and I had the most terrible case of hat hair, which was suddenly quite fascinating.

"Come on," said Antony, handing me my hat. "You'll have plenty of time to look at yourself later. Like all night after you get home from this party. How do you feel?"

"Well, I feel great actually. Thanks again for looking after me, Antony."

"Quite alright. Stop going on about it. Interesting place to keep a lipstick, incidentally. How come you aren't using one of your famous handbags?"

"How on earth do you know about that?"

"I told you you were famous. I saw your apartment in *ELLE Decoration* last year. You had a divine little cupboard to keep your handbag collection in, and the special ones were displayed on the wall like works of art. You were living with some kind of genius art director, weren't you? What happened to him?"

"I'm surprised you don't already know," I said. "You seem to know everything else about me. It's a long story. I'll tell you sometime, if you don't find out on your own. And I very rarely take my handbags out with me. They're too special. I would have spent this whole party worrying about it, so wherever possible I travel hands free."

He stopped and looked at me and once again I had the feeling of being seriously appraised. Then he smiled sweetly and chucked my cheek.

"You're nuts," he said. "And you're going to love living in Sydney. Let's go and sock it to them."

Chapter Two

I put my hat back on and we swaggered along the corridor, looking into each room, while Antony gave me a very loud running commentary on all the people who looked out at us with startled eyes.

"Now, what do we have here? Two bankrupts, a plagiarist and three men I've slept with. Next. Ugh, too hideous, a room full of actors, trip away trip away . . . Now who's in here? One quite amusing artist—hello Tracey darling, loved your show—and one of your colleagues in the fourth estate, Mr. Nick Pollock surrounded, as usual, by women. Let us move on. And here we have the Persian room, as previously announced, and someone I think you already know . . ."

Antony and his eyebrows turned and looked at me enquiringly as I peered in and saw, amid a circle of sleepy-looking people, Jasper O'Connor, slouched on an old armchair with a very young, very thin, very beautiful Asian-looking girl on his knee. She was wearing a big bright red satin bow in her very long, inky-black hair. Her lips were painted as red as the ribbon. She made me feel like a potato. Antony continued his voice-over.

"Jasper's latest honey, Lin Lee Smith. Seventeen. Just moved here from Broome to be a model. Still thinks he's a famous fashion photographer. Someone will tell her the truth sooner or later and he won't see her for dust. Part of a continuing saga . . ."

I pulled my head in quickly. For some reason I didn't want Jasper to know I'd seen him with her—and I was hard to miss in that hat.

Antony was still wittering. "And finally—ah, this is more like it—a room full of my adorable friends. Old queens, fag hags, drunks, functioning drug addicts, millionaires, paupers, liars, neurotics, egomaniacs—and very amusing, quite brilliant, creative types all of them."

So Antony introduced me to a roomful of people, who appeared to hang on his every word while I stood next to him smiling like a goon.

"This is my new best friend Georgiana Abbott," he announced. "She's just moved here from London and you must all be charming to her, because I like her. You can call her Georgia for short. Georgia, mind, not Georgie. She's come here to work at *Glow* (God knows why—she used to work on *Pratler*, my favorite magazine, as well as *Kitty*, which I suppose explains it). As you all know what darling Debbie and Maxine and Liinda are capable of, I'm sure you will all be very kind to her—she'll need it."

And they greeted me with a big cheer. Hip hip hooray. I couldn't believe it. Then it was a blur of smiling faces and handshakes, kisses and invitations to dinner, from these total strangers. I couldn't help comparing my reception from this crowd with what any of them could have expected from my friends had they arrived in London. A row of blank uninterested faces, with a brisk "Hellohowareyou?" if they were lucky.

The introductions over (and all names instantly forgotten by me), Antony and I sat down and were pulled into the conversation, which was very funny even though I didn't have the slightest idea who any of them were talking about.

"Do you think it was fair that I was suspended for having a little sleep at work?" a kind-faced man with messy blond hair asked us. "It was Wednesday and everyone knows all the gallery openings are on Tuesday night, so of course I'm going to be a little bit hung-over . . . Mind you, I suppose it was a bit cheeky to use the managing director's office."

"I love being suspended," said another fellow with a shaved head and a large stud through his lower lip, and everyone laughed.

Amid all the fun, another of Antony's plates appeared and came round to me. It was like playing pass the parcel, and it seemed the most natural thing in the world to wet the end of my forefinger, dab it in the powder and rub it on my gums. It tasted really nasty, but soon after I got that tickly feeling again and everything seemed funnier than ever. The effect of the pot had completely gone and Antony passed me glass after glass of champagne, which I swilled happily.

This cheerful little group, ensconced on silver bean bags and cushions in what I realised was a dressing room for the photographic studio, never stopped talking and laughing. The faces changed constantly as people came and went, with new arrivals greeted like they'd just returned from an Antarctic expedition. Eventually I realised that Antony had disappeared, but I was having such a good time with all my fabulous new friends I didn't mind. And the champagne and the plate just kept coming round and round.

Eventually a familiar face appeared. It was Billy Ryan.

"Billy darling!" I cried out, forgetting that I'd been offended by his behaviour, because I was so thrilled to be able to greet

someone myself. Especially someone so ridiculously good looking. "Come and sit with me," I said, patting the bean bag next
to me.

He looked a bit surprised at the warmth of my welcome, but
came over anyway.

"Having fun?" I asked, beaming at him.

"Not bad at all, er, Jodie . . ."

"Georgia. Georgia Abbott. But you can call me Georgie." I
thought this was very funny and for some reason I'd started
laughing like Antony. HA HA HA HA HA.

"So tell me, Georgie," said Billy. "How do you come to be at
this party and how come I've never met you in Sydney before?"
He looked around the room. "We seem to know a lot of the
same people."

"Actually, I don't know any of these people. I don't even
know you. HA HA HA. I've only lived in Sydney for two weeks.
I came out here to work on *Glow* magazine."

"Ah, *Glow*." He nodded. "Do you know the beauty editor
there, Debbie Brent? She's my cousin. My mother is her father's
sister."

"No! But that's amazing. Of course I know her. She's gorgeous. I mean she's a lovely person. I really like Debbie. Yes, I
really like her. Is your mother very beautiful? Debbie is unbelievably beautiful. She looks so beautiful every day, you never
know what she's going to turn up in and she always looks gorgeous. I've heard her father is gorgeous too. Gorgeous gorgeous
gorgeous, all those Brents, I've heard, and you're half Brent so
you must be half gorgeous, HA HA HA."

Oh, I thought I was hilarious. Billy didn't seem to mind—he
was smiling indulgently. He shook his head as the plate came
round and I took just another little dip—oops, on it goes—and
passed it round. Billy seemed a bit distracted.

"Rory!" he suddenly shouted, "Roar!" and did one of those piercing whistles through his teeth that only Real Men can do. The tall fellow I'd seen him with earlier popped his head round the door.

"Bills, mate," he said. "What are you doing?"

"Just chatting to my new friend Georgie here. Come and say hello."

Rory came over and shook my hand. He had lovely pale blue eyes.

"Rory Stewart, g'day," he said, doffing his hat. I noticed that although he had very black eyebrows, his hair was silver all over. He wasn't pin-up perfect like Billy, but there was something very attractive about him too.

"Georgia Abbott, how do you do?" I replied, suddenly a bit shy and formal, but also wanting to burst into hysterical giggles because he had actually said "g'day" and tipped his hat. He was dressed the same way as Billy and I decided on the spot that moleskin pants do something for a man. Specially men with nice long legs like this Rory person.

"Georgie's just moved here from London," said Billy. "She's working on *Glow* with Debbie."

"Yeah? Well, I'm sure you'll have lots of fun there. Say hi to Debs for me, would you?"

I nodded, starting to wonder if Debbie Brent had first dibs on every attractive man in Sydney. Rory then turned to Billy and said, "Mate, I was looking for you to tell you I'm going. I've left Scooby in the ute and I've got to let her out. I'll see you back at the house, OK? Bye Georgia, good to meet you."

And he left. Shame, I thought, he'd actually got my name right, but at least I still had darling Billy to flirt with.

"Was he speaking in tongues?" I asked him. "Didn't make a word of sense to me."

"Oh, that's just old Rory. Been my best friend all my life. We grew up together. We're like family. Great guy." He laughed. "God, we've had some funny times together."

"Yes, I saw you laughing after you stuck your tongue in my mouth earlier . . ."

"Uh—oh, that was something else . . ."

I let him squirm a bit. "Anyway, he does seem very nice, but isn't he a bit young to be grey?"

"Yes, he is. He's the same age as me, but he had a big shock and his hair went grey."

"What on earth happened?"

Billy turned quiet. "It was really sad. Rory comes from quite a big family—he had three brothers and one sister. He's the youngest. Eighteen months ago all three of his brothers were killed in a light plane accident on their property. It was terrible—all over the papers here. Debbie Brent was engaged to the eldest one, Drew."

"Oh no—I had no idea. She just seems like one of those people who have a perfect life; how really awful for her. It must have been terrible for all of you."

"You're not wrong. That accident devastated so many people. Rory's father has never recovered from it. He had a stroke not long after and now he's paralysed down one side. Rory had to leave Sydney and go and take over the farm, which he never wanted to do. His brothers were always the farmers. Rory was the youngest and thought he was free of it—now he spends his life trudging around in cow shit. But he never complains about it. I get him down here to stay with me as much as I can. Make sure he has a good time."

It was a very sad story, but I must confess I was paying as much attention to the movements of Billy's beautiful mouth as he told it, as I was to what he was saying. Those lips . . . yum. I had to keep him talking.

"Who or what is Scooby?" I asked him, not caring in the slightest.

"Rory's cattle dog. She's a character. You've never seen a dog who can jump higher than Scoobs. They ride along in the ute and she sticks both her front legs out the window."

"What's a ute?" I was practically cross-eyed, trying to squint down his shirt. He looked at me like I was an alien.

"A utility . . . a van for the farm. You know, you have a little cabin in the front and a big tray in the back where you can put bales of hay, or sheep, or women. Ha ha ha."

"Oh, a pickup . . ."

"Yeah, that's what the Yanks call them, isn't it?"

He didn't get my joke. Antony would have, I thought. Oh well. Billy shifted around in his seat and shuddered a bit.

"Still gets to me, talking about the Stewart boys. They were all like brothers to me. Drew was my hero when I was a kid. The best shot in New South Wales . . ."

He looked into the distance for a moment and then suddenly turned to me and grinned. "Let's dance."

He stood up and offered me his hand. Then he pulled my hat off my head and threw it on the floor, followed by his own.

"Too hot," he said and led me to the dance floor, where they seemed to have lined up all my favourite dance tracks. Out they came . . . "Car Wash," "Groove is in the Heart," "Love Shack". . .

Billy was a great dancer. He understood all about being funny on the dance floor, about dancing stupidly and ironically as well as dancing sexily, doing the Hitchhiker and the Pony and singing along. He knew all the moves for "My Sharona" and "Night Fever." We did the Twist. We did the Mashed Potato. We even did the Macarena, during which I thought I was gong to wet myself, because he did the wiggle in such a funny way. And when he took my hand and spun me around, out and back and into his arms, I was in heaven.

It was wild on that dance floor. Suddenly it seemed that every person at the party was dancing. Danny Green, cameras still around his neck, was prancing around like the Mad Hatter on speed. I could see Jasper and Lin Lee on the other side of the dance floor and noticed with satisfaction that she had absolutely no sense of rhythm, although he had a louche hip-swivelling style.

Antony and his eyebrows went by a few times, accompanied by a series of laughing women, each one very attractive. All of his friends from the dressing room were on the dance floor too and they kept coming up and kissing me on the cheek in the middle of a track for no apparent reason. "Having fun, Georgie?" they'd ask.

"Go girlfriend!" said a drag queen in a red sequin kaftan, with a platform shoe as a hat on top of a blood-red wig.

"Woo hoo!" we all sang. Especially me. Woo bloody hoo. "How do you like Sydney, eh Georgia?" asked Antony, appearing suddenly and whispering into my ear. How did I like Sydney? I bloody loved it. That's how much I liked it. I hadn't had this much fun for years. And Billy spun me out and in and round and round, never missing a beat, until I was breathless with excitement.

"Water! Water!" I cried, slumping on a gold salon chair, while he went off in search of liquid refreshment. It wasn't until I stopped for a minute that I realised it was dark outside and that the room was beginning to thin out. I'd arrived at the party at four o'clock and now it was nearly eleven. I'd been carrying on like this for seven hours.

Billy came back with water and champagne and, as he crossed the room, I had another good look at him. He may have been only half a Brent, but he was all gorgeous. His shirt was now unbuttoned to the waist so I could clearly see a perfectly smooth, muscular chest. He had slightly bandy legs, which I've always found very attractive, and his riding boots were fetchingly worn in. His blond, slightly wavy hair flopped over one eye. Crikey. What a dreamboat.

"There you are, darl," he said, taking the seat next to me. I skulled the water and then we sat sipping the champagne in a happy silence.

Billy turned and smiled at me. "Where did you learn to dance like that?"

"I could ask you the same question," I said. "I've always loved dancing. My whole family loves it. My parents had a lot of parties when I was growing up and there was always wild and crazy dancing. And we used to go to my grandparents' in Scotland for hogmanay and there'd be reeling, so I suppose I've spent a large proportion of my adult life skipping the light fantastic."

Now I'd started, I couldn't stop talking.

"One of the things I'd started to hate about London was that there was nowhere to go dancing. All the nightclubs were about being eighteen and cool, or they were ghastly pick-up joints with men in white shoes, or Annabel's, which I really have to be in the mood for—i.e. drunk. And none of my friends have proper parties any more. They've all got children and you'll be invited to hideous Sunday lunches with thousands of kids everywhere, or drink parties where you all leave at nine-thirty and go out and spend £40 a head on dinner, which you don't get until ten-thirty . . ."

I could see his eyes glazing over. "Sorry, I'm going on, aren't I?"

"No worries," he said, clearly oblivious. "I love this song. Come on."

It was a slow one. Don't ask me what it was. I couldn't hear it. All I was aware of was the smell of Billy's neck, a combination of soap and sunshine and clean shirt, as he held me tightly and slowly moved us round the floor. It was divine. There were lots of slow songs after that and we danced until my knees were practically buckling. I could feel the hardness of Billy's body pressed against me. He felt like he was made entirely of muscle—he may have been a stockbroker during the week, but he felt like a farmer. Was it the champagne, the music, the powder plate, or just pure pheromones? Maybe it was the way he was humming along with the music in my ear. I don't know what it was but I would have followed Billy Ryan around on my hands and knees at that moment. I think for the first time in my life I really understood the meaning of the word "lust." I was practically drooling.

Then the music stopped. Coming back to consciousness, I saw that the room was empty, apart from the DJ packing up, Danny Green asleep on a sofa and his poodle sniffing around the empty glasses and full ashtrays. I could hear naughty giggles coming from one of the side rooms.

"We'd better go," said Billy. "I think this party is officially over. I'll take you home. Where do you live?"

"Elizabeth Bay," I murmured, blinking up at him. "Billyard Avenue."

"Well, that won't be hard then. We're already in Elizabeth Bay. I'll just go and get our hats."

He came back wearing mine and handed me his. I put it on. When we stepped outside the night was still warm and very starry.

"This city never stops showing off, does it?" I said, looking up at the huge vaulted inky sky, with its unfamiliar constellations.

"Mmm?" He didn't seem to have heard me. "Did you say you live in Billyard Avenue? Let's go the long way round."

He took my hand and instead of walking straight to my street, he turned left down some steps to a park. It was so peaceful. The water in Rushcutters Bay was completely calm; the lights reflected in it were barely twinkling. Even the air was barely stirring. We leaned on the seawall for a while and then I asked Billy if he could show me the Southern Cross.

"Too right," he said. "But let's get away form these lights."

He led me to the darkest part of the park, where we lay on our backs on the grass.

"OK. See that bright star there? That's your guide star. Then you just go along and you can see the five stars of the Southern Cross. It's kind of upside down at this time of year. See it?"

I did see it. It was beautiful.

"And if you draw a line from the head of the cross to the foot and continue over—that bright star is called Achenar. Now come back in a circle towards the Southern Cross—see those three stars in a row? That's called the Peacock. Don't ask me why."

"What's that very bright one there?"

"That's Sirius. Aborigines call him the Eagle. Come across from there . . ." He was holding my hand while he said all this, tracing the direction. "See those three bright stars in a row? That's Orion's belt. That little cluster is his head and—if you follow the line down here—his left foot is called Betelgeuse. It's a red star. Great name, isn't it?"

I looked and looked and, while I was looking, he kissed me. Not a yucky kiss like the one he'd given me on the dance floor when I first met him, but a really nice kiss. Lots of really nice kisses. Slow ones. Confident ones. Confident kisses and confident hands, moving and exploring and unbuttoning. I was lost. No one had kissed me like this since Rick. But the point came, lying as we were in the middle of a public park, when I thought, we could get arrested if we carry on like this. Billy had his shirt off and in the light of the moon he looked like he was carved out of soap. It was a very fine thing, I must say, but suddenly his trousers were unbuttoned too and the top of my catsuit was all over the place. When he rolled on top of me I decided I'd better do something quick. So I rolled him straight over the top.

"Eugh! Oh no. Yuk!" he cried out as he hit the ground on the other side and an all-too-familiar smell filled the air. "I've rolled in dog shit."

"Yuk! You poor thing."

Talk about destroying the moment. We both sat up and there it was all over his back. I didn't know whether to laugh or throw up.

"Why is dog poo so vile?" he said. "Kangaroo or sheep poo won't do you any harm if you roll in it, but dog poo is evil. I feel sick. Pass me my shirt, will you, Georgie? Would you rub it off me? I can't stand it being on there."

"With your shirt?"

"It's all we've got. I'm not rolling in the grass, I'll just get more on me."

I wiped it off with his shirt as best as I could.

"It's really sticky. Oh yuk." The smell was making me retch. "It really is disgusting. I think you'd better come back to my place and have a shower." I said it without thinking. Honestly.

We got up and walked back through the park, Billy holding his shirt out from him as if it was radioactive.

"What a waste of a good shirt," he said, dropping it in the first garbage bin we came to. "And I loved that one. It was my special Easter Show shirt. I always had a good time in it. But it doesn't matter how many times I wash it, it would always be the dog shit shirt now. People who don't pick up their dog's droppings should be shot. Why would you have a dog in the city, anyway? God, I feel stupid walking around with no shirt on."

He didn't look stupid—even though he still had my hat on. He looked magnificent. His back was muscly, he had marvelous shoulders and, I noticed, a tattoo of a tiger on his left bicep.

"Nice tat, Billy."

"Oh yeah, had it done when I was sixteen. Rory and I got drunk and went together. It was his idea."

That surprised me—Rory had seemed so straitlaced. "What has he got?"

"A Maori symbol he found in a book. It's pretty cool. It means strength."

"What does yours mean?"

"Grrr!" he said, making tigery faces and pretending to claw me.

When we got to the door of my building I suddenly realised I hardly knew this guy, and here I was letting him come up to my apartment. This was foolish behaviour. But he *was* Debbie Brent's cousin, I told myself, and I did work with her, so he wasn't a total stranger. I turned the key. I just hoped he understood that I was only inviting him in because his back was covered in excreta. It didn't mean I was asking him to stay the night.

"I wouldn't normally expect to come up to your place, Georgie," he said as I opened the door to my flat. Mind-reader. "But they *are* slightly unusual circumstances—and I also need to apologise for kissing you on the dance floor ten seconds after we met. I'm sorry about that. It was rude, but I was just showing off to Rory. In fact, he dared me to do it . . ."

A dare? What was he talking about? Why would Rory dare Billy to kiss me? Was it because I was so ugly? Not judging by his performance in the park. I didn't know whether to feel insulted or just to let it pass. It was all so weird.

"Oh, that's fine," I said, suddenly all brisk. "The bathroom's in there. There are clean towels in that basket and you can use my back brush—or maybe not . . . I'll get you a T-shirt."

He disappeared inside. I didn't pour any drinks. I didn't put soft music on. I didn't take my clothes off. I just paced around, not knowing what to do with myself. One of the most beautiful men I'd ever seen was naked in my shower—I could hear the water running and him singing 'car wash . . . woo ooo ooo . . .'"

through the door—and my heart was still racing from a combination of all those little platey licks and our passionate snogfest under the stars. So I did what I always do when I don't know what to do. I had a drink of water. When I turned round from the sink, Billy was standing in the kitchen doorway, his hair wet and slicked back, a white towel around his waist and that smile on his face.

Seconds later we were in my bed.

Now, I'd been working on women's magazines long enough to know that the best way to kill a romance before it begins is to sleep with a guy on the first date. But he was gorgeous. All over. Not an ounce of fat on the man. I felt like I was losing consciousness.

Then something funny happened. Or rather, it didn't happen. His body was hard as rock all over—except for the one place it really mattered.

"Georgie," he said, as it became patently obvious to both of us that things were not quite right. "I don't think this is a good idea."

"You're right," I said, secretly relieved. "I'm sorry. I never should have let it get this far, but it was unusual circumstances like you said." Not to mention that I'd ingested about twenty-five fingerfuls of Class A drugs, two bottles of champagne and several puffs of supersonic hydroponic Sydney smoko.

"I'm the one who should be sorry," he said. "I didn't mean to take advantage of you, but it was such an amazing night and it just sort of happened. I think I'd better go home. Would you mind?"

"No, it's a good idea, before we do anything else stupid. I'll get you that T-shirt."

I got up quickly, glad he was going—it meant I wasn't a slut after all. But I was also sad, confused, disappointed and embarrassed. What had gone wrong? He'd been like a raging bull in the park and then, when we were in a more appropriate locale, it had all closed down. Had he suddenly realised I was repulsive?

What was the matter with me? First I had made Rick turn to hookers and now I'd made macho-man Billy Ryan turn to jelly. Was this all part of the dare with Rory?

"Georgie, give me your phone number. Please. I'm not a bastard, really. I would like to see you again. I'd really like to be friends."

Friends? What was that supposed to mean? I found a business card and gave it to him. If he wanted to be "friends" he could ring me at work. He looked at it and looked back at me, with a winning half smile.

"Can I have your home number as well? I'll call you tomorrow. We can go and have brunch or something."

Yeah right, I thought, but I wrote my home number on the back anyway. He gave me a warm kiss on the cheek and left. I pulled horrible faces at the closed door for a while and then, after five more glasses of water, I got into bed and screamed into the pillow.

Chapter Three

I don't want to dwell on how I was feeling physically when the phone woke me up the next morning. It was not good. It took a while for the far-away bell in my dream to register as the phone. My voice must have sounded even huskier than Liinda's.

"Hurro?"

"Georgie! I was just about to give up on you. Thought you'd gone out for a jog. How are you?"

"Uh?"

"It's Billy. You know, Dog-shit Billy."

"Oh Billy, hi, how are you." That's romantic, I thought. Dog-shit Billy. Lovely.

"How am I?" he replied, in a disgustingly perky voice. "I'm bloody starving and I thought you might like to come and have some brekkie. I presume you don't have to go to work today? Too bad if you do, because it's nearly eleven-thirty. Why don't you come and have breakfast with me at Bondi? Get some sea air into your lungs, that'll wake you up."

I felt a bit better already at the thought of seeing Billy's face again. And Billy's shoulders.

"That would be lovely. Where shall I see you?"

"I'll come and pick you up. Can you be ready in fifteen?"

Years, maybe, I thought as my mouth said, "Sure, sure. Great. See you in er . . . fifteen, then?"

"Beauty," he said and hung up.

I flopped back onto the pillow. I was feeling so sick—just moving my head was torture. But I was grinning. Beautiful Billy, the farming broker, the disco king, the perfect man with perfect manners (apart from the odd unannounced tonguer), had rung me less than twelve hours after I'd last seen him. Rock and roll. I now had twelve minutes to get ready.

I spent six of them in the shower, hoping that the therapeutic effect of water on the head would make me feel better. After forcing down a banana as a pill cushion, I swallowed two painkillers and six glasses of water, while fantasising about Antony's bottle of Coca Cola. The phone rang. It was Antony.

"Hello. How are you this fine and glorious morning?"

"I are terrible, how is you?"

"Oh, I'm marvellous. Just walked in the door. Starving. Want some breakfast?"

I couldn't believe it. "You just walked in the door? From last night?"

"Ye-es," he said, as if I'd asked a peculiar question. "And I don't feel ready to sleep yet, so I thought you might like to have some bloody marys and a steak sandwich with me at the Bourbon and Beefsteak."

"That would have been lovely, Antony, but I'm already doing something. I'm just rushing out the door, actually. Perhaps we could do it some other time?"

"Whatever. Have a nice time. Goodbye," he said, completely unperturbed.

A quick look out of the window revealed a perfect summer day, so I threw on a very short, striped T-shirt dress, a pair of slides and my old Panama hat, with the lack of care that comes only from feeling extremely ill and having one minute to get ready. The doorbell rang at exactly 11:45. And it wasn't until I was riding down in the lift that I remembered I hadn't given Antony my phone number.

Billy was waiting for me on the pavement, looking just as attractive in daylight as he had by the light of the Milky Way. He was wearing jeans and a checked shirt and his hair was wet again. I wondered idly what kind of car a farmer broker would drive and was secretly thrilled when he walked up to a really beaten-up old "ute." He opened the passenger door for me and I was met by a hot wet tongue.

"Scoobs, stop it!" came Rory's voice from inside. "Don't worry, she's just being friendly. Scoobs, stop it. Come here."

"Hello Rory," I said, surprised. "Hello Scooby. How lovely to meet you. I see even Australian dogs like to tongue-kiss people they haven't been introduced to. Did you dare her as well, Rory?"

He laughed heartily and Billy went red, which made me feel vindicated. Then, with Scooby sitting on Billy's knee, both front legs and her entire upper body hanging out the window, and me sandwiched between the two men, we set off for Bondi.

The three of us made jokey chit-chat about the party and the outrageous hats, while I tried not to let the throbbing diesel engine and the smell of Scooby make me feel even sicker. Behind the talk, my head was racing. Was I abnormal for thinking that it was a little strange of Billy to bring Rory along?

It was Billy I had snogged. It was Billy who had lain naked in my bed (not for long, admittedly). Rory seemed nice enough, but I thought I was having a let's-get-to-know-each-other-better breakfast with Billy, not Rabbit's friend, relations and pets as well. Perhaps they were gay, I thought for a moment, but then I stopped caring.

The sun was shining and Crowded House came on the radio singing "Weather with You." The happiest guitar break in history always makes me smile and when Rory turned it up, saying "I love this song," we all sang along. Scooby howled. OK, I thought, my hot date is a foursome, including a dog, and my mouth feels like the inside of a junk-shop handbag, but my life could be worse. And as Billy's leg pressed into me on one side and Rory's hand touched my knee every time he changed gear, I thought, yes, it could be much worse.

All too soon we pulled up at a café with outside tables and views right over the surf. It was only the second time I'd been to Bondi and it still amazed me. Such incredibly ugly buildings and then that jaw-dropping beach. But even covered with people as it was on this bank holiday morning, once you turned your back on the awful cheap brick apartment buildings and burger shops, it had such a powerful vibe.

"You should go for a swim after brekkie," said Billy. "Get your head under the surf. Guaranteed to cure a hangover."

"What makes you think I've got a hangover?" I asked him, crossing my eyes.

"Just an informed guess." That smile again.

Scooby came with us, carrying her own bone, which Rory had thrown to her from the back of the ute. She sat quietly under the table and was given a bowl of water by a waiter who knew her name. Rory poured some milky coffee into it.

"Love your coffee, don't you Scoobs?" he said.

She certainly lapped it up eagerly. When she seemed settled I slipped off my slides, and put my feet on her warm, furry back and scrungled my toes in her smooth fur. Dog therapy. She turned her head and licked them a bit and then went back to her bone.

The boys had the full hangover breakfast, but I was still feeling sick so I ordered plain toast. This was unusual. I'm normally the one who has two fry-ups, a brace of cream cheese and smoked salmon bagels and then heads to Burger King to fill up after a big night out. This morning, though, the thought of crispy bacon was repellent. I didn't want to own up to myself that this might have something to do with Antony's dinner plate and the magic white powder. Not good, I thought, wondering if there were any public loos in the vicinity. They could come and film some up-to-date anti-drug propaganda for schools starring Georgiana Abbott as the Class A desperado.

Rory was speaking to me.

"Sorry? What?" I said.

"How long have you been in Sydney?"

"Oh, um, two weeks yesterday."

"How do you like it?"

"It's great. I've found a really good place to live in Elizabeth Bay—I can see water, which is thrilling—and the job seems OK. It's all very new still, but everyone's been so friendly."

"What do you do?"

"I work on *Glow*—"

"Oh that's right, with Debs. How is she?"

"She's great. Really great," I said, wondering if we always had to talk about Debbie, who seemed to have quite enough male attention as it was, judging by the amount of flowers that arrived at the office for her every day.

Billy was rather quiet. In fact, he was reading the paper. Great. And it was the real estate section, not even the times of movies or something interesting like that. Rory leaned down to give Scooby some bacon scraps and smiled up at me when he saw my feet on her back.

"I hope you don't mind me er . . . borrowing your dog," I said, feeling as if I'd taken a liberty.

"Not at all. I'm glad you like her. Do you have a dog back in England?"

"Yes." My eyes immediately filled with tears. "He lives with my parents, but he's my dog. Gaston. He's a French bulldog."

"What's the difference between a French bulldog and a British one?"

"Well, the main thing is he's not nearly as ugly as a British bulldog and he's as black as a liquorice allsort and he has a white bib on his chest and his ears stick straight up and when he runs his front legs go from side to side, it's the sweetest thing . . ."

A sob escaped. How embarrassing. "I'm so sorry, but I really miss him. Scooby's fur feels similar."

"Well, you can borrow Scooby as a footrest any time you're missing Gaston. You'd be happy to help, wouldn't you Scoobs?"

We both put our heads under the table to look at her at the same time. She glanced from one to the other and gave a big doggy yawn. Rory really did have a sweet smile.

Billy was now absorbed in the business news, eating with one hand and holding the paper with the other. Rory clearly felt it was his responsibility to make conversation with me. I was glad somebody did.

"So why did you move here?" he asked.

I still didn't have a pat answer for this question worked out.

"Oh you know, I just felt like a new challenge and I've always liked *Glow* and I was sick of London—terrible traffic jams, too hard to do anything, so expensive, and it seemed like an exciting time to come out here."

And my fiancé was shagging PROSTITUTES and all the men were wacko and hated me . . . I changed the subject.

"So, Billy tells me you're a farmer."

"Yes. So they tell me."

"My brother is a sort of farmer. He went to agricultural college, to do something called 'estate management,' which just seemed to involve going to lots of parties at big houses and shooting a lot of innocent creatures. Did you do anything like that?"

Rory's expression changed. His shoulders went a bit slumpy and I had the feeling I'd said the wrong thing. Oh no—the brothers. The father. The farm. I'd forgotten the full horror of the story. What had Billy told me?

"No. I went to art college," he said. "Not very useful for cattle farming, I know, but then I never expected to be a farmer."

I decided to go by my grandmother's principle and seize a difficult subject rather than tiptoe around it. "Billy told me about your brothers, Rory. I'm so sorry, it must have been awful for you. Such a terrible shock."

He looked surprised, but also relieved that he didn't have to explain the tragic story to me himself.

"Thank you," he said, quietly. "It has been pretty tough."

"What were you doing at art college?"

"Painting. I had an MA already and I was hoping to get a part-time teaching job and carry on doing my own work, but I had to go and help Dad with the farm. I couldn't let him sell it—not on top of everything else; that would have been the last straw. The property's been in the family for over a hundred years—that's a long time in Australia."

"Sometimes doing the right thing is so hard," I said. "You're very brave to stick to your principles like that. Do you still paint?"

"No. I just closed that part of my brain down. I couldn't bear to be a weekend painter. It was never a hobby for me."

It didn't seem like the right moment to tell him it was very much a hobby for me and that I was actually searching for a good life-drawing class to go to in Sydney. Rory looked very sad. I turned to Billy for help—he was studying the stock prices. This was the strangest date I'd ever been on, I thought. First he brings his friend and then he ignores both of us. Rory seemed to feel the awkwardness of the situation too.

"Hey, Bills," he said, winking at me. "I think I made thirty cents profit last week, at the sheep sale. Seen any can't-miss shares I should buy with it?"

Billy looked up. "No, just hold on to the land, mate. Most valuable asset you have. So, Georgie, how are you feeling? You haven't eaten your toast." Oh, so he had remembered I was alive. "Maybe you should have another coffee. Rory? Another latte?"

Rory nodded and Billy went inside to find a waiter. When he came back he was pushing his wallet into his back pocket and looking at his watch.

"Well, I've got an appointment at one, so I'd better be off. Good to see you, Georgie. Let's catch up again soon. I've got your numbers; I'll call you. See you at the Four in Hand later, Roar? I've fixed this up. OK, bye you two."

And that was it. He hailed a taxi that was just coming round the corner and left. I was glad I was hung-over. In my stunned state I couldn't process the full weirdness of Billy's behaviour. We met. We danced. We snogged. He called me. We went out. He left me. This cycle normally takes more than twelve hours. Rory didn't seem too perturbed by it. Was I missing something here?

"Have you got something to rush off to, Georgia, or do you fancy a walk when we finish these coffees? Scoobs would love to take you for a walk, wouldn't you Scooby?"

Great. Perhaps Rory was planning to leave too, so it would just be me and the dog.

"I'd love a walk," I said, all the same.

So we finished our coffee and strolled down the hill to the promenade. It was very hot and the beach was packed with people enjoying the public holiday. There were families, with big fat grannies in black dresses and cardigans, but most people seemed to have improbably good bodies. Girls in tiny bikinis and guys in brief Speedos Rollerbladed along the concrete walkway. There were buskers playing pan pipes and a circle of drummers in front of the pavilion.

"Those drums remind me of the crazy jungle drum pedestrian crossings here," I told Rory. "I think they're hilarious. They always make me feel I should limbo dance across the street."

"What else have you noticed since you arrived here?" he asked and I felt that, unlike Billy last night, he was genuinely interested in hearing my answer.

"Well, everyone is really friendly. Even the people on the phone when you ring the gas board. In England they hate you, on principle. And taxi drivers here are amazing. They don't always know the way, but sometimes they round the fare down when they give you the change. That would never happen in London."

Rory was a good listener and one I get started I can really go on. But he didn't seem to mind. He listened and laughed and smiled and nodded and Scoobs padded along by our side, sniffing everything keenly.

I wanted to ask him more questions, about his life on the farm and his life before it, but it seemed too intrusive and I felt it was better to keep prattling. And of course, this was an ideal opportunity for me to probe him subtly about Billy. About how long they had known each other and all the things they'd done together—the tattoos, the first youthful drinking binges, the sporting achievements—until I managed to drag the subject round to what I really cared about: girlfriends.

It's useful being a journalist sometimes. It trains you to be able to get things out of people without them realising. We did first girlfriends and important girlfriends, girlfriends fought over and girlfriends still pined over, and then I directed him to the subject of current girlfriends—as in girlfriends, current, did Billy have one? No. No, he didn't have a girlfriend and neither did Rory. He was very firm about it. And then I masterfully changed the subject. Oh wow, look at those skateboarders . . . Shall we stop and watch?

We sat on a park bench and watched them do their impossible leaps and flips until Scooby decided it was really boring and we walked back to the ute. By now I was feeling ready for my afternoon nap and as Rory drove me home I fell asleep, with Scooby draped across me, her head out of the window, ears blowing in the breeze.

I woke up with a start when we stopped outside my building. With manners as impeccable as Billy's, Rory jumped out and came round to open the passenger door. No man under the age of sixty had ever done this for me in London. I was about to kiss Scooby goodbye when I remembered something.

"Rory—Billy told me that Scooby is a champion jumper. Will you show me?"

"Sure," he said, grinning. He put his head back into the ute and came back holding a dog biscuit. "Scoobs!" he said, holding it above his head. "Biscuit!"

Scooby leapt straight up in the air. It was amazing how high she went. I clapped and Rory gave her the biscuit.

"You should be in the Olympics, you clever old high jumper," I said to Scooby, giving her a big kiss. She gave my face a good licking in response. Rory was beaming as he walked me to the door. Then there was a slightly awkward moment.

"Well, that was really fun," I said shyly. "Thanks for driving me home and thanks for the dog-replacement therapy."

"It was our pleasure. Wasn't it, Scoobs? Well, I'll be off then. It was great to meet you, Georgia. Hope to see you again next time I'm up in Sydney."

"Yeah, that would be great. As long as you bring Scooby."

I kissed him on the cheek and he stayed still for one extra beat. There was something hanging in the air at that moment. I didn't know what to do, so I just went inside.

.   .   .

I was cream crackered. What a weird twenty-four hours. I put on my comfiest nightie and lay on the sofa with a packet of Kettle Chips (the grease craving had just kicked in) and pondered all the events since I'd arrived at Danny Green's party the day before.

Jasper O'Connor's dickhead hat and jungle joints. Antony Maybury and his dancing eyebrows. Billy Ryan's unannounced tongue kiss and unerect penis. About twenty-five new best friends whose names I couldn't remember. The wicked plate. The heavenly dancing. The heavenly snogging. The unheavenly dog poo. The stupidity of the bed incident and subsequent embarrassment. The surprising morning phone call followed by the incredible disappearing date. Rory Stewart's kind smile. Scooby dooby doo.

What was Billy playing at? Talk about hot-cold hot-cold. One minute he was kissing me, then he was running away laughing, then he was nearly ravishing me in a public place, then he was running away, then we were having a cosy breakfast, then he was running away. If he wasn't so gorgeous I probably would have dismissed him as a kookalooka, but he was the perfect package. The full *Town Like Alice* fantasy. My parents would adore him. Even my brother would like him. My grandfather would be beside himself. He'd hated Rick—too urban. Couldn't comprehend a man who didn't like fishing. Billy was bound to like fishing, and shooting too. Perhaps we could divide our time between Australia and Scotland. Wouldn't that be the perfect life? I wondered when he would call me again.

But as I fell asleep, my mouth full of half-chewed crisps—or chips, as I was learning to call them—I realised what was odd about the moment with Rory at the door. I think he'd been about to ask me for my phone number. And I was slightly disappointed that he hadn't.

Chapter Four

"OK, how about 'Why Running Away from Heartache Never Works'?"

"No, too depressing," growled *Glow*'s editor, Maxine Thane. "It's just a statement, it doesn't offer a solution. Who's going to buy a magazine that promises to make them depressed? Could you all think before you open your mouths, please? Liinda, this story was your idea, what have you got?"

"Well, how about 'You've Left Him, But You're Still Carrying the Baggage'?"

"Not bad, we're getting somewhere—baggage is a good word and it's quite funny, but it's a bit clumsy. Have you got any ideas, Zoe?"

"Er . . . 'The Great Guy Who Got Away'?"

"What? Pay attention, will you?" said Maxine, not a woman inclined to put tact before getting her point across. "I know you're thinking about all the lunch you're not going to eat, but 'The Great Guy Who Got Away' is another story entirely. Actually, it's not a bad idea—make a note of it, Liinda. We could get single women in their late thirties to talk about the one guy they still think about. Put it on the list for the May issue. It would be cheap to do. We can ring all our friends and ask them. Now, what are we going to call this bloody man-baggage feature? Debbie?"

Debbie was looking down at her manicured nails and hardly lifted her glossy blonde head towards Maxine to answer. She sighed deeply.

"Oh, I don't know. What's it about? Dumping a man and not being over him? That's never happened to me. I can't imagine it. I just dump them and never give them another thought."

"Oh, you make me sick," said Maxine. "I don't know why I have you at these meetings. You might look like Grace Kelly, but I've met more intelligent handbags. Just sit there and look beautiful, darling, it might inspire somebody. OK, come on the rest of you, someone has an idea, surely?"

Up until now I'd been gazing vacantly out of the window, mesmerised by the vivid blue sky. I turned back to the other four women in the room and sat up.

"So what we're really looking at here," I said, "Is 'Why a Perfectly Normal Person Might Move to the Other Side of the World to Get Over Some Stupid Man.' Is that right?"

"Exactly."

"Well, funnily enough, I think I might be able to come up with some input on that—"

But before I could finish I was interrupted by a very pale woman with an enormous tower of black hair piled up on her head like an out-of-control bird's nest, with a large pink hibiscus flower that appeared to grow out of the middle of it. Liinda Vidovic.

"How about 'You've Left the Country, But Have You Really Left Him Behind'?" she said, determined that the editor's attention stay on her and "her" story idea.

"Mmm . . . That's pretty good, but it's a bit long," Maxine replied.

"I've got a better idea," I said, turning towards Liinda. The bird's nest swung around in irritation. "What about 'You've Left Him, But Have You Left Him Behind'?"

"That's brilliant, Georgia," said Maxine, smiling delightedly. "We've got it. Now you can all fuck off and leave me alone."

"And incidentally, the answer is yes," I added. "I have left him behind. Thank you all for your interest."

It was a good line, but then it should have been, seeing as it came from my own painful experience, which Liinda, as predicted, had lifted wholesale as a coverline. Of course it was outrageous of her to use my heartbreak as a story idea—and I now realised she'd bought me lunch on my first day in the office expressly to get all the grisly details—but I was in such a good mood that morning, I was prepared to forgive anything. Plus, I quietly gloated, it was me who had come up with the final editor-pleasing line. That'll learn here, I thought. Ms. Vidovic may have had the smartest mouth on *Glow* magazine for the past seven years, but now she had a little competition.

I was in a particularly good mood because of the fabulous long weekend I'd just had, but I was also still generally high on the newness of living in Australia. Just walking along a street was thrilling. Going to the supermarket was an anthropological expedition. Everything had different brand names—I tried three brands of loo paper before I discovered that the Australian equivalent of Andrex was called Sorbent. I spent quite some time watching water going down the plughole to see if it really did go the other way. (It does—and I'd made a special point of watching it in England just before I left, so I would know the difference.)

The birds were different. The sirens were different. The radio announced "golden oldies" I had never heard before. The newsreaders were strangers. You went north towards the sun. A southerly wind was a really cold one. I bought a postcard that showed Australia was the same size as the whole of Europe, and another that showed the world with Australia at the top. "No longer down under" it said. Too right, mate, I thought.

Sometimes I would be strolling along and the thought would literally stop me in my tracks. I'm in Australia. *Australia.* It thrilled me to the core. There I was on the other side of the world, as far away as I could be from Rick the Prick Robinson and his surgically enhanced sperm receptacles. From him and all the other weak-willied goons my homeland could come up with, under the heading of Men.

I was yonks away from all the superannuated public-school boys who were terrified of a woman with a job and a libido. Miles from the working-class blokes who thought I was a snooty bitch the minute I opened my mouth. Twenty-four hours from the idiots who said, "Oh, you're one of those feminists, are you?" because I ticked the "Ms." box on forms.

If *Glow* had a Mars edition, I might have taken a job on that, but for the time being Sydney was as far as I could go. And judging by the ones I'd met at Danny Green's hat party, the men here seemed to be a whole lot more attractive than Martians.

When we came out of the meeting I told Liinda I wanted a word with her in my office.

"You are appalling," I told her, shaking my head, but smiling. "You're shameless. You just lifted a great segment of my life to make a coverline. Unbelievable. Do you do this to all your friends?"

"Yes."

"Don't they get mad at you?"

The bird's nest teetered dangerously as she nodded. "Yes, but they carry on telling me all about their love lives anyway, so I carry on using them for inspiration. They know the deal. I always change their names."

I couldn't help laughing and she smiled back at me like a naughty child who knows they've got away with it.

"Oh, that's a relief. And who's writing this story about leaving a country to leave a man, anyway?" I asked.

"I've already written it."

"But you've never been out of Australia, have you?"

She shrugged. "No, but I have a good imagination."

"Did you actually speak to anyone about what it's like to change country?"

"Yes. Three psychologists. And you. And my mother. She moved here from Croatia in the 1950s, so she knows what it's like to move country."

"You are a piece of work," I told her, but I couldn't help liking Liinda. She was so barefaced about her treachery. I knew I was going to be one of those friends who carried on telling her my secrets, because apart from anything else she was a good listener and I needed someone to talk to. I sorely missed my girlfriends back in London and even after two weeks I knew that the time difference made it impossible to communicate with them properly.

If I rang them late at night for a good chat they were in the middle of their busy days and vice versa. I'd already received a couple of drunken phone calls in the morning at my desk. Even with emails it wasn't the same. Because I was also realising that if they didn't understand the context, my romantic tales just wouldn't be the same. It was no good if I had to start out explaining who Danny Green was and what moleskin pants were. I needed someone who already understood the subtle nuances of Sydney life, which I was only just beginning to grasp myself. Like the vast gulf between living in Elizabeth Bay, where I lived, and in Paddington, where Billy lived, for example. Separated only by a busy road and a couple of parks, but different universes in terms of values and beliefs. One bohemian and sophisticated, but with a dark side, the other chic and sophisticated, but with a dull side.

"Want to have lunch?" I heard myself ask her. I was burning to talk to someone about Billy's weird behaviour.

"Sure, I'll take you to a Sydney landmark. Do you like Chinese food?"

"Love it."

"Good. Because I only eat Chinese food."

I didn't even bother to ask why. I knew she'd tell me.

"Because you can smoke right through the meal."

BBQ King looked like a 1950s truckstop, all laminated tables and tatty lino. A jolly Chinese man barked, "Hello mate! Hello Riinda!" at us when we came in. Everyone in there knew Liinda. They didn't even ask for her order, they just brought it. The chairs were red vinyl, the floor was sticky and the noodle soup I was slurping down was like nectar. Already on her third Diet Coke, Liinda picked at her plate of plain boiled chicken and plain boiled rice with one hand, holding a cigarette in her other.

"I don't normally 'do lunch,' you know," she was telling me. "I like to eat alone, or there's a great lunchtime NA meeting in Macquarie Street, so you're very honoured."

"NA? Is that Narcotics Anonymous?"

"Yes."

"How often do you go to NA meetings?"

She took a long, deep drag on her cigarette. "Most days. I go to AA as well. And Codependents Anonymous. I have been known to do three meetings in a day."

"Crikey. That wouldn't leave you much time for a social life."

"That's the whole point. The last thing I want is a social life. Social lives in Sydney have drugs in them. As I'm sure you discovered on Sunday. How was it? Did you trash yourself?"

"Yes. I trashed myself. And nearly my reputation as well."

Linda looked very interested in that idea. I let her stew for a bit while I took a mouthful of soup.

"Tell."

"Do you know a guy called Billy Ryan?"

"Yes. He's a stockbroker. We had him as one of our 50 Most Eligible Bachelors one year. He's not bad looking if you like men who look like Liberal Party campaign posters."

"What kind of reputation does he have?" I asked.

"Don't know. He's more Deb-rett's territory. Overprivileged Paddington pond life. He knew the guy she was engaged to who died, I think, so I don't advise asking Debbie about him. I did try to get her to have some grief counselling when that happened but she started throwing stiletto shoes at my head. And when I left a few Codependents Anonymous brochures on her desk, she just threw them back onto mine. On fire. So I've left her to get over it her own way—hard drugs and casual sex. Was everybody totally shitfaced at the party?"

"Yes. Totally blasted. I've never seen such an orgy of drink and drugs. Why do they do that?"

Liinda shrugged. "Haven't a clue. It's just the way Sydney is. We all live in paradise and most of us can't wait to get out of it as soon as possible. Me included. If I hadn't woken up one morning in bed with two bikers I'd never seen before, in a room full of sawn-off shotguns, I'd still be behaving like that myself. Except I'd probably be dead."

I stopped with my chopsticks halfway to my mouth. The noodles fell back into the bowl with a plop.

"When did that happen?"

"Seven years ago. Just before I started at *Glow*. Maxine knows all about it. She saved my life, really. She might seem like a queen bitch but she has a really good heart. Her father was an alcoholic, like mine. I actually met her at Al Anon—it's for adult children of alcoholics. She sponsored me and she gave me a job. I owe her a lot—that's why I put up with her verbal abuse. That's why I try so hard to give her the best possible coverlines and why I haven't left *Glow* even though I've been offered lots of other jobs."

I paused to take it all in, giving up on the noodles and just sipping the delicious broth. Liinda pushed her plate away.

"But why is Maxine so awful to Debbie?" I asked. "She had a terrible thing happen to her and Maxine was giving her such a hard time at the meeting this morning. I was really embarrassed."

"Maxine does it deliberately. She's known Debbie all her life. They went to school together. Maxine's family used to be even wealthier than Debbie's but her pisspot father gambled and drank it all away and then killed himself. When she was twelve, Princess Maxine went from living in a huge house in Bellevue Hill to a two-bedroom unit in Bondi Junction. She could only stay on at her swanky girls' school because she had a scholarship."

Liinda paused for dramatic effect.

"Her genteel mother had to take in ironing. That's why she comes over so tough and that's why she hates seeing Debbie, who still has all her money and privilege, ruining herself over Drew's death rather than working her way through it. I think Maxine's hoping to shock Debbie into doing something about it. And then, of course, she's fantastically jealous of Debbie's beauty and money. It's a mixture of both, I guess."

"Blimey," I said. "I feel like I've walked onto the set of *The Young and the Restless* or whatever it's called."

"Oh, that's nothing. We've only just scratched the surface of what goes on in that place."

I used the spoon to slurp up a few noodles. Liinda took a couple more deep drags on her cigarette and then ashed it in her chicken. I had to ask her, I couldn't help myself—it was that journalist's curiosity again:

"Liinda, I hope you don't mind me asking, but how did you become a . . . er . . . junkie?" I hoped she wasn't going to say it started with a white plate and a little fingerful of hoochy coochy, as Antony called it.

"Do you really want to know?"

"Yes, but only if you want to tell me."

"It's not a pretty story, but I've told it so many times at meetings I don't mind who I tell it to anymore. It might put you off your noodles, though."

I shrugged.

"My father was an alcoholic," she began. "He beat my mother. He beat my brother. He beat me. Then he left us, which broke our hearts. He wasn't a bad man, but after they moved here from Croatia it never worked for him. He never learned to speak the language properly and felt frustrated and shut out. He thought he'd failed us, so he beat us. But he was still my daddy, you know?"

I didn't, but I tried to imagine it, nodding to encourage her.

"It was terrible after he left, but we survived. We had no money but we had each other. Then my mother got a boyfriend. He was much worse than my father. He beat my mother and he raped me. Had enough yet?"

I shook my head. "No. Tell me everything."

"OK. When I was fifteen I left home. I lived with one of the teachers from school right through my HSC and she was great. I graduated Dux of the school—and in the top five per cent of the state. Then I went to uni. Happy ending, right? Wrong. Because then I got a boyfriend and the only example I had for how to choose boyfriends was my mother. Not a great example. Not a great boyfriend. He smoked a lot of pot. So I did too."

Liinda paused and lit another cigarette.

"I'd never drunk alcohol because I'd seen what it could do to people," she continued, blowing a long stream of smoke out through her nose. "But I thought pot was fine. For some people it is, but when you have an addictive personality nothing like that is a good idea."

I'd lost interest in my noodles and was just stirring them around in a daze while Liinda continued.

"I smoked pot all the time. I stopped going to classes. I dropped out. Then my boyfriend got into heroin and so did I. First I smoked it. Then I started injecting. I didn't even think about it. It was in me. I was going to get addicted to something. Look at me now. I'm still addicted to cigarettes, to Diet Coke, to going to NA meetings and to work. I'm addicted to astrology. I'm an addict. That's what I am. It defines me. I've just learned to choose addictions that won't destroy my life."

I felt sick. The happy, golden simplicity of my childhood made me feel guilty. Of course there were sad moments and difficult times, but compared to Liinda's story my life had been a Disney script. The episode with Rick was a mere comic aside. I had tears in my eyes. I couldn't say anything; I just grabbed her hand and squeezed it.

"Don't feel sad for me, Georgia," she said. "I know it probably sounds like a horror story to you, but it's my reality and I've learned to live with it. I'm really proud that I've risen above it. I didn't talk to my mother for ten years, but now I do and I help her financially. My brother is doing fine and has two really sweet kids. I have a few good friends who love me, I'm good at my job and I'm not using drugs. And I've managed to help some of the people I've met at NA. That's a good feeling."

I was gawping at her miserably—I couldn't help it. I'd never heard a story like that before. She smiled at me gently.

"I know my life is weird to some people," she continued. "But I'm happy now. I'm happier than Debbie Brent, and she supposedly has everything. She's the one smiling out of the social pages while I go home on the train to the suburbs, but she's the one who has to fill her body with chemicals in order to feel elated. I feel elated just walking down the street knowing my body doesn't have any of those toxins in it anymore."

"You're amazing, Liinda," I said. I meant it.

"Oh, get out of here." She put her cigarette out. In my noodles. "Now, tell me about the orgy on Sunday. I want to live vicariously. Why are you so interested in Billy Ryan? Did you root him?"

"No, I did not *root* him, as you so delightfully put it. I came stupidly close to it, though." And even though she'd used my love life as a coverline that morning, I felt that after the story she had just told me, she'd earned a confessional in return. So I told her about my weekend. The whole lot. She listened, she laughed, she bugged her eyes, she lived it with me. And of course, she asked me what star signs they all were.

"Liinda, I don't know what sign Billy is. I don't even know what street he lives in. I know very little about him apart from the fact that he's a great dancer, he knows the names of all the stars, he's good fun and he has an unusually good body. And an unusually flaccid penis."

"You nearly slept with the guy and you don't know what sign he is?"

"How am I supposed to ask him? Hello, my name's Georgia, I'm a Gemini—what sign are you?"

"Exactly," she said out the side of her mouth as she lit up again.

"Oh, come on! That sounds so corny."

"It's better than falling in love with him and finding out afterwards that he's a Taurus."

"What wrong with Taureans? My grandfather's a Taurus and I adore him."

"There's nothing wrong with them, but it would be hopeless for you."

"Are you telling me you ask every vaguely attractive man you meet when he was born?"

"No. Not just the attractive ones. All of them. And until a law is passed making it compulsory for all men to have their date, time and place of birth tattooed on their foreheads I will continue to do so. I ask all women too."

"Well, I promise I'll ask him next time I see him. And Rory. But you should know what sign Jasper O'Connor is already. He said he knew you."

She looked up at me quickly and shifted in her seat.

"Yes, I do know him. Well, I used to. The scumbag. He's a Gemini like you but there's also a lot of Pisces in his chart, and as you have Scorpio rising there would be an attraction there, but—"

"Is he really a scumbag?"

"No, he's not really, but he smokes too much pot and it makes him behave like a scumbag. He forgets to pay back money to people. He's always late. He doesn't do what he says he will. It's boring."

She was rubbing her forehead and not meeting my eye. Suddenly what was going on in the restaurant seemed a lot more interesting to her.

"How did you meet him?" I persisted.

"Oh, you know," she shrugged, "around. We worked together a lot at *Glow*."

"Why doesn't he work for *Glow* anymore? He wasn't very flattering about Maxine . . ."

Her left hand came down on the table with a surprisingly loud *thwack* and she finally leaned forward and looked at me, with a big sigh.

"Or me, I bet. Jasper's getting really bitter because he knows he fucked up. At first it was great working with him—he was so much fun on a shoot—but then he messed something up and we stopped using him. It was no longer amusing. We were good friends for a while, but I just can't be around people who won't acknowledge their addictions. That's it."

I didn't think it was, but it did sound like the end of the conversation as far as Jasper O'Connor was concerned. Liinda lit another cigarette. I thought I'd try another gambit.

"Do you know Antony Maybury?" I asked.

"Know of. He's that dressmaker guy. Really camp queen. Big friend of Deb-rett's, in fact I think he was making her wedding dress . . . Not my type, darling."

"What do you mean? Because he's gay?" I said, stiffening with indignation.

Liinda shook her head. "I've got nothing against homosexuals. There's a leather queen I really like who goes to one of my groups, but I just don't like really camp men. I don't get them and they don't get me because I don't shave under my arms."

I couldn't imagine life without my gay friends. The campier the better. They were the centre of my universe. The chilli on my hot dog. The pom-poms on my mules.

"I thought all strong women loved gay men," I said, suddenly missing my boys in London terribly. "They're like oxygen for me. I prefer them to straight men most of the time."

"That's an interesting pathology," said Liinda, getting her coverlines expression. "Why?"

"Because you know they like you just for you. With straight men there's always that element of thinking: Does he think I'm attractive? Do I think he's attractive? Would he make a good husband? With gay men you don't have to worry about all that."

"I think that's really weird," said Liinda. "But then I'm not sure I really like any men much, and I certainly don't trust gay ones any more than straight ones. I think that's such a fallacy. They all hate women deep down."

I didn't agree with her, but it wasn't the time for an argument, seeing as she'd just told me about her horrendous childhood and then listened to me droning on about my silly little five-minute romance. We walked back to the office, with Liinda smoking all the way.

When we got there I thanked her for telling me her story and for listening to my recent adventures. Then she left my office, only to stick her bird's nest around the door again.

"And if I were you, I wouldn't bother finding out Billy Ryan's birthdate. He sounds like a complete flake. But I'd be interested to know about that Rory," she said, and disappeared.

I spent most of the afternoon rewriting an unintelligible article we'd paid someone a fortune for when I heard Maxine barking my name through her office door. A summons.

"GEORGIE! GEORGIE! COME HERE, I'VE HAD AN IDEA."

When she was excited about something, Maxine didn't need a phone. She was a human megaphone. I ran in.

"What?"

"I've had a great idea for a picture story and I want you to write it. We'll rope in five couples and get the men to direct make-overs on the women—you know, hair and make-up, that kind of thing. What do you think? I love it. 'How He Would Really Like You to Look.' It's a good coverline. Could you go and talk to Debbie about setting it up next week?"

I'd be delighted to, I thought, thrilled to have an excuse to go and talk to Debbie. Just being near her made me feel closer to her handsome cousin Billy. I dashed into the beauty office, where Debbie was standing on her desk wearing the most beautiful dress I had ever seen. I wolf-whistled.

"Va va va voom. You look incredible. Where did you get that gown? It's magnificent."

"Gown" was the only word for it. It was sculpted around her

upper body so it lifted her breasts and made her waist look tiny. Then it fell in bias-cut panels revealing layers of leopardskin-print silk and georgette with huge red roses on it. There were bits of silk plaid and paisley all mixed together, but somehow it worked. I was just about to ask her again where she got it from, when a spiky black head popped up from behind the desk with eyebrows in full flight.

"Antony!"

"Hello, Georgia. So glad you like my little creation."

"I've never seen anything like it—it's wonderful."

"Oh, just an amusement. Anything looks gorgeous on Debbie."

And Debbie certainly seemed to think so. She was completely ignoring me, so transfixed was she by her image in a full-length mirror being held up by her assistant, Kylie, who was pink with exertion.

"Kylie, keep that mirror still, would you. You're making me seasick. Antony, don't you think the décolletage should be lower?"

"No, darling. Let's leave something to the imagination. Anyway, you've only got an hour for hair and make-up before you go and I still have to get this hem fixed up—there's no time to do anything else. You're being picked up at seven, remember? It is now five to six."

"Kylie, did Christian call?" said Debbie. "He's meant to be doing my hair and face. Ring up and see where he is and then I want you to go down to the courier dock again to see if my shoes have arrived."

"Christian just called," Kylie replied. "He's on his way, and Ted in the courier dock is going to ring me when the messenger arrives with the shoes."

Debbie seemed happy now she knew all her minions were in order.

"Is she going out in that tonight?" I asked Antony. There didn't seem any point in addressing any more remarks to the Tsarina on the desk.

"No, it's for a charity ball in Melbourne on Saturday night. It's white tie or fancy dress—very smart. This is just the dress rehearsal." His left eyebrow nearly met his hairline.

"But I thought you said she was being picked up at seven . . . and the hair and make-up artist is on his way."

"Oh, that's just for tonight's date. Dinner."

"Which is not fancy dress?"

"Right."

We waggled our eyebrows in perfect synch.

"OK . . . Well, you look amazing, Debbie. I'm sure you'll be the belle of the ball on Saturday," I said.

She smiled at me absently, intent on mastering the art of opening and closing a huge fan with suitably coquettish grace.

"I'll come and talk to you tomorrow about a story idea Maxine's had, OK? Debbie?" I said, raising my voice as if she were deaf, than gave up. "Antony, why don't you come and say hi in my office when you've finished?"

"I'd love to."

At five minutes to seven, after he'd styled Debbie's dinner outfit and supervised her hair and make-up, Antony came and flopped down on a chair in my office. He was talking to me, but his eyes were wandering all over the room, taking in every detail of the pictures I had stuck up on my pinboard.

"Sweet of you to wait, Georgiana dear. Jeez Louise, what a princess!" he said, sniffing the roses on my desk. "Ten minutes ago she wanted me to ring the manageress of Bulgari—at home—to ask her to come and re-open the boutique so she could borrow—*borrow,* mind you—a necklace she saw in the window today. She was serious."

"How did you get out of that?"

"Told her the line was busy and then distracted her by telling her how beautiful she is. Sweet dog," he said, picking up a framed photo of Gaston on my desk.

"Why do you put up with it?" I asked.

"Debs? You know what happened to her fiancé, don't you?"

I nodded wearily. I was almost sick of hearing about it. "But does that justify her behaviour?"

"Believe me, Drew Stewart was really divine," said Antony, getting up to look at the books on my shelves. "I would have married him myself. He was funny, too. It was a devastating thing to happen to anyone. I was doing a fitting on Debbie's wedding dress when she got the phone call. When you go through that with someone you can't just desert them afterwards. Ooh, you've got a book about Cecil Beaton I haven't seen before."

"But is indulging her whims really going to help her in the long run?" I persisted as he turned my teacup upside down to look at the mark on the bottom. "It's Spode, Antony. Doesn't she need to face reality and see a shrink or something?"

"Yes, I like that pattern. Oh, I don't know, it's up to her. I'm just going to support her in any way she wants. Plus I'm madly in love with her father." He grinned, wickedly. "Wait till you see him. He makes Robert Redford look like an ugly man. But it's not just his looks, he oozes charm and sex—and money. I want a cigarette. Can we please leave this horrible building?"

So we left that horrible building and went to another horrible building. Well, it looked horrible on the outside, but as for the inside, I'd never seen such an amazing place. Antony lived in an ugly old warehouse, built of cheap brick, on a mean little street in Surry Hills. There was a dark entrance that smelled strongly of stale urine, and a nasty metal lift that creaked and groaned.

The place felt distinctly dangerous, but when he unbolted a metal front door it opened onto a kind of paradise—a big white space with floor-to-ceiling fold-back windows on one side, leading out to a huge roof garden. And it was a garden, not just a terrace. There were full-sized trees, many of them in bloom; there was even a stretch of lawn and flowerbeds edged with lavender hedges. I could see water features and real butterflies. Yet it was surrounded by the roofs of semi-industrial buildings.

"*Voilà*," said Antony, pushing open the sliding wall of glass and indicating the view with a flourish. "*Les toits de* Sydney, which make a pleasant change from *les* twats *de* Sydney, don't you think?"

"Antony—this is so gorgeous. But how come you have full-grown trees up here? How long have you lived here?"

"I've lived here five years, but the person who had it before me lived here for ten and the trees were half grown when he put them in. He was a film director—he could afford that kind of thing. He left me this place in his will. I would rather have him back, but I'm glad that something good has come from the plague."

"The plague?"

"AIDS, darling. That little *fauteuil* over there was another bequest. Hello, Stephen darling. And that mirror. Hello, Roger. And hello, Lee darling, of course. Lee was the one who left me the studio. Not that he has entirely left the studio. I can feel him here sometimes. The lights flicker on and off when he finds something amusing."

Although it was huge the main room had very little in it. There was a kitchen along one wall, with a gleaming stainless-steel bench, a matching fridge and stove, and a long line of stainless-steel pans hanging from a ceiling rack. A row of bar stools ran along one side of the bench and there was a large tray at the end crowded with bottles of alcohol. The opposite wall, the only one with no windows, had a steel rail stretching the length of it with about six dresses on it, each as extravagant as the one I'd seen Debbie in. Hanging above them were enormous hats covered in plumes, like something from a Gainsborough portrait. There was very little else apart from the small red armchair, the gilt mirror mounted with two imperial eagles and an ormolu console table stacked with invitations.

The only other furniture was a bed, standing on a Persian rug right in the middle of the room, and covered in pillows and cushions, with a huge chandelier hanging over it. Next to it there was a small table with just one book on it. This surprised me, as I thought Antony would be the reading type.

There was no sofa, no dining table, no TV and no curtains. And there was no sewing machine, no pins, threads or patterns, or any sign at all of where he made those extraordinary dresses. Music had started playing—Ella Fitzgerald—although I couldn't see the hi-fi. Antony was opening a bottle of champagne and didn't seem to mind me gawping at his home.

"I suppose you get used to people staring," I said.

"Not many people see it—I do all my fittings at clients' houses—but I thought you'd enjoy it," he said, handing me a long flute of champagne. "I imagine you are wondering three things: Where are his books? Where does he go to the loo? And where does he make those funny dresses?"

I laughed.

"I'll show you."

He walked out onto the roof garden and I saw that there was another room running perpendicular to the main room and about half the size. This was his studio. Great bunches of patterns hung from hooks next to a long work-top with a cutting table, a sewing machine and an overlocker. Along one wall was a shelving system filled with bolts of fabric. There were two dressmaker's dummies, another set of shelves stacked with cardboard boxes marked "ribbon, silk, tartan, red," "buttons, pearl," etc., and a whole shelf of Barbie dolls in fabulous outfits. The other walls were covered in . . . stuff: pages torn from magazines, little snippets of fabric, feathers, plastic toys, badges, shells, stickers, matchbooks. Magazines were piled up everywhere. Unlike the rest of the place, the workroom was a total mess.

"This is where I make the dresses," said Antony. "And this is where I ablute." He gestured towards two doors between the shelving units. He opened the left one, revealing a bathroom that was like a cave. Apart from a loo and a basin, the rest of the space was filled with large grey rocks. A giant showerhead dominated the centre of the ceiling and the entire floor sloped down towards one central drain.

"It's a steam room," said Antony. "Lee put it in. My workroom was originally his bedroom, but I like more space to sleep in."

The other door opened into a square room lined from floor to ceiling with books, with one of those old-fashioned library ladders to get to the top shelves. In the middle stood a round table with more books on it and a very comfortable-looking dark red leather club chair.

"This is wonderful, Antony. I can't believe this place. It's my fantasy to have a library. I just have books everywhere—all over the floor in my new place, actually."

"This used to be Lee's gym. I have different interests. Are you hungry?"

I nodded.

"Omelettes," he announced.

We went back into the big room and I sat on a stool while he whirled around with eggs and whisks. He sent me out into the garden to get some fresh basil and oregano.

"Well, you passed that test," he said when I came back with them. "You didn't ask me where they were."

We ate our omelettes, which were very good, finished the champagne and started on another bottle. We told each other our life stories. They weren't that different: Antony had grown up in the New South Wales countryside, five hours from Sydney. His father was the doctor for a huge area. Mine is a country solicitor. My blonde hair and freckles come from my Scottish mother, Antony's dark skin and black hair from his half-Spanish mother. He has two older sisters, I have one older brother. We both went to local junior schools, then boarding school, and we both hated riding although we liked the idea of horses. And we both played obsessively with Barbies. Well, Antony's was actually an Action Man, but he wore women's clothing, systematically pinched from Antony's sisters' dolls or created out of anything he could find.

"I had never heard of drag queens," he told me, polishing a fresh glass for each of us, because he thought the first ones were a bit stale. "I didn't know they existed, but one day I had the idea of making Action Man a wig. I made the first one—a beehive— out of a cotton-wool ball, which I coloured yellow with a felt-tip pen. It was quite successful, but I really wanted hair I could comb. So I paid a girl at school $1 for a lock of her straight blonde hair. I mounted it on sticky tape and attached it with glue. It didn't look quite right, so I made a scarf out of a bit of material and tied it over the top, to hide the join. It looked fine with day wear, but I wasn't so happy with the effect for after six."

It was a funny story the way he told it, but I could detect a little sadness in his eyes. "My father found Action Madame one day," he said, sighing. "In his wig and a fine silver lamé gown. It was the only time he ever beat me."

He drained his glass in one and demanded to know more about me.

I told him tales about my glorious years at Edinburgh University and Antony explained that he'd gone to art school to study fashion, but had dropped out after a year. He really only wanted to make fabulous dresses, he said—he wasn't interested in the commercial side of things. So he scraped together a living making evening gowns for his female friends, until one of them was spotted by a woman who worked in the wardrobe department of Opera Australia.

After ten years working at the Opera he had gone freelance, and now he made a few costumes when they needed something really spectacular, but he mainly specialised in wild gowns for costume parties—which Sydney seemed to have a lot of—and charity balls.

"I don't make much money, but I don't need much," he told me. "Lee left me quite a bit of capital along with this place, so I don't have to work any more than I feel like. I really just do it so I can look at beautiful women in beautiful underwear."

I must have looked very surprised. He started chuckling and doing the eyebrow thing—he'd obviously guessed what I was thinking.

"Yes, darling, I am gay, but I still like looking at beautiful underwear. And I can still find women attractive, you know—there are no rules against window shopping."

I opened my mouth to say something, but he got in first.

"Yes, I have slept with a woman. More than one, actually. No, I didn't find it revolting. I found it quite pleasant, but I prefer having sex with men. I like the roughness of it. I like to keep sex and emotions separate and that's easier with other men. Especially if you don't know their names. Don't looked shocked. I use protection. I just like anonymous sex. Oh! Hello Lee!"

The lights were flickering on and off.

"See?" Antony smiled. "Say hello."

"Hello Lee," I said. The lights flickered one more time and stopped.

"I think he likes you," said Antony. "Anyway, enough about

my sordid sex life. I want to know more about you. How did you get into journalism?"

So I told him how I'd got into magazines when I was working as a bilingual secretary for the managing director of a publishing company. Then he asked me why I had moved to Sydney and, for the first time since I'd arrived, I told the whole story. I had only told Liinda the bare outlines—fiancé found with other woman—and I hadn't told her what the other woman did for a living and what the fiancé was doing at the moment of discovery. For some reason, though, I told Antony everything.

He laughed so much I thought he was going to have a conniption. Tears were rolling down his cheeks.

"That's the funniest thing I have ever heard. A gym slip. HA HA HA. He thought you wouldn't mind, HA HA HA." Suddenly he snapped out of it and looked at me seriously. "What a complete asshole."

"Well, he is and he isn't. Rick has his good side."

"His money?"

"I didn't care about that. It was nice sometimes, but it wasn't why I was with him. He made me laugh. He was exciting to be around."

"Especially when he got his cane out . . . Oh I'm sorry, poor you. It must have been such a blow to think you had your future all set out and suddenly, a blank page. So have you come out to Sydney to meet a broad-shouldered Australian man?"

I think I blushed.

"Well, I hope you won't be disappointed. And I hope you don't think Jasper O'Connor is it, because he really isn't. He's nice looking, I can see that, but he's a total flake."

"Yes, I have been warned." All these pronouncements about Jasper were beginning to irritate me. I'd only talked to the guy and everyone was warning me off him like he was radioactive or something. If anything it made him sound more interesting.

"Did you meet anyone else on Sunday?" asked Antony. "Who were you dancing with? I can't remember. Got too out of it later and blasted those particular brain cells."

I hesitated, not sure if I should tell him. He might tell Debbie and I didn't want to short-circuit the whole thing, whatever kind of thing it was. Yet even as I thought this, I could hear my mouth saying "Billy Ryan."

"Billy! That's right, I remember now. You *are* a fast worker." He narrowed his eyes and did some eyebrow dancing. "Or did he hit on you?"

"Well, he dragged me onto the dance floor and put his tongue in my mouth."

Antony sighed deeply.

"What's wrong? Is he notorious for snogging girls he hardly knows?"

"No, he's not notorious, it's just that through Debbie, I know a bit more about Billy than most people. He's a lovely guy, but he's rather confused. What happened between you two?"

I told him. I made it into a funny story, complete with me falling asleep with a mouth full of crisps. I waited for the HA HA HA—it didn't come. Another bottle of champagne did and Antony looked uncharacteristically serious. The dancing brows were meeting in a frown.

"Georgia, I've only know you five minutes, but I really like you. We are going to be friends. I don't make new friends very often, but when I meet someone and we click, that's it. So I'm going to tell you exactly why Billy behaved the way he did, because I don't want you to be disappointed."

I felt a bit sick. "Is he gay?" At least I got a laugh that time.

"No, he is not gay. It would be easier if he was. No, Billy's problem is that he's in love with his own brother's wife."

"He's what? I don't believe this town. His best friend is Rory

Stewart, whose brother was engaged to Debbie Brent, who is Billy's cousin . . . oh, I give up . . ."

"It gets better. Or worse. The woman Billy is in love with—the one married to his brother, Tom—is . . . wait for it . . . Rory's sister."

"Rory's *sister*? Hang on, doesn't that also make her the sister of Debbie's dead fiancé?"

Antony nodded.

"This is ridiculous. You'll have to draw me a Venn diagram. Is everyone in Sydney related?"

"Pretty much. At the top end of 'society' they are, anyway. The Ryans, the Stewarts and the Brents are three big country families. They all grew up together. That awful plane crash makes the whole thing seem a lot more gothic, but they've all been marrying each other for a hundred years. That's why Debbie's ghastly little common mother was a good thing—some fresh blood. Debbie and Drew's children would have been really something, but I think it will be good if she marries outside the clans now."

"But hang on, tell me more about Billy. He's in love with his sister-in-law, Rory's sister. What's her name, anyway?"

"Elizabeth Ryan, née Stewart—known as Lizzy."

"Is this Lizzy in love with Billy?"

"Yes."

"Are they doing something about it?"

Antony nodded as he drained his glass.

"Does her husband—hang on, Billy's *brother*—know?"

"No. Tom doesn't know about them, but he does know something weird is going on."

This was incredible. "Does Rory know?"

"Yes."

"How does he feel about it?"

"He's not very happy about it, but he doesn't say anything. Remember, his sister is his last living sibling and she suffered a lot after the crash too. I guess he reckons it's her—er—affair, so he and Billy just never talk about it. They both pretend it's not happening. That's why Billy kissed you like that—to show Rory he's still chasing women."

"But Rory dared him to do it . . ."

"That's typical too. He hopes Billy will meet someone else and leave Lizzy alone. All part of the game."

I must have looked crestfallen. I was just a pawn. A porn.

"But why was he so passionate in the park?"

Antony paused and seemed to look at me closely.

"Georgia, you are a very attractive woman, you know."

I pulled a Quasimodo face.

"Stop that," he said, flicking me with his napkin. "I'm sure Billy would have been chasing you for real a few months ago, before he got together with Lizzy. But really, this thing between them has been going on since they were teenagers. Everyone was mystified when she married Tom—it was like, uh? Wrong brother. But Billy just left it too long to ask her. He wanted to play the field, just one more year, one more year . . . So she married Tom, because he did ask her."

"A Ryan in hand—"

"Is better than a Ryan in the park, as you discovered."

"Well, I feel like a total idiot, but it does explain his weird behaviour. You know when he left the café on Monday—would he have been going to see Lizzy?"

"Definitely. Tom would have been playing golf."

"Does everybody in Sydney know about this?" I was beginning to wonder if Liinda knew and that was why she'd told me to forget about Billy.

Antony patted my hand. "No. Absolutely not. I only know because Debbie tells me everything. And I've only told you because I want you to put him out of your mind. He's basically a nice guy—a bit thick, but very attractive, I do admit—and Debbie says it's tearing him up behaving like this. But he really does love Lizzy. It will all come out in the end, I'm sure."

"So I guess he won't be ringing me then."

"Well, he might, because he's a gentleman and I'm sure he enjoyed your company, and in his doltish way he'll think it would be nice to be friends. Plus it will help him cover if he's seen around town with a beautiful girl like you."

"Oh Ant, you're so gallant. I wish it was true. Anyway, it's nice to have an esteem boost when I've just found out that my dream man is involved in a psycho-incest love triangle. What an unholy bloody mess. But to tell the truth, he is a bit of a dunderhead really, it was just the package that got me going." I held out my glass. "Give me another drink, bartender."

Maybe it was all the champagne and Antony's effervescent company, but I wasn't desperately upset about Billy. It was such a ridiculous mess I couldn't take it personally, but I did thank God I hadn't slept with him. Then I would have felt used. And somehow being told by Antony made it OK. He was scrabbling around doing something under the kitchen bench. Suddenly the music changed and the Astrud Gilberto which had been playing was replaced by the opening bars of "We Are Family."

"Let's dance," said Antony. "I want to see you shake that cute arse of yours."

So I did. And Antony turned out to be a pretty good dancer too, whirling around in that big white room. It was a hoot. We danced until we were pooped and then we flopped onto Antony's big bed, because there was nowhere else to flop. It had a headboard and a footboard carved with flowers and washed with white paint, which were very comfortable to lean against.

While I had the chance, I wanted to ask him about all the new people I'd met.

"Antony," I said, getting comfortable. "What do you know about Rory Stewart?"

"Very nice man. Sometimes I wish Debbie would marry him, but he's actually too intelligent for her. She'd drive him mad. Although they did go out when they were sixteen and she was having a temporary falling out with Drew . . ."

"Oh God, don't tell me any more. It's a miracle this lot don't all have two heads."

He looked at me closely. "It's a shame, really, because Rory would have been nice for you."

It was my turn to do some eyebrow raising. "Well, I must say I don't find him unattractive. He's not as stunningly good-looking as Billy on first sight, but when you get to know him, he's so nice and kind you start to find him gorgeous in his own way. To be honest, I was a bit disappointed he didn't ask me for my phone number . . ."

Antony's brows were doing the cancan.

"Good God, no!" he cried. "He couldn't possibly do that—you're Billy's squeeze."

"What? But Rory knows Billy is having it off with his sister—he knows he's not really interested in me."

"I know that, you know that, they know that, but they're pretending it isn't happening, remember? That's all part of the double bluff: Rory couldn't ask you out, because he'd be moving in on Billy's turf. They're mates. Mateship is a great Australian tradition," he continued. "A real Aussie bloke would put his mate before his girl—and Billy and Rory have been friends since they were born. They're maaaates."

I shook my head, bemused. "They're nuts, that's what they all are. They might be heavenly looking dream husbands, but they're all barmy. I thought the English middle classes were hung up, but this lot are positively constipated—I'm going to give them all a very wide berth."

"I think that might be wise. And whatever you do, don't tell Debbie about it. Don't even tell her you met them. She'll be ridiculously jealous. She thinks all those men are her property, and in a way they are. Nothing has really been right in those three families since Debbie Brent grew breasts."

I looked at my watch. It was after one and I was facing my second hangover in a week. And it was a school night. Good going, Georgia, I thought. You've been in Australia two weeks and you are already a drug-taking alcoholic embroiled in an ugly family scandal. I told Antony I had to go and he called me a cab.

When it arrived he came down in the lift with me and put me in it.

"Bye darling," he said, kissing me warmly on both cheeks. Then he stopped, looked at me for a moment, and kissed me full on the lips.

Chapter Five

The next day I didn't feel quite as bad as I had on Monday morning. And a bacon sandwich at my desk first thing made me feel even better. Then I remembered that I had to pin Debbie down to arrange the shot for the couples makeover story that Maxine was so excited about.

I walked round to the beauty office. She wasn't in yet. It was ten-thirty and Kylie looked embarrassed. She was too nice a girl to be able to lie with any conviction and I had the strong impression that Debbie wasn't "doing appointments," as Kylie was now telling me.

Then Debbie strolled in. With wet hair. I raised an eyebrow at Kylie, wondering if I'd caught the habit from Antony. Debbie was smiling broadly. She didn't take her sunglasses off.

"Hello girlies. How are we today? Having a little chinwag? Anything I should know?"

"Yes," I said. "We're planning to steal your ball dress. How was your dinner last night?"

She wrinkled her perfect little nose. "Really boring. I met Peter at a weekend party in Bowral. I thought he was fun, but he turned out to be a major snore. Didn't have any coke on him and didn't even want any of mine when I offered it, which I thought was bloody rude. And he didn't want to go dancing after dinner. He said he wanted to 'talk' more. What a drag."

"So did you have a nice early night then, Debbie?" asked Liinda, popping her head round the door.

"Oh no, darling—five a.m. I made him take me to the Blue Room for some drinks and then I met this really nice guy. Quite yummy, actually. We had a really good time. Ended up at the Midnight Shift, can you believe it?" She started singing "Believe" by Cher and snapping her fingers; she was even dancing a bit. Liinda gave me a look and mouthed the word "ecstasy."

"Debbie," I said to her boogying back. "Maxine has had an idea for a shoot involving ten real people—"

She turned round and made a face. "Real people are so ugly. The pictures will be hideous. What is her stupid idea, anyway?"

Liinda sloped off—not enough raw emotion for her.

"She wants us to find five real couples and get the men to direct makeovers for the women, to see what kind of hair and make-up men really like on women."

Debbie brightened up. "Great, if they're re-styling each other you won't need me, the stylist, will you? Kylie can organise the shoot and they can make each other look disgusting while I do something useful instead. OK? Now, Kylie, can you go and get me two coffees? Skinny lattes. Would you like a coffee, Georgie? OK—add a fat latte to that, Kyles, and whatever you want. I'll give you the money later—I need to go to the autobank. Actually, you could go for me, here you are. Get me $500. You know the number. So Georgie, how are you, anyway? How are you settling in to *Glow* and to Sydney?"

She was being amazingly friendly. She was smiling at me. Even if it was drug-fuelled, I liked it. No one could be unmoved by Debbie's smile on high beam.

"It's great, thank you. So far I really love it. Everyone is being so friendly . . ."

"That's great. I'm sure you'll fit in here. Have you met any nice men?"

"One or two. I went to Danny Green's hat party on Sunday, that was really fun."

"Oh, I normally go to that but I couldn't be bothered this year. Had a big night on Saturday and I forgot to get Antony to make me a hat, so I had nothing to wear."

"I met your friend Antony. He's really lovely."

"Well, don't go falling for him, will you—he's gay. A poofter. Useless."

"I meant he's lovely as a friend. He's so much fun."

"Oh yes, he makes beautiful frocks, but you don't want to be seen hanging around with gay men in public too much. Puts real men off. So, did you meet anyone else?"

"Jasper O'Connor."

"Yeauuch. So you've met a screaming queen and a pathetic failure—not doing very well are you? I know all you English girls come out here to get laid, so we'd better do something about it. Mind you, I don't blame you. I spent a year in London after I finished school and those Pommy guys were hopeless in bed. One of them kept apologising." She started laughing. "I'm so sorry," she said in a good take-off of an English public-school voice. "I'm frightfully sorry, I'm afraid I just had a little orgasm. I do hope you don't mind." She laughed and laughed. "What a waste of time. So I can understand why you moved out here. I wonder if we know any people in common in London. I go there so much. Where did you go to school?"

My obscure Scottish boarding school didn't impress her,

but when I told her my brother had been to Winchester she perked up.

"Oh, do you know Freddie Swinton and Toby Ayres? They both went to Winchester. They're both gorgeous. Toby's mother is Italian . . ."

It went on like this for quite a while and then she opened her diary and pulled out a big pile of invitations.

"Now what do we have this week? What can I take you to that will be throbbing with Australian manhood . . . Mmm, an opening at the Glenmore Road Gallery—oh, that was last week; launch of a new Ralph Lauren fragrance tonight, which I'm going to, but there won't be any men, just single beauty editors—although there will be free perfume, which makes it worthwhile. Someone's launching a new mobile phone next week—that'll be good for suits, we should go to that—but I want to take you to something this week, so you'll realise that there are men in Sydney apart from queens and potheads. What else? Another gallery opening tonight, which I'll call in at on my way to Ralph Lauren. Do you want to come to that?"

"No, I'm too tired. And I look awful—I had a big night last night."

She looked at me over the top of her shades.

"Yes, you do look a bit blotchy. Let's see what else is here. The welcome party for some boring person at Opera Australia—give that a big miss, wall-to-wall poofters. Opening of a shoe shop in Mosman—over the bridge, forget it. Aha! This is perfect—tomorrow night's the fashion parade at David Jones. It's the preview of the new winter collections and it's always a good party. Lots of men at that. OK? We'll leave straight from here, no time for hair and make-up—I'll get Marco to blow-dry my hair in the morning—but you'll have to dress up a bit."

She looked me over like a horse she wasn't at all sure about buying. I wondered if I should show her my teeth.

"Yes. Wear a dress. Something skimpy. And you might try combing your hair. Do you ever go to the hairdresser?"

"It has been known. Don't worry, I'll wash it. And thanks, Debbie. It's really nice of you." I sat on my hands so she couldn't see my nails.

"You're most welcome." She gave me one of her arc-light smiles, and once again I could see why the entire Stewart and Ryan families had been in love with her. "I'd hate you to get the wrong impression of Sydney. And you can introduce me to all your brothers' friends next time I'm in London. So, you'll tell Maxine that Kylie will organise her shoot—OK?"

I nodded, aware that my audience with Her Highness was now over. Sure Debbie, I thought, as I went back to my own office, I'll take all the flak for you not wanting to do a shoot specially requested by the editor, if you'll introduce me to some men. What was I coming to?

Debbie was right about the smorgasbord of suitable men at the David Jones fashion parade—I just wish I'd inspected the buffet a little more closely before filling my plate. Because the one I chose was Nick Pollock. Also known, by quite a large sector of Sydney's female population, as P.O.F. —which stood for Pants On Fire. But I didn't know it then.

It was a great party, I must say. Lots of ladies in Chanel suits accompanied by their po-faced husbands, and a good smattering of Bright Young Things to make it look less like a plastic-surgery convention. I was an honorary BYT, tagging along with Debbie, who'd been to All the Right Schools and told me she knew All the Right People for me to meet. Because I had gone to an OK school in Scotland and my brother had gone to a very OK one in England, I was granted instant membership to her exclusive group of polo-playing, beach-house-owning, BMW-driving, bond-dealing, cocaine-snorting buddies.

Fired up with all the excitement of a new city, a new country, a new job and a new life, I was ready to go along with anything. Especially if there were a few free glasses of champagne thrown in. But what really amazed me was that after a fashion show of stultifying frumpiness, they didn't just turf us out into the night with a miniature scent sample, champagne halitosis and an incipient headache, as they would have done in London. Instead, they dimmed the lights and let the dancing begin. We had a full disco in the shoe department. It was marvellous getting down between the mules—and that's where I met Mr. P.O.F. Pollock, shimmying his hips with great aplomb to "It's Raining Men."

Clearly he was one of Debbie's Right People, because she introduced us straight away.

"Nick darling, this is Georgie Abbott. She's just moved here from London. She went to St. Leonards. Her brother went to Winchester. She used to work for *Pratler*. She's come to work on *Glow*. She knows lots of people on newspapers in London—you've probably got friends in common."

With a swish of her hair Debbie was off to dance with her broker of the week and left me to talk to a dark-haired fellow with boyishly pink cheeks who was smiling at me rather coyly. Dark hair, blue eyes . . . mmm . . . reminded me of Rick a little. First Jasper, now this guy. Was I seeing Rick in every man I met?

"Let's dance," he said, grabbing my hand, spinning me round and pushing his groin into me from behind. I had never known anything like these Australian men for dancing. Maybe it was used as a substitute for contact sports in social situations.

The Weather Girls were playing and Nick sang along jubilantly into my ear, grinding his hips in time, until suddenly he spun me round, stared into my eyes like a crazed ferret and yelled "ABSOLUTELY SOAKING WET!"

I couldn't help laughing, and seeing he had my full attention, he suddenly stopped dead and said, "What is this disco crap, anyway? Let's go and have a drink."

With one hand still firmly holding mine he made for the bar and got us two glasses of champagne. Then he led me to a table right in the corner, where he sat with his back to the crowd and gazed into my eyes.

"So, Georgie, is it?"

"Georgia, actually. Georgiana, not Georgina, so it's Georgia."

"Georgie. Georgie. I've got Georgie on my mind..." He seemed to enjoy singing. He was quite good at it, it was just a shame he couldn't get the words right. "Georgie, Geooooooorgie . . . I'm on the midday train to Georgie boo boo bo boo bo bo bo boo boooo . . ."

"Or you can just call me George, if you like—"

"Boy George. Girl George. Georgie Girl. Girl Friday. Thank God it's Friday . . . Forgive me, I go on a bit, sorry. It's just that words are my thing. Words are my lifeblood, my life's work, my work life, my word life. I word to live and live to word—"

"Are you in newspapers?" I asked him quickly, keen to stem his stream of consciousness. It didn't work.

"Yeah, I'm in newspapers. I'm on newspapers, I'm of newspapers, I am newspapers. I'm a senior writer at the *Sydney Morning Herald,* although I'm thinking of taking a gig back in your old town on the *Sunday Times,* or I might head for Washington. There's some really interesting stuff over there I want to check out about corruption in the Pentagon."

"So what do you write about? Are you an investigative reporter?"

"Sure, I do investigations. I do major arts profiles. I write about food. I do big sport round-ups when there's something interesting going on. And I'm getting a weekly opinion column soon—you know, just thoughts and observations, politics, corruption, the big issues. I like to keep it all loose."

He was leaning forward over the table, playing with the stem of his glass suggestively.

"You must be terribly busy . . ." I said.

"Yes, and I've got a couple of book projects on the go too. A biography of Paul Keating and a history of the Wallabies—the rugby team, not the marsupials. Just a few little things to keep me interested."

"So what would I have read by you in the *Herald* in the past few weeks?"

"The past few weeks?" He looked shifty and took a big gulp of his champagne.

"Yes. I've lived in Sydney for nearly three weeks, I read the paper every day, what would I have seen of yours?"

"Oh, I don't write every week. Only when there's something really worth saying. I'm more of an essayist, although I might throw a couple of scraps to the back page. You know, 'Stay In Touch'?"

"Oh yes, I think so. Sort of gossip around town. Do you work on that?"

He shrugged and drained my glass.

"Well, I just help them out with a few tips. My contact book, you know. So what do you do on *Glow*? Orgasm Editor? Special Correspondent, Fellatio?"

I was beginning to find this arrogant smart arse really annoying, but something about him kept me at the table.

"I'm the deputy editor, actually. I'm involved with every aspect of the magazine. I write as well. I really enjoy it. In fact I won an award for it last year . . . I wrote a piece about Harley Street doctors who perform clitoridectomies on Arab princesses . . ."

But he didn't seem very interested in hearing about my award and that's when he analysed my handwriting, showing me how like his own it was. Then he asked me what my favourite books were and we seemed to like all the same ones. *The Tempest* was his favourite Shakespeare play too, and he said if he ever had a daughter he was going to call her Miranda. We both agreed on Benedick for a boy.

The next thing I knew we were leaving the party. I snapped myself back to reality long enough to run and tell Debbie I was leaving. When she saw who I was leaving with, a look of amusement crossed her face but she didn't make any comment beyond, "Have fun. See you tomorrow."

Nick rode down in the lift with me, gazing into my eyes all the way. It was a bit much, actually. I was glad when he came back to earth. I still wasn't sure whether I liked him or not, but there was something fascinating about his awfulness.

"Let's go eat something," he said when we got outside and I couldn't think of a good reason not to. After a ten-minute ride in his red open-top MG, we arrived at a cosily lit bistro. I had no idea where we were, but all the staff knew him and greeted him warmly, apart from one of the waitresses who looked at him rather stonily, I noticed.

Although the restaurant was packed, they immediately found a table for us in a small courtyard out the back. The air was fragrant with frangipani flowers, which periodically fell off the trees and landed on us. Nick tucked one behind my ear and leaned over to sniff it, nuzzling my neck at the same time, which I thought was a bit familiar. A bottle of rosé appeared immediately and Nick only broke my gaze long enough to shoo away the menu and ask the waiter to bring us a dozen oysters and two rocket salads. I hate oysters, but—like the neck-nuzzling—it seemed rather rude to mention it. I'm British. I can't help myself.

"Tell me everything," he said.

"Everything what?"

"Who you are, where you come from, why a beautiful woman like you has moved to our tiny little city from the great metropolis. What you love, who you hate and why you aren't married . . ."

"How long have you got?"

"As long as it takes. But start with where you were born and why you've moved to Sydney." He put his head in his hands and gazed at me with a fascinated expression.

"Well, I grew up in Wiltshire, but I went to school in Scotland—"

"Oh, I love Scotland," said Nick, sitting up and brightening visibly. "I went there with my father when I was a kid. He had a year as a writer-in-residence at Edinburgh University."

"That's where I went. I did French and English literature—"

"Oh, you'll be familiar with my father's work then. James Pollock." He looked at me confidently. The name rang a small bell. A very small bell, somewhere in another part of the house.

"You've probably read *Dingo Man Donger* or *Hard-Belly Blowflies*," he continued, as the surly-looking waitress brought our food over and plonked it on the table. "I've always felt that *Dust Dancers* was his best, although they wrecked it in the movie when they put Paul Hogan in the part of Slingo. It should have been Bryan Brown. Hogan didn't have the *gravitas*."

I'd seen that film. On a plane. It was so awful I went and flicked through the book in a bookshop afterwards. Some terrible tripe about Real Men finding themselves in the Outback and Finding Themselves. Absolutely the worst kind of macho bullshit served up as serious literature, although I had to admit James Pollock was a pretty good writer. It was just his attitude to women I found so offensive. They only appeared in the book when Dingo or Slingo or Pingo or one of his neanderthal hard men needed a quick shag. But Nick was still going on about him, in between helping himself to oysters. I should have seen the warning signs then, but something about his undintable self-confidence kept me interested.

"Yeah, they're having a exhibition on him at the State Library next month, where they're displaying his manuscripts— he always writes them by hand with a fountain pen and never rewrites a line, you know. I wanted to use pen and ink at the *Herald* instead of those computers that just confine your creativity into a square box, but they couldn't understand what I was trying to do."

Neither could I, but I didn't get a chance to say so. Nick was still droning on, with a rather beautific smile on his broad-cheeked face.

"Yeah, so they'll have the manuscripts and photographs of the parts of the bush where Dad finds his inspiration and on the opening night they're going to have performances by some elders of the tribe he was initiated into in Far North Queensland. You'll have to come as my date," he said, squeezing my hand.

Even though I still wasn't sure if I hated him or not, that was an attractive prospect. I always like a man who uses the future tense and me in the same sentence.

"Dad will love you," he said. "He loves other writers. That's why he's so happy I'm a writer now. I'll take you out to the property to meet him one weekend, although he'll give you a hard time about being a Pom. Hates bloody Poms. But he's always wanted to see me with another writer. 'Nick,' he says, 'what you need is the right woman to knock some sense into that thick head of yours. Preferably one who can read and write.' The old bastard. He's always carrying on like that."

Nick smiled to himself and shook his head, stuffing in a few more oysters at the same time. The platter was empty and I'd only eaten one (forced myself, revolting), and when I was a bit slow with my rocket salad (too concerned about bits of it getting stuck in my teeth) he hoed in and helped me. Then he asked a passing waiter to bring us two double espressos, which I thought was a bit much at that time of night.

And on he went, telling me more about his father and all the wonderful books he, Pollock Revisited, was going to write when he could persuade the *Sydney Morning Herald* to let him go. They found his unique voice just impossible to replace, apparently. He knocked off his coffee in one go and when I'd only taken a couple of cautious sips of mine, he finished that too. And all four of the complimentary chocolates.

Without even waiting for the bill, he tossed a couple of $50 notes on the table and stood up. "Shall we?" he said, smiling down at me, one lock of very black hair falling onto his forehead. It was all very fetching. After scooping up the last bit of bread to eat on the way, he escorted me to the door, waving to all his waiter chums and only frowning slightly when the chilly waitress said sarcastically, "Bye, Mr. and Mrs. Pollock. Sleep well."

At the time I thought it was a very peculiar thing to say. Now I realise she was just another member of the handwriting-analysed sorority, who had truly believed for a few sweet hours that she was possibly going to be the next Mrs. Pollock. At that time I was just another innocent lamb headed for the barbie.

Nick didn't even ask me if I wanted to go home with him. He just took me. And of course he was absolutely right in his assumption that I found him sexually attractive. It might sound odd, that a man who talked about himself and his stupid father for most of the evening could have any appeal, but it was the way he talked that was so bewitching. He made you feel as though you were the one woman he had ever met who it was even worth telling these things to. And, as I say, I've always had a thing for men with black hair and blue eyes. It's so Celtic.

While Nick was banging on about his bewildering childhood—being whisked around the world while Daddy P. took up writer-in-freebie-residence at a succession of major universities—he gazed at you slightly sadly and vulnerably, as if pleading with you to understand that being the son of a genius wasn't easy at all. Meanwhile, he was rubbing your thigh under the table, and popping his fingers into his mouth to lick off the oyster juices. And letting that shiny black curl flop into his eyes.

God, he was a piece of work.

But the truly tragic thing about Nick, with all his hang-ups about not inheriting his father's genius, was that he did have a real talent all of his own. Nick Pollock could flirt for Australia. I think he could seduce a statue.

But I hate people making assumptions about me, and as we pulled up in front of a block of flats in Bondi, my self-preservation instinct kicked in. It was only a few days since the incident with Billy Ryan, after all, and I wasn't going to find myself accidentally in bed with a stranger again so soon.

"Er, Nick. This is not where I live. I live in Elizabeth Bay and I need to go home now."

He looked very surprised. "What? Don't you want to come up and see my poems? I've got some of Dad's manuscripts up there too—you'd really enjoy them."

I couldn't tell if he was joking. I didn't care. I just knew I must not go up there with him.

"Maybe some other time, Nick. I've really got to get home to bed. New job, you know."

"Sure, sorry, I should have asked you. I just thought we were getting on so well, you might like to continue the conversation on my balcony looking over the Pacific Ocean."

"Perhaps you could show me some etchings of it, as well," I said. Really, it was too much. "But some other time—it's midnight already and I have to be brilliantly witty and creative in nine hours' time."

He looked at me for a moment—in retrospect, I realise he couldn't believe what he was hearing—then he drove me home.

Chapter Six

When I got to work the next morning Nick had already rung and left a message on my voicemail. Singing.

"Georgie, Georgie . . . I've got Georgie on my mind . . ." He was playing the guitar while he sang it. "Good morning, beautiful. It was great to meet you last night. I'm just ringing to say have a fabulous day. I feel like seeing a movie later—I'll give you a call and see if you want to come. Ciao."

I have to confess I was thrilled. Until the last word. I hate it when people say "ciao." Unless they're Italian, of course—then I adore it. But the rest of the message was so lovely I let it pass.

I thought about calling Antony to ask him what he knew about Nick, but decided not to jinx the whole thing. I didn't want to hear another Victorian melodrama. I could talk to Debbie about him, of course, because she had seen me leave with him, but at eleven she still wasn't in the office.

I was out in the hall at the water cooler when she came in just after midday, carrying two coffees and wearing sunglasses again.

"Debbie, hi!" I said, thrilled to see her—I could have a mini-post mortem at last. She just shook her head and walked past me. I was dumbfounded.

"Don't take offence," said Seraphima, the office junior, who had witnessed the scene from her position on the front desk. "She's having a toxic day."

"A what?"

"A toxic day. What you and I might call a hangover. When Debbie has one it's her toxins coming out from whatever new vitamin, diet, or alternative therapy she has just discovered. It never has anything to do with five bottles of champagne and three packets of cigarettes. In about an hour she'll be able to speak. Then she'll go down to the gym, work out, have a sauna and a massage, then a little nap. After that she'll come up with just enough time to open her post, return a few calls, and read the cards on today's bouquets of flowers . . ."

She held up a huge bunch of old-fashioned roses as she said it. "These are from someone called Dominic. 'To a beautiful lady. Thank you for a night to remember.' I hope he does remember it, because with a card like that he won't be getting a repeat."

I looked at Seraphima with fresh eyes. She only looked about sixteen—actually I think she was nineteen—but she was a smart kid.

"Then she'll start getting ready for tonight's party," she continued.

"Is this a normal week for Debbie?"

"Oh, yeah."

"When does she find time to do her work?"

Seraphima said nothing and reassumed her customary innocent expression. "Can I get you a cup of tea, Georgia? It's milk, no sugar, quite strong, isn't it?"

"That would be lovely, Sera, thank you so much."

I didn't get to speak to Debbie until five-thirty. She seemed much better and was smiling again. Her hair looked freshly blow-dried.

"Great party, Debbie. Thank you so much for taking me. I had a great time."

"Oh, good. Did you meet any nice men? When did you leave? One minute you were there and then I didn't see you again."

I looked at her—she really had forgotten about me leaving with Nick. I made a snap decision not to remind her about it, and not to tell her that he'd just rung me and we'd arranged to meet after work for a drink and a movie. I wanted to keep my fledgling romance my own little secret. Big mistake.

But it certainly didn't seem that way at the time. We had a great night, with dinner after the movie, then he looked at his watch, said he knew I liked to get my beauty sleep, and took me straight home. And by the time I got up to my flat, there was already a message from him on my machine. He'd called on his mobile while I was in the lift. He really was something.

It went on like this for a week. On Saturday we went for breakfast at the same café I'd gone to with Billy and Rory, followed by a day on the beach and another movie in the evening. When he put on the tape in his car it started playing Lou Reed's "Perfect Day," one of my favourite songs. Then he dropped me home.

On Sunday we did the Art Gallery. On Monday he called me at work and I told him I was busy for the next two nights. He sent me flowers. Pale pink roses: "For an English rose . . ." On Wednesday I cancelled our date at the last minute, because we were having a production crisis on the magazine and I had to work late. And on the Thursday night we had dinner at a beautiful restaurant on Balmoral Beach looking out over the water. He held my hand through most of it and in between talking about himself and his father, he laid compliments on me, thick, like fondant icing. Just like the first time we'd had dinner, he drank two double espressos, but this time I went home with him.

And at five a.m., as the glorious fireball rose over Bondi Beach and he bent me gently over his balcony railing for a tender sunrise rogering (the fourth joining of various kinds since we'd arrived back at his place), I understood why Nick drank extra-strong coffee after dinner. He had no intention of going to sleep. Oh no, he was Mr. Long and Strong and All Night Long. Action Jackson. The Eveready battery man.

And while he did not have the most amazing body I had ever seen, he was very finely equipped for such endeavours, if I may be so coarse. (Oh, alright then, he had a great big stonker, smooth as a puppy's belly, hard as a hammer, long as a baby's arm, straight as an outback road and fat as a VB stubby, OK?)

I couldn't stop smiling. Although I should have got the hint when, at one point in the proceedings, he wished me to turn over and directed me to do so with a gracious hand gesture and all the politess of an usher. I couldn't help wondering if it wasn't a little bit lacking in spontaneity.

But in between rumpy pumpys he was as tender as ever, spinning me more tales of the imminent visit we would make to his father's farm, until I began to wish I'd packed my riding boots in my evening bag. He wanted to know everything about me: What were my beliefs about child rearing? Did I think mothers should work before children went to school? He even asked me what I thought about the whooping cough immunisation debate. Holy bloody moly.

He told me about his favourite beaches and of an ocean swimming pool he'd always wanted to make love in, and how he was going to take me there one moonless night to do it. One moonless night very soon, was my impression.

I must have been stupid—I was certainly spunk drunk—and he knew exactly what he was doing, even if he was acting more from instinct than intellect. Nick was playing me like my grandfather used to play a trout, while I sat on the bank in my little wellingtons to watch. Choose the right lure, cast it out into the river and when the fish bites, tease it so gently that it bites down hard on the hook, then a quick flick to fix it, so it hardly knows what's hit it, and slowly, steadily reel it in. Then you smash it over the head with a blunt object.

At six a.m. we went to sleep. At nine my automatic internal alarm went off—two hours late. I wriggled about a bit to try to wake him but he wouldn't stir. I lay there hopefully until the clock said 9:25 and I knew I had to get up and go to work. I washed and moisturised my face with his impressive range of Clarins products (clearly he was a man who liked to look after his skin) and wrote him a note.

> "Nick—Thanks for dinner. It was great. And the dinner. See you soon. (Naked.) Georgia (just in case you wondered who this was from)."

Well, that was prophetic, wasn't it?

By the time I left it was after ten. I was really late and it was still only week four of my new job. I had no choice but to head straight there in yesterday's clothes, with the intention of buying some clean knickers at lunchtime. I took a calculated gamble that the reaction of my colleagues at *Glow* would be the same as my old friends back at *Kitty* in London. Gentle ribbing and a tinge of admiration.

But when I entered the reception area, Seraphima took one look at me and produced from under the counter one of those nasty toys that emits coarse laughter when squeezed. She squeezed it. Women came running from all directions.

"Who's the dirty stopout?" demanded Maxine, emerging from her office and seeming quite thrilled that it was me. Debbie was right behind her, laughing silently but hysterically. Cathy, the art director, popped her head round the art room door to look and Zoe, the fashion editor, came out holding a yoghurt which she was eating by dipping one finger in it and licking it off. Various young assistants and trainees gathered in a clutch by the front desk, giggling nervously. Last out was Liinda, an unlit cigarette clamped between her teeth.

"Nice work, girlfriend," she said, without removing it. "Four weeks on the job and you've already been out doing some practical."

I looked at them all in amazement. I was used to a fair amount of rough teasing from my London workmates, but this was something else.

"You know what this means, don't you?" said Maxine, smiling broadly.

"No?" I wondered if I had to pack up my office straightaway.

"You have to buy morning tea."

"What?"

"Morning tea. A cake. A big cake for all of us. Sera will go and get it, but you'll have to cough up for it. You have my permission to go down to the gym for a shower and Debbie will show you where we keep the spare undies. And by the way, was he any good?"

Before I could help it a big grin spread across my face, and my insides (my lower insides) gave one of those involuntary backflips as they remembered just how good he'd been.

"Hmmm, I can see he was very very good," said Maxine. "Try and remember some of it for our next sealed sex section. OK, everybody, back to work. Morning tea at eleven-thirty in my office. May I suggest a sticky toffee pudding?"

There were general murmurs of agreement and I sloped into my office, relieved to no longer be the centre of attention. I was scanning the *Herald* for Nick's byline, as I'd been doing (unsuccessfully) every day since I met him, when Liinda appeared. She was wearing one of her characteristic outfits: an enormous pair of denim dungarees over a stripy cropped T-shirt, an arm crowded with multicoloured plastic bangles, pink rubber thongs, purple toenail varnish and, today, an orange gerbera in her nest of hair.

She still had the unlit cigarette in her mouth, where I now realised it stayed all day apart from the many times she went downstairs to smoke it, standing outside the back entrance with all the other nicotine addicts and replacing it with a fresh unlit one the minute she returned to her desk.

"So, what sign is he? Get his exact time of birth, did you?" she said as she sat down in the chair opposite me.

"I don't know what sign he is. It didn't come up. Not his date of birth, anyway."

"What?" she said, letting the cigarette fall from her mouth and slapping her forehead with her hand. "You didn't ask him? Are you mad? You did it again?' You slept with a man without finding out his star sign? That's unsafe sex."

"Well, we did use a condom. Condoms*sss*, actually. . ."

"Really?" She replaced the cigarette and leaned back in the chair, looking thoughtful. "Must be Aries, or Scorpio, then. Maybe Venus in Scorpio, they're horny little devils. I can't believe you didn't ask him. What was his name, anyway? Was he really good in bed? And why are you looking at the *Herald* with such interest all of a sudden? Have they put in a horoscope at last?"

"No, they haven't. I'm looking for his byline." I was so light-headed from my night of passion I didn't care who knew. I wanted to shout it from the rooftops. "He works on the *Herald*. His name is Nick and he's gorgeous beyond belief. He's the killer shagmeister from Bondi and I'm just seeing if he has anything in here today, to see if he's as mighty with his pen as he is with his penis."

I was still grinning, but Liinda suddenly looked serious and took the cigarette out of her mouth again.

"Nick, you say? Bondi . . . *Sydney Morning Herald*. Hmmm. Was his second name Pollock, by any chance?"

"Yes! How on earth did you guess? Do you know him?"

"Yes, I know him. And if I can give you a little bit of unsolicited advice, I wouldn't tell anyone else here the name of the man who made you late for work this morning."

"OK, if you say so, but why not?" Liinda was starting to be a bit of a pain. I was so happy, I just wanted to enjoy it.

"Oh, you know, they might get jealous or something—rich, famous father and all that. And I wouldn't waste your time looking for his name in the paper. He's worked there for eighteen months and he's only had five things printed. He's famous for it. Spends most of his time checking the spelling of the names of people in Stay in Touch and frequently gets those wrong. Everything else is a work in progress. He only got the job because Daddy pulled strings behind the scenes."

Liinda smiled quite evilly, but then looked worried. She put the unlit cigarette back into her mouth. "See you at morning tea."

And she got up and walked out. Then the bird's nest suddenly appeared round the door again. "And by the way. He's a Pisces."

I threw the paper in the bin and spent a few stunned moments staring into space. Why was Liinda being so weird? And why was she being so horrible about Nick? First she was nasty about Jasper, now Nick—was she just plain jealous? But if so, why had she looked so concerned? And why had Nick made out he was like Woodward and Bernstein, but more talented? Oh well, I could ask him all that tonight, or tomorrow, or whenever I next saw him.

Too restless to get down to work, I went looking for Debbie and the spare undies drawer. She was in her den at the back of the office, a grim windowless room where the sun never shone, but it was like Aladdin's cave to us because it was always full of fabulous—free—beauty products, which it was our duty to take home and try.

I'd decided that despite her obsession with only being seen with the Right People at the Right Places and her unbelievable turnover of men, Debbie was not a bad sort. And she was so unbelievably stylish I couldn't help being fascinated by her.

I'd had the entire family history from Antony, who was clearly very impressed by it. Debbie's mother had been a successful model in the 1960s, who lucked out in the new socially permissive age and married a handsome polo player who just happened to come from one of the country's wealthiest and most established families. As Antony told it, Johnny Brent was as close as it comes to aristocracy in Australia, and once young Jenny Kelly had wrapped her long brown legs around his neck there was no way she was going to let him go, even though she'd been brought up practically on the railway tracks and gone to All the Wrong Schools.

It appeared Debbie had inherited the best physical attributes of both parents—she even had nice hands and feet, which seemed to be taking it a bit too far—but you just had to accept it, she was one of nature's better achievements. She'd been a model for a few minutes but quickly got bored with it and much preferred being a fashion stylist. There were more opportunities to boss people around.

Debbie had a natural flair for bossing and styling, and as she'd been to school with Maxine (who happily admitted she had been in love with Debbie's glamorous father from the age of eight), she just glided her way into the job as beauty editor at *Glow* with the same ease as everything else that came to her in her charmed life. Charmed until that fatal plane crash, at least, when the thing she'd loved the most was taken away.

She was looking particularly golden this morning, in a tiny white summer shift dress with white varnished finger- and toenails, one simple gold bangle and a pair of orange Gucci slides. She wore something different every single day and always looked amazing. She could get the entire staff wearing silk scarves one month, bootleg pants the next.

The only person uninfluenced by Debbie's perfect taste was Liinda, who had her own style entirely. She didn't give a fig for fashion; she just wore what she liked, which most days was something denim, something junk shop and that outrageous hair. One day she'd wear pink plastic jelly sandals, the next she'd have on white lace 1950s stilettos. She always looked great in her way too, but no one would have been game to imitate her.

Back in the beauty office, I had the impression Deb-rett's—I realised I'd picked up Liinda's nickname for her—was being a bit funny with me. Talking on the phone and not looking me in the eye. She hissed at Kylie to show me where the undies were kept and all but turned her back on me. I couldn't understand it, she'd been so friendly to me before. I wondered if Liinda had already told her about me and Nick Pollock. Perhaps she was jealous too. After all, she'd taken me to the party and I had scooped up quite a prize. Oh well.

I was certainly glad Antony had warned me not to tell her I'd met Billy and Rory, if this was the way she was reacting about Nick. I hoped it wouldn't make life difficult at work. I chose a pair of knickers out of a large bag full of them and left wondering exactly what was on Debbie's mind. Then I had another hot flush of memory from the night before and forgot all about her.

I thought momentarily about going down to the company gym for a quick shower but decided to get on with some work instead. Actually, I didn't want to be away from my phone that long. I quickened my pace into my office, half expecting the message light on my phone to be flashing already. It wasn't. I ducked out again and asked Seraphima if there were any messages for me. She smiled knowingly and shook her head.

I read the Pisces horoscope in four different magazines. Then I finally turned on my computer to do some work. The phone rang. My hand shot out, but I forced myself to wait four rings before picking it up. It was a contributor chasing a payment. I opened up a story I had to edit for the next issue, called "Ten Signs He's the Man for You." I'd completely forgotten that was the title of it. That was a bloody sign in itself.

I started scrolling through the copy, which we'd bought from a US magazine, to see if there were any gross Americanisms I needed to remove and replace with Aussie alternatives. I tore through all the introductory blurb and the usual crapola—"says psychologist Dr. Deandra Dingdong" and "Harriet, twenty-six, knew Tod was the right man for her when . . ."—changed Tod to Brent, a few thrus to through, gray to grey and then got onto the good bit—the list.

Ten Signs He's the Man for You
1. You Enjoy Doing the Same Things

No problem with that at all. Dancing, talking, eating, poetry, Shakespeare and . . . sure, we like the same things, I thought.

2. He Talks About His Future—with You in It

Well, we were going to his father's exhibition together and then there was the moonless night at the pool and his father's farm— that was the future, wasn't it?

3. He Looks You in the Eye When He Kisses You

I was just trying to remember whether he did or not, when Seraphima appeared in the doorway grinning and holding a huge bouquet of red roses.

"For me?" I asked.

She nodded, put them on my desk and sat down. I looked at her pointedly. She stayed sitting.

"So who are they from then?" she asked, cheeky little bugger.

I could feel myself blushing hugely as I fumbled with the card. A very tasteful small white card that said: "Dear Georgia, Welcome to Sydney—from everyone at Revlon."

"Revlon," I croaked, trying to force a smile. "Isn't that lovely of them? So kind."

Seraphima grimaced and went back to her desk. My phone rang.

"Hi Georgie, this is Nerilyn Keyes of Thunderstuck PR. How are you today?"

I resisted the temptation to say "thunderstruck." "Very well, thank you."

"That's great. Now, I wanted to check if you've received our release about the new Bravington lawn trimmer? We thought it would make a perfect giveaway for your women's page."

"This is *Glow* magazine, Nerilyn."

"Yes . . ."

"All our pages are women's pages."

"I'm sure it's a product your readers would love to know about."

"Well, thank you very much for thinking of us, but unless it has a built-in vibrator and a bikini-waxing attachment, I don't think they'd be interested at all. Once again, thank you. Goodbye."

Where was I . . .

4. He Has a Good Relationship with His Mother

Mmm. Nick had never mentioned his mother, but he'd talked about his father solidly for what would amount to several days, so that probably made up for it.

The phone rang. Contributor. Where was her payment? I neither knew nor cared and it probably showed. Phone. PR. More press-release bollocks. Phone. Revlon. Did I get the flowers? Lovely, thank you. Ooh—call waiting. PR. Are you coming to our mascara launch? Yes. Can hardly wait. Phone. Mad reader. Why are all your models so thin? Because they don't eat much? Ooh! Must go. Call waiting. Accounts department. We can't pay invoices unless they're attached to correct dockets. OK, will docket more assiduously in future. Phone. PR. Did you get our press release? Get fucked. Phone. Wrong number.

At 11:25 loud pig-honking noises emanated from the front desk outside my door. It was Seraphima with another gadget, *Glow's* answer to the dinner gong, inviting us to enter Maxine's office for morning tea. I began to wonder how many more noise-making devices she had stashed under there. Perhaps an air-raid siren for when one of management approached, or a recording of the Red Army choir singing "The Red Flag" for those days when the entire staff started their period simultaneously.

In Maxine's office, everyone was gathered around the desk, where there was a baking tray filled with a steaming sticky toffee pudding, dotted with strawberries, with bits of card to use as plates and pieces of loo roll as napkins.

Everybody had brought in their own tea and coffee and Seraphima made me one. Liinda drank only obscure South American herbal teas and was dunking her tea bag in her cup, which had the word "GET" on one side and "LOST" on the other. Her cigarette was behind her ear. Debbie was holding her usual Kylie-delivered skim-milk latte from a trendy café. Maxine had a large plunger of coffee on her desk beside a metal cup and saucer. Most of the other girls clutched mugs of tea. Zoe had a glass of water.

It was my job to cut and distribute the cake. Zoe stood very close to me while I did it, making yum-yum comments about how she couldn't wait for her piece.

"So, who was the lucky guy?" said Maxine, licking her fingers, her feet up on her desk.

"Oh, I'd . . . er . . . rather not say," I said, longing to tell her, but remembering Liinda's advice. "It's all a bit new . . ."

The phone in my office rang. I started to run for it, but Maxine waved a manicured hand and said, "Let it go to message bank, that's what we have it for."

I felt a terrible rictus pass across my face and before I could hide it, I saw Liinda and Debbie exchange a look. What was going on?

Several of the girls had seconds of cake, but I could hardly eat a mouthful, a fact that I thought should be the next point in my Ten signs list: *You Are Unable to Eat Whenever You Think of Him.*

Zoe seemed to be in love too. She'd gone back to her office, leaving her hotly anticipated piece of cake completely untouched except for the strawberry. Maxine saw me notice it.

"I see Zoe's been pigging out again," she said. "But don't worry, she won't go hungry—she'll have eaten the whole strawberry. Even the stalk."

"She does seem to eat in very strange ways," I said. "That business with the finger in the yoghurt. I can't believe she's worried about her weight."

"Zoe's terrified that if she relaxes for a moment the fat girl lurking inside her will come out and take over. That's why she's in the gym every spare minute too. She looks gorgeous, but it gets really hard to be around. I've tried talking to her about it, but she gets very shitty and says it's none of my business if she wants to be healthy." She shrugged and reached for another piece of cake.

Although she was what you would kindly call "strapping," Maxine seemed totally confident about her appearance. She was very tall, with the kind of body that looks like it should be in hockey gear, and an equally strong-featured face. But the overall package was very attractive—particularly to men who liked to be dominated, or so Liinda had told me.

"What shall I do with the rest of this cake?" I asked her. "There's about half of it left. We can't possibly finish it."

"Just put it in the kitchen," said Maxine. "How are you going with those articles I gave you? We need all the copy for the April issue ready by next week for layouts."

"It's going fine. I'm just reading through it all and then I'll go over it with Liinda this afternoon. I think there are some articles that cold do with some more boxes and lists."

Maxine nodded. "Sounds great. We love boxes and lists. There's your phone again."

This time I ran. PR. There were three messages on my voicemail. Danny Green inviting me to go to a party with him. Another angry contributor—I really would have to get Seraphima to explain the docket system to me. And Antony asking me if I wanted to go to the same party Danny Green had invited me to. It was weird. Nick's messages were usually waiting for me when I arrived at work and he'd rung me by lunchtime every day since the night I'd met him. I desperately wanted to ring him, but part of me wanted to see how long he would leave it before calling. The other part wanted to ring all the hospitals to see if anyone with the initials NP had been checked in with two broken arms.

By one p.m. I was starting to feel hysterical. I decided to go to the gym and have that shower. A workout wouldn't do me any harm either; it would take my mind off things. I had my swimsuit with me, so I went to look for Zoe to see if she'd take me. She wasn't in the fashion office and I asked Seraphima if she'd seen her leave. She looked at her watch, fixed me with her innocent look and suggested that I should look in the loo. Sure enough, one minute later Zoe emerged from the Ladies. With fresh lipstick on.

"Are you going down to the gym?" I asked her.

"Yes—now. Do you want to come?"

So we went to the gym and I swam up and down the pool thinking about Nick, while Zoe ran about a hundred miles on the treadmill. She ran without a break for an hour. It was funny, she looked really great in her clothes, but seeing her in a tiny Lycra bra top and little boy-leg shorts, she just looked thin. Her face was locked in a grimace and sweat was pouring off her. She was still running when I emerged from the changing rooms, dressed, hair dried and ready to go. I told her I'd see her upstairs.

There was still no message from Nick. Maybe a really big story had broken at the paper and they'd sent him off to Papua New Guinea to cover it. I decided to risk ringing his work number in case he'd left a special message on his voicemail, but it was just the usual one:

"Hi. You've reached Nick Pollock, senior writer and essayist, *Sydney Morning Herald*. I'm either on another call, or away from my desk breaking a major story, so leave a message and I'll catch you later. Ciao."

I didn't leave a message. By four I was really feeling the effects of a night without sleep and thought I'd have another little piece of the sticky toffee pudding to give myself a sugar hit. But when I got to the kitchen the baking tray was empty. Washed and dried. Nobody knew what had happened to it. I even looked in the bin to see if some busybody had thrown it away. Not a crumb. It was weird. On the way back to my office I asked Seraphima if she knew what had happened to it.

"You could ask Zoe," she said. "But I wouldn't."

"Zoe? Zoe didn't have any. And she hasn't thrown it in the bin—I looked."

"Zoe didn't have any while you were looking, Georgia. And she might have thrown it somewhere—but not in the bin." She nodded her head towards the loo.

I stood there dumbly absorbing what she'd just said. "You

mean she ate the whole thing and threw it up in there? Is that why she was in the loo?"

Seraphima shrugged. "Could be. I saw her eat a couple of carrots before morning tea. That's always a sign."

"A sign of what?"

"A sign that a bulimic is planning a binge. The carrot acts as a marker—when the carrot comes up you know you've got it all up."

I stared at her horrified. "Oh god. That's hideous. Are you sure?"

"No—but I saw the carrot and I saw her go into the loo and I saw her come out a long time after and then I saw her go to the gym."

I remembered Zoe's desperate little monkey face on the treadmill.

"How did you figure all that out? Especially the carrots. That's so awful it's quite brilliant. I never would have thought of that."

"My sister used to be bulimic. You can spot the signs."

I went back to my desk. Antony had called again. Nick had not. I rang Antony back and told him I was too tired to go anywhere, but that I'd love to see him another time. I rang Danny Green and told him the same thing. In truth, though, I didn't want to be out when Nick rang.

But he didn't ring. He didn't ring me that night. And he didn't ring over the entire weekend. I spent the time veering wildly between thinking Fuck You, Nick Pollock, I Never Want to Speak to You Again Anyway, and desperate weeping. Then I'd get all fired up with confidence and think, damn it, I'll just bloody well ring him. We're both grown-ups. I'll just leave a casual message saying "Hi, How are you? Can you call me please?" But I knew I couldn't trust myself to be casual. I knew it would sound forced and hysterical. And what if he answered?

I'm ashamed to say that on Saturday night I had a bottle of wine on my own and rang his home number. The machine was on. It was on all day Sunday as well.

On Monday I rang his work number and got the voicemail again.

Tuesday—still no call. I had my mobile permanently turned on and I rang my home message machine every hour. If it hadn't been so bloody upsetting it would have been bizarre. I think the girls in the office knew something was up. Debbie and Liinda were avoiding me and when I walked into the beauty room to ask Debbie something, they broke off their conversation suddenly.

Later on, Seraphima came into my office and told me, "Estee Lauder have sent you some flowers. I looked at the card first, because I know how disappointing it is."

I thanked her sincerely and told her she could have them. Somehow life went on. Zoe came and collected me for the gym at lunchtime. Even Maxine was being particularly nice to me. She came in a couple of times and asked me if I was happy in Sydney, and invited me to her house for a drink after work. What was going on?

There was no word by Wednesday—it was nearly our one-week anniversary and I still hadn't heard from him. So I hatched the marvellous idea of sending him a note instead. Just a bright and breezy little note, which I convinced myself could be passed off as a thank-you card for a lovely dinner.

This breezy little note took me the whole afternoon to write, composing various versions on my computer.

Nick—I'm a bit surprised you haven't. . .
Nick—How about giving me a call?
Nick—I believe tonight is a moonless night. Coogee awaits us.
Georgia xxx
Nick—Are you dead? Give me a call. Georgia.

*Nick—It was really fun seeing you last week. Let's do it
again soon (and dinner). G.*
*Nick—Thanks for a great dinner. Shall we do it again? Give
me a call. Georgia.*

That was it. The last one. That's what I sent. On a postcard that
featured a Victorian picture of a vicar skating from the Scottish
National Gallery. We'd talked about that picture. We both loved
it. I felt sick as I put the card into the mailbox, but at least I'd
done something.

Oh, it's no good, I can't lie. I wish it had been that one. Ac-
tually, I sent him the Coogee one. And the postcard was that
Brassai photo of the couple kissing in Paris. AAAGH. What was
I thinking? How could I do it to myself? But I did.

And still there was no call. By the Sunday morning—a week
and a half, including two weekends, after we had sex—I knew
he was never going to call. And I knew he wasn't in Papua New
Guinea, because there'd been pictures of him in the social pages
of the Sunday papers. Pictures of him at the opening of his father's exhibition at the State Library. The one he had promised
to take me to. Pictures of him with a girl who looked not hugely
unlike me, except she was wearing a much shorter dress than I'd
ever wear. And she had rings on her forefingers.

"Wordsmith Nick Pollock with fiancée Phoebe Trill, back
from two months in Europe," said the caption. Fiancée. Yes.
And from what I could see in the photograph Phoebe had very
nice skin, which explained Nick's well-stocked bathroom.

I cried for an hour. I ranted and raved and threw things
around the flat. I couldn't believe it. I rang his work voicemail
intending to leave a coruscating message for him, but chickened
out at the last minute. Too humiliating. I cried a bit more and
then I rang his home phone. He'd changed the message. It now
said: "Phoebe and Nick can't take your call right now . . ."

I cried some more because I couldn't ring any of my friends in London and tell them what had happened. It was three in the morning over there. So I rang the only person I could think of—Liinda Vidovic. She was in.

"Hello?" The usual Marlboro-man rasp. I just sobbed into the phone.

"Li-ii-ii-ii-nda . . . It's Georgia. I'm really sorry—*sniff*—to call you like this, but I don't know who else to turn to."

"What's happened? Is it Nick Pollock by any chance?"

"Yeee-eeee-es," and I was off wailing and sobbing, which of course, Liinda adored. "He's in the paa-aa-per," I wailed. "With his fi-ia-aa-ncée."

I could hear her lighting up a cigarette. "Oh no. I thought this would happen. I should have told you, but I just couldn't. You remember that morning when you were the dirty stopout and had to buy us morning tea and I warned you not to tell anyone it was him? That was why—I wanted to protect you. But when you didn't mention him again, I thought maybe it would be alright. Had you met him the night before?"

"No. I'd met him over a week before and I'd seen him practically every night since. I wasn't sure at first, but then he was so *lovely* to me. He sent me flowers. He called me five times a day. I didn't sleep with him for a week. We had a wonderful dinner together and by that point I felt I knew him. I thought I could tru-u-ust him." That set me off again. "But Liinda, why didn't you tell me he was engaged?"

"I didn't know he was until I saw this morning's paper. I knew he'd been seeing Phoebe Trill but—"

"Who is she, anyway? She dresses like a hooker."

"She's a TV game-show host."

"I bet Big Daddy Pollock is impressed with her intellectual prowess."

"Bet he's made a pass at her too. It's congenital with those two." Liinda paused. "I'm sorry, George, I should have warned you. Debbie and I didn't know what to do. We wanted to tell you, but at the same time it seemed so cruel to say, 'The guy you are so excited about is the biggest womaniser in Sydney.' Debbie felt awful she hadn't warned you about him, because she says she remembered afterwards that she'd introduced you."

"What do you mean—the biggest womaniser in Sydney?" I felt sick.

Liinda let out a big sigh. "OK. Did he analyse your hand-writing?"

"Yes."

"Did he ask you where you stood on child care?"

"Yes."

"Did he leave a message on your voicemail, playing the gui-tar and singing 'Georgia On My Mind'?"

"Yes. How did you know? Although I suppose it's obvious with my name."

"It's bloody ironic with your name—but he sings it to everyone. It doesn't matter who, he just inserts the appropriate name."

I was speechless. But I had stopped crying.

"I'm really sorry, George," she said. "If only I'd known you met him in the first place, I would have told you not to touch him with a ten-foot cattle prod. But you'd already slept with him by the time I found out, and even with a rat like him there's always a grain of hope that once in his low-down ugly life he might do the right thing. I mean, even slimeballs like Nick Pollock are going to fall in love someday and I just thought, what if it's George and I've told her he's a shit? But when I saw you starting to mope, I feared the worst."

"Is this his usual pattern? Adoration until sex and then total shutdown?"

"Yes. What exactly happened?"

I told her everything. Liinda listened attentively, making soothing noises. I should have known better.

"Don't be too hard on yourself, George. You did nothing wrong. At least you put up a good fight—very few of his victims hold out a week. I mean, I hate the shit, but I have to admit he is quite handsome—in an obvious kind of way—and he can spin a yarn like no one else. What a shame he can't write them down. Of course, he has massive emotional problems. I sent him some Co-DA pamphlets anonymously once and he actually turned up at a meeting. He talked all about how awful it is having an incredibly rich and famous father, and every woman in the room was nearly sliding off her chair with desire.

"Afterwards I saw him chatting up the most attractive one, who had just told the group that she was still recovering from an abusive relationship and that her therapist had told her to stay single for a year. He was onto her like a blood-sucking leech. I got hold of him in the car park and told him never to come back if he wanted to keep his famous family jewels intact. I was holding a large knife at the time, so I think he took me seriously."

She had actually made me laugh. "A knife? How come you had a knife?"

"I always carry a knife. I used to live on the streets, remember. I know what goes out there."

"Isn't it illegal to carry a knife?"

"It's illegal to carry, buy, sell or take heroin and I did all of those things for long enough. I don't care. I don't get it out in public, I just like to know it's there."

"Liinda, you are a one-off. Thank you for being there for me today. I feel like the biggest idiot who ever drew breath, but at least I know why he didn't call. That was what was killing me. It was torture. Phone torture."

"Phone torture," said Liinda, slowly. "Mmm . . . Terrible.

As a matter of interest, why didn't you call him? I would have been on his doorstep."

"With your knife?"

She chuckled. "Yes. But why didn't you call him? You don't seem like a sap."

"I'm not normally. But I felt so stupid. It seemed too undignified to ring up and say, 'Why haven't you rung me? Don't you like me anymore?' I wanted to retain a shred of self-respect—and in the light of what you've just told me, I'm really glad I didn't ring him. Although I nearly wore my fingers out ringing his voicemail."

"Of course if it was me I'd be on the bus to Bondi right now, to tell him face-to-face what I thought of him, but I don't suppose you'll do any of that, will you?"

"No, I will not. I can't think of anything more embarrassing. I just never want to see him again."

"In Sydney that might be hard to arrange," said Liinda. "But you can have the pleasure of ignoring him in public a lot. Anyway, I'm really sorry you found out about Pants On Fire Pollock the hard way. Do you want to come to a meeting with me this afternoon? There's a really good all-women's one in Chatswood at three . . ."

I declined. I wanted to stay home and feel sorry for myself. The whole thing had sent me spiralling back into the depression I'd felt after Rick and the years of being single in London.

I stayed at home all day, eating ice cream and watching the cricket on TV because it was so mind-numbingly boring it stopped me thinking. I kept one eye on the clock hands, which slowly crawled forward to a time when I could ring the one person who could always cheer me up—my brother, Hamish.

At last it was ten a.m. in England. That was late enough.

"Hello, this is Hamish Abbott. You know the drill. . ." Just as I was about to start howling with frustration he picked up.

"Hurrrgh?" said a very croaky voice.

"Hamish?" I asked. I wasn't sure.

"Hurrghggggh . . ."

"Horsehead?"

"Hey, Big Bum—is that you?"

"Yes, it's me—what on earth is wrong with you?"

"Point-to-point. Fell off. Wagon. Fell off . . . Got in at six, feel indescribably awful—thought you might be someone who was at the Cross Foxes last night ringing to remind me what I'd done. Was trying to keep my options open re: identity, mine."

I had homesick tears in my eyes, but I was grinning. Billy Ryans and Nick Pollocks may come and go but some things never changed, including my party-animal brother, his flair for getting into trouble and his ability to make me laugh.

"Hamish, you are terrible. How many girls did you kiss?"

"Hueeurrrrgh . . ."

"That bad, was it?"

"I'm a very bad boy, Porgie. I think somebody put something in my drink."

I snorted. "Yeah, more drink probably."

"Hmmm. How are you, anyway? How are the colonies? Found me a job yet? Found yourself a husband?"

"No, to all of the above. The colonies are great, but Hame . . ." I let out a very wobbly sigh. "Oh, why are men so awful?"

"I wish I knew. Then I might be able to stop myself. It's just that women are so very attractive . . . Want me to come over there and kill him for you?"

"Yes."

"Find me a job on one of those big farms they have in Australia, where all I have to do is ride around all day and there's a decent pub within two days' hack, and I'll come over and kill him, OK? No, I'll horsewhip him, that's even better. Preserve the Abbott honour."

I couldn't help smiling, Hamish always made me feel better. "OK, it's a deal. Now go back to sleep and try not to break any more hearts than is strictly necessary."

"Wilko. Bye-bye, Big Bum. Lots of love."

"Lots of love to you, Horsehead."

Chapter Seven

So that was my Sunday, and on Monday morning I went in to work and an ideas meeting where I couldn't believe my ears.

Liinda was suggesting a story called: "Phone Torture—Why Guys Don't Call."

"Not bad," said Maxine. "Torture's a good word and you feel like you're getting some inside info, but it's still a bit bald. Have you got any ideas, Zoe?"

"Er . . . 'How To Make Him Call You'?"

"No, not tortured enough. We need pain and suffering, hope and possible catastrophe. The tension of the unringing phone. Debbie?"

"What's it about? Men who don't call when they say they will? That's never happened to me . . ."

"Somebody please hit her. Why did I even ask you? Just go back to sleep and when we're working on a story called 'What It's Like Being a Goddess,' I'll wake you up. OK, come on the rest of you, someone has an idea, surely?"

I had a very good idea. It involved a sharp implement and

Liinda Vidovic's head, but as we were in a public place I thought I'd better restrain myself.

"So what we're really looking at here," I said between gritted teeth, "is, 'Why Some Total Shits Lose the Use of Their Arms and Don't Call You When They Say They Will'?"

"Exactly."

"OK," I continued. "What about—"

"How about 'Why Guys Say They'll Call and Why They Don't'?" This was Liinda, of course.

"Liinda, shut up for a moment, would you?" I snapped at her and turned back to Maxine. "What about 'The Date Was Great, But Will He Call Again?'"

Maxine beamed to me. "That's brilliant, Georgia, we've got it. But I think we'll use the 'Phone Torture' line as well."

"Or," I added, "we could just tell the truth—'The Fuck Was Great, But Will He Call Again?' . . . eh, Liinda?" I punched her arm in a gesture that could have been seen as playful, except I was deadly serious. I had to get out of there before I did her some grievous bodily harm.

"Maxine," I said. "I've got to make some calls to New York, before it's too late. Can I duck out?" I stood up. "And I'll see you later," I hissed into Liinda's ear as I passed her.

I was furious with her. OK, so we'd had that conversation about her using friends' experiences for inspiration, but she knew how upset I was about Nick Pollock and I couldn't believe she was doing this while it was all so raw. I was amazed that she could be such a good friend one day and so totally treacherous the next. Of course I shouldn't have been stupid enough to tell her, but I'd needed somebody to talk to and I really didn't think she would be so shameless.

I sat at my desk and fumed for a while until I heard the meeting break up. Then I phoned Seraphima and told her to go and tell Liinda I wanted to see her immediately.

"She's just gone downstairs for a cigarette break," said Seraphima.

"GO and GET her," I said, instantly regretting being short with Sera, whom I was beginning to adore. I don't get angry often, but when I do I can spark nuclear fission with a look. And I was furious with Liinda. Although of course the person I was really furious with was Nick Pollock and, more than anyone, with myself. But Liinda would do.

At that moment the phone rang.

"Pinkie?" It was Jasper O'Connor. Great. Just what I needed. Another slimeball who comes on like Elvis Presley at a clambake and then turns up moments later with a supermodel on his knee. I pretended not to know who it was.

"Hello? This is Georgiana Abbott, deputy editor, *Glow* magazine, how can I help you?"

My voice could have etched glass. It has been pointed out to me on more than one occasion that Alfred Hitchcock would have loved me in this mood. The ice maiden cometh.

"Pinkie—it's Jazzie."

"I'm sorry?"

"Jasper—Jasper O'Connor, I met you at Danny Green's hat party. We danced on the roof . . ."

"Oh, yes. I remember now. How are you?"

"I'm perfect, Pinkie. How are you?"

"Very well, thank you. Rather busy, actually. Is there something I can help you with?"

There was a pause. I was being a total bitch. I didn't care.

"Well, I was wondering if you'd like to come and sit on my verandah this evening and have a long drink."

"Oh that's terribly sweet of you Jasper—" no one can make the word "sweet" sound more patronizing than a pissed-off Pom, "—but I've got something on. Perhaps we could catch up for a coffee sometime? Why don't you call me next week? Anyway, I must go. Goodbye."

I hung up. At that moment the creature from the black lagoon walked through my door, her mouth open ready to say something.

"Shut the door. Shut up and sit down." Liinda looked a bit surprised, but she did what she was told. I folded my arms and just looked at her. She didn't have her bag with her. Good, no knife.

"How could you?" I said after a long silence.

"How could I what?"

"That coverline idea of yours— 'Phone Torture.' I used those exact words to you on the phone yesterday. How could you do it? The very next day!"

She turned up her palms. "I warned you, Georgia. I warned you that I do this. You still rang me. My conscience is clear."

"But you were so supportive and kind to me yesterday and then this morning—this! How could you be so insincere?"

"I was completely sincere yesterday. And I'm still really sorry that he hurt you like that. But I never let a good coverline pass me by. I owe that to Maxine. And it is a brilliant coverline. Phone torture has happened to every woman at some time and that will make them buy the magazine. Stop being so self-centred. Think about the common good."

"Is this magazine a communist regime?"

"Oh come on, George. I'm sorry I hurt you, but that's me. I told you—I do it to my best friends all the time."

"Well, you could have waited a few weeks." I stood up and paced around the room, kicking things. "This is not what I call friendship, Liinda. This is sick behaviour and I'm not as stupid as your so-called friends. I will not be coming to you with any of my problems in future. I think everyone on this magazine is gone in the head. You're all junkies or bulimics or tragic princesses, and all the men in this town are psychos too. I don't know why I came here. You all smile and dance all the time and the sun's always shining but you're all totally fucked."

And I burst into tears. Liinda got up and came and put her arm round me.

"FUCK OFF! Don't come near me with your fake friendship and your twelve-step bloody bullshit. I'm sick of it. Go away and leave me alone."

She did and I sat at my desk crying. Seraphima came in with a cup of tea and a box of tissues and went out without saying anything, little treasure that she is. I didn't stop crying until I glanced up and saw Debbie looking at me. Great. Now the beautiful Debbie Brent was going to see me with snot running down my face and a red nose. She put a jar of Chanel eye gel on my desk.

"This will help the puffiness," she said and went to the door. "I'm sorry I don't have anything for red noses . . . And Georgie, I really am sorry about Nick Pollock, we should have warned you. I just never dreamed he'd move in on you like that—I thought he was serious about Phoebe and I didn't think he'd do it. There are good men in Australia, Georgie. Believe me."

She looked very sad and, with her glamorous front let down for just a moment, she looked more beautiful than ever. I knew she was thinking about Drew.

"That's OK, Debbie," I said, in between sniffs. "It's not anyone's fault except his. I'll get over it, but it's all been a bit much when I'm so far from home. I've been so buoyed up with the excitement of moving here, but this has made me feel really homesick."

"Do you like the bush?" she said suddenly.

I must have looked dense. I was thinking, what bush? What is she talking about? A rhododendron? The burning bush?

"The country," she explained.

"Oh, yeah. I love the country. I grew up in the country."

"Good. Well, perhaps you'd like to come to my parents' farm one weekend. It's really beautiful. You can ride or walk, or just lie around. My parents would love to meet you."

I looked up at her in surprise. She was genuine. "I'd love that. Thank you."

She smiled and left.

It was very sweet of Debbie, I thought as I sat and drank my tea, not to mention bloody amazing for her to think about someone else for a millisecond. It would be nice to spend a weekend in the country, but I wondered if seeing someone else with their loving parents might just make me miss mine even more. Because at that moment I was missing them like crazy.

If I'd ever felt as miserable in London as I did that Monday at my desk in Sydney, I would have got straight on the phone to my mum. Hamish always made me laugh, but Mum really knew how to comfort me. She'd never have grasped the particular subtleties of the situation (and I certainly wouldn't have told her the grisly details), but in her endearingly vague way she would tell me funny stories about what Gaston had been doing and the latest chapter in his ongoing love/hate relationship with her haughty cat, Clarissa (Gaston loves Clarissa, Clarissa hates him). Or she'd tell me about a new rose that had bloomed for the first time, and my father's latest mad project for a watercourse in the garden.

But all that cosiness was 12,000 miles and twenty-four very uncomfortable hours away, and I couldn't ring them because it was the middle of the night there. Maybe moving to Sydney hadn't been such a bright idea. I knew nobody here—not a soul apart from the lunatics I worked with and a few people I'd met at parties.

I went out on my own at lunchtime into the still-unfamiliar streets. All the people looked weird. The women were wearing appalling suits. The men looked too tall and lummocky. The buses were too noisy. The crossing signal sounded gross and stupid. It was incredibly humid and my clothes stuck to me. I wandered around in a hideous underground food court looking for something I could bear to eat. In the end I just bought an apple and drifted into Grace Bros., thinking some retail therapy might help. But one look at a display of terrible handbags sent me straight out into the street again, more depressed than ever. As I walked back to the office, a thought suddenly stood me still in my tracks. What the fuck was I doing here?

Back in my room I took one bite of the apple, which had a thick, highly waxed skin and floury flesh. I threw it in the bin, thinking of the crisp Cox's Orange Pippins in my mother's orchard.

I turned to work for distraction, reading through the regular contributors' columns for the April issue before passing them on to the sub-editors. I was pleased to note that Geminis like myself could look forward to "the chance to meet new people and have a lot of new experiences. But you also have an important lesson to learn, Ms. Gemini. Trust your instincts and life will seem a lot less mysterious."

Well, my instincts hadn't done me much good with Nick Pollock who, as a Pisces, could anticipate "new starts in many parts of your life. Your horizons are expanding, but maybe the real love of your life is closer to home than you think."

Yeah, I thought, in the mirror . . . and the new starts would be the five other women he'd slept with since me.

The phone didn't ring all afternoon and nobody came into my office. Maxine was out at a meeting with an important advertiser. Seraphima had been taken on a fashion shoot with Zoe as a treat, and Liinda was giving me a wide berth. Who knows where Debbie was—probably having a free facial somewhere. At five p.m. I decided I couldn't stand it anymore and went home. Or "home," as I thought of it.

It was quite a nice flat in a 1920s block, with views of a little marina full of boats and out into the harbour, which was so thrilling after living in London. It was light and spacious, but practically empty. I'd assumed I would be moving into a furnished place and hadn't brought a thing with me apart from clothes and essential books and photos. Not that I owned anything practical anyway, because although I'd lived with Rick for five years, it was very much his place and his stuff—his Alessi kettle, his Fornasetti china, his Conran Shop cutlery. So I'd spent my first two days in Australia buying a bed, a kettle, one mug, one plate, one bowl, one knife, one fork, one spoon, one saucepan, one wooden spoon, and hiring a fridge and a telly.

Looking at my sad little kitchen, with one of those lonely half-pint milk cartons in the fridge, I remembered all the mad dinner parties we'd given at our place in Holland Park. A Burns Night with four fat haggis and Rick, looking wonderful in a kilt, reciting Robbie Burns's "Ode to a Haggis," while Hamish played his bagpipes. The Ebony Dinner when everyone had to wear black and all the food was black to match. The Guilty Secrets Evening where everyone had to wear their secret garment and bring their secret food fetish—sweetcorn out of the tin, uncooked cake mix, condensed milk out of the tube, that kind of thing (mine was some of Gaston's biscuits). The dinner when everyone brought their pets and Rick's show-off friend Tony brought his horse (which I later found out had been drugged to keep it docile—I was furious) and someone else's ferret went missing.

I turned on the TV. *The World's Funniest Home Videos. The World's Worst Drivers.* A film from Iraq. A documentary about the last days of the Third Reich. And there, on Channel Seven, *Pick the Pony*—a brainless game show involving plastic horses in a pretend race with "our glamorous hostess—Phoebe Trill" wearing a red satin gown. I nearly puked as she flashed her silicon breasts and silicon smile at the camera. Mind you, it wasn't her fault her fiancé was a philandering bastard—I actually felt quite sorry for her—but that didn't mean I wanted her in my living room.

To distract myself, I started unpacking some of the boxes that had just arrived from England. The first thing I came across was a photo album. There were pictures of my entire family at a point-to-point, where Hamish had been competing. He looked so handsome and sweet with his cheeks bright red from exertion and his jodhpurs plastered in mud. There were pictures of me and crowds of loving friends sharing happy days at university. Pictures of a hilarious villa holiday in Greece with my three best friends. Me and Rick in Mexico and Iceland and Japan. I sobbed. What was I doing in this strange country where I didn't know anyone, when there were so many people (and dogs) back in Britain who loved me?

Suddenly the intercom buzzed and I picked it up, assuming it was a mistake.

"Special delivery," said the voice of someone who was clearly holding their nose to disguise their identity.

"Who is it?"

"Special delivery for Ms. Abbott."

I pressed the buzzer and opened my front door, ready to slam it again if necessary.

When the lift opened Liinda, Debbie and Zoe sprang out.

"Surprise!" said Zoe, holding up a plastic carrier bag containing several takeaway containers.

"We've brought you dinner," said Debbie. "Sushi . . ." and they all collapsed into laughter and stumbled past me into the flat.

"Oh dear—reckon we got here just in time," said Liinda. "She's been looking at photo albums . . . Mmm, like the guy in the leather pants . . . very Dylan McDermott. Look Debs, here's one for you, he's on a horse . . ."

I took it out of her hands and slammed it shut.

"Where are your glasses?" asked Debbie, shoving several bottles of white wine into my fridge.

"I've only got one and it's next to my bed, full of dusty water," I said. "Is this a home invasion?"

"Yes," said Liinda, who was banging kitchen cupboards and drawers open and shut. "Where are your ashtrays? Here's the corkscrew, Debs. Catch."

"I haven't got an ashtray. I don't smoke. Why don't you use my head, Liinda?" I still hadn't forgiven her. She gave me the finger, but she was smiling.

"I'll go and ask your neighbours," said Debbie. "I used to date a guy who lived in this building. He was a real spunk—maybe there are more of them." She disappeared.

Zoe was unpacking the food. There were boxes and boxes of raw fish all over my floor.

I heard Debbie through the open front door and could tell by her voice that she was talking to a man. She came back with three wine glasses, an ashtray and a full report.

"Not bad, actually. Nice hair, but he was wearing a cheap watch."

She opened a bottle of wine and sat on the floor with Zoe. Liinda joined them, opened a can of Diet Coke and lit a cigarette. They all picked up a piece of sushi and looked up at me.

"Come on," said Zoe. "Come and have some sushi."

"To what do I owe this honour?" I asked, sitting down. Debbie handed me a glass of wine. Zoe handed me a piece of tuna-topped rice. Then they all raised their pieces of fish and touched them together like they were making a toast. Debbie indicated I should do the same. Too depressed to argue, I did.

"Sushi sisters!" they said in unison, eating the fish followed by a large swig of wine or, in Liinda's case, Diet Coke.

"Come on," said Debbie, and I ate mine too. "OK, now pick up another bit and say it with us."

"Why?"

"Just do it," said Zoe. "Humour us."

What the heck, I thought, it was better than watching *Pick the Pony* on my own.

"Sushi sisters!" we cried.

"What's this all about?" I asked. "Why are we sushi sisters?" They were grinning.

"We're sushi sisters . . ." said Zoe.

"Because we've all slept with the same man . . ." said Debbie. I looked at each of them in amazement.

"Nick Pollock," said Liinda.

"All of you?"

They nodded.

"Sadly Maxine couldn't join us," she continued. "Or Kylie."

"Kylie?"

More nods.

I couldn't believe it. "Has the entire *Glow* staff slept with him?"

"No," said Debbie. "Only the really pretty ones."

It was so appalling it actually made me feel a bit better.

"So I wasn't the only idiot to be taken in by his unctuous charms and the stories of his genius father?"

"No, we've all been fully sucked in," said Zoe.

"And spat out," added Liinda.

"I swallowed," said Debbie, and they all roared with laughter. I was still too stunned by what they'd just told me to join in.

"But didn't you warn each other? And why didn't you warn me?"

"It's always too late," said Zoe.

"He makes every woman think *she* is the special one," Liinda explained. "Even multiply psychoanalysed me. Even devastating Debbie. Even Maxine the mighty. Even tiny little Zoe. Even smarty pants you. That's his talent. He can make intelligent, in-dependent, normally rational women believe his bullshit. That's why we call him Pants On Fire—because he's the most unbeliev-able fibber and he is permanently horny."

I looked at her in amazement. "But how does he do it? He's not that gorgeous . . ."

"He has an unerring instinct for what will work for each vic-tim. With me it was endless discussions of the psychopathologies of our twisted families—and astrology."

"For me it was shopping for clothes and going to the gym," said Zoe, putting half a piece of raw fish back in the container.

"For me it was sex." Debbie smiled at me as she drained her glass and poured us more wine. "And great drugs. He's got some secret source of the most wicked ecstasy I've ever taken . . ."

And that's when I started laughing. It was so ridiculous. All that crap about Shakespeare and books and what we would call our children. I told them about it and we laughed and laughed. And then we compared notes on his sexual performance, which we all agreed almost—*almost*—made it worthwhile.

And that led us on to the next bottle of wine and the filthy de-tails of all our other disastrous romantic encounters and sexual escapades. By the third bottle I knew the exact circumstances in which all of them had lost their virginity (Liinda went to the loo at that point, I noticed), their first big loves, their favourite sex-ual positions, the best sex they'd ever had, their number-one turn-offs and the most treacherous things men had done to them. High on all our lists was Phone Torture, except for Deb-bie, who said her problem was men who wouldn't stop calling, but she could see it was a dastardly concept.

I grinned evilly at Liinda. "There's a coverline idea for you—oh, too late, we've already thought of it . . ." which was my way of letting her know I'd forgiven her.

At eleven-thirty I started yawning.

"I think I'd better go," Zoe announced. "My personal trainer is coming at six tomorrow morning."

"And I've got to get back to Wahroonga," said Liinda.

"Where's that?" I asked.

"It's miles away," said Debbie. "It's on the Upper North Shore—a really boring suburb."

"It's a lovely suburb," Liinda corrected her. "Full of nice middle-class families and their lovely children—and nowhere to get drugs, thank you Debbie. And it takes a while to get to work, which gives me plenty of time to read. You know, Debbie—books. Remember them? Those things you had at school, with pages."

"Ha ha, very funny. Do you want to come out, Georgie? These two bores can go home and we can go to the Soho Bar, or the Blue Room. It's only quarter to twelve."

"Debbie, it's Monday night . . ."

"Oh yeah, the Blue Room is closed on Mondays, but I think the International's open. Or Fix. Come on, it'll be fun."

"No. I think I'll be boring and go to bed too, thanks. This has been fun, though. Thanks so much, all of you. I was feeling really homesick before you came—I was about to ring Qantas to find out the next plane I could get on. It was really nice of you."

"Oh, get out of here," said Liinda. "We couldn't let a sushi sister suffer."

I went to bed laughing to myself. Bollocky Pollocky Pants On Fire.

Chapter Eight

The next morning we were all back in Maxine's office, sharing Panadols and laughing at new private jokes. For the first time I really felt part of the gang.

"Well, you're all in a good mood," said Maxine. "Let's hope you're still smiling when we've finished looking at these cover pictures, eh? SERAPHIMA, CAN YOU BRING US SOME COFFEE AND TIM TAMS!" she shouted through the door.

Zoe had turned out the light and drawn the blinds and was now fiddling with a projector. She seemed nervous and kept dropping slides on the floor. Maxine was leaning back in her chair with her feet up on the desk and her hands behind her head.

"These had better be good," she said. "I don't have money in the budget to keep shelling out for vastly overpriced pictures from American magazines. As I've told you time and time again, *Glow* is an Australian magazine and I want Australian models on the cover."

Zoe knocked the entire carousel of transparencies onto the floor.

"Oh Jesus," said Maxine. "Get your shit together, Zoe. Why do I have a sinking feeling? SERAPHIMA, WHERE'S THAT FUCKING COFFEE?"

I caught Liinda's eye. She took the cigarette out from behind her ear and clamped it between her teeth.

"Fasten your seat belt," she growled out of the side of her mouth. "It's going to be a rocky ride."

Seraphima came in with Maxine's coffee and a packet of biscuits.

"Ah," said Maxine, tearing it open. "Tim Tams."

"What's a Tim Tam?" I asked, looking at them curiously.

Maxine stopped with the biscuit halfway to her mouth and stared at me. "Are you telling me you've never eaten a Tim Tam?"

"I've never even seen one. What are they?"

She leaned forward conspiratorially and turned on her desk lamp. She held an oblong chocolate biscuit under the light and turned it over with reverence, as if she was showing me a precious artefact.

"This," she said, "is a Tim Tam. Not just a chocolate-coated crispy biscuit sandwich with creamy chocolate filling, but a totem for Australian womanhood. This biscuit is our source of comfort when men turn bad, jobs turn boring and life, in general, sucks. Retiring to bed with a packet of Tim Tams is a crucial part of the heartbreak recovery process. It is with Tim Tams that we break our diets and mend our hearts."

She looked at the biscuit with love, turned off the light and bit it in half.

"I'd better have one of those," I said. It was great. Really munchy. "Mmm . . . these are good."

"You should try one when you've had a few joints," said Debbie.

"You should try them on a hot day after they've been in the fridge," said Liinda.

"You should try one that's been frozen—you can use it as a straw to drink your coffee through," Zoe chimed in between bites.

We all looked at her, astonished. She was actually eating a chocolate biscuit. And I hadn't seen any carrots in the vicinity.

"Do you really not have these in England?" asked Maxine. I shook my head. "You poor deprived little Pommy. Do you have an equivalent?"

I thought hard. "Well, milk chocolate digestives are popular, but I've always considered them overrated. Maybe Jaffa Cakes— I love the contrast of the crispy dark chocolate, the smooth tangy orange filling and the rough sponge—but they pall after a while and some people hate them. Club biscuits are good, especially the orange ones, but it's a bit hard on the teeth to eat more than one. A Penguin biscuit would be the closest, but I don't really like them. They were always a disappointing substitute for real chocolate. But these—" I took another bite, "—these are something special."

Maxine bestowed one of her radiant smiles on me.

"You are definitely going to fit in here, Georgia," she said. "Now Zoe, what about these cover shots. This is for April, so it's going into winter, but we're not ready for woolly jumpers."

"I've got the cover tries we did on that trip to New Zealand in December," said Zoe. "They're swimsuits, but I think they work for April and it is an Australian model."

She turned on the projector and clicked the carousel round to the first shot. I stared in amazement. Was she serious? The picture showed a girl in a tiny turquoise bikini standing calf-deep in water. She was so thin you could practically see her internal organs. Her head looked like a skull. Her rib cage looked like a percussion instrument.

"What the fuck is that?" said Maxine in a deadly voice.

"It's a new girl from Perth called Katrina, and that's a Bondi Babes bikini," Zoe replied.

"Oh, it is human is it?" said Maxine. "Are you sure it's not a chicken? Because I've never seen arms that thin on a human being. Did you take her pulse, Zoe? I find it hard to believe someone that thin is still breathing. And look at that—the goose pimples on her thighs are bigger than her breasts. Isn't that lovely?"

"Well, maybe this isn't a very good shot," Zoe mumbled. "Let's look at some others." She started clicking the carousel round. They were all just as bad and there were some side views that made the model look even thinner.

"STOP!" Maxine roared. "I don't want to see any more pictures of this human skeleton."

"There's a different cozzie here somewhere," said Zoe, clicking wildly until a picture appeared of the plucked chicken wearing a black bikini with a bandeau top. It was even worse.

"I said STOP!" Maxine thumped her fist on the desk. "Zoe. How many times have I told you? I will *not* have anorexics on the cover of my magazine. This girl is sick—and so are you. What were you thinking when you cast her and why didn't I get to see her book before you went on the trip?"

"You were away—"

"So who approved the casting? Debbie, was it you?"

"Yes, Maxine," said Debbie. "I did see her book—but she didn't look like this. She was much bigger. Really. But I didn't see her in the flesh, I admit."

"Great help you are. Thank you. You fucked up big-time. And tell me, Zoe," she said, turning her icy gaze to her. "Did you actually see this model before you got to the airport?"

"Yes."

"And was she this thin?"

Zoe looked surprised. "I don't think she's thin."

There was a moment's stunned silence. Zoe's left hand was crumbling up the Tim Tam she'd been nibbling. I held my breath.

"Zoe," said Maxine, quietly. "If you don't think this girl is thin, there is something seriously wrong with you."

"She's got beautiful bones," said Zoe.

"Bones are all she's got!" said Maxine. "We can't use these pictures—they're dangerous to young women. Please take them off the projector. You and I will have a little talk later. In the meantime, does anyone have any other cover suggestions? Or will I have to draw a picture? We have two days to get it ready for the printer."

Zoe slumped into a chair, shell-shocked.

"I've got some shots I did for the May beauty story," said Debbie. "They just came in—I'll get Kylie to bring them through."

She picked up the phone. Maxine had her head in her hands. Liinda passed me the Tim Tams.

"Welcome to the snake pit," she said.

Kylie came in with the pictures and Debbie indicated with one imperious gesture that she should load them onto the carousel.

"So what are these about, Debbie?" said Maxine.

"It's a skin story, so there isn't much make-up, but the hair is nice. She's an Aussie girl. Go on, Kylie."

A radiant face filled the screen. Dead-straight honey-blonde hair framed her face. She had big blue eyes with ridiculously long lashes. Big pouty lips. It looked exactly like Debbie.

Maxine sighed loudly. "Ten thousand ways with a blue-eyed blonde. Did you know, Debbie, that some people actually consider dark-haired women like me and Zoe and Liinda quite attractive?"

Debbie was totally unperturbed.

"Nice shot, isn't it?" she said. "Click on, Kylie."

They were lovely shots, but all pretty much the same, very close up and not smiling.

"Yes, they are beautiful, Debbie, like all your pictures, and I think *Harper's Bazaar* or *Vogue* would love to have them on their covers. But they don't make a *Glow* cover, because she doesn't look like someone our readers could sit down and have a chat to about men and mascaras. She's too snooty. Funny that—SERAPHIMA, CAN YOU GET THE COVERS FILE OUT PLEASE?"

She turned to me.

"You know, Georgia, I have two very talented stylists on this magazine, who work with all the best photographers in this country and have their pick of the models, yet month after month they are incapable of producing *one* little picture I can use on my cover. Fortunately, however, I am a little more resourceful. Would you mind loading the carousel, Sera? My fingers are covered in chocolate." She took another Tim Tam. So did I.

"Thank you Seraphima, I'll take over now." Maxine stood up and came over to the carousel. "OK, what do we have here?"

She clicked and up came a beautiful picture of a blonde model laughing in a red and white gingham bikini top. "Might save that for summer," said Maxine. She clicked again. A magnificent-looking brunette in a fuschia stretch bikini. "Not bad after a baby," said Maxine. "But I'm saving it for the body issue in September."

Click. Up came a gorgeous dark-haired girl with beautiful green eyes and very full lips wearing a dark denim shirt unbuttoned to reveal a phenomenal cleavage.

"Now *that* is a *Glow* cover," said Maxine. "The improbably named Laetitia—do you think they call her Titty for short? What a fantastic girl. She's stunningly beautiful, but approachable. You feel like you might know a girl like that. I mean, you wouldn't introduce her to your boyfriend, but she looks like she'd enjoy a laugh. That is a *Glow* cover. Not anorexics. Not snotty-nosed bitches. Beautiful, nice women. Have you got that, Zoe? Debbie? Because I've had to buy this picture from *Madame*

Figaro in France and it's cost me $2,000. I can't afford to do that every month and I'm sick of running myself ragged negotiating with nightmare agents in New York to buy French pictures and doing calculations in three foreign currencies to cover your arses." She patted the carousel. "So this is our April cover—but for our May one I want an *Australian* model taken by an *Australian* photographer. Do I make myself clear? OK. Good. Now get out. Except Zoe. I want you to stay. And Liinda—can you stay in your office, for an hour or so? I might need you."

Debbie followed me into my office. She didn't seem at all bothered about what had just gone on and I decided not to say anything. I'd had enough drama for one day.

"I've spoken to Mum about you coming up to Bundaburra," she said. "That's the name of our property—and she suggested this weekend. It's the annual rodeo in Walton, near where the farm is. Mum thought you'd enjoy it. It's heaps of fun."

Debbie's naughty smile told me she was implying heaps of cute men. The words "fun" and "attractive men" seemed to be interchangeable in her language.

I must have looked a bit doubtful. I was rather off men as a concept.

"Real men, George," she added. "Wearing chaps—and not to go to Mardi Gras. And you only have to look, we don't have to talk to them or anything."

"Mmm," I said. "I love cowboys. Will they be wearing big hats and cowboy boots too?"

"Shit yeah."

"Yee haw. Tell your mum I'd love to come. Oh and Debbie, explain something to me—why did Maxine want Liinda to stay behind? Is she going to get a bollocking too?"

"No. Maxine wants her to hang around because she might need her counseling skills for Zoe. Liinda's had her own head shrinked so much she's actually quite good at helping other people, although she does get a bit carried away with it. She tried to get me to go to some godforsaken AA meeting once, can you believe it? I told her to get fucked, but Zoe does need some help. I wonder if they've got something called Pukers Anonymous that Liinda can take her to. See you later."

Debbie was appalling, but I couldn't help liking her. She was spoilt and excessive and selfish, but she didn't pretend not to be. And I really liked the sound of the rodeo. At lunchtime I went out and bought myself a pair of RM Williams boots to celebrate. I already had a beaten-up old straw Stetson I'd bought in Texas years before on a trip with Rick, and the boots would complete my look. I always like to be correctly attired.

When I got back to the office Seraphima had a look on her face that I'd come to realize meant she Knew Something.

"OK Sera," I said. "Spill it."

She took a deep breath as she sat down in my office. "Maxine has sent Zoe home. Liinda's taken her in a taxi. It was her third warning in three months, so Maxine's decided to suspend her—on full pay—until she 'shows she is prepared to do something about coming to terms with her bulimia.'"

I could tell by Sera's voice that this was a direct through-the-office-door quote.

"I've just given Maxine the name and number of the specialist who looked after my sister and she's on the phone to Zoe's mum with it."

"Zoe's mum?" I couldn't believe Maxine would do that.

Sera shrugged. "Maxine says there's no point in pretending it's not happening—it's much better to get it all out in the open."

I'd had enough drama for one day and went back into my office to try to do some work. I was admiring my new boots when the phone rang.

"Hello," said a loud happy voice.

"Ant, how nice to hear from you. How are you?"

"I'm very well. More to the point, how are you? I hear you got bitten by one of Australia's most venomous creatures—Pants On Fire Pollock. I wish I'd warned you, not that it ever does any good . . ."

"How on earth did you know about that?"

"No secrets in this town, sweetie. It's good you found that much out quickly."

"Who told you, Antony?" I persisted.

"Debbie."

"I don't believe it—I thought she was a friend . . ."

"Georgia, it's just the way this town is. Debbie is no worse than anyone else. It's like a big village. You'll get used to it. Soon you'll be gossiping along with the rest of us, spreading rumours, making up juicy details, planting joke rumours to see how quickly they come back to you. It's hilarious. Don't people gossip in London?"

"Of course they do. But unless you're world famous it is possible to maintain a level of privacy. You can keep different parts of your life in separate compartments—that doesn't seem to be possible here."

He snorted. "Sounds boring to me. Anyway, do you want to come out with me and drown your sorrows?"

"I drowned them at birth, but I'd love to come out. Where are we going?"

"Art galleries—it's Tuesday. Then we can have dinner. Have you had your nails done yet?"

"No I haven't, but Debbie's already sent her assistant into my office with her manicurist's card."

"HA HA HA . . . So have you made your appointment? Consuela's impossible to get in to."

"No, I have not! I threw it in the bin. I don't have manicures. They're a total waste of time and money. I used to know Princess

Diana's personal hairdresser in London and he told me she always did her own nails. If it was good enough for her, it's good enough for me."

"At least she had her hair done. I'll be waiting for you downstairs at six. Goodbye."

What was wrong with my hair and nails? My nails were clean and short, my hair was—well, it was hair. I went into the loo and had a look at it. Seraphima came out of one of the cubicles and washed her hands next to me. Her blonde curls were pulled back neatly with a tortoiseshell slide. My lank locks were pulled back in an elastic band I'd found on my office floor. I inspected an incipient pimple on my chin. Seraphima got lip pencil and lipgloss out of her pocket and applied it carefully. Maybe I did need to look at the grooming issue, I thought.

I went back to my office and started reading the last few articles for the next issue, including "Phone Torture," which I had to admit made a bloody good read. As I was finishing it the most extraordinary sound came floating through my office window. It sounded like a maniac was outside.

I looked up and a small, squat, no-necked bird was sitting on my windowsill—on the fourth floor of an office block, in the middle of the Central Business District. I realized it was a kookaburra. And it was laughing.

Chapter Nine

The art openings were great fun. The first one was in a converted factory in Redfern and the second was in an old shop in Surry Hills. Don't ask me about the art—I didn't get a chance to look at it. Antony knew everybody at both parties and introduced me to so many people I was starting to get dizzy.

Then I saw Danny Green, who accosted me with his usual kisses and pushed me together with someone for a photo opportunity. It was Jasper O'Connor, without penis hat or bright pink trousers and looking rather attractive for a scumbag.

"Jazzy!" I greeted him with the fervour born of knowing no one else in the room. He put his arm round me and we smiled for the camera.

"Gorgeous, you two," said Danny, kissing us again and then running off to fuss over his next subjects.

"Hello, Pinkie darling. What a nice surprise this is. Who brought you to this major event for Sydney's bohemian A list?"

"Antony Maybury."

Jasper pulled a face and I suddenly realized there was something different about him.

"You've shaved off your goatee."

"Yes," he said, rubbing his chin and making an endearing little moue. "You like?"

"Oh yes, it's much better. I can't bear facial hair. You know, all that stuff about looking like you're trying to hide something."

"I was. My age." He laughed infectiously, and I could see how he would charm his subjects when he took their photos. He was certainly charming me.

"Is your underage girlfriend here tonight, Jasper?"

"You don't miss a trick, do you Pinkie?" Jasper put his head on one side and looked at me through those narrowed green eyes. "I'd like to take your picture, Pinkie," he said. "In that hat you were wearing at the party. 'Pinkie in the Pink,' we could call it."

"Don't try and worm out of it with your devastating charm. Where is Little Lotus Blossom tonight?"

"Fucked if I know. Somewhere with her new boyfriend, I expect. Riding around in his Porsche, probably, seeing as that's the kind of thing that impresses her. She refused to be seen in my car because it was more than a year old."

"How old is it?"

"About twenty-five years." He laughed again. "So how's life at the convent?" he asked. "Debbie still the only woman in that place getting her portion and everyone else's?"

I'm not sure if I blushed or looked shocked.

"It's well known that the *Glow* girls talk and write about sex incessantly but never actually get any themselves," Jasper continued. "Liinda's too crazy, Maxine's too ugly and Zoe's too thin. Debbie is another matter altogether and almost more of a worry for it—she seems to be a nymphomaniac—but you, Pinkie, you strike me as a normal girl with normal appetites."

I didn't know what to say. Luckily Antony did, sliding up behind me.

"Well, I hope she has got a normal appetite because I'm taking her out to dinner. Now. Goodbye Jasper."

"And goodbye to you, An-thu-ny," said Jasper, putting a special emphasis on the middle syllable. Then he turned to me. "Goodbye Pinkie. I'll give you a ring again soon—even though you were a total bitch the last time I called."

"Sorry about that. I was having a really bad day. See you." I smiled at him sheepishly. As Antony frogmarched me to the door, I turned back and caught Jasper winking at me. That wink of his was very sexy.

"Whatever were you talking to that deadbeat for?" demanded Antony. "I can't stand people who call me AnTHUNy. It's TUNNy. Tunny, like the fish."

"I like Jasper. He's funny."

"Funny in the head. Anyway, I must tell you what Sophie Paparellis was just telling me. Apparently the entire *Chic* fashion department is going to resign if . . ."

And he chattered on like this in the taxi all the way to the third gallery. I didn't have a clue who any of the people were that Antony was talking about, but he was enjoying himself so much that I did too.

"I've saved the best party to last. This one's going to be hilarious," he said, as we walked through the door of a lovely old terrace in Paddington. "Trudy! Trudy! Come here, I want you to meet Georgia."

I met Trudy. He was lovely. Trudy was a man. So was Betty. And Norma. And Mary. And Antony had suddenly turned into Dolores. They weren't drag queens, they were Antony's best friends and they all called each other by their mother's names.

"It works," said Antony. "Look how the names suit them."

I smiled at him. "You're right. Especially Dolores. It's perfect for you, Antony. I'm going to call you Doll."

"What's your mother's name, Georgia?" asked Trudy, a tall, slim man with rather bouffant hair, dressed in head-to-toe Prada.

"Shouldn't it be my father's name?"

"Oh no," said Betty, a short, chubby-faced fellow with a shaved head, a big earring and stubby beard. "We only like girls' names."

"Well, my mother's called Hermoine—"

"Ooh, that's a love name," said Betty. "Are you Greek?"

"—but everyone calls her Pussy . . ."

Dolores was laughing so much his wine came down his nose.

"Pussy! Oh, that is too good. I'm always going to call you Pussy from now on."

Then he proceeded to introduce me to everybody at the party as Pussy. I was past caring. I thought Dolores was so funny I didn't mind being Pussy a bit—and he was right, it was a fun party. Eventually I had to go to the loo and on my way back to find Delores, I finally got to see the art. It was an exhibition of Robert Mapplethorpe's black and white photographs. I'd seen them before in a book, but blown up into huge prints they were a bit confronting. One of them was called "Man in a Polyester Suit" and featured a beautiful black man in a cheap suit. Except he had forgotten to do up his fly and something very large and surprising was hanging out of it.

"Gorgeous, isn't he, Pussy?" said Betty, taking my arm in a chummy way and guiding me on a tour of his favourite penises in the exhibition. As we walked around the gallery I became aware that I was one of only about ten women in a very crowded room. And the only one wearing lipstick.

"Is this a gay art gallery?" I asked Betty. "Or just a gay show?"

"Well, one of the guys who owns it is gay, but it's a regular gallery—or as regular as anything gets in Sydney." He shrieked like a pantomime dame. I liked Betty. He was cosy, which isn't easy to achieve in leather chaps and steel-toed boots. Under his leather waistcoat I could see his nipples were pierced with thick silver rings, and on his bicep there was something that looked like a cattle brand, which said "100% AUSSIE BEEF." He looked quite terrifying but he sounded as if he was just going to pass the vicar some nice hot scones.

"This show is part of the Mardi Gras arts festival," he told me. "You are going to come to the party, aren't you? You'll love it."

"Pussy! Pussy! Where are you? Here puss, puss, puss!" I could hear Antony shouting from the other side of the gallery.

I pushed my way back through the crowd.

"Hello Dolly," I said.

He grinned. "Come on, Pussy Galore, we're going to dinner."

He drained his glass, deposited it with a passing waiter and walked straight out of the door, with me obediently following along behind him.

"I never say goodbye," he explained. "It takes too long. I saw all of those people on Saturday night and I'll probably see them all tomorrow. No point. We can walk to the restaurant."

We were on a lovely street of terrace houses with curly wrought-iron railings on their balconies. There were lofty leaf-laden trees all along it, with branches meeting in the middle.

"This is a beautiful street," I said.

"Paddington Street. Yes, it is lovely. Your friend Billy Ryan lives just down there." He pointed to a side street. "And Debbie Brent lives round the corner that way. It's her own house, lucky bitch. Really, she doesn't need a rich husband—it's such a waste—but she'll get one. I used to live in Paddington but I was glad to escape to my grungy little corner of Surry Hills. I got sick of seeing *le tout* Sydney every time I went out for the paper."

The restaurant was a large oblong space with a bold black and white mural of people having dinner all along one wall. The waiters wore long aprons and all the diners looked polished and well fed.

Antony kissed the maitre d' on both cheeks. "Hello, darling. We'll need a table for eight."

As we sat at the bar waiting for a table to become available, Trudy, Betty, Norma and Mary came in, with two new fellows I hadn't met before—Joanna and Ingrid.

"So," said Ingrid, once we were introduced, "how is your spanking ex doing without you? Still with your friend, is he?" I turned to glare at Antony, but he was telling Joanna all the *Chic* gossip.

"No, I believe Rick has decided to join an order of gay Franciscan monks," I told Ingrid, straight-faced. "In Iceland." Right Antony, thanks for the tip, I'll just wait to see how long it takes before that little pigeon flies home.

The dinner was riotous. A lot of the talk was about the Mardi Gras—who was in the parade, who was having liposuction to get into their costume, who had the most reliable source of good ecstasy, who didn't have tickets and who the surprise performers were going to be.

"I heard Madonna," said Betty.

"Yeah, right," said Antony. "She'll probably do a duet with Barbra Streisand. And Elvis. I heard Cher is coming but I don't believe it."

"Yeah—and Tom Cruise, Prince Edward and Richard Gere are the go-go dancers," said Norma.

They were screaming with laughter. So was I.

"So, are you going to come to the party?" asked Antony. I'd noticed they all called it that.

"I'll think about it," I said.

"Well, don't think too long. I'd have to make you an outfit. Probably something topless." He looked me up and down. "You'd look good in one of those outfits the women wear at the

Rio carnival. You have just the right body shape—little perky tits and a big round bottom. I'd like to see you in a G-string and a feather headdress. A sparkly G-string. Fuschia. Lots of fake tan. Mmm . . ."

After dinner there was much hugging and kissing and lots of see-you-soons and gorgeous-to-meet-you-darlings. Then we all jumped into cabs and went our separate ways, except that Antony insisted on dropping me off first "on his way," which it wasn't.

"I want to see where you live," he admitted.

"I should warn you I have no possessions," I told him. "I thought I'd be living in furnished digs and I brought hardly anything with me apart from some clothes and handbags, and a few books and CDs I can't live without. Actually, that was all I really had anyway. I've had to buy things like kettles. So boring."

"I've got a load of stuff like that you can have—I've got all my own gear and then I inherited all Lee's things, so now I've got two of everything. My place is like Noah's ark . . . I see what you mean about bare," he said, wrinkling his nose when we got inside. He marched straight into my bedroom and opened the wardrobe doors.

"Where do you keep the handbag collection then?"

"Well, I only brought a few with me. They're in this hat box."

"Divine. I love hat boxes. Mmm, I like this little one shaped like a pot of violets. That's very sweet. This is cute—is it vintage?"

He looked at every one, then he commented on my bed linen, which he approved of because it was old and embroidered. Then, after looking through all my CDs and thrusting Frank Sinatra at me to put on, he sat on the floor and asked if I had any photo albums with me.

"Yes I do, actually."

"Oh, good. I love photo albums."

He wasn't kidding. Antony looked through all my albums, demanding a running commentary on every picture. After some initial embarrassment I happily went into all the details of who was who. He got the hang of it all very quickly.

"Oh, look at your brother Hamish. He's gorgeous. I love that high colour in his cheeks. Very Scottish. He looks like a handsome version of James Hewitt."

I hit him with a cushion. "He does *not* look like that cad."

"Does he play polo? Look at his shoulders. All polo players have those gorgeous shoulders. Even Prince Charles. Oh look, there's Real Pussy."

"Real Pussy?"

"Yes, you're Pussy now, so your mum is Real Pussy, otherwise it gets too confusing."

"Right . . ."

"Why is she called Pussy, by the way?"

"I honestly don't know. She does like cats, but she's been called Pussy since she was a little girl."

"Oh, is that one of your father's water features? Marvellous lion's head. Look at you here—how old are you? Eight? Is that needlepoint you're holding? How sweet. Oh, look at Real Pussy in a straw hat and espadrilles, she was glamorous, wasn't she? Is that in Provence? Thought so. Got any pictures of your grandparents? Look, they're both in tartan skirts, how funny! Yes, I know his is a kilt, but you know what I mean. Dear little dogs. Look at Gaston's ears sticking up. OK, now I want to see pictures of Rick."

"Do you really?"

"Yes. Give me that. Ah! He is heaven. Look at those long legs. Leather pants. He's a major spunk. Darling, I can see why your friends thought you were mad to leave him. All that and money too. And there he is in a suit. Got any pictures of where you lived?"

And so it went on until Antony had worked his way through my entire life—and a fair amount of my whisky—like termites going through a house. He seemed as interested in the physical and material details of my previous life as Liinda was in the emotional ones. I felt validated and violated at the same time—but at least Antony wasn't going to be in a coverlines meeting with me in the near future.

"He may have gone too far, though from what you've told me, that Rick is going to be hard to replace. Shame Nick Pollock came along when he did, but you're over him, aren't you? I'll have to get you out as much as possible meeting people. What are you doing this weekend?"

"I'm going to Debbie's parents' farm."

He turned and stared at me with his mouth open.

"What? I've never been there. I'm furious. Debbie knows I long to go to Bundaburra, the bitch. I want a complete report. Will you take lots of photos please? Just think, you'll be spending nearly forty-eight hours with Johnny Brent. Of course, you'll have to be with that ghastly Jenny Kelly as well, but it'll be worth it."

"Why are you so horrible about Debbie's mother?" I asked.

"Oh, she's such a social climber. She got pregnant deliberately, you know—she only wanted to marry Johnny Brent because he was handsome and gorgeous and rich."

"You were just telling me I was mad to leave Rick for exactly the same reasons."

Antony made a noise that can only be described as "humph."

"What have you really got against Jenny Brent?" I used her married name just to annoy him.

"I don't think she's good enough for him."

"Well, if Debbie is the result she can't be all bad."

"Oh, she was beautiful—that's how she got him—but her father was a labourer, for God's sake."

"Ah, so you think she wasn't *posh* enough for him? That's

what all this is about, isn't it? And I thought there wasn't supposed to be a class system in Australia. Well, I promise to take lots of photos and give you a full report, but I do not promise to dislike Jenny Brent because her father lifted bricks for a living. I bet she's lovely."

And I was right. Jenny Brent was lovely. From the moment she picked Debbie and me up from the airport at Tamworth I adored her. She kissed me straightaway even though we'd only just met, and then asked me to hold her dachshund, Choccie, while she threw our bags into the back of a beaten-up old ute. Next to French bulldogs, my favourite dogs in the whole world are dachshunds, partly because I was never allowed to have one as a child—my father always said they were deformed. Choccie sat on my lap for the entire drive to the homestead, which took over an hour.

"Oh, I see Choccie has a new friend," said Jenny, smiling at me in the rear-view mirror. "He doesn't love everybody, you know, but when he does it's for life. I hope you won't find his devotion a pain."

"No, I'll just love him back," I said.

I watched her as she chatted to Debbie about our journey and the preparations for the rodeo. She was still beautiful. Tall and slim like Debbie, and although her face was deeply lined it added character—they were happy lines, not frowny ones. Her hair was an unassisted mixture of warm blonde and grey, simply pulled back in a ponytail. She was dressed in khaki pants, RM Williams boots (just like mine, I'd been thrilled to notice), and a white singlet, with a khaki shirt open over the top. I could see where Debbie got her style from. For the finishing touch Jenny had a pair of diamond stud earrings the size of peanuts.

Once we got away from the town the countryside was beautiful. Rolling hills that reminded me of England a little, except they were more peaked and pointy than the high country around my parents' house and, rather than thick green hedges and pastures, everything looked golden—the grass, the rock, the earth and the light all had a golden glow.

After a while I became aware of something else my eye was missing—there were no church steeples—and I realised how used I was to there always being a steeple somewhere in the landscape. Here the only regular man-made features, apart from the roads and the fences, were windmills.

After we'd driven for about forty-five minutes Jenny announced in a jokey voice that we were now driving through Brent Land. Ten minutes later we came to an elaborate wrought-iron sign over a cattle grid which said "Bundaburra." It was another ten minutes up the drive, going steadily uphill until finally, after cresting a little ridge, we came to the homestead.

"Oh look, isn't it lovely!" I heard myself saying. Jenny stopped the car.

"This is a good place to get a perspective on the property," she said, clearly pleased that I liked it.

It was a big square house with a corrugated-iron roof and verandahs all round it, with creepers growing up them. A covered walkway led to another smaller house and beyond that lay stables, forming three sides of a square. The place was huge, and although I could see a swimming pool and a tennis court, it still had a farming feel to it. There were a couple of smaller houses on the other side of the stables which looked lived in, and a big barn with bits of old farm machinery lying around outside it. Three cattle dogs were lying in the sun—working dogs, Jenny told me (apparently Choccie was the only hound with house privileges.).

And then I saw the main attraction of the homestead. Leaning against the open double doors, with his arms folded, was the famous Johnny Brent. He was wearing polo gear. There were a couple of mallets lying on the ground by his feet. His breeches were dirty. He had floppy blond hair and he was smiling at us warmly. When he shook my hand his grip was ridiculously strong. His teeth were ridiculously white and his eyes were ridiculously blue and warm as they looked into mine. I couldn't look back at him properly—I was too shy. He had all the separate elements I'd found attractive in Billy and Rory and Nick and Jasper, but more of them.

OK, Antony, I thought. I take your point.

"Aren't I the lucky boy then?" he said, giving Debbie a big hug. "Three beautiful women all to myself. I reckon I'm going to be king of the rodeo dance tomorrow night, walking in with you three."

What dance? Debbie hadn't told me anything about a dance. I had nothing to wear. But looking on the bright side, maybe I'd get to see Johnny Brent strut his stuff on the dance floor, because no doubt he would be a great dancer as well as everything else. I could just imagine him getting down to "Brown Sugar" . . . I'd certainly torture Antony about that.

Debbie wanted to go out riding straightaway, but I stayed behind with Jenny, while she and her father went to saddle up. With Choccie trotting along beside us, Jenny showed me around the house and grounds. We visited the stables, which housed Johnny's polo ponies and the work horses they still used to move the cattle around. I met the working dogs and Jenny showed me how high they could jump. They were good, I thought, but not as good as Rory's dog, Scooby. That was when I realised that the Stewarts' farm must be somewhere in the vicinity, although having an idea of how big the Brents' property was, I didn't think Rory would be popping over to borrow a cup of sugar.

Then, most thrillingly for Pommy me, Jenny introduced me to her two tame kangaroos, Rocky and Chomp. They were so cute, with a funny way of moving slowly, using their tail like a third leg to ease themselves forward. I scratched them behind their ears and their little heads were so soft.

"I found Rocky a couple of years ago," Jenny explained. "He's such a big boy now, but he was a tiny joey in his mother's pouch than. She'd been knocked over by a car, but he was still alive. I brought him home and bottle-fed him, and I made him a pouch out of an old jumper with a hot-water bottle in it and strapped it to my front."

"Ooh. I'd love to do that. Did you have to hop?"

She laughed. "No. He was very happy—he came shopping with me and everything. Didn't you, Rocky? I found Chomp this spring."

"Did you have them in the house while you were rearing them?" Getting animals into the house had been one of the primary obsessions of my childhood.

"Oh yes. They'd come hopping along the hallway; it was so funny. I know a lot of farmers hate kangaroos, but I just can't leave them to die by the road."

Then she showed me the swimming pool and the rose garden and the vegetable and herb gardens she'd planted herself.

We filled two baskets with vegetables for dinner and sat on the verandah podding peas together. I felt completely comfortable with Jenny. She wanted to know all about why I'd come to Australia (I gave her the censored version) and what I thought of it. And what's more she called me Georgia, not Georgie.

Then she asked me a question I'd rather been dreading.

"How is Debbie getting on in Sydney, Georgia? I'm assuming you know that eighteen months ago we had a great sadness in the family . . ."

"Yes. Someone told me about the plane crash. I was so sorry to hear about it. It's a terrible thing."

"It was. We all loved Drew and nothing's really been the

same since that accident. We had known him all his life. His poor father, Andrew, had a stroke, and his mother, Margaret, has a terrible lot to deal with. I mean, it would be hard enough to lose three sons, but now she has to look after Andrew as well. At least they have their daughter and their youngest son, Rory. He's so good to them."

She wiped away a tear.

"Anyway, it happened, so we just have to deal with it. I do worry about Debbie in Sydney, though. I wanted her to stay here for a while—maybe a year or so, to really get over it and be around people who had known Drew—but she insisted on rushing back to Sydney. She said she needed to get straight back into her working life. I worry that she hasn't really dealt with the grief, and I hear little bits and pieces from friends who have children down there. I think she's got in with a bit of a fast crowd . . . What do you think, Georgia?"

She looked so worried, I desperately wanted to say the right thing.

"I don't know Debbie that well yet, Jenny, although she's been incredibly kind to me since I arrived . . ."

I looked at her intelligent face, waiting so keenly for my answer.

"She does go out quite a bit and there are a lot of late nights, but that's true of most of the people I've met in Sydney. It seems to be a party town."

What was I supposed to say? Your stunningly beautiful daughter has a far-reaching reputation as a drug-fucked nymphomaniac?

Jenny looked thoughtful.

"Georgia," she said. "I know you've only been here a minute, but I feel I can trust you and I'm going to ask you a favour: Would you keep an eye on Debbie for us? All I ask is that if you think she's getting in trouble, you'll ring me. Will you do that?"

How could I say no? I promised I would and was relieved to hear a distraction approaching, as Debbie and her father galloped into the garden on their horses.

"Mum! Mum! He's chasing me," cried Debbie, as they disappeared around the side of the house.

"Mind my roses!" called Jenny. She smoothed back her hair and appeared consciously to pull herself together. Then she turned and smiled at me.

"Anyway, you didn't come for a relaxing weekend in the country to hear about all our family dramas. Why don't you go and have a nice long bath and a rest before dinner? We'll have drinks out here at seven, so just do what you like and make yourself completely at home."

Dinner with the Brents was a lot of fun. When I joined them on the verandah, Johnny (with hair still wet from the shower, I noted for future Antony-baiting) already had the champagne open. We ate outside, with citronella candles burning to keep the mozzies at bay, and had steaks from cattle "grown on the property," as Johnny put it, along with several bottles of red wine.

Johnny regaled us with stories of his japes on the polo circuit as a young man and I told him about my brother's equestrian exploits in England, Scotland and Argentina.

"So, your brother's a polo man, is he?" said Johnny, topping up my glass. "What's his handicap?"

"An overfondness for pretty girls and good champagne?" I suggested.

Johnny roared with laughter. "Well, he definitely sounds like my kind of guy. Reckon if he's worked on a cattle ranch in Argentina he could probably survive out here. Tell him if he'd like to come and spend some time working at Bundaburra he'd be more than welcome."

"That's really kind of you. I will tell him—I think he's finding it a bit hard to settle back down in England."

I was really enjoying dinner, but talking about dear old Horsehead suddenly made me feel very homesick. It must have shown on my face, because Jenny took my hand across the table.

"Why don't you ring him right now and ask him?" she said. "I know what you Poms are like, you're so polite you'll be too shy to ask us again if we 'really' meant it—and we do really mean it, don't we Johnny?"

"Sure," he said. "I'd love another bloke around the place. Specially one I can recruit for the team."

Jenny went inside and got the phone. I did some mental arithmetic. Eleven hours difference, it was Friday night in Australia, so it was Friday morning in England, he should be talkable to. He picked up on the first ring.

"Heeeuuuurgh?"

"Oh Horsehead, you can't have a hangover on Friday morning . . ."

Johnny laughed and slapped his thigh in amusement.

"Big Bum? Is that you?" I hoped Debbie hadn't heard his nickname for me. "Well, yes, I have rather, but it's only a minor one. It's so bloody cold over here and I had to do something to keep warm. How are you, anyway?"

"I'm fine—listen. Remember that guy I wanted you to kill?"

"What's the arsehole done now?"

"Nothing, but remember our deal? I had to find you a job out here? Well, I've found you one."

"Have you really, Big Bum? That would be marvelous, I'm jack shit of this bloody weather, let me tell you. Is it a big place? Can I ride?"

Johnny was grinning and making beckoning gestures.

"Why don't you ask the owner? Here's Johnny Brent." I

handed him the phone. "He wants to know if he can ride here, Johnny."

"Hamish, how are you? Johnny Brent here. Heard a lot about you from your ravishing sister. She says you're a polo man. What's your handicap? Really? That's pretty good. Well, we can always use another man on the team and Georgia tells us you worked on a ranch in Argentina, yes? So you know what it's all about. That's great. OK, well I'll hand you back to your sister, she can give you my number and we'll be in touch. OK, mate. Bye."

I took the phone.

"Happy?" I asked Hamish.

"Rock and roll, Big Bum. He sounds like a good bloke. Is there a decent pub?"

"Hamish wants to know if there's a decent pub here, Johnny . . ."

They all laughed.

"Tell him the Walton Hotel is a fine old establishment," said Jenny.

"Yes," I told him. "There's a pub."

"Excellent," said Hamish. "I'll be over there before you know it to disgrace you. Thanks, Big Bum."

"My pleasure. I'll call you soon, you bad dog. Goodbye. And give your liver a rest."

They all shouted cheery 'bye's as I put the phone down. I couldn't stop grinning. It had been so nice to have some connection between my new life and my old life.

"Thank you so much for that," I said to Jenny. "I do get a bit homesick sometimes and it would be great to have him here."

"We look forward to meeting him," said Jenny, smiling kindly at me.

I glanced at Debbie, who was looking thoughtful. She was

picking at something on her jeans. Jenny noticed too and put her bright face on.

"So, Johnny," she said, filling our glasses. "Are you going to do some steer-roping tomorrow?" She nudged Debbie and winked at me.

"Yeah, Dad," said Debbie. "Let's see you up on one of those bucking broncos. Or perhaps you're just a polo pansy and couldn't handle a real horse."

"I'll handle you two in a moment, if you carry on like that," said Johnny, clearly loving having both his "girls" with him. "Actually, I'm running a rodeo of my own tomorrow."

"Oh yeah?" said Debbie. "What's that? The seniors' event?"

"Nooo . . . it's the junior rodeo," said Johnny, shaking with laughter. "I'm going to be leading the nippers around on a Shetland pony."

As we were carrying all the plates back into the kitchen later, Debbie sidled up next to me and spoke out of the side of her mouth, so Jenny wouldn't hear.

"Hey, Georgie," she said, "I didn't know your brother played polo. What does he look like? Is he cute? Or is he ugly like you—Big Bum!"

And she slapped me on the backside and ran off shrieking, with me in hot pursuit.

Chapter Ten

"Is this a rodeo or a festival or erotica?" I asked Debbie the next morning, as we sat on the fence by the corral watching the cowboys strut around in their jeans and boots, all bandy-legged and lanky. "Why do you think cowboys are so attractive?"

"I think it's the hats," said Debbie. "They're like dinner jackets—they make all men look gorgeous. If you saw one of these blokes walk into Wine Banc without his hat on you wouldn't give him a second look."

"I guess you're right. It only works in their natural habitat, which I must say feels very much like my natural habitat. Do you think the hat does it for me?" I tipped my old straw Stetson at her.

"Ten-four, rubber duck. You look like you were born wearing it. Do you have rodeos in England?"

"Not that I know of, although I believe boot-scooting is very popular. I suppose the closest thing would be point-to-points, or Pony Club. Not quite the same."

"Did you do all that?"

"No, too hearty for me. Hamish, as you'll have gathered, is

horse mad, but I got thrown off one when I was ten and never really fancied it after that. I can ride and I like horses, but it's not a big passion for me."

"I love it. Not as much as Dad, though. These days I just do it to make him happy, really." She paused. "Drew and I used to ride a lot. We'd go out for a couple of nights and sleep under the stars. The Stewart property joins ours, so we could ride for miles and miles and never see a soul. Heaven."

It was the first time I'd ever heard her mention him.

"Do you miss him terribly?" I asked her.

"When I'm up here I miss him almost more than I can bear. That's why I don't come home very often—and it's really nice to have you with me, let me tell you. Anything that makes it different from the past is good. I would have been to this rodeo maybe twelve times with Drew. We started out in the kiddies' rodeo, where Dad is helping right now. We grew up together."

"Did you always think you'd marry him?"

"I think so. I did have other boyfriends and I went out with all of his brothers over the years, and of course we went through those stages where boys and girls just taunt each other, but he was always special to me. I'm pretty sure he sent me a Valentine's Day card every year from the age of ten until he died. He'd never have admitted it and they were never signed—and of course I always got so many—but I could always tell which one was from Drew. I have twenty-two of them."

I nodded, swallowing.

"You see, there was always one card with a rabbit on it. He used to call me Bunny—he said I had buck teeth and big ears and looked like a rabbit. The first Valentine's Day after he died I got fifteen cards and not one of them had a rabbit on it."

She kicked the wooden paling a bit and then pulled herself together just as her mother had done the night before, pasting that big smile back on her face.

"I'm thirsty," she said, jumping down. "Let's go get us some beers."

In the beer tent I just toyed with my drink, but Debbie drank three or four stubbies in close succession. Some cowboys standing around the beer tent watched us with interest. Interest which increased with every beer Debbie downed. A couple of times I suggested we go back out to see what was happening at the corral, but she always wanted another beer instead. Soon there was no mistaking it—she was pissed. She was starting to stagger and sing along loudly with the country music that was playing. I didn't know what to do. Jenny was off helping with the sausage sizzle and Johnny was with the junior rodeo, and I didn't dare leave her to go and find them.

Then two of the cowboys came over to talk to us.

"You two girls look like you're having a good time," said the tallest one.

"Yes, thank you," I answered in my best clipped snotty Pom voice, which didn't make any difference because Debbie had already thrown her arms round his neck and said, "We're having a faaabulous time, big boy."

Then she started dancing with him in the middle of the beer tent. It was a total nightmare. There were no other women in there and somehow the boys had edged us over to a corner where people coming in to grab a beer couldn't see us. The other cowboy realized his mate was cracking on to a good thing with Debbie, so he thought he'd better make some fast progress with me.

"So are you going to have a good time like your mate and dance with me?" he said, putting his arms around my waist, with his groin thrust well forward.

"No, thank you," I said, pulling myself sharply away and sounding like Julie Andrews in full Mary Poppins mode.

"Oh right, you're a snobby little Pom, are you?"

"Yes. I am." Well, it seemed the only reply.

Debbie was nuzzling the tall one's neck and I could hear him suggesting they go off "someplace private."

"Debs," I said, looking at my watch theatrically. "It's nearly three o'clock. We're supposed to be meeting your father JOHNNY BRENT now. We'd better go."

I'd hoped the name would register, but these guys were on the rodeo circuit and had never heard of Johnny or any other Brent, and Debbie—now on about the twenty-fifth beer Buffalo Bill had bought her—didn't even seem to hear. There was only one option—I had to go and find Johnny and bring him back as soon as possible.

"I've just got to go for a pee," I said, suddenly smiling at my cowboy as though I thought he was adorable. "Why don't you just wait here until I get back?" I tapped him playfully on his lariat. Debbie didn't notice me leave. She had her hand down John Wayne's jeans.

I ran out of the beer tent with no idea where to find the junior rodeo. All the formerly gorgeous cowboys hanging around suddenly looked like prospective rapists. Then I heard a voice say: "Georgia? Is it you under that hat?"

It was Rory Stewart.

"Rory! Oh thank God, you've got to help me, quick—Debbie's drunk in the beer tent and a hideous cowboy is about to rape her."

"Which tent? Show me."

I grabbed his hand and we ran back to the tent just in time to see the cowboy bundling Debbie out the back of it.

"BUNNY!" shouted Rory. "Get back here."

She instantly stood up straight and looked at us. The cowboy tried to push her out of the tent but Debbie pushed back past him.

"Hey, what's going on?" said the cowboy. "I thought we were mates . . ."

"BUNNY, COME HERE NOW!" said Rory, his hat pulled down low over his face.

The cowboy gave Debbie another shove, but she managed to squeeze past him and came running over to Rory.

"Drew!" she said. "DREW?"

Rory just grabbed her hand and pulled her out of the tent as the cowboy came running after her.

"Hey! What the fuck are you doing? She's with me," he yelled.

"Not anymore, she isn't," I told him, running after Debbie and Rory.

When I got outside she was screaming at him. He held her wrists while she pummeled his chest.

"How could you do that to me? How could you pretend to be Drew? You know your voice sounds just like his. How could you *do* that? No one calls me Bunny except Drew. You bastard. I hate your fucking guts. Why didn't *you* die?"

She burst into racking sobs and Rory just grabbed her and held her tight in his arms. I could hear him making soothing noises like you'd make to a frightened horse. Then he looked up at me, an expression of pure pain on his face.

"I think you'd better go and find Johnny," he said.

I went over to the corral and asked a friendly looking family where the junior rodeo was. It wasn't far and I found Johnny holding a tiny toddler on the back of a Shetland pony. It was hard to say which of them was enjoying it more.

"Hello Georgie," he said. "Having fun?"

"Yes thank you, Johnny. Um . . . Johnny, Debbie's a bit upset. I think you need to come and see her."

His face dropped immediately. He gave the child back to its mother and handed her the reins to the pony.

"What happened? Where is she?"

"She um . . . we bumped into Rory Stewart. He had his hat on. She thought he was Drew."

"Oh, God." He stopped and looked at me. "Had she been drinking?"

"Well, we did have a couple of beers."

I took him over to where she was still sobbing in Rory's arms.

"I'm really sorry, Johnny," Rory said. "I had my hat pulled low against the sun, and Drew had a similar one . . . it was a terrible mistake."

I was glad to see he didn't give Johnny the whole story either.

"That's OK, Rory—thanks for looking after her. Hey, where's my little baby? Come on. Daddy's here. Everything's going to be alright. We're going to go home. Come on, let's go and get Mum." And he led her away.

I put my face in my hands and groaned. I felt awful. It was all my fault. I should have stopped her drinking. Rory pulled my hands away.

"Georgia, it's not your fault. Debbie still has a lot of grieving to do and she's going to be a mess until she does it."

"Thank God you came along, Rory. It was getting really ugly in there."

"I can imagine."

We just stood there for a moment, still in shock.

"Are you staying at the Brents' place?" he asked.

"Yes—we came up for a relaxing weekend in the country . . ." We both laughed more than this remark warranted.

"Well, it's good to see you anyway." He smiled. "Do you want to go for a drink? Not in that beer tent, don't worry. There's a really nice pub just up the road. And then I'll take you back to the Brents' later. It's thirty ks so I don't think you'll want to walk."

The Walton Hotel was a nice pub, old—by Australian standards—with verandahs round the front and a big garden at the back. Rory and I sat outside with our beers.

"It's really beautiful here," I said.

"You reckon?"

"Absolutely. How far away is your place?"

"Twenty ks that way." He gestured in the opposite direction from the road to Bundaburra. "Yeah, it is beautiful. You're right," he said after a while. "But I think I've stopped noticing it. It's just where I have to be. I look out at all this and dream of sitting outside a café in Darlinghurst, or looking at the books in Berkelouw's, or walking along Bondi checking out all the crazy people. Like we did that time."

He smiled his sweet smile at me. Then he seemed to snap to attention.

"Have you seen Billy recently?"

"No," I said, slightly too quickly. Not since that weird morning and not since I found out he was rogering your sister . . . There was a silence.

"Are you always looking after people, Rory?" I asked. I don't know what made me say it. I could have commented on the weather.

"What do you mean?" he said, surprised.

"Well, you looked after Debbie before and you're looking after me now, and I know that the reason you're not sitting outside a café in Darlinghurst is because you have to look after your mother, your father and the farm . . . That's a lot of looking after."

And you're looking after Billy's messy little secret, I thought. And your sister's reputation.

"Well, I suppose you're right. I hadn't thought about it that way. It just happened . . . It's just the way things are right now." He shrugged. "I do miss the life I had in Sydney, but I wouldn't enjoy it if I knew my parents were suffering here without me. And Georgia, I'm very happy to look after you. That's a pleasure, not a duty. Come to think of it, I'd better give Jen a ring and let her know you're OK."

He came back a few minutes later with more drinks.

"Well, that's all sorted. Debbie's in bed—they got the doctor to come and give her a shot. Jen said she's sorry they won't be going to the dance tonight, but why don't you go and have a good time with me? Which I thought was an excellent idea."

"Were you going anyway? Are you sure I won't be cramping your style?"

"Are you kidding? I'd love to take you. It's really fun—they have it in a big old shed."

"Will there be as a live band?"

He nodded. "Too right. You can't have a bush dance without a live band."

"Great. I can't wait. But won't I need to change or something? I'm not exactly dressed for a dance."

"No, you're perfect," he said. "It's a bush dance, everyone will be in jeans and boots—and anyway, you'd be the most beautiful girl there whatever you were wearing."

Well, I don't know whether that was true or not, but I certainly danced more than any other girl there. Bush dancing was quite similar to Scottish reeling and while shaking your thing in a free-form way is fun, there's something very satisfying about doing a dance with a set format and getting it right. Especially if you get to hold hands with Rory Stewart while you do it.

I couldn't stop laughing—it was all such a hoot. I was a long way from home, but I was doing one of the things I love most. It would have made my grandparents so happy to see me charging around that hall. Especially, it occurred to me, with someone with a name like Rory Stewart.

"Rory, is your family Scottish?" I asked him, as he whisked me round in polka time.

"Well, we're Australian now, but my great, great, great—er . . . something like that—grandfather was a Scottish soldier called Andrew Stewart."

"My family's Scottish too."

"Is that right?"

"My grandparents live on the island of Mull. My brother Hamish can play the bagpipes."

"So can I," said Rory, grinning.

"You're kidding."

"No, I'm not. I went to Scots College and they have a school pipe band. I was in it."

Then we were whirled away from each other because it was one of those dances where you keep changing partners. We met up again a few minutes later, red-faced and gasping.

"You really are having a good time, aren't you Georgia?" said Rory, as we skipped up and down two lines of clapping people.

"I'm having a fabulous time. But I'm about to collapse—can we sit the next one out and have a drink?"

And that's when they played the Tennessee Waltz, which happens to be one of my favourites.

"You're going to have to wait for your rest, Georgia," said Rory. "I love this one."

And he swept me onto the floor. Round and round we went in perfect time. He actually knew how to waltz—no shuffling and definitely in control.

As we danced I tried to look steadily over his left shoulder, as per Mrs. Emerson's dance classes, but then something made me pull my head back a little to sneak a look at his face. He was looking straight at me. He didn't automatically smile or move his eyes away, but kept them locked on mine in a steady gaze. I felt a distinct flutter in my stomach and looked away again as my face started to burn. At the end of the song he dropped me back into a deep dip. People clapped. They were clapping us.

"Thank you, Ginger," said Rory, kissing me on the cheek.

"Thank you, Fred."

This time we did go and have a rest, and I suddenly felt breathless and shy. It had been a very intimate dance and I didn't quite know how to be with Rory after it. It seemed he felt the same say.

"Well, I'd better get you back to Bundaburra then," he said briskly, after we'd sat looking at our hands for a while. "I've got to be up early."

And that was it. We left. He put the radio on quietly in the ute and I watched the night country go by. Sitting in the dark, I felt more at ease with him again.

"What are your paintings like, Rory?" I aside him.

He laughed. Not a mad bark like Antony, or a kookaburra's cackle like Jasper, but a mild, gentle laugh.

"That's what I like about you, Georgia. You always get straight to the point." He turned and smiled at me.

"What are my paintings like?" He let out a sigh between his teeth. "Of course I haven't done any for a while, but I suppose you could say that you're looking at what they're about right now. They're about this country. These hills. I was always trying to capture the shapes and colours of this country. Not what it actually looks like, but what it feels like. How I remember it sitting in my studio in the city."

"Golden."

"Yes, that's right. Golden." He turned and gave me a look. "That was a big part of it for me. Are you interested in art, Georgia?"

"Yes. I love it. A . . . um . . . a friend took me round the Art Gallery of New South Wales a couple of weeks ago. I loved it. All those great artists I'd never heard of before."

"What did you like?"

"I liked the early paintings—I can't remember the names— the Australian impressionists, I think they were. Pictures of the bush. But I liked Arthur Boyd most of all."

I wondered if he thought I was pretentious.

"Tell me why you liked the Boyds."

"Um . . . I liked the way he combined the landscape with mythological things like that dog creature. How is Scooby, by the way?"

"Scooby's very well. She's in disgrace for an incident with the butter dish, but basically she's a happy puppy. She's entered for the dog high-jump competition tomorrow. She's a dead cert . . ." He paused before continuing. "Yes, that's pretty much why I like Arthur Boyd too. The gallery is one of the things I miss about living up here."

He was silent for a while and then we were at the gate to Bundaburra.

"Nearly home," said Rory. And all too soon we were.

"I won't come in," he said, pulling up outside and jumping out to open any door. "Give Jenny my love, will you? And tell her that if Debs wants to stay on for a few days, I'd be happy to drive you to the airport tomorrow."

"Thanks, Rory. You've been really kind all day."

"It was my pleasure, believe me. I don't get much of a chance to discuss Arthur Boyd up here." Then we just stood there smiling at each other and I realised I had to go in.

"OK, bye then," I said and kissed him on the cheek. As I stood in the doorway and waved him goodbye, I wondered why he still hadn't asked me for my phone number.

Chapter Eleven

Well, Debbie did not want to stay up at Bundaburra. She wanted to leave as soon as possible. She couldn't wait to get back to Sydney and she couldn't wait to get away from me. She was furious about missing the bush dance. She was furious with her parents for getting the doctor to knock her out with a tranquilliser. She was furious with Rory Stewart for stopping her when she was having "a good time." But most of all she was furious with me.

"I'm sorry, Debbie," I said through her bedroom door. "I'm really sorry, but I don't think that cowboy had your best interests at heart. I was just trying to do the right thing."

"Fuck off, you bloody dobber," she shouted back at me. I could hear her throwing things around inside. "I brought you up here to have a good time and the minute I started to enjoy myself you went running off to tell my parents. Jesus! Why does everybody want to stop me having fun? I thought you were cool, but you're just as bad as the rest of them."

She opened the door for a minute. She was red in the face.

"Have a nice time with Rory at the bush dance did you, you

little Pommy traitor? That's probably the only reason you came up here. You're just another pathetic social climber. Well, fuck you."

She slammed the door. I felt like I'd been slapped. After that tirade I didn't quite know what to do with myself, so I went and packed my things.

Through the bedroom window I could see Jenny and Johnny talking on the verandah, looking pale with worry. Then Johnny disappeared off somewhere and Jenny came inside. I went to look for her in the kitchen. She was standing at the sink just staring out of the window.

"I'm so sorry, Jenny," I said.

"It's not your fault, Georgia, please don't feel bad," she said, turning to look at me. "Debbie's being completely irrational. She's had a terrible shock—she really thought Rory was Drew."

"I know," I said. "It was awful." And even worse if you knew the full story, I thought.

"She needs to cry," said Jenny, hitting her hand against the edge of the sink in frustration. "She needs to feel it and let it out, but she just rages against anyone who's nearby."

She put her face in her hands and shook her head, then looked at me again. Her eyes were full of tears.

"I really hoped this weekend would help her come to terms with being up here," she said. "But it's just made things worse. I don't know what we're going to do with her."

I went and put my arm around her. She wiped her eyes.

"Don't worry, Georgia. Debbie won't hate you for long—it's not her nature—and it would be a real comfort for me to know that she has a friend like you looking out for her. Does our deal still stand? Do you still promise you'll let me know if you think she's getting into trouble?"

After the tongue lashing I had just received it was a scary thought. My face must have given me away.

"I know it's a heavy responsibility," said Jenny. "And you

hardly even know us, but I just feel I can trust you." Her eyes filled with tears again.

"I'll do my best, Jenny," I said, praying I wouldn't have to.

"Thank you." She smiled weakly. "How was the bush dance? Did Rory look after you?"

"I had a really good time. I wish you all could have been there, it was great fun."

I felt shy talking about Rory. The link with Drew was so strong—how could I have been out having such a good time with him while they struggled with their bereaved daughter?

"It would have been nice for Rory to have some young female company too," said Jenny. "Must be very dull and lonely for him up here, poor love."

And if I wasn't mistaken, she gave me a knowing look.

Debbie didn't say a word to me all the way to the airport and when we got there she just stormed out of the car, without even saying goodbye to her mother.

"She'll get over it soon, Jenny," I said, nervously.

"Yes, I'm sure you're right. Well, it was lovely to meet you— I hope you'll come back and see us again. And if Debbie's still being a horror, you're always welcome to come up on your own. Here's our phone number, so you won't even need to ask Debbie for it, and don't be a shy Pom—our offer to Hamish still stands."

"Bye Jenny—and thank you," I said, kissing her cheek. "Try not to worry."

Debbie ignored me all the way home on the plane and at the other end she just swept off to her car, leaving me to get a taxi.

On the way to Elizabeth Bay I wondered how much to tell Antony about what had happened. I didn't have long to think about it—my phone was already ringing as I opened the front door.

"Well?"

"Hello, Antony. How are you? How was your weekend?"

"Bugger my weekend. How was Johnny Brent?"

"Well, I must admit he's not bad looking . . . he looks very nice with his hair wet."

Antony was making gurgling noises.

"Did you see him on a horse? Was he wearing his polo boots?" More gurgling. "What's the house like? Is it divine?"

"It's heaven. The whole thing is heaven. Ralph Lauren would spontaneously combust if he went up there. So would you, probably. But Antony, tell me something—have you ever actually met Jenny Brent?"

"Good God, no. Ghastly little *arriviste*."

"She's not ghastly. She's lovely—the nicest woman you could ever meet. And she's just as beautiful as he is. I won't hear you say one more horrible thing about her. And Johnny is clearly still mad about her too."

"Oh, you are boring. Debbie says she hates your guts, by the way, and that you only went up there to social climb."

"Oh really? When did she tell you that?"

"She rang me from her car ten minutes ago. That's how I knew you were back. What happened?"

I told him everything. Everything except what a good time I'd had at the bush dance with Rory—I didn't want that getting back to Debbie and making things worse. But Antony Maybury QC didn't miss anything.

"So Debbie got sent home to bed like a naughty girl and you went gallivanting off to *her* bush dance with the last remaining Stewart brother. Pheweee, she wouldn't have liked that at all. No wonder she's having a tantie."

"Does she really think I had her taken home deliberately?" I said. "She was about to get gang-banged by a bunch of cowboys—I bumped into Rory by sheer chance when I was looking for her father to come and save her. And I'm really glad I did bump into him because it meant Johnny Brent didn't have to see his precious little princess with her hand down the Lone Ranger's pants."

"Is that what she was doing? Oh, she is a naughty girl. HA HA HA. Was he cute?"

"Antony, it wasn't funny. It was horrible. If I hadn't found Rory I really don't know what would have happened."

"Well, she's certainly furious with you," he said. "You stepped into her territory and I warned you, she's not rational about anything with the name Stewart stenciled on it."

"I suppose I can understand that, but she was the one who got drunk. I was looking forward to going to the bush dance with all of them. I wanted to see Johnny Brent dancing so I could torture you about it."

"Did you have a good time with Rory then?"

Nice try, Antony.

"Yeah, it was OK," I said casually. "It was a funny little dance in a funny little country town. You can imagine."

"Did you have the last waltz with Rory Stewart. Just like the song?" He started singing it in a high falsetto.

Was he a witch? How did he know? Had someone told Debbie?

"Oh, I can't remember, I danced with lots of people. You know what those things are like, you keep changing partner. I danced with a lot of arthritic old men and spotty adolescents and one enthusiastic six-year-old. It was fun. There were dogs running around and babies."

"Hmmm. Well, I wish you luck with Debbie at work tomorrow. I've been through all this before with her. She nearly took a contract out on Maxine when she had a fling with another brother—Alex Stewart. I'd just give her a wide berth for a day or two—she'll get over it pretty quickly. Anyway, stuff all that, I wanted to talk to you about something else. We've got lots of parties to go to this week. Get your diary."

And that was just the way it was. Debbie was vile to me for a couple of days and then gradually thawed, until we were back on our old footing and things settled down at work. But she never mentioned the weekend at all. It was like it had never happened.

Over the next week, leading up to Mardi Gras, Antony and I went out every single night, sometimes meeting for lunch and breakfast as well, to post-mortem the night before. The parties got more and more charged, as Antony's crowd became increasingly excited about the big night on Saturday. And it wasn't just his crowd. The whole city was cranking up into a fever of sexual tension. You could feel it in the air.

Hordes of gay tourists had arrived from all over the world and were marching around the CBD hand in hand, wearing backpacks, big boots and no shirts. Lesbian couples kissed passionately on street corners. Nobody gave them a second look. Oxford Street was pumping twenty-four hours a day and Seraphima told me she'd seen a man sitting at a pavement table completely nude except for a pair of chaps and a hat. At lunchtime.

Despite Antony's gang telling me what a marvellous time I would have, I'd decided not to go to the party itself. I knew that "breeders" did go and I was sure it would be a great night, but I just didn't think a honky straight chick had any business muscling in on such hard-won fun. But I wasn't going to miss the parade for anything.

Antony was really pissed off with me, telling me my attitude was totally "suburban," until Debbie announced she was going to go with him and he got caught up creating an outfit for his favourite human Barbie doll.

I wasn't quite sure how I was going to watch the parade until, to my great surprise, Liinda strolled into my office on Friday morning and asked me if I wanted to go with her.

"I thought you didn't like gay men," I said. "And I thought you never went out at night."

"I never said that. I said I didn't have gay men as close friends. But I love watching the parade. Gays and lesbians are a repressed minority—as are women everywhere—and I find the parade really inspiring. Just twenty years ago they were arrested for having it, now it's sponsored by major banks and goes out on national TV. It shows what you can do if you fight consistently for your rights." She grinned. "And I like seeing the Dykes on Bikes. I still have a thing for big throbbing motorbikes left over from my previous life."

"Well, I'd love to watch it with you. What's the plan and pack drill?"

"I go in the afternoon and bag our pozzie at Taylor Square," Liinda explained. "I have milk crates. I have my Walkman. I have cigarettes. I'll be quite happy. Then you come along and meet me at about seven. It's worth coming a bit earlier for the people watching. Zoe's going to come with us."

"That's great. How is she?"

"OK. She's seeing a shrink and she's coming to Al Anon meetings with me. It's early days, but I think she'll make it."

"Do you really think she'll feel like going out?"

The bird's nest nodded vigorously. "Yeah, she lives at home, you know—and needless to say her family is the reason she's in this state—so it will do her good to have a break from them."

"Not another messed-up family. I don't think I can stand it. Don't tell me any more."

"OK, I won't. I gather you've got yourself rather involved in Debbie's psychodramas, which seem to involve three dysfunctional families, so I can see you don't need to hear about another one."

How did Liinda know about all that? Had Debbie told her about the disastrous weekend as well?

"I can hear all Debbie's phone calls," she said, reading my

mind. "You were getting a hell of a serve for a time there. Anyway, you and Zoe should go out after the parade. I'll go home with my knitting, of course, but you two could go out and have some fun." She shook her head. "Ah, fun—I remember fun . . . Want Zoe's number?"

"Sure."

I'd spent the weekend with a nymphomaniac alcoholic drug fuck, so why not a big night out with a neurotic bulimic?

Chapter Twelve

The parade was hilarious. I'd never seen anything like it—and I'd never experienced an atmosphere like it either. The crowd was really mixed, young and old, trendy and suburban (thank you, Antony) and everyone was friendly and excited. The police arrested some young thugs who were shouting homophobic remarks, but most people were just grinning at each other.

Antony had rung me in the morning to wish me "Happy Mardi Gras."

"It's our Christmas, you know," he said. I'd never heard him so excited. He was babbling on about his outfit—black leather pants and a black singlet. Totally simple, very comfortable, but all *ultima qualita,* he insisted.

"Won't you be a bit hot in leather?" I asked.

"That's the whole point, darling."

"Well, have a wonderful time. Call me when you surface. And another thing, Antony—be bad."

"Oh, I will, Pussy, I will. Love you. Goodbye."

Liinda had found the perfect spot on a corner near Taylor

Square and we were right at the front, so I had a great view even without standing on my milk crate. First to come along were the Dykes on Bikes, hundreds of them and as magnificent as Liinda had said they would be. After them came a huge band of marching boys in tiny shorts, marching in perfect time.

Then came a big group of leathermen in all manner of outrageous ensembles. Betty was marching along, his hairy bum hanging out of a pair of leather chaps.

"Betty! Betty!" I shouted. "You look gorgeous." He turned and saw me and gave me a big wave.

"Thank you, Pussy darling! Happy Mardi Gras!" Then he darted over and gave me a big hug and a kiss. Which made me feel very special, before running back to join his gang.

The intense spectacle whipped me up into a high emotional state. One minute I was laughing hysterically as a float in the shape of a giant penis went by, with ten men in sparkly shorts and cowboy hats riding it like it was a bucking bronco. The next I was choking back tears when the Proud Parents of HIV Positive Children walked past with their heads up high, holding hands with their sick sons. One or two were pushing them in wheelchairs. I thought of friends I had lost in London and said a little prayer for Henry, Malcolm and Les. Never forgotten, I told them. Never forgotten.

Some of the floats were works of art and some were sweet and homemade. Some represented tiny little community groups from Tasmania and rural New South Wales, and others were sponsored by enormous corporations. A troupe of about a hundred Monica Lewinskys walked past—all men, in blue dresses, holding big cigars. A clan of bear men marched by in their jeans, check shirts and Tuff boots, looking like something out of *Little House on the Prairie*. On acid. Drag queens were strolling along in the most amazing outfits and beautiful lesbians paraded by wearing no tops and great big boots. Everybody was grinning. I hoped they could all feel the love from the crowd.

"Happy Mardi Gras!" I was shouting. "Happy Mardi Gras!" I said to Liinda and Zoe, hugging them both. It was great. Then, suddenly, it was all over. The Mardi Gras revellers had disappeared up to their party at the old Showground and Liinda was right, I certainly didn't feel like going home to some cocoa and a good book. I was in the mood to parteee. Fortunately, so was Zoe. I wanted to go dancing, but where could two straight girls go on Mardi Gras night?

"Don't ask me," said Liinda. "I only ever went to clubs where I knew I could score drugs. I'm going home. Bye, you two. Have fun." And she disappeared.

Zoe and I looked at each other. I was determined to have a good time, because I was wearing a fabulous new dress in a wild tropical print and my party high heels—Linda had kindly taken my trainers home with her.

"What time is it?" said Zoe, who was looking very fetching in a turquoise lace shift, trimmed with red. "OK, it's only just after nine—why don't we go on a bit of a bar crawl and see where we end up?"

We started in the champagne bar of a groovy boutique hotel and then moved on to a very stylish place with a great cocktail list and views over the city. There were lots of people up there and quite a few nice-looking guys, although after my recent Pollocking and the business with Billy, meeting new men was not such an attractive prospect. But Zoe knew lots of people in there, so we teamed up with a gang of them and it all seemed quite jolly. They weren't as much fun as Antony's friends but the music was excellent and the place was cool. I thought I was going to have a good night.

After a while I noticed Zoe was looking round the room with a slightly puzzled expression on her face.

"What is it?" I asked.

"It's been bugging me ever since we walked in here—you know, What is Wrong With this Picture? I knew something was different and I was trying to figure it out. Have they changed the lighting? Is it different carpet? I've just worked out what it is . . ."

"What?"

"There are no gay men in here."

I looked around. It was true.

"This is the one night of the year you can go out in Sydney and not see a single homosexual," said Zoe.

"Weird, isn't it?" I said, having another look round the room. "I wondered why everyone was so badly dressed."

We had a good laugh. But now she had pointed it out I felt a bit uncomfortable. This was probably the best night in the whole year to meet a man in Sydney and I couldn't have felt less like it. The truth was I missed Dolores and Betty and Trudy. I missed their humour and their excessive behaviour. I missed the sense of security I felt with them. With these men I felt judged entirely on my attractiveness. I could see them looking at my legs.

I wondered what Antony was doing at the party. I missed his eyebrows and his honking laugh, although I dreaded to think what he and Debbie were getting up to together. And then thinking about Debbie made me think about Rory Stewart. Had he watched the parade on TV up at the farm and felt totally left out of everything? Poor Rory . . .

"This is earth calling Georgie, earth calling Georgie, come in please," said Zoe.

I blinked and glanced around me. The crowd we'd joined up with had split up into men and women. The men were talking about football and the women were talking about men. I stifled a yawn.

Zoe rolled her eyes and laughed. "You really are on sparkling form."

"Looks like you need a little jump," said one of the girls we were with. "We were just going to take a walk to the 'powder' room, if you wanted to come."

"Oh, no, it's OK thanks," I said. She gave me a funny look and she and two other women minced off in their tight dresses.

"I think she just offered me Class A drugs," I said to Zoe.

"That would be right."

"Do you take them?"

"Only slimming pills and laxatives. Just kidding. I used to take the lot," she said. "Except pot, of course, because it gives you the munchies. I've been hanging around with this crowd since we were teenagers and we've always done drugs. Cocaine and ecstasy, mainly. We're sort of part-time weekend party people, not like Debbie, who takes them all the time. But I'm not allowed to do them at all now. It's one of the conditions of my therapy. I had to make a deal not to 'act out'"—she made inverted commas with her fingers—"in any of my 'addictions.' Do I sound like Liinda?"

"Only in a good way," I said.

"I'm not really supposed to be drinking either, to tell you the truth. Cheers!"

We clinked glasses.

The girls were coming back. Fresh lipstick all round. I saw the one I'd talked to pass something to one of the men, and then the four of them went off to the loo. It was like watching a Swiss clock. The girls were even more inane now, but faster. They were talking about men again, and then one of them mentioned some great shoes she'd seen in a shop in Double Bay, which somehow led to a discussion about their favourite episodes of *Friends,* and that brought them right back to men—the men who had just gone to the loo, in fact.

Now I love shoes as much as the next girl and I'm pretty keen on men and even *Friends* can be fun on a dull night, so it wasn't the subjects they were talking about that were getting to me, it was the *way* they were talking about them. There was no debate or discussion, they just went round and round in circles, making flat statements, with everything relating back to them.

One would say, "Oh, I liked the episode when . . ." and then another would just butt in saying, "Oh no, I liked the one when . . ." and another would say, "I think Joey's really cute, I like him best . . ." and the first one would come back saying, "Oh no, I like Ross . . ." and on and on like that. It wasn't conversation, it was mutual monologuing. And to make it worse, the girls who had boyfriends talked only in the royal "we," as in "WE went to Bowral at the weekend because WE are buying a horse."

To make matters worse, my feet were beginning to hurt. Isn't it funny how, when you're having a good time, you can run for miles in the highest stilettos, but the minute you're bored, every second is agony? I was shifting from foot to foot and I saw Zoe notice, but I couldn't very well tell her that her lifelong friends were boring me to death, could I?

The boys had come back from the loo pumped up with inhaled masculinity and the sexes mingled a little. One of the boys started chatting me up. At least I think that's what he was doing.

"Seen any good movies recently?" he said.

"Yes. It was called *Salo—100 Days of Sodom*."

"Really? Never heard of it. My favourite movie is *Terminator*."

"Oh, you should try and catch *Salo*, you'd love it. It's quite like *Terminator*. Lots of violence. Arnie has a bit part in it." He plays an anus.

"So," he said, getting a frisky look in his eye. "I hear you work with Zoe."

Oh here we go, I thought. This old chestnut.

"Yes, I work on *Glow*. I'm the orgasms editor."

"Is that right?" He looked thrilled. You could see him thinking: she works on *Glow*, she must be a pushover and know hundreds of kinky sexual positions.

"Sorry Ben," I said. I think his name was Ben. "Would you excuse me? I've just got to go and find my G-spot."

I don't know why I dislike men like Ben so much, but I do.

He was quite good looking, he was tall, he had all the right gear on and he had nice hair. I hated him. I went to the loo and sat there a long time. I left the cubicle and reapplied my lipstick for something to do. I was just pulling some faces at myself in the mirror to pass the time when Zoe came out of another stall.

"Don't worry," she said. "I wasn't throwing up in there."

I liked Zoe. She was bright and sparky, when she wasn't starving herself to death.

"We're all going to go on to the Blue Room now," she said. "You can sort of dance there. Want to come?"

"Sounds great." I replied weakly. But when we were all downstairs and they turned right down Victoria Street, I caught Zoe by the arm and told her I was going to split.

"I'm going to go home while I can still walk there. It's been really fun, but I don't feel like having a big night. I'll see you on Monday. Have a good one."

I stood and watched them for a moment as they headed towards Oxford Street, hanging on to each other and laughing and joking. Why don't I like nice, simple, stable blokes like that crowd? I wondered. I'm sure they all had good jobs and would want to have nice big weddings and lots of kiddies, who they would send to private schools. I could have a nice life with a man like that, but I found them insufferably dull.

That's why I'd ended up with Rick in London. It was a choice between him or the English equivalent of these guys. Rick certainly wasn't dull. He was so creative that he was slightly unbalanced at times, but he was never dull. And that's why I liked my darling Antony so much too. He wasn't dull either. But wasn't there another type of man anywhere? One who wasn't unbearably boring, without being gay, or totally mad? I think that was Nick Pollock's genius. He'd appeared to be the missing link.

I stopped in Kings Cross and got myself in a large portion of fries and ate them as I walked home, barefoot.

. . .

On Sunday morning I was really glad I hadn't had a big night, because Liinda rang me at eight a.m.

"Hello," she said brightly. "How was your big night?"

"Small."

"Really? I thought you'd be out until dawn when you would have dragged home some unsuspecting youth, to help you road-test all the sex tips in our next sealed section."

"You thought that and you rang me at eight?"

She ignored that one. "So what time did you get in?"

"Before twelve."

"Really? What went wrong?"

"Oh, nothing. We went to a couple of bars, but then I just didn't feel like it. Must be your influence."

"Did Zoe have a good time?"

"Yes, I think so. We bumped into some friends of hers and she kicked on with them."

"Well, she probably needed to cut loose."

"That's exactly what she said. But I loved the parade. Thanks for bagging that spot for us."

"No problem. So what are you doing today? I was wondering if you felt like meeting up later."

"I thought I might walk over to the Brent Whiteley studio museum thing in Surry Hills. But I'd love to catch up later."

"That's a great idea—you can go via Oxford Street and check out all the tragedies staggering home from the party. It's really fun. I sometimes come into town just to watch it. It's like the anti-parade. And we can get together later for a Turkish pizza in Cleveland Street. Sound good?"

"Sounds great. Where will I meet you?"

"I'll call you on your mobile at one-twenty and give you directions."

"Thirteen-twenty hours? Roger, over and out."

At nine a.m. Oxford Street was full of Mardi Gras casualties. Drag queens carrying their shoes, make-up running down their faces. Lithe men and women in tight Lycra shorts, chewing gum ferociously. Everyone was exhausted and very pale but they all looked happy. There were lots of couples holding hands, some of them in a great hurry—presumably to get home to bed— while others were oblivious to their surroundings, just gazing into each other's eyes.

It was great people-watching, as Liinda had said, so I sat at a café in Taylor Square and watched them all go by. Then I studied my map to work out how to get to the Whiteley Studio from that spot. It didn't seem very hard.

I crossed Flinders Street and found a lane which would take me through to Bourke Street, but there seemed to be a party going on in it, with a DJ and the works. Quit a few of the people I'd seen going by earlier were there, looking like they were about to do it all again, and I realised this must be one of the recovery parties I'd heard about. I stopped to let a gaggle of very large drag queens go by and just happened to glance to my left, where there was a smaller, really filthy lane. I stopped dead. There, sprawled on a milk crate, was Debbie.

She was naked apart from gigantic platforms and a sparkly fuschia G-string. Her make-up was all over her face. She was leaning against the filthy wall with her head back and her eyes closed. Her left arm was hanging down by her side and there was a man crouching next to her. Did he take something off her arm and throw it on the ground? He moved so quickly, it was hard to tell. I was so surprised I took an involuntary step forward. At that moment the man looked up and saw me and mouthed "fuck off" at me with such venom that I jumped and turned back up the main lane. I didn't know what to do. Then I saw Antony. I couldn't believe my luck.

"Dolly!" I called out to him. He was staggering a bit and didn't look up.

"Antony! It's me," I said, standing right in front of him. I tapped his shoulder. He looked up at me with completely blank eyes. "Fuck off," he said.

I thought he must have mistaken me for someone else.

"Antony, it's me, Georgia . . . Pussy."

"I don't give a fuck about pussy," he said and pushed me away, stumbling down the lane.

I felt like I'd been punched. First Debbie, naked in an alley. Then Antony—my dear Antony, who I thought was my best friend in Sydney—had told me to fuck off. The party in the alley seemed like a nightmare, full of ghouls and strange wasted creatures. I pushed my way through and walked down Bourke Street as fast as I could. It was a steamy humid day but I was shivering.

I came to a café and sat down. I needed a glass of water; I was still in shock. What was Debbie doing with that horrid man? Had he been injecting her with something? Now I felt really ill. Was I going to have to ring Jenny Brent and tell her Debbie was a junkie? But how could I be sure? I didn't actually see a syringe. What if I rang and told Jenny that and I was wrong?

And as for Antony, I couldn't bear to think about what had just happened with him.

Then my mobile rang. It was Liinda.

"Georgia? Hi. Look, I'm going to have to cancel lunch. One of the women I'm sponsoring at my NA group is in crisis and I can't leave her. I'm really sorry."

I was relieved. I didn't really want to tell anyone what I'd just seen until I'd had time to digest it.

Chapter Thirteen

"It's a shame you didn't come to the Blue Room with us," said Zoe on Monday. She was back at work and looking very happy to be there. She sat on the chair across from my desk and swung her legs like a schoolgirl.

"Yeah? Did you have a late night?"

Zoe smiled. "Very late . . . I didn't go home at all—or rather, I went home with Ben."

"Really?" I wondered if he had a *Terminator* duvet cover. "How was that?"

Zoe looked just as I had the morning after a good Pollocking.

"It was divine. He's fantastic in bed. Gorgeous bod. He plays soccer."

Well, waddyaknow? Maybe he could have helped me find my G-spot after all.

"It meant a lot to me," continued Zoe, in full post-coital glow. "I haven't been with a guy for nearly a year. It was a big breakthrough." She looked serious for a moment. "I thought I was too fat to let anyone see me with my clothes off."

"Therapy must be working then," I said. "That's great. Was there a good crowd at the Blue Room?"

"Great, it was pumping and there was a guy looking for you . . ."

"Really, who?" I said. Pollock Repentant? Billy Unbound?

"Jasper O'Connor. The photographer. I didn't know you knew him. Anyway, he asked me where you were and seemed very disappointed I told him you'd gone home."

Jasper, I thought. Hmmm.

At midday Antony called.

"Hello," he said in us usual chirpy voice.

"Fuck off," I said.

"Well, that's nice isn't it? I ring up to tell you all about the party and that's the reception I get."

"Fuck off."

"Pussy—is something wrong?"

"I don't give a fuck about Pussy."

"What are you talking about?"

"That's what I wanted to ask you, because those were the last things you said to me."

"What? Fuck off?"

"That's right."

"I distinctly remember telling you I loved you the first time we spoke. My first eccie was just kicking in, but I did mean it. What's wrong with you? This is quite boring, I want to have lunch and tell you what Betty did at the party."

"So you don't remember seeing me in a lane in Darlinghurst, or Surry Hills or wherever it was, yesterday morning?"

"What? Yesterday? Where was I yesterday morning? Oh, I was at the More-di Gras after party. It was a riot. Were you there? Did I tell you to fuck off? How hysterical. Sorry, Pussy darling. I was really off my tree. Anyway, Betty got to the party and he—"

I couldn't believe he could just brush it aside like that. I'd hardly slept a wink worrying about him and I wasn't ready to pretend it hadn't happened.

"Antony, I'm sorry, but I have rather a lot on this morning—we're just clearing the issue and I have to read all the proofs. I can't make lunch today. I'll call you."

He slammed the phone down. I didn't care—let him be pissed off. I had been deeply wounded by what he'd said to me the day before. I didn't care how off his tree he was, I was shocked that Antony could be so horrible to anyone.

The phone rang again.

"Fuck off," I said down the receiver.

"Pinkie?"

"Jasper! I'm so sorry. I thought it was someone else . . . Oh dear." I got the giggles.

"Well, someone must have done you wrong for you to answer the phone like that. Want me to go round and rearrange their features for you?"

"No, I think the person in question is quite capable of doing that by himself. How are you, anyway?"

"I'm perfect. Shame you didn't make it to the Blue Room on Saturday night—it would have been much better if you'd been there."

"Oh, you silver-tongued persuader. You're full of shit, but I do find it cheering."

"What's uncheered you? Who was that 'eff off' aimed at?"

"It's a bit of a long story."

"Is it a long, romantic story?"

"No, just a long, sordid one."

"Pinkie, you're not helping me here—I'm trying to find out by subtle means if there's a love interest in your life."

I couldn't help liking Jasper. There was all that puff and bluster and then he would just lay himself bare.

"Well, there was a bit of love interest," I said. "But it lost interest. OK?"

"Good, that means you can come and have a drink with me."

"I'd love to."

"Really? Great. When?"

"Let me look in my diary. Oh, yesterday was St. David's Day and I didn't even know. Mmm . . . what about Wednesday? Where?"

"Wednesday is great. My house. It's in Elizabeth Bay Road. You just have to walk around the corner from your place. I'll be waiting outside. Is seven OK? See you then, Pinkie."

After I put the phone down I realized I had never told Jasper where I lived.

"SERAPHIMA, GO AND GET DEBBIE FOR ME. WE'VE GOT TO GO TO THE BIG ESTEE LAUDER LUNCH."

Maxine was having one of her loud days. Instead of going round to Debbie's room, I heard Seraphima go straight into Maxine's office.

"WHAT DO YOU MEAN SHE'S NOT HERE? WE'VE GOT TO BE AT ROCKPOOL IN FIVE MINUTES."

Then something was hurled across the room. I got up and went to my office door. Seraphima scuttled past rolling her eyes at me as she went by. I watched her dial Debbie's mobile number. There was no reply. Then she tried her home number. Machine. Now I was starting to feel really worried. Should I say something to Maxine? But I still wasn't sure what I'd seen in that alley, and I didn't want Maxine to go into hard love overdrive if it was nothing. Maybe she'd just been having a rest. Walking around in those platform shoes would have worn out Elton John. Of course, the best person to ask would have been

Antony, but if he couldn't remember what he'd done himself, what use would he be about Debbie?

I went round to see Liinda. She had one unlit cigarette behind her ear, another between her lips and the packet open on her desk. This meant she was writing.

"Seen Debbie today at all?" I asked casually.

"No. And I don't expect we'll see her until Wednesday. She's probably still at a recovery party somewhere. Then she'll have Ecstasy Tuesday to get through tomorrow and she might grace us with her presence on Wednesday."

"Ecstasy Tuesday?"

She took the cigarette out of her mouth and looked at me strangely.

"Are you for real? It's the day the come-down hits you. Take ecstasy on Saturday night and the full come-down doesn't hit you until Tuesday. On Sunday you're still in love with the entire world. On Monday you're still a bit warm and fuzzy. On Tuesday you're suicidal. What goes up, must come down. That's how it works."

I thought about it a bit.

"What forms can you get ecstasy in?" I asked her. "Is it just tabs?"

She looked at me intensely again with her head on one side. "Why are you so interested in drugs all of a sudden, Pollyanna?"

I ignored the jibe. "Is it possible to inject ecstasy?"

"I suppose you could. There is that GBH stuff, which is supposed to be liquid ecstasy, and I suppose you could inject anything if you ground it up finely enough, but I've never heard of anyone doing it. The slow build as it comes on is all part of the ride. Are you thinking of trying it?"

"Er . . . no. I just wondered."

I thought I'd better change the subject; she had put my mind at rest about Debbie's absence and I didn't want any further questions.

"What are you working on?" I asked brightly.

"Putting a Gloss on It—Beauty's New Shine."

"Isn't that Debbie's story for the next issue?"

"Yes."

"Why are *you* writing it?"

"It was due last Monday. I don't want her to get into any more trouble with Maxine than she already is."

"So you're going to pretend Debbie wrote it?"

"Yep."

I just looked at her, with what I imagine was a stupid expression.

"Look, I think Debbie is a spoiled little princess," said Liinda. "She drives me mad with her snobbery, but she's basically a good person. We've worked together a long time. She was very different before Drew was killed, you know. She had such a spark to her which has completely gone. It went out like a light. She tries to put it back with drink and drugs and sex, but I think eventually she'll realise it's not the answer. I just want to see her get that spark back."

"You are an extraordinary person," I said.

"And then I'm going to make her help me write an award-winning story called 'My Lover Was Killed—One Woman's Story of Surviving Heartbreak.'"

That was more like it. I hooted with laughter.

"You are stark-raving mad, Liinda Vidovic, but underneath it all you're a good woman."

She grinned and I put her cigarette back in her mouth for her.

Chapter Fourteen

When I turned into Elizabeth Bay Road, Jasper was waiting outside his house as he'd promised. And what a place it was. The only old mansion left in a road of big apartment buildings looking over the harbour. It was enormous and, with a cupola on the roof, it looked like something out of a Hammer horror film.

"I can't believe you live here," I said. "I've been looking at this house ever since I moved here, wondering who lived in it."

"Now you know. That's why I said I'd meet you at the gate. I wanted to share the entire Caledonia experience with you."

"Is that what the house is called—Caledonia?"

He pointed to a sign on the gate.

"That means Scotland," I said. "Hail Caledonia."

Jasper gave me the full tour. The interior had hardly been touched since it was built in 1905. It still had the servants' bells in the scullery, with labels saying "Dining Room," "Drawing Room and "Library," and it was all falling to bits in a romantic way.

"I'm so glad it hasn't been done up," I said. "So often people get hold of these lovely old houses and renovate them to death, so they look like characterless hotel rooms. I love genteel decay. It reminds me of my family."

He laughed. There was a huge hall, with an old dinner gong in it, a library with worn-out leather club chairs, a dining room and an elegant drawing room, full of tatty junk-shop furniture. Then Jasper took me downstairs and showed me the big space he used as a photographic studio. Upstairs there were so many bedrooms I lost count, but I was thrilled to see two bathrooms with lovely old claw-foot baths and ancient loos with flower patterns in the bowls.

Finally, we went up into the cupola, which was like four window seats joined together, with a 360-degree view of Sydney and the harbour, right over to the ocean.

"You've done it again, Jasper," I said, shaking my head in amazement. "You just keep taking my breath away."

He grinned, in his likeable boyish way.

"Vodka and cranberry?" he asked, gesturing towards a tray with two glasses, a plastic ice bucket shaped like a pineapple and a tall glass jug full of ruby liquid.

I nodded and he poured the drinks while I walked round and round the cupola trying to take it all in.

"I feel like I'm in the crow's nest of an old schooner," I said. "This place is unbelievable. It has such a welcoming atmosphere. How long have you lived here?"

"Sixteen years. I moved in here when I was a callow young art student and now I'm the longest-standing resident. The place has been passed down through Sydney's boho generations for over thirty years. The same family has owned it since it was built. There was six of us here. We pay $100 a week rent—in total."

I whistled. "That's amazing."

"There are some house rules," Jasper continued, passing me a drink. "You have to be involved in some form of creative endeavour to live here. I'm a photographer/filmmaker. We've got two artists, two writers and an animator. And if anyone's income goes over a certain level, they have to move out. It's always worked really well."

"It must be a great party house."

"It sure is, and we'll be having a major one sometime soon."

"Yeah? What are you celebrating?"

"The end of an era. The owners have sold the house."

"Oh, no! You must be heartbroken. Why did they decide to sell it after all this time?"

"The property developers finally got to them," he explained. "They've been trying to buy it for years, and this time they offered so much money the family just couldn't say no. But I reckon I'm lucky to have lived here as long as I have."

"What are they going to do with it?"

"It's going to be a boutique hotel."

"Well, that's better than knocking it down, I suppose."

We sipped our vodkas, Jasper rolled a joint, and I risked a couple of puffs because he assured me it was a mild one. Then we just sat and talked. I hadn't enjoyed myself so much for ages. The wild hysteria of Antony's gang was all very well, but this was what I enjoyed the most: chatting to someone and hearing about their views and experiences. No competitiveness or point scoring, just an exchange. Everybody had told me what a scumbag Jasper was, but they clearly hadn't spent much time with him, I thought.

I told him about the one-dimensional chit-chat on Saturday night and about telling brainless Ben he should go and see *100 Years of Sodom*.

"I think that's why God invented dancing," Jasper said, laughing. "So we don't have to talk to each other at parties."

I felt so relaxed I lay back on the window seat and stared up through the glass roof of the cupola. Jasper did the same, so our heads were at right angles, as the sky grew darker.

"That looked like a bat!" I said, as something black flew past.

"It was a bat," said Jasper. And then there were scores of them, flapping their leathery wings. "They do this every night. They leave the trees where they sleep during the day and fly over the house going about their batty business."

We carried on talking about this and that, but nothing really personal. No past relationships, or work, or why I had moved to Sydney, but rather what we felt about what was going on in the world. It was like a long, refreshing drink of water. I'd lost all track of time and deliberately didn't look at my watch—I just wanted to go with the flow. The mood was finally broken by the sound of someone beating the dinner gong.

"Great," said Jasper, springing up.

I must have looked surprised.

"One of the girls works in a restaurant and she brings home all the excess food for the house. It's good nosh. Come on."

When we got downstairs I could see candles on a big table outside with about ten people sitting round it. Jasper introduced me to the crowd, who were a pleasantly motley crew.

The table was covered with an equally odd assortment of food on mismatched plates and several bottles of wine. I was feeling ravenous after Jasper's pot and hoed into bread, paté and rocket salad, followed by a large helping of chocolate mousse.

"Weren't you at Danny Green's hat party?" said a fat fellow, with a shiny bald head and a big silver ring through his nose like a bull. I recognised him as the one who'd been wearing bunny ears.

"I never forget a face," he said. "Which is pretty funny considering I'm in radio." He had a girlish giggle that matched his hands, which were genteel and fluttery, but not the rest of him. I wondered if he knew Betty.

A young woman with bright blue hair was reminiscing about India with an attractive blonde of about forty-five, who was wearing a long purple velvet dress and a cheap tiara. Jasper was talking to Matt, a performance artist, about doing a joint project with him and the animators. I was happy just listening, as I gazed down at the boats in Elizabeth Bay and the reflection of the moon on the water.

"Having fun, Pinkie?" Jasper murmured, squeezing my hand. I smiled at him and nodded. "Like a homecoming, Jasper."

"That's the go."

Eventually the party started to break up and I told Jasper I had to be going too. My block of flats was only round the corner, but he insisted on walking me home. When we got there I kissed him on the cheek.

"See you soon, Pinkie," he said. "Just drop in on us any time you feel like it. We never lock the door. Even if I'm not there and you feel like sitting in the garden, just come in and help yourself. While we still have it, Caledonia is for everyone."

"That's really sweet of you, Jazzie. I'll see you soon."

I found it hard to settle when I got to bed—the cocktail of vodka, pot, wine and chocolate mousse was churning around in my stomach, and mixed thoughts about Jasper were churning around in my head. I'd never been warned off a man by so many different people, but I found his company so stimulating, and I felt totally at ease with him.

I didn't see Jasper as a potential husband, the way I had with Billy and Nick within about two seconds of meeting them, and the last thing I needed after Rick was another bohemian creative type, liable to spring unwelcome surprises. But I still felt there was a little more developing between us than friendship. He certainly made no secret of the fact that he found me attractive. After all the hidden agendas and dark secrets everyone else I'd met in Sydney seemed to have, I found that very appealing indeed.

· · ·

At eleven-thirty the next morning he rang me.

"Pinkie darling, how are you?"

"Hello, Jasper. I was just thinking about you. Well, I'm slightly hung-over, but it was worth it. Thank you so much for last night, I really enjoyed it."

"So did I, Pinkus. And I hope you'll come over again very soon. I meant what I said about just dropping in."

"I'll take you up on it—oh and Jasper, while we're at it, can I have your phone number?"

He proceeded to give me his home number, a separate number for the downstairs studio, plus numbers for his mobile and pager.

"Now I am entirely at your service," he said. I promised to call him soon.

I was just settling in to read the last few proofs for the issue when Seraphima came in with a cup of tea for me. She put it on my desk and sat down opposite me.

"Georgia," she said, top marks for that. "I think you should know that Debbie hasn't been in all week and Maxine's just told me she wants to see her after lunch. So I rang her at home and she told me to tell Maxine to 'get fucked because it's the week after Mardi Gras and how could anyone expect her to come in like it was a normal week . . .'"

She paused for dramatic effect, then continued.

"Anyway, Maxine's already angry with her about missing that Lauder lunch on Monday, so I told her Debbie had rung in sick and I hadn't seen the message until just now, and then I asked Zoe to ring Ben—he's a doctor—to get him to write a sick note for her, and I've sent a courier over to collect it. OK?"

I just looked at her in amazement. Nineteen years old and such a smooth operator. I was in awe.

"Is that OK, Georgia?"

"That's very OK, Seraphima. You've definitely done the right thing—and thank you for letting me in on it. I won't tell Maxine."

"That's alright," she said. "I knew you'd be cool." She returned to her desk.

I leaned back in my chair and pondered what she'd just told me. The way they all protected Debbie was extraordinary, but I was ready to go along with it until I found out exactly what had been going on in that lane on Sunday. I knew the only way to find out more about that was to swallow my pride and ring Antony. I was still furious with him, but he had given me an excellent excuse to call—that morning he'd sent me an enormous bouquet of pale mauve roses. The card had said:

Pussy cat, pussy cat, where have you been?
I've been to Sydney to meet an old queen.
Pussy cat, pussy cat, what did you do there?
I frightened a vile old degenerate from under the chair.

Pussy Galore—please forgive me. I hate myself. I am your slave. Dolly.

It was impossible to resist—and they were the first flowers I'd had since Nick Pollock that weren't from a multinational corporation. I rang him.

"Is that the vile old degenerate?"

"Oh, Pussy. I hate myself. Did I really say those awful things to you? Well, I know I probably did because I've had other reports about my shocking behaviour. You weren't the only victim. I really didn't know it was you, you must believe me."

"I forgive you. But if you didn't know it was me, why did you say 'I don't give a fuck about Pussy?' It's your name for me, after all."

"I probably thought you meant pussy as in female genitalia . . . Which I'm really not very interested in."

I had to laugh.

"Antony, you are appalling, but I still love you. What on earth had you taken to get like that? Hemlock?"

"Quite a few eccies . . ."

"I thought they were meant to make you love all mankind."

". . . some cocaine, several lines of speed, and then the real killer—copious amounts of vodka."

"What's wrong with vodka?"

"It turns me into Vlad the Impaler. On everything else I'm just various sorts of silly, but vodka turns me into a mass murderer. I shouldn't drink it. On champagne I'm quite delightful, as you know, wine makes me merry, tequila makes me take my clothes off—not a good look—beer makes me sleepy, whisky makes me droll, but vodka turns me into a sociopath."

"That must be why they call it vodka."

"Uh?"

"It stands for Vile Old Degenerate. V.O.D.—you're a Voddie."

He shrieked. "That's it! I'm a voddie. A voddie and tonic. I'm so glad there's a reason. Anyway, I'm sorry you saw me that way."

"Don't worry, I forgive you completely. We'll never mention it again."

"So will you come over and play tonight? Just we two? A little dinner *à deux chez moi*? *À sept heures*?"

"*Oui, ça sera bon.*"

"*Au revoir.*" And he put the phone down in his usual peremptory fashion.

Dinner was quite a production—Antony must have been feeling really bad about what he'd said to me. There was a little round table out on the roof garden with candles, a starched white cloth to the ground and enormous napkins. It was set with beautiful silver (which I recognised as Tiffany & Co. pattern), fine crystal glasses (which Antony told me were Baccarat) and Limoges china (I looked). He met me at the door, wearing a frilly white apron and holding a bottle of Cristal.

"It's so hard to get *staff* these days," he said.

The food was wonderful—a huge platter of prawns (with silver finger bowls to rinse our fingers), grilled barramundi with a lemon sauce and purple potatoes, which he said he'd bought as a joke, mashed and piped into little castles.

"Have you really got one of those piping bags?" I asked. "I haven't seen one for years."

"I inherited all this from Lee. He loved cooking and had a very *Women's Weekly* circa 1972 style. I've got a fondue set too."

After we'd enjoyed a nice peppery rocket salad, Antony produced a great mound of meringue, whipped cream, strawberries and kiwi fruit.

"Is that a pavlova?"

"Bien sûr. La Pavlova du Lee."

"Why have you started speaking in French, Dolores? I've never heard a worse accent."

"I met a gorgeous French flight attendant at the party . . ."

And he proceeded to entertain me with a blow by blow—literally—story of his evening. His impersonations of Betty up on a go-go boy's dancing podium left me helpless with laughter, but I noticed his account didn't mention Debbie very much.

"Didn't Debbie go to the party with you?"

"Oh yes. She looked amazing. I made her that outfit I wanted you to wear and she walked all over town with her boobs on display—and they're much bigger than yours, let me tell you."

I poked my tongue out at him. "Did she have a good time?"

"I couldn't tell you. We got ready together here before going to Trudy's house for a pre-party, then we watched the parade right at the end of the route and afterwards we went into the Showground, where we immediately lost each other."

"Didn't you see her again all night?"

"Come off it, Pussy darling. There are twenty thousand people there, you know, most of them gorgeous-looking men. There was no way I was going to go trailing around looking for her, and I knew I'd see her at the recovery party anyway. She can look after herself."

Can she? I wondered.

"I thought I saw her in that hideous alley where—" I started to say, but Antony interrupted.

"You said you'd never mention it!"

"OK. But I thought I saw her."

"Probably. Like I say, we always meet there—it's a well-known recovery party."

"She was down a side alley."

"With a man, I suppose."

"Yes."

"Was she giving him a head job?"

"Antony! No, she wasn't. Don't be disgusting."

He pulled a face.

"Sorry, I forgot I was having dinner with Mary Poppins for a moment. What was she doing?"

"She was sort of resting ... Antony—do you think Debbie's OK?"

"No. She's completely out of control."

"Are you serious?"

"As serious as I ever am."

"What I mean is, do you think she might harm herself?"

"Well, all that alcohol certainly isn't doing her skin any good and her reputation is shot ..."

"Do you think she might be injecting drugs?"

His eyebrows broke the land speed record.

"Whatever makes you think that?"

"Oh I don't know, just something I saw ..."

He looked serious.

"Now that would be a bore. Injecting is so *déclassé*. I tell you what, I'm fitting her for a dress at the weekend, I'll check her over for track marks. Although I draw the line at looking between her toes. Will that keep you happy? I really don't think you need to fuss too much—she just likes to have a good time and, since that plane crash, I'm quite happy to go along with anything she wants to do that makes her smile. But don't worry, I won't let anything really bad happen to her—if I see a track mark I'll let you know immediately. Anyway, did I tell you what Trudy said when I told him about Jean-Luc? Well . . ."

And off he went.

Chapter Fifteen

On Friday morning, while I was in a planning meeting with Linda and Maxine (who'd been totally mollified by Debbie's bogus doctor's note), Seraphima took a message from Jasper for me. He'd invited me over to Caledonia that night for what he called "a film show."

It turned out to be an open-air showing of various short films made by Jasper, the animators, and their friends, projected onto a big sheet in the garden. There was the usual Caledonia crew of weird and interesting-looking people sitting on the grass, talking, drinking and smoking, while we waited for it to get dark enough to start the show. Jasper floated around being host, coming over regularly to check I had someone to talk to, a fresh drink and—most importantly—that I was having a good time. I was.

The films were pretty average, and the remarks shouted out by the crowd were far more entertaining. Two of the films were by Jasper and the awful thing was that I really couldn't see the point of them. I was dreading him coming to ask me what I thought. Luckily he made it easy for me.

"Well, that was a piece of shit wasn't it?" he said, sitting down on the grass next to me.

"Um, well, yes it was, really," I said. "I have to say I didn't get the point, Jasper—I was hoping you would explain it to me."

He roared with laughter and then leant over and gave me a big kiss on the lips.

"That's my Pinkie. No bullshit. That film isn't about anything. It's garbage. I'm going to set fire to it so I can't ever show it again by mistake. I'd been smoking this really heavy hydroponic weed for about two weeks and I was convinced I was the new Tarkovsky. What was I thinking? A two-minute static shot of an empty bus shelter. I thought it was a fantastic symbol of suburban ennui."

"So is that why the next two minutes was a static shot of a man trying to start a four-wheel drive? Was he desperately trying to escape his ennui?"

He nodded and began to laugh silently, until he was shaking uncontrollably and tears were running down his cheeks. I couldn't help joining in and it just made him worse when I said, "And I couldn't see the Turkish bread in it either . . ."

"Aaah," said Jasper, falling back onto the grass. "Oh, I'm such a pretentious git. I really must stop smoking dope. What total garbage. God, I'm a tosspot. Well, at least it didn't have any of my terrible dialogue in it."

Then he sat up again and looked at me.

"Hey, you work on a magazine—you must be able to write. You could write a film with me."

"Well, I do write things now and again, but I don't think I'm up to a film script."

"Of course you are. I know—we can have a girl leafing through a copy of *Glow* and then we can cut to her trying to apply what she reads to her own life."

"It might be classed as pornography in that case."

"Good! Good! This could be really interesting . . ."

Fired with enthusiasm, he went off to find the animators to see if they'd do animated sex scenes for us so we wouldn't have to hire real porn stars. Then he decided I should play the *Glow* reader as well as write the script and so it went on. A load of harmless, entertaining nonsense.

About one in the morning I'd had enough and told Jasper I was off. Once again he insisted on walking me home.

"Well, here we are at your castle gate again, Princess Pinkie. Perhaps one day you will allow your suitor to accompany you up to your ivory tower."

"Right now the Princess is about to turn into Sleeping Beauty. Good night, Jasper."

Saturday morning, at five minutes to eight, my phone rang. Vidovic.

"Are you alone?"

"Believe me, Liinda, the morning I'm not alone, I'm going to leave my phone off the hook in anticipation of your wake-up call."

"Thank God you're by yourself," she rasped.

"Why? Are you coming over?"

"No, it's just that you were seen getting very chummy with Jasper O'Conner last night and I was worried that in your vulnerable state you might have fallen victim to his charms."

"What? Where on earth did you get this from? And what vulnerable state?"

"Post Pollock. I thought you might need some uncomplicated validation of your attractiveness to men and accidentally fall into bed with Jasper."

I couldn't believe this. "You didn't answer my first question—who told you I was 'getting chummy' with Jasper O'Connor? And why did they think it was any of your business?"

"So you were!"

"Liinda, what are you playing at? Is this your way of warning me that Jasper is an even bigger bastard than Nick Pratface Pollock? Because if he is, just tell me. I don't want another sushi sister evening; this time I'd like to know in advance."

"No, it's just that he's a big pothead flake like I told you and I don't think he's what you need in your life."

"Liinda, I appreciate your solicitude," I said with heavy sarcasm. "Although it makes it even more bizarre that you didn't warn me about the P. person. But this is really none of your business. And I'm not having a relationship with Jasper, he's just very friendly and I like all the nutty people who hang around that mad old house—apart from whichever creep came snitching to you. Who was it, anyway."

"Oh, somebody I know just happened to mention it in passing."

"Well, they must have been up early. And how would anyone there have known I knew you? Oh, who cares. So, tell me, what are you up to this weekend? Got anyone else to stalk?"

As the weeks went by, Liinda's weekend wake-up calls became a regular feature of my existence, as my new life in Sydney started to fall into a kind of rhythm. Hysterical nights out with Antony and the boys and round to Antony's place on my own for long chats and a bit of dancing. Mascara launches and boutique openings with Debbie. Workday lunches with Liinda and Zoe—who was eating more normally, encouraged by Dr. Ben—and on Saturday afternoons I would often meet up with Zoe and sometimes Debbie to go to the beach, or shopping in Oxford Street.

And in between all that I got into the habit of dropping in at Caledonia. There was always someone interesting to hang out with, even if Jasper wasn't there. When he was around we usually ended up in the cupola, talking, or watching whatever obscure foreign-language movie was on SBS.

I really enjoyed his company and the more I got to like his mind, the more attractive I found his body. But Liinda was right about one thing—I was vulnerable after the Pollocking and, although it pissed me off, her warnings had sunk in.

Work settled into a routine too. I was into my fourth *Glow* issue and I found the monthly magazine cycle very familiar and comfortable—ideas meetings, commissioning articles, reading them, editing them, checking them on proofs, coming up with catchy headlines with the subs and helping Maxine and Cathy, the art director, choose the best photos. I had great fun with visual ideas like "Which Celebs Look Worst with No Make-Up?" and "Beached Whales—Celebrity Swimsuit Cellulite." Then it would be time to choose the cover shots with the team, followed by the coverline meeting.

Now I was part of the monthly loop, Liinda could no longer spring unexpected coverlines at me and I had a few laughs with ideas of my own, such as "Ten Surefire Ways to Spot a Bastard—Before It's Too Late," which Maxine thought would make a great coverline. I stuck my tongue out at Liinda and whispered, "Beat you to it that time, eh?" So she came back with an idea about how to stop a friend getting involved with the wrong man, which I was delighted to hear Maxine say was a stupid idea.

"Our readers have enough problems with their own love lives without interfering in their friends' relationships," she said.

"Two all," I hissed, thumbing my nose at Liinda.

Chapter Sixteen

It was Saturday morning. I'd had my hour-long conversation with Liinda as per usual, but unlike previous Saturdays, Zoe and I weren't meeting as she was now into the stage of wanting to spend every spare moment with Ben. Perhaps I should take a cue from Liinda, I thought, and suggest a story along the lines of the "Man Trap—Women Who Desert Their Girlfriends for a Man." I didn't feel like staying in the flat so I decided to walk from Elizabeth Bay to the Art Gallery of New South Wales.

I stopped at the top of the steps in Victoria Street that look down over Woolloomooloo. It was one of my favourite spots in Sydney—it seemed to sum up the whole place in one view, right down to the ugly new units half blocking the view of the Domain. But I loved seeing the Australian Navy ships right in the middle of the city and the funny old pie cart, Harry's Café de Wheels, standing proudly in front of the poshly renovated old wharf. In the main harbour beyond, the Saturday sailors were out in their yachts, and the city skyline looked proud and prosperous beyond the green of Mrs. Macquarie's Point.

What a pretty city, I said to myself for about the hundredth time. Sydney did that to me—every time I got complacent about living there it would leap out at me from another splendid perspective, grabbing my attention all over again. Look at me! Aren't I something? Did you ever see a city as pretty as me?

I spent a couple of hours in the Gallery, then wandered through an exhibition called Australian Works on Paper—New Acquisitions. Idly looking at the exhibits, I stopped in front of an almost abstract landscape done in warm yellow and ochre chalks. I admired it for a while and then looked at the plaque on the wall next to it: "*Back Acres III*. Rory Stewart. Chalk on paper."

There it was, the golden landscape around Walton, its dreamy quality perfectly captured. It was a wonderful drawing. No wonder Rory was frustrated at being cut off from his artistic life, he had serious talent. And he was so modest about it. Nick Pollock boasted about books he hadn't even written yet and Jasper summoned half of Sydney to come and watch films he admitted were terrible. But even though we'd had that conversation about the Gallery, Rory had never mentioned that he had a picture in it himself.

Seeing Rory's drawing unexpectedly like that was a bit of a shock. I wanted to tell someone about the coincidence, someone who would understand the full significance of it, but it dawned on me that there was no one in my newly divided life, in either England or Australia, to fill that role. The sudden realisation made me feel acutely homesick. I came out of the Gallery and decided to take a walk through the Botanic Gardens, with my latest food discovery—a chocolate Paddle Pop—for company.

It was so peaceful in there, even on a sunny Saturday morning it didn't seem crowded. There were a few people setting up picnic rugs under big shady trees, and families with small children went riding by on a brightly coloured miniature train, but you would hardly have known you were in a major city at all. It was a good place for a long think.

I'd been invited to a big party that night—it was Trudy's fortieth birthday and Antony's gang were all very excited about the celebration, which was being held at the Diggers Club in Bondi. They'd booked out the whole place for the night and there was going to be hot music, lavish food and endless drinks for 300 guests. Antony and Betty had spent the last few days organising the decorations, which were going to have a Moroccan theme. Trudy ran a PR company which specialised in fashion labels and other groovy products like vodka and sunglasses, and it was set to be a very glamorous affair. "Dress: UP" the invitation had said.

Debbie had bought a bright orange and pink stripey bias-cut backless dress from Scanlan & Theodore specially for the occasion and she'd made Kylie spend most of her week trying to find a pair of matching shoes. Zoe had a primrose yellow satin dress from Collette Dinnigan, which looked gorgeous with her olive skin, especially now that she'd put on some weight. And I was looking forward to giving my favourite Chloe dress its first Sydney outing.

I knew the party would be really fun in a frenzied way, with lots of dancing and larking around, but there were three reasons I wasn't sure about going.

The first was that through some cunning research (asking Trudy when he was drunk), I had found out that Nick Pollock was going to be there with Phoebe Trill.

The second was that much as I adored Antony and his boys I knew that, apart from Pants On Fire Pollock, Zoe's Ben and whichever bonk-of-the-week Debbie had in tow, it would be pretty much a gay affair. I knew that I'd have a hilarious time and then go home to bed alone, pissed, feeling empty inside.

The third reason involved Jasper. He had called me on Friday afternoon and asked me what I was doing over the weekend. I'd been deliberately vague to keep my options open and he'd said if I wanted to have a really good time, I should come to Caledonia at two p.m. on Saturday with a jumper and a swimsuit. That was all he'd tell me, but he warned me not to be late, or he'd leave without me.

Now it was twelve noon. I had two hours to decide one way or the other. I wandered down to the water's edge at Farm Cove and leaned against the sea wall. The sound of the waves slapping against the stone was very restful. I felt quite sleepy and the thought of a big noisy party with Antony and Debbie off their faces didn't appeal at all.

I'd assumed Jasper's secret plan was a beach picnic, but there was something about the way he'd said "he" would leave without me—not "they" would leave without me—that made me wonder if it was an outing for just two. Did I want that?

Yes and no. I certainly didn't want to start a serious relationship with anyone—did I? But if not, why had I got so dizzy so quickly about Nick Pollock? And why had I started choosing schools within moments of meeting Billy Ryan? Also, Liinda had been so persistent in her warnings about not getting involved with Jasper. Should I take notice of her?

What I really wanted was some uncomplicated male companionship of the close kind. I longed to be held in someone's arms. I wanted to kiss someone. Long, deep, slow kisses. Apart from a quick snog with Billy and a night of wild humping with Bollocky Pollock, it felt like a lifetime since I'd had sustained physical contact with another human. My whole body yearned for it. Skin on skin.

I stood there gazing at the water with my thoughts going round and round like clothes in a washing machine. Jasper. Flake. Pothead. Skin. Antony. Rory. Liinda. Jasper's laugh. Flake. Pothead. Skin. Antony. Liinda. Round and round and round.

And then, almost without realising it, I was walking home. I hadn't consciously made a decision, but my feet had. I was going to go with Jasper—wherever he was going. But as I walked along, with the washing machine on the spin cycle, I came up with a disqualifier clause. I was going to be ten minutes late deliberately and if Jasper had gone without me, I would go to Trudy's party.

When I got home I rang and left a message on Antony's work number—which I knew he wouldn't answer on a Saturday—saying I wasn't feeling too good, but I would see him at the party as long as I was feeling better. That way he wouldn't feel offended when I didn't show.

I walked into the gate of Caledonia at ten past two. Jasper was sitting on the bonnet of his car wearing his gold-rimmed Vegas-period Elvis sunglasses and a large straw stetson—even bigger than the one I was wearing. He had his pink pants on, a brightly striped business shirt and Jesus sandals. His toenails were painted the same colour as his pants. He looked totally nuts—and very very cute.

"Pinkie!" he cried. "You took the challenge. I wore my pink pants in the hope they would conjure you up and they did."

"Jasper—you look very fine. Here I am with my jumper and swimsuit. What's the secret plan?" I noticed there was no one else around.

"Jump in and I'll tell you."

Jasper's car was an old sky-blue Holden with a bench seat across the front. There was no radio, but he'd brought a portable cassette player. A large cooler box and a couple of picnic rugs were stowed on the back seat.

"So are we going on a picnic?" I asked him.

"Well, a picnic is part of it . . ." He put a cassette into the player and hit play.

The B52s came blaring out.

"Are we going to the Love Shack?" I asked him.

Jasper slammed the car into gear and set off out of the gates at great speed.

"Road trip!" he cried as we swung onto Elizabeth Bay Road. "Woohoo!" he yelled. "Yeehaw!" I cried in agreement.

I didn't mind being kidnapped in the slightest. There are few things I like more than a road trip, and Jasper really understood the rules of the road. He had a whole glove compartment full of specially made compilation tapes with good driving music on them, including one on which every track mentioned a road, a car, driving, or a destination.

We happily yodeled "Twenty-four Hours from Tulsa" and crooned along to "Wichita Lineman" and "Galveston" with the mighty Glenn. Jasper was thrilled I knew all the words.

He had pre-rolled a little tin of his pleasantly mild joints, and the cooler in the back was full of iced tea he'd made himself and poured into empty Coke bottles. Jasper didn't approve of Coca Cola on moral grounds—but he was quite happy to stop at a petrol station and load up on cheap "lollies" as he called them.

"But these are sweets," I said. "Lollies are things on sticks."

"That's a boiled lolly you've got in your gob right now, darlin'."

"No, this is a boiled sweet. A Chupa Chup is a lolly. A Paddle Pop is an ice lolly."

"A Paddle Pop is an icy pole," he corrected me.

"A what? That sounds like something an Eskimo would make a tent with."

"Or something an Eskimo lady would be happy to warm up . . ."

We had the windows down, the music up high, and in no time at all we were out of suburbia and bowling along a highway through some kind of national park. The water was on our left, so I figured we were heading south.

"Where are we going?" I asked, as we bypassed somewhere called Wollongong.

Jasper shrugged his shoulders.

"I guess we'll know when we get there. We're south of the Gong on the open road. We've got a full tank of gas . . ."

"We're wearing shades . . ."

"Hit it!" we cried in unison.

And on we went through twee little towns with cutesy high streets which Jasper dismissed as muffin zones, and then through nowhere much at all, both just happy to look out the window at the pastoral countryside, sing along and smile. I took my watch off and zipped it into a side pocket in my bag. Jasper smiled.

"I knew you'd get it. No time, no appointments, no plans, no rules."

"No deadlines."

"No worries." We grinned at each other.

After a couple more hours—at a guess, the shadows were lengthening anyway—Jasper suddenly turned left off the highway.

"Let's see what's down here, shall we?" he said.

The side road wound through stands of gum trees and large shrubs, a sort of scrubby forest. Jasper drove at a dangerous lick through a few funny little towns until eventually we came to a high area from where I could see we were on some kind of peninsula with water on two sides. On the right was the open ocean, on the left there was a huge round bay, edged by white sand beaches.

We turned off again and wound down a hill until we came to a much more picturesque settlement of weatherboard buildings, right by the shore. Jasper drove past them and then along quite a rough track, ignoring a sign which said No Entry. After a couple of miles through dense trees he parked, and we just sat there and listened. Apart from the waves and the odd bird call there was complete silence.

"No man-made sounds at all," I said. "Heaven. Do you know there is practically nowhere in the British Isles where you can find this kind of silence anymore? There always seems to be a motorway in the distance or a plane overhead. This is amazing."

We sat there for a while, just listening. Then Jasper said, "Let me show you to your accommodation, modom," and he took my hand and led me through the trees to the beach. It was pristine. There were no plastic bottles on the shore, just shells and seaweed. Then I saw something jumping in the water.

"Look!" said Jasper. "Dolphins."

A whole pod of them were swimming and leaping, not far off shore.

"You've done it again," I said to Jasper. "You've stood me still." And then it seemed the most natural thing in the world for him to take me in his arms and kiss me. For a long time. Slowly and sweetly, just as I had imagined it.

We swam. We built a fire and baked potatoes in it. We drank pinot noir out of real glasses—"No need to slum it," said Jasper—and we ate salad and ham and cold watermelon out of an "esky."

"The same one who had the icy pole?" I asked him and he kissed me some more.

When night fell and the stars came out, we lay on our backs, as we'd done so often in the cupola, and smoked a few joints and talked and talked until we fell asleep. Well, not asleep exactly. Jasper had a double sleeping bag in the boot. He'd also brought two single ones, he told me.

"I'd hate you to think I was making assumptions," he said.

The next morning we woke with the sunrise, running into the sea to wash and wake ourselves up. Jasper disappeared for a while with the car and came back with coffee and bacon and egg rolls. All day we swam and sunbathed and slept and talked and made love. Skin to skin. I felt like sunshine was running in my veins.

"We're living like savages," said Jasper.

"And aren't savages on to a good thing?"

When the sun got up high I wondered sadly if he would soon say it was time to go. Instead, he leaned over and tickled my face with a blade of grass and said, "Want to stay another night?" I just nodded. Bugger work. I'd made enough excuses for Debbie Brent over the last two months—now I was going to chuck a little sickie myself, as I'd heard Liinda call it.

I had deliberately left my mobile behind, so I drove Jasper's car (which we had christened "The Whale") into the little village to find a phone box and left a message on Seraphima's voicemail at work. I said I'd been struck down with food poisoning on Saturday and still felt really rough on Sunday afternoon, so I wouldn't be in on Monday. That would cover me for Saturday night too, I thought. Debbie would hear and she could tell Antony and it would all hang together. And I was sleeping a lot, I told Sera's tape, so if anyone called I might not answer the phone. I didn't feel remotely guilty. I just felt high on the pure pleasure of being with Jasper.

That feeling didn't go away for all of Sunday and it was still there on Monday morning.

"I feel like we've been away for weeks," I told Jasper. He nodded.

"We can do this anytime you like," he said. "It's only four hours from Sydney. We could come here every Friday night if you wanted to."

I smiled at him. He might be a flake, but his dreams were charming. There was nothing dangerous in them. And he was a wonderful lover. Maybe it was the pot, but he took it all so slowly and easily, he wound me up to fever pitch. And even when we weren't skin to skin, I felt completely relaxed with him. I knew he liked me, because he'd told me so many times before we'd even kissed, so I didn't feel I had to be on scintillating form every second as I had with Nick Pollock. And I knew I was never going to marry him. With Jasper, I was quite happy to live in the moment.

But eventually the time came when we had to kiss our Blue Lagoon goodbye. There was no brutal "better be off then," it just seemed to happen. One minute we were lying in the sun, the next we were carrying things up to the car. When it was all packed away Jasper took my hand and led me along the beach to a sheltered spot where he'd written J & G in the sand with shells. He picked up one of the shells and gave it to me.

"Every time you look at this shell for the next week, I will be thinking about you," he said.

"Only a week?"

"We can renegotiate that each Monday morning."

The journey home was easy and companionable, with a suitably soppy compilation tape playing. Briefly I wondered if he had made another one to fit the mood if I'd opted for the single sleeping bag. I fell asleep on the bench seat with my head on Jasper's lap and woke up to find him stroking my hair. And then we were back in Elizabeth Bay.

He left the motor running while we kissed goodbye. I wondered for a moment if he was expecting me to ask him up to spend the night there, but I wanted to keep our precious weekend separate from the reality of the alarm clock going off in the morning. We kissed for a long time and as I started to get out of the car I turned round and asked him what he would have done if I'd been late for the rendezvous.

"I would have waited all afternoon," he said and I went inside, humming "Galveston" on the way up in the lift.

The next morning there was a bunch of purple bougainvillea outside the door to my flat—no note, but I knew it was from the garden at Caledonia. It made me smile and my insides did a quick somersault when I had a sudden image of Jasper walking out of the sea naked, shaking his long dark hair. I was going to have to make a real effort not to have too obvious a case of post-coital glow when I got into the office.

Sometimes it's a real pain working with a bunch of women and their collective intuition—you can't get away with any-thing—but for once they didn't seem to notice. To be on the safe side, I told Debbie and Zoe I was still feeling too sick to have lunch, so they wouldn't have the chance to observe me close up.

At three p.m. precisely Jasper called me.

"I left it until three, because I didn't want to seem too keen," he said and told me he would have loved to see me that night, but he had something on. That was fine with me—I wanted a bit of time just to enjoy remembering how wonderful it had been, before seeing him in reality again.

Later on Antony called to see if I was over my food poison-ing—the bush telegraph was working perfectly—and to tell me tales of Trudy's party, which had been the expected wild and crazy night. He wanted me to go over to his place for drinks, but I used the sick excuse again and we made arrangements to go to the var-ious lipstick promotions, gallery openings and product launches that made up the next ten days in Sydney's social calendar.

I did want to see Antony and the rest of the gang, but I also wanted to make sure that I'd booked in plenty of nights when I would be unavailable to Jasper. After feeling so helpless and cast adrift by the fiery-panted Pollock it felt really good not to feel desperate about this man.

When I did see him again, everything was as easy as ever. We had a Mongolian meal, watched a Mongolian movie and then went back to my place for a spot of what Jasper called Mongo-lian horizontal folk-dancing.

It wasn't as romantic as the beach, but Jasper seemed to have a natural flair for creating atmosphere—he'd brought some tea lights with him, so we could create a more conducive mood in my bare little room.

After that it seemed quite natural to see him again on Friday night, and we spent the whole of Saturday together going round Surry Hills markets and various junk shops to buy things to make my flat less like a nun's cell. I bought a mad old 1950s lamp in the shape of a gypsy dancer, complete with original pleated shade, a multicoloured bead curtain to put up in the kitchen and a framed school map of the world with Australia right in the middle. Jasper bought me a plastic pineapple ice bucket like his.

And so we drifted into an easy companionship. We didn't see each other every night and when we did stay together, he always came to my place. We didn't declare ourselves a couple, but inhabited our own secret universe whenever we were together and our separate ones when we were apart. It made me think of that country-and-western song—it's not love, but it's not bad. And it was exactly what I wanted.

Not long after our weekend away, Jasper started going on about the Royal Easter Show, which he kept telling me was a Sydney institution I mustn't miss. It sounded like just my kind of thing— it involved animals *and* men in Akubra hats—and I desperately wanted him to take me. But Jasper refused, saying he had boycotted it ever since they'd moved it from the old Showground to new buildings in Homebush. "I've heard that new place is just like a multi-storey car park," he said.

So I went on my own. Jasper had a point about the buildings; it was all grey concrete and seemed more urban than country. There were a few young fellows in hats, but I couldn't even get a whiff of cow shit. At first it just made me feel really homesick, it was so very different from the county shows I used to love when I was growing up. I wished that Hamish was there to share it with me—agricultural shows are his idea of bliss—and I wondered if he had done anything yet about coming over to work for Johnny Brent. I'd have to give him a call. Meanwhile, Jasper had given me a list of essential Easter Show experiences and I was determined to have a good time.

According to Jasper I had to watch the wood chopping, look at the prize-winning scones and cakes, check out the tableaux in the Hall of Industries, go on a terrifying ride, get him a Violet Crumble showbag and eat something called a Dagwood Dog, followed immediately by fairy floss, while watching the Grand Parade.

So I found myself eating a vile thing which seemed to be a deep-fried battered hot dog on a stick, followed by what I knew as candy floss. I'd already marveled at the amazing rural scenes made entirely out of soya beans, lentils, pumpkins and wool, I'd inspected the cakes, watched the wood chopping, cooed over the piglets, battled through 10,000 screaming children in sugar shock to get Jasper's showbag and decided which ride I was going to pretend I'd been on. All that remained was the Grand Parade, where the winning beasts in every class were led around the big arena in concentric circles. I loved it all.

I particularly loved the cattle. I couldn't believe that such mighty animals could be so gentle, and when I went to look at them more closely in their stalls, their bodies made such beautiful shapes, it made me want to draw them. I still hadn't found a life-drawing class to go to in Sydney, so I got my notebook out of my handbag and started sketching.

They had such lovely big curves, I found them even more engrossing to draw than humans. They were very good at keeping still too and soon I was lost in concentration. People stopped to look, as they always do when you are drawing in a public place, but I didn't take any notice until one of them said my name.

"Well, look at that—it's Georgie. Hey, that's not bad."

I looked up and saw Billy Ryan, accompanied by an attractive dark-haired woman. It was such a surprise to see him I felt myself blush.

"Hello, Billy, I'm just drawing the cows . . . they have such lovely shapes . . . Hello," I said to the woman, putting out my hand to shake hers and dropping everything on the floor. "Georgiana Abbott, how do you do?"

"Oh, Georgie," said Billy. "This is Lizzy . . . er . . . Stewart."

"Hi Lizzy," I said, a little too brightly.

She had a good handshake. I hated what she was wearing (an A-line denim skirt and a white blouse, which made her look like a transplanted Sloane Ranger), but at least she could shake hands properly. So this was Lizzy Ryan, Billy's sister-in-law and secret love. Rory's sister. The scarlet woman of Walton. How interesting that he'd introduced her by her maiden name. And how interesting that they were out in public together.

"I didn't know you were an artist, Georgie," said Billy. "I think these are quite good, don't you, Lizzy? Perhaps you'd like to come up to the farm and draw our cows."

"They're lovely," said Lizzy. "I can see how much you like animals."

I smiled at her. She was growing on me.

"Actually, I know someone else who draws cattle. My brother." She looked at me steadily.

I could feel a serious blush starting, but luckily Billy blundered on in his usual gung-ho way.

"Does Roar draw cattle?" said Billy. "Well, I knew he got bored up on the farm, ha ha ha. Lucky he just draws them, eh? Just kidding, Georgie. So how have you been? How are you settling in to Sydney?"

"Great, thank you," I said, marvelling at what a dunderhead he could be. A likeable dunderhead, though. A terrifically handsome and likeable dunderhead.

"Glad to hear it. We'll have to get you over for supper one of these nights. Can we get hold of you at *Glow*?"

I noted he was talking in the royal "we." I wondered how his poor old brother Tom would feel about that.

"Yes, that would be lovely," I said, lily-livered Pom that I am.

Lizzy was looking at my drawings.

"Georgie, I don't suppose you'd sell me one of these, would you?"

"Oh Lizzy, you can have one, they're only silly sketches. Please, take one, I'd love you to."

She gave me a sweet smile which reminded me very much of her brother.

"How is Rory?" I asked. "Is he down for the show?"

"No, he hasn't come this year. Too much to do up there. But he's pretty well. I hear you two had a good time at the rodeo."

I think I blushed again. Sometimes it's terrible having fair skin.

"Yes, it was really fun," I mumbled.

"Well, we'd better be off, Picasso," said Billy. "It was good to see you. Take care." He kissed me on both cheeks. "We'll be in touch about that dinner. Introduce you to some fun people."

"Bye, Billy. Bye, Lizzy, good to meet you. Say hi to Rory for me, won't you?"

"Oh I will," she said. "I definitely will."

Chapter Seventeen

Over the next few weeks Jasper and I carried on our happily casual liaison and although I quite often woke up to find flowers on my doorstep, I was glad he kept it all light. We still only saw each other about three times a week, leaving me plenty of time to go gallivanting with Antony, so he didn't suspect anything. Not that Jasper and I had anything to hide, I just didn't feel like having to explain it to anybody. It was nobody else's business—and a whole lot of fun.

One evening I came home from work and found a big J & G drawn on the pavement outside my door in pink chalk. Arrows led from it along the pavement, with hearts every few feet. I followed them down to Beare Park where Jasper was sitting on a picnic rug with a bottle of champagne and two glasses. Another time he found a great set of old china covered in pink roses in a junk shop. He presented me with the teapot and told me he'd hidden the rest of it around Caledonia and I had to find all the pieces. The clues were in the teapot.

Of course, one of the reasons Jasper had so much time to

spend on me was that, as far as I could tell, he had very little work to do. He had a few regular things he did for old friends and he always had some crazy creative project on the go, but Jasper O'Connor, famous fashion and portrait photographer, was certainly not getting any new clients.

I didn't let any of that bother me because I didn't consider it a "serious" liaison, just simple fun.

So when Jasper told me he'd been invited to a party that was being given by an ex-Caledonia resident called Cordelia, now a successful florist, living in a big house in Watson's Bay with her new barrister husband, I said I'd love to go.

"You know this will be our first real public outing, don't you?" he said. "Do you feel comfortable with that? I mean, let's play it a bit cool, but people will get the picture."

I thought for a second and said I didn't mind going. From what I already knew of Sydney I could see it was impossible to keep our little fling a secret much longer. Plus I had another motive for wanting to go to Cordelia's party on Jasper's arm; Nick Pollock was going to be there.

I knew this because Antony had already told me about the party. He and Debbie had both been invited but they couldn't go because they'd already accepted invitations to a big society wedding in Melbourne on the same night.

"It's so annoying, Pussy," he had said to me. "That awful Nick Pollock is going to be there and I could have given you a big pash right in front of him to show him how much you don't care."

"What's a pash?" I'd asked him.

"A big wet French tongue kiss. With groping."

"Ooh—a snog. Cool. That would have got people talking."

One lunchtime a few days before the party, I took myself on an anthropological expedition up to the north end of the Central Business District, where all the suits worked. Liinda had told me that she went there sometimes, just to sit outside with her cigarettes (equals lunch) and watch the passing parade. She said it was a "top perve" and that the food court at the bottom of Australia Square was the prime spot.

I bought a sandwich and sat down at one of the outside tables. Liinda was right—there were attractive men in suits everywhere you looked. One of them was Billy Ryan. We saw each other at the same moment. He looked even more handsome in his suit than he did in the country togs I'd always seen him in up to then and I felt myself blush scarlet yet again, as he called out "Georgie!" and came over to sit with me. After my years in lonely London, I still wasn't used to the Sydney thing of bumping into people you know every five seconds. I felt like I'd been caught doing something naughty.

"Well, we can't go on meeting like this," he said, with his usual endearing predictability. "Are your offices round here too?"

"Oh no, I, um, I just had a meeting up here and I was starving, so I thought I'd have a quick sarnie."

We chatted a bit about the Easter Show and then he asked me again if I was enjoying Sydney. He always made me feel like I was being interviewed for acceptance at a boys' prep school.

"Met Mr. Right yet, have you? I bet men are queuing up to take you out. I'd be in the queue myself if I wasn't already, er, involved with someone. Met anyone in particular?"

As I didn't consider Jasper a proper boyfriend I said no.

"I've been seeing a few people . . ." Like you, I thought, stark naked. "But I'm not involved in anything serious."

I didn't feel I was betraying Jasper. That was the way I saw our situation. Then Billy surprised me by asking me if I was going to Cordelia and Michael's party on Saturday.

"Cordelia the florist?" I asked. He nodded. "Funnily enough I am. What a coincidence."

He didn't seem to find it surprising at all.

"Cords is very tied up in that fashion scene, so I thought

you'd know her. Great girl, Cords. Very arty. I went to school with Michael. Well, I'll see you on Saturday then. We can have another dance." And with a flash of that dazzling smile he kissed me on the cheek and was off.

On the day of the party Jasper rang me and said I should walk round for drinks at Caledonia and then a gang of us could go on together. He also told me that the dress theme was All Things Bright and Beautiful.

"Which means you won't need a costume of course, Pinkus."

When I got there everyone was dressed up in their finest, with a group theme of flowers in tribute to Cordelia's profession. Lulu, the artist with the blue hair, had stencilled a flower onto the top of her crop with purple dye, which looked very arresting teamed with an old flowery frock and big black boots. The older woman, Tania, looked like Ann Margret in a psychedelic flowery print halter neck, and one of the animator boys was wearing a Hawaiian shirt, with a loud hibiscus motif. Jasper was resplendent in flowery trousers and a bright green shirt, with his painted toenails on display again.

"Jasper, where do you get those pants?" I asked him. He wore the most ridiculous clothes, but somehoe he could carry it off.

"Places no one else would think of looking," he said, with one of his winks.

On Jasper's instructions, I'd put on my loudest outfit—a scarlet flamenco dress with huge bright pink polka dots, cut very low in the back and very tight over my bum. Rick had bought it for me years before in Spain. It was 100 per cent polyester and 100 per cent fabulous, as he'd said when he'd given it to me, and I was delighted to have a chance to wear it. Jasper put a hibiscus flower behind my ear and we all piled into his car.

From the moment we arrived at the party Jasper seemed to know everybody we passed, so I left him to meet and greet and followed Lulu and Tania through the house and onto a huge sandstone terrace looking over the harbour. It was a really lovely old house, with gardens running down to Camp Cove, my favourite beach. I took a glass of champagne from a passing waiter and happily surveyed the scene.

I was surprised to see that I knew quite a few people there and soon became involved in a conversation. Jasper came out to find me and I reassured him that I was quite alright on my own and didn't need to follow him round like a dog.

"I knew you wouldn't be a party cling-on, Pinkie. Come in and find me if you feel like a smoke," he said and disappeared inside.

It was a good crowd—a mix of colourful Caledonia bohos, Antony's shiny fashion set and straighter-looking types, whom I assumed were Michael's legal friends, although I couldn't see Billy anywhere. Betty and Trudy were there and they introduced me to lots of other people.

Then Nick Pollock walked in. I felt sick. I should have forced Jasper to stay with me until he made his entrance. I'd had such a clear picture of myself standing laughing with Jasper when he came in, but at that precise moment I was completely on my own.

It was one of those natural breaks in party conversations when a large conglomeration of people splits up into several smaller groups and, in my shock at seeing the Poisonous Pollock, I hadn't joined any of them. I saw his eyes pass over the crowd, flicker at me and move straight on. Maybe he was counting how many women in the room he'd shafted, I thought.

The very lovely Phoebe Trill didn't seem to be with him— maybe she was off giving a blow job to whoever had given her the gig on the game show—so Pigface would be on the prowl. I was damned sure he wasn't going to prowl anywhere near me, but I still felt so humiliated by the way he'd treated me I didn't trust myself to come up with suitably lacerating remarks if he should front up. I knew I'd be all tongue-tied and pathetic. Now he appeared to be coming my way—I could hear him thanking Trudy for his party. I bolted.

I needed a few moments alone to compose myself and headed down the steps into the garden. I had my sights on an old stone bench which wouldn't be visible from the terrace, when someone came down the steps from the other side and got there first. It was Rory Stewart.

"Rory!" I called and ran the last few steps to meet him.

"Hello Georgia," he said, giving me a big kiss on the cheek. "I was wondering when I'd run into you—Billy said you'd be here. Wow, look at your dress. That's quite something. Give me a twirl."

I twirled and stamped my feet, stopping in a flamboyant flamenco pose. Rory laughed and clapped his hands.

"Olé! It looks great on you. But why are you down here and not up there eclipsing all the other women at the party?"

We both sat down on the bench.

"I could ask you the same question—well, almost—why aren't you up there charming all the women at the party?"

"I asked you first."

I slumped a bit.

"Oh, someone just walked in that I really didn't want to see."

"A man?"

"I wouldn't honour him with that title. A total plonker is a better description."

Rory laughed again. "That's such a great English word. Plonker. Well, he must be an idiot if he's done anything to hurt your feelings."

"Anyway, enough about that toad, you haven't told me why you're skulking around down here."

He paused, looking as if he was trying to decide whether to tell me something or not.

"I just feel a bit low," he said quietly. "Cordelia used to be engaged to Alastair—one of my brothers who was killed. I'm really happy for her that she's found someone else—Michael was at school with all of us, although I didn't really know him, he was older—and she seems very happy, but it still makes me really sad."

I took his right hand in both of mine and stroked it. It seemed like the right thing to do.

"So Debbie wasn't the only bereaved fiancée," I said.

He looked at me with an expression that reminded me of his sister Lizzy at the Easter Show.

"You've got it in one," he said. "Drew is the one that everyone talks about—he was the oldest and Debbie and he were Sydney's golden couple—but it pisses me off sometimes, because three of them died. Drew and Alex were sporty and played polo and all that stuff and were always in the social pages, but Alastair was much quieter. Sometimes I feel like everyone's forgotten he ever lived."

"Tell me about Alastair," I said. "What was he like?"

"He was a botanist and a biologist—even when he was a little boy, he was fascinated by insects and plants—and he was doing a PhD in organic farming. He was trying to persuade Drew to give him a section of the property to farm bio-dynamically, to prove that it would be more profitable. Alastair was an idealist, he wanted to change things."

"How did he meet Cordelia?"

"Plants. She was trying to source organic flowers for her shop and that was how they met. They were such a special couple. Just as special as Drew and Debbie—but much softer and less showy."

I could hear a wobble in his voice. He paused and I squeezed his hand.

"Alastair was the one I was closest to and he's the one I miss the most. To be honest, I just don't see Cordelia with a big flashy barrister. I think she just married him for this garden."

And a big fat tear rolled down his cheek. I put my arm around him and smoothed his hair. He wiped his eyes.

"Thanks, Georgia. I'm sorry to lay this on you. I'll be really embarrassed later, but sometimes the gap where Alastair used to be is like a yawning chasm, and when I saw Cordelia I just kept thinking Al should be next to her."

He sighed deeply then took a deep breath.

"Why don't you go back up to the party now and I'll come up in a minute. I don't want to cramp your style."

"It's no bother whatsoever. And if you're ever feeling down, Rory, just call me, please. My ears are always available."

Then I suddenly remembered Rory had never asked for my phone number and at this sensitive moment I was not about to push it on him.

"You know you can always ring me at *Glow*," I said quickly. "And as for going back to the party, you wouldn't be cramping my style at all. In fact, you'd be doing me an enormous favour if you would walk up those steps with me, looking at me as if you consider me the most fascinating woman on the planet. Just in case the plonker is lurking."

"Ah—the plonker gambit. That would be a pleasure. And I have to tell you I don't think I'll find my role very hard to play . . ."

It worked like a dream. We walked around the garden a bit, because Rory didn't want anyone to see he had red eyes, and then he presented his arm to me and walked me up those steps as though we were entering an embassy ball. Plonker Pants On Fire Pillocky Pollock was standing in the perfect position to see us as Rory bent down and pretended to whisper sweet nothings in my ear.

"Nothing nothing nothing" is what he actually said, so I found it easy to laugh coquettishly. In fact with Rory's head so close to mine, I didn't find it hard at all.

Unfortunately Plonker was talking to Jasper.

"There you are, Pinkie," Jasper cried. "Come and meet my very good friend, Nick Pollock."

Then he surprised me by doing a shoulder manoeuvre that effectively closed Rory out of the group. I moved aside to let him in again.

"Nick and I have already met," I said through a steely smile. "Where is your lovely fiancée tonight, Nick? Spinning a barrel somewhere?" Then I copied Jasper's shoulder trick and turned my back on Plonker. "Jasper," I said. "This is *my* very good friend, Rory Stewart."

Rory put out his hand. Jasper shook it as if it were a wet fish. I couldn't believe it. He was standing in a really stupid slouchy way and chewing gum. I'd never seen him chew gum before.

"Yeah right, hi Rory, howareya? Anyway, catch you on the flip side, dude, Nick and I have some serious shit to talk about. See ya." And he made to put his arm around my waist in a proprietorial fashion. I wriggled away. There was no way I was going to be stuck listening to his "serious shit" with Plonker. Dude? What was he talking about?

"Rory's just taking me to meet Cordelia," I said and turned to him with a panicked expression on my face. I mouthed "HELP" and crossed my eyes.

"Oh yes," said Rory, getting it immediately. "She's inside. Come on, Georgia."

"I can see why you call him Plonker," he said, once we were in the house. "What's with the American accent? 'Catch you on the flip side' . . . Puhlease."

Oops, I thought. Wrong plonker. I couldn't believe Jasper's

behaviour. I couldn't believe ghastly Real Plonker was a friend of his. But I was beginning to realise that there was about half a degree of separation between everyone who lived in Sydney.

"Shall we get a drink?" I said quickly. "And if we see Cordelia, I really would like to meet her."

"Here she is now . . ."

She looked exactly how I thought a Cordelia should look— tall and willowy with long wavy auburn hair. She was wearing a long green dress with tiny glass beads embroidered over the pattern and a headdress made of real calla lilies. She gave Rory a huge hug.

"Oooh, you gorgeous thing," she said. "I'm so glad you decided to come after all. I really want you to have a good time— and I *really* want you to like Michael. He's not a horrible greedy lawyer—he's a nice one, or I wouldn't have married him."

She paused and looked Rory straight in the eye.

"I wouldn't have married anyone I didn't think Alastair would have approved of, Rory," she said gently and he smiled back at her, sadly.

"I'll look forward to meeting him then," said Rory. "I haven't seen him since I was thirteen and he was a big scary boy in Year Twelve. Cords, this is Georgia Abbott."

"Hi Georgia," she said and kissed me, which I thought was charming. "I'm so pleased to meet you. I've heard such a lot about you. You'll have to come over for dinner one night when it's not so manic here. I suppose I can get your number from Rory . . ."

Yeah, right, I thought—not. I glanced at him, but he was staring studiedly off into the distance.

"You can always get me at *Glow*," I said. "On the switchboard number."

"Oh, that's easy," said Cordelia. "I know that number off by heart, because we send Debbie so many bouquets. I've learned always to ring first, because there are so many days when she's out working on location."

Something like that, I thought.

Then Cordelia swept us off to meet Michael, and she was right, he was a nice lawyer. As well as his money-making clients, he also represented anti-logging groups and environmental charities—for nothing—and that was how he and Cordelia had met. She'd been chained to a tree at the time. Despite Rory's misgivings I could see that he did like Michael, so I thought I'd leave them to bond and went off to find the loo.

Cordelia directed me upstairs to her private bathroom where I found Jasper—doing cocaine with Plonker.

"Pinkie darling, there you are," said Jasper, throwing his arms open extravagantly. I didn't run into them, but I saw Plonker's eyes flicker as he registered the intimacy between us. I really hoped he'd have the restraint not to fill Jasper in on our previous acquaintance. It made me feel like a slut. From what I'd heard Plonker was the biggest slut in Sydney, but it was OK for him, of course, he was a bloke.

"I see you boys are powdering your noses," I said, icily. "I'll see you downstairs, Jasper."

"Don't you want a little line, Georgie?" asked El Plonko.

"I'd rather set fire to myself." I flashed a big fake smile and left them to it.

Back downstairs, the party was beginning to take off and people had started dancing. Trudy and Betty were out shaking it on the dance floor, so I joined them. Rory was sitting on a sofa chatting happily to a fair-haired girl I didn't recognise.

It soon turned into the usual Sydney mayhem. Trudy was jiving with me. Betty was doing some kind of tango with a very attractive Asian guy. Lulu and Tania were doing the twist. Rory was dancing with the fair-haired girl. I asked Trudy who she was and he didn't know, so she clearly wasn't part of the "in" crowd. In between spins and turns, I took a good look at her.

She was wearing a dark red suit with a very short skirt, natural-coloured pantyhose and black shoes. Lots of fussy gold jewellery. And too much lipstick. The girl in the polyester suit. Not someone I'd want to go on a villa holiday with, I said to myself, sniffing.

After a few more songs I saw her leave the room and Rory came over to me.

"May I have the pleasure of the next dance?" he asked, bowing low.

"I would be enchanted," I said, dropping into a curtsy, and we grooved and shimmied and generally got down. After we'd danced to a couple of tracks I saw the girl in the red suit come in, spot us and walk straight out again. Rory didn't notice, taking me into his confident waltz hold and spinning me around the floor to a dance mix of "I've Got You Under My Skin." And as he dropped me down into that familiar dip at the end, I realised I was beaming up at him.

Then, as the music changed to the unmistakable opening bars of "Groove is in the Heart," somebody grabbed me, quite roughly, from behind.

"There you are, Pinkie my darling," said Jasper, pulling me close and shoving Rory out of the way. "Sorry mate," he said to Rory, "but I think it's time I danced with my date. Hop it."

I opened my mouth to say something, but Jasper had turned me round and propelled me to the other side of the dance floor, where he started pumping his groin into mine in a grotesque way. I looked over my shoulder to see Rory stare with amazement and then turn on his heel.

"Jasper, what are you doing? That was so rude."

"Oh sorry, did I offend your nice middle-class friend? I'm so sorry if I don't know the correct etiquette." He had a really un-pleasant tone in his voice and a hard glint in his eye. Maybe it was the coke, maybe it was Plonker's evil influence, but I hadn't seen Jasper like this before. Suddenly I didn't feel like dancing anymore. Specially not the pervy way he was swivelling his hips.

"Jasper, I'm going to sit this one out," I said, coldly.

"What's wrong? I'm not good enough for you now? You only want to dance with the private-school boys?"

"Get over yourself, Jasper. I'm going to get some fresh air—the atmosphere in here just got a big muggy. I'll see you later."

I went outside and sat on the wall of the terrace. What had got into him? I'd never seen this side of him before and I didn't like it. Through the open doors I could see him dancing with Lulu and Tania and he seemed quite happy. Plonker appeared with a very pretty girl who looked about seventeen. He was gaz-ing into her eyes and singing along with the words to "It's Rain-ing Men"—all very familiar. Cordelia and Michael were clasped around each other, apparently oblivious to their guests. After a while Rory came back onto the dance floor with Red Suit. She had her arms around his neck and was pressing her large breasts into him. He didn't seem to mind. But I realised I did.

After a while I saw Jasper leave the dance floor and Tania came out and sat with me.

"Why the long face, Georgie?" she said. "You seemed to be having a good time earlier."

"Oh, I just don't feel like dancing any more."

"Is Jasper being an arsehole?"

I looked at her. "Yes. How did you know?"

"Cocaine. Doesn't suit him." She rolled herself a cigarette from a little embroidered pouch she always had with her.

"How did you know he'd been doing coke?"

"I've known the guy since he was twenty. I know Jasper better than just about anybody, I suppose." Tania was smiling smugly to herself. "He's always been a pain in the arse on coke. Makes him paranoid and brings out his pent-up anger. And coming to houses like this makes him aggro too."

"But he lives in a house bigger than this."

"Yes, but he doesn't own it. He likes to pretend he's Mr Laid Back King Boho—and if he smokes enough pot he is—but deep down he's really bitter about the way his career has tailed off." She lit the roll-up and took a deep puff. "It all started to go wrong for him when he got involved with that Liinda Vidovic," she said, with smoke pouring out of her nostrils.

I stared at her. "What?"

"Doesn't she work with you on *Glow*?" Croatian. Big hair. Great writer, total nutcase . . . used to be a junkie, now she's a one-woman Salvation Army."

"What do you mean by 'involved'?"

"She was madly in love with him. He was screwing every model in town and wasn't interested. He liked her intellectually, but he didn't fancy her. Jasper likes blondes . . . Like you. And me. Anyway, one night he was stoned and horny and she was the only woman around, and he fucked her. That was a biiig mistake. She stalked him relentlessly—she thought he should marry her because they'd slept together once. She was relentless. Phoned him day and night. Followed him. Left threatening messages for any woman who went near him. It was insane."

I couldn't believe it. No wonder Liinda had warned me off him so intensely.

"Is she still in love with him?"

"If she is, she's not so obvious about it. But she's the reason Jasper can't work for *Glow* anymore and a lot of other places. Terry would be the one to ask."

"Who's Terry?"

"You know Terry, big guy, bald, nose ring, works at Radio

National, you've met him at the house. He's a very good friend of Liinda's—they're both AA, NA and all the rest of it.

Aha, a mystery solved—that was how she knew I'd been to Caledonia that time. I wonder what else he'd told her.

"I haven't seen him around for a while," I said.

"No, he's been in Melbourne for weeks—there was a big NA convention and he stayed on."

Tania carried on smoking and I just sat there feeling winded. I really liked Liinda—I didn't want to become her love rival. She took feuds very seriously. And she had that knife. I'd enjoyed my time with Jasper—until tonight—but I didn't like him enough to risk making my life at work total misery.

"Thanks for telling me all this, Tania. I wonder why Jasper didn't warn me not to tell Liinda . . . I could have gone into work and told her I'd met this wonderful man."

"I think he reckoned you were strong enough to take Liinda on."

"I think he's overestimated me," I said, stunned. This was too much. Did every man in Sydney come with several steamer trunks of emotional baggage?

"I hope I haven't spoiled your evening," said Tania, grinding the butt of her roll-up into the terrace. "Jasper's a good guy really, but his career's on the skids and he needs people to blame it on. And he needs all the help he can get to put it right again." She smiled at me innocently.

What exactly was Tania telling me now? Was she implying that Jasper was only seeing me in the hope of getting work from *Glow* again? I'd had enough unpleasant revelations for one evening so I decided not to pursue that line of thinking. Maybe Tania was a bit of a stirrer. And then another thought occurred to me—maybe she fancied Jasper for herself. I'd noticed her looking at him in a certain way and she certainly spent an awful lot of time at Caledonia for someone who didn't actually live there.

Living in Sydney's tangled web of relationships was beginning to smarten me up. I was going to check out everything
she'd told me before I acted on it.

"Well, thanks for letting me in on the background, Tania. I
think I'll go in and see if Jasper's mood has improved."

The look she gave me as I got up made me think I'd been
right in my deduction. Perhaps she thought her sordid revelations would make me go home. Well, tough luck.

Jasper was back on the dance floor.

"Pinkus, Pinkus—there you are. Come and dance with me. I
know I was a pain earlier, I have to admit I was jealous. Those
middle-class boys make me feel like the peasant I am. Gets me
every time. Do you forgive me?"

"Not entirely. But I'll consider it if you don't take any more
coke tonight. It makes you aggressive."

He saluted me smartly. "Yessir. Nosir. No more cocaine. Sir."

"OK. At ease," I said. "And please don't do that pervy dancing. It's embarrassing."

My feelings about Jasper were rather confused. Part of me
wanted to walk out and never see him again, but I wondered if
that was overreacting. And anyway—it was a great party and I
was determined to enjoy what was left of it. I danced with Trudy
and Betty and their friends for a while, but when a slower track
came on, Jasper sensed my weakness and pulled me into a clinch.

I looked over his shoulder and saw Rory doing the same with
Red Suit. At that exact moment he glanced straight at me and I
saw something—Surprise? Irritation?—flicker across his face.
Probably the same thing that had just flickered across mine. I
looked away immediately and surrendered myself to the music
and Jasper's incorrigibly wiggling hips. Then he kissed me, one
of his long, slow, dreamy kisses, and I forgot all about everyone
else. He may have been more complicated than I'd thought, but
Jasper was a blissful kisser.

After a couple more slow songs I was beginning to feel drowsy and Jasper picked up on it—he knew he'd been out of line earlier and was being his most tender and adorable.

"Want to go home, little Pinkie? Had enough excitement for one night?"

I nodded with my eyes closed like a sleepy puppy.

"OK, come on then, little girl." I let him lead me towards the door.

As we left the room I saw Rory sitting on a sofa with Red Suit on his knee. They were smogging madly.

"Bye, Mr. Silvertail. Have fun," said Jasper, quite unnecessarily, tapping him on the knee as we went by. I looked back and saw Rory open one eye. It opened a bit wider when he saw who had spoken and who was with him. Then it closed again. Tightly.

Chapter Eighteen

I was standing on a stool in Antony's workroom. He was kneeling at my feet with pins in his mouth, wearing the white coat he always wore to work in, like they do in the Paris couture houses.

"I don't want to get threads on my beautiful clothes any more than they do," he said, when I suggested it was just a tiny tad pretentious. (Actually he said, "I on't ont oo et freds on y ootiful close any or an ay oo.")

I pointed out that he was wearing white Levis and a white T-shirt, not a Saville Row suit—and that he'd never make it as a ventriloquist.

"Ay are ootiful oo e," he said and told me to keep still. He was pinning the hem on an evening gown he'd insisted on making for me after hearing that I'd worn a polyester flamenco dress to Cordelia's party.

He sat back on his heels and took the pins out of his mouth.

"Whatever possessed you, Pussy? None of my girlfriends can go out looking trashy. I don't allow it. It reflects so badly on me. I made Cordelia's dress—did you like it? It was her wedding present. That beading cost me a fortune. Of course, I know why you wore it—it's the influence of that trashy Jasper O'Connor. He loves a bit of polyester. Mad for it. Probably has dark brown nylon sheets. I can't believe you're seeing him, after all I told you—and I can't believe you didn't tell me."

"Oh, give it a rest, Antony," I said crossly. I was still pissed off with Jasper for his behaviour at the party and I didn't feel like defending him. "I didn't tell you because I knew you'd go on and on about how unsuitable he is—like you are. Get over it. I've got no intention of marrying him and I'm not really seeing him anymore anyway. I just wanted some male company . . . no strings attached and no judgments from well-meaning friends. It can be a terrible strain going out with potential husbands and having to be fascinating all the time. Exhausting. I find non-potentials much more relaxing."

"Oh, I see, you just wanted a root—or a 'shag,' as I believe you English girls say. So, is he a good fuck?"

"Oh Dolly darling, you do have a way with words. Yes. He's a top root."

"How does he compare with Nick Pollock and his pneumatic penis?"

"Well, I have to admit that Nick could compete internationally—it's a spectacular display. But it rather loses its gloss when you find out that it's really just a matter of practice makes perfect. Jasper is much more sincere and you get the feeling the experience is spontaneous, rather than a well-rehearsed medal-winning routine, the way it is with Plonker."

"HA HA HA . . . Plonker. I love that."

Which meant the rest of Sydney would soon love it as well, I thought. Good.

"Oh well, if he's a good fuck, what the heck," said Antony. "Enjoy yourself, but remember that he won't enhance your stock around town."

"Am I in a cattle auction?"

"Pretty much."

"Lovely. I suppose Betty and Trudy told you I was smooching with Jasper at the party."

"That's right. I must say you've done very well to keep it quiet for so long."

"Well, as I told you, it was never a relationship. It's my version of your anonymous sex."

"Good. Keep it like that."

"Yes, dearest," I said meekly.

After he'd finished pinning and fussing we sat on the roof garden and Antony opened his customary bottle of Cristal.

"Actually, I've got some far more juicy gossip than you and that grubby photographer."

"What?"

"You know your friend Billy Ryan?"

"Yes. I've bumped into him twice recently—once was at the Easter Show and the famous Lizzy Ryan was with him. Except he introduced her as Lizzy Stewart, which I thought was kind of interesting."

"That's it exactly!" said Antony, clearly filing away this new detail and thrilled with it. "They've gone public. Can you imagine? Billy told his own brother that he was in love with his wife, that they'd been having an affair for a year and that she was leaving Tom to come and be with him. It happened the night of Cordelia's party."

"That explains why I didn't see him there. So how come he was with her at the Show? That was a couple of weeks before."

"Tom was in New York on business. Billy told him when he got back."

"Poor old Tom. What did he do?"

"Punched his lights out. Billy had to have three stitches—in his eyebrow, of course, which will just make him look more handsome than ever. Isn't it heaven?" He clasped his hands together with delight. "Oh, I wish I could have been there. Imagine those two gorgeous Ryan boys fighting it out. But the best thing of all—Billy told him in the Four in Hand. Can you imagine, with all those rugby boys around? 'Sorry, mate, I'm rooting your wife. And she's going to be mine.' Pow! Crash! Oh, Patrick White would have loved it. Primeval." He paused and looked at me. "Of course, this lays it all open for you and Rory Stewart."

"What are you talking about?"

"Billy doesn't have to pretend he's seeing other women anymore, so Rory can now hit on all the gals who were previously in Billy's harem of pretend girlfriends, without betraying his maaate. You were one of them, sweetie."

"Oh, I think it's too late for that."

"Why?"

"Well, I see Rory as a friend now. You know how that initial attraction fades if you don't act on it? He was at Cordelia's party, actually—last seen snogging a busty girl in a horrible suit. Looked very happy about it."

Antony's left eyebrow shot up. He was looking at me with his evaluating face, exactly as he had when I first met him at the hat party. I looked back at him boldly and drained my glass.

"The attraction fades, does it, Georgia? Hmmm. I wonder who the chick was . . . Probably very rich if she was wearing nasty clothes. We'll have to find out. Ask Debs about it—then tell me. Does she ever come into the office these days?"

"Debbie? Oh yes, from time to time. Not like every day or anything and never before eleven a.m. and often in a filthy temper, but we do see her. How was the wedding in Melbourne?"

"Oh it was *fabulous*. We had the best time. We behaved really really badly. Debbie has been banned for life from the Australia Club."

I must have looked blank.

"It's a very snooty club. The members are mainly senior lawyers, you have to wear a tie to breakfast and all that bollocks. Very establishment. Beautiful old building, billiard room, the works."

"So what did Debbie do that got her banned for life?"

"She gave the best man a head job in the breakfast room—members were having breakfast at the time."

I couldn't believe my ears. I just gaped at him, appalled.

"Isn't she hilarious?" he said.

"No. I think she's seriously deranged. She needs help and your attitude just encourages her. She could get arrested for doing something like that. I mean what does she have to do to get some attention? Was she totally off her face?"

"Oh, you are boring sometimes, Pussy. She'd had a little cocaine possibly and maybe some eccies and rather a lot of champagne, but I wouldn't let something really bad happen to Deb—or Bed, as I now call her, HA HA HA."

Was this bad enough for me to ring Jenny? I wondered. How would I tell her? Your daughter was caught giving oral relief to a man in the dining room of a major Australian establishment? I couldn't do it. And it's not like it was actually endangering her health, just her poor destroyed reputation.

Despite her recent disgrace Debbie (or Beddie, as I now couldn't help thinking of her) seemed to be in a better mood around the office and as Liinda was away for the week doing a travel story in Hawaii, I thought I'd grab the opportunity to talk to Debbie about the Jasper stalking incident.

"Shame you missed Cordelia's party," I said to her casually, while we were going through photos of supermodels with spots for her next beauty story: "Bad Pore Days—Supermodels' Skin-Saving Secrets Revealed."

"Yeah, I heard it was good," she said. "And I heard you were smooching publicly with Jasper O'Connor. Yukko. You really have got the most appalling taste in men. Antony told me you just wanted a root, but really you can have meaningless sex with stockbrokers and rugby internationals, you know, you don't have to resort to penniless failed photographers."

"Did Antony tell you about me and Jasper?" I wanted to understand the complete workings of Sydney's jungle drums.

"Antony and about fifty other people. Trudy told me. And Rory Stewart told my mum he'd seen you with—and this is a quote—"some kind of drug addict," and now Jenny's really worried about you."

"Bloody cheek. Fancy telling Jenny that. Tell her not to worry, it was just a fling. And Rory wasn't exactly behaving like the pope himself either. He was snogging someone like mad."

"Oh yes, Mum told me all about that too. That was Fiona Clarke." Debbie pulled a face. "Apparently he's really keen. She's going up to the Stewarts' farm this weekend. Mum's pleased he's got a girlfriend at last, because he hasn't had once since . . ." She sighed. "Since he had to move back up there."

I gave her shoulder a squeeze.

"But you'd think he could have done better than her, for Christ's sake," she said vehemently.

"Apart from the fact she was wearing a bad polyester suit, what's wrong with her?"

"Was she? That's typical. She's just so ordinary. A real wannabe. The kind of girl who goes to polo matches in a baseball cap and too much make-up, hoping to meet a rich husband. That's all she cares about—the rich bit. She's such a social climber. Can't stand her. She'll be so excited to think she has her hands on a Stewart too."

I was used to Debbie's appalling snobbery and let it wash over me, while getting as many details about Fiona Clarke as I could.

"What does she do?"

"She does PR for a big property developer. The sort that is putting up all those Hong Kong slum buildings and calling them 'lifestyle apartments.' She sends out invitations saying things like 'Be a part of Sydney's new status address' and they're these hideous little poky units you couldn't stand up in wearing Manolos. Heinous."

"She doesn't sound like Rory's type at all," I said.

"Oh, he's just desperate to get laid, I reckon. Stuck up there on the farm. He was ripe for the picking." She paused and leaned on the light box. "I have this theory that men ripen like fruit—when they're ready to fall off the tree it doesn't really matter who the woman is, he'll drop into her lap. It's all about timing."

"Actually, she was all over *his* lap," I said. "But that's a good theory. It explains why some of the most gorgeous men you meet are with the most ghastly women. I always thought it was something to do with their mothers. You know, at the risk of sounding like Liinda, we could do a story based on your theory. We'd get a great coverline out of it, although we'd have to come up with something better than 'Why Men Are Like Fruit'—let's think about it. You should bring it up at the next ideas meeting."

Debbie looked at me with a thoughtful expression. Yet again I noticed that she had the longest eyelashes I'd ever seen. A few cows at the Easter Show came close, but no other human.

"That's very nice of you, Georgie. Liinda would have just stolen the idea and I'd have forgotten about it until I heard her passing it off as her own at the next meeting."

So she did pay attention in those meetings.

"Don't worry," I said. "I have an ideas file on my computer. I'll tap it in there and remind you before we go in."

"Well, it would be nice not to feel completely retarded in an editorial meeting for a change. You and Liinda sit there having brilliantly witty ideas, but when Maxine starts screaming and shouting I just clam up and can't think of anything to say."

And you sit there looking like you couldn't give a damn, I thought. How easy it is to misjudge people.

"Debbie, on the subject of La Vidovic, can I ask you something?" I wanted to grab my opportunity while I could.

"Someone told me that she used to be madly in love with Jasper O'Connor and stalked him and all that. Do you think she's still in love with him? Should I tell her I've been seeing him, rather than let her find out? She has warned me off him several times . . ."

"Oh, that was hilarious. The way she carried on you'd have thought he was a real catch, although it did get messy in the office and we had to stop using him. I did think that was a bit rough on him actually, because he was a good photographer."

She let out a bored sigh. I knew she couldn't understand why anyone would possibly want to give Jasper O'Connor a moment's thought, but she struggled valiantly to answer me.

"I don't think she could possibly still be in love with him but she did stalk him pretty heavily. It got pretty ugly."

She went back to flicking through the slides. I could tell her attention span for other people's problems was running out.

"But I don't think you need to tell her, no. Why open yourself up to all that aggro? And if she does find out you can just tell her it's none of her fucking business, which it isn't. Hey, look at this zit on Linda Evangelista's nose. Needs its own postcode. Excellent."

So maybe I didn't need to talk to Liinda about it—good. But what about Jasper? I needed to have things out with him anyway. After his behaviour at Cordelia's I'd seriously cooled off on him. I had let him come home with me after the party, but I hadn't seen him since, and I hadn't returned his last five phone calls. However, I still wanted to know if there was a good reason he hadn't warned me that one of my workmates was liable to have a psychopathic freakout when she found out we'd been seeing each other. And also, my conscience was nagging me a bit—I'd been talking about him to all these other people, surely it was only fair to let him tell his side of the story.

That night I walked round to Caledonia and found him up in the cupola.

"Pinkie, darling," he said, smiling beatifically and opening his arms. "Is your phone broken? I've called you so many times. Sit down, I've just been watching this amazing 1970s Brazilian film. It was the story of—"

I jumped in before he could get going on one of his endless rambling theories of the universe and his precise place in it.

"I've got a better idea," I said, sitting opposite him and folding my arms. "Why don't you tell me the story of when my friend and colleague Liinda Vidovic stalked you?"

His ebullinet mood vanished and he got the ugly look on his face I'd seen at Cordelia's party.

"Who told you that?"

"It appears to be common knowledge. Common to everyone but me."

"So that's why you haven't rung me." His face contorted with anger and he slammed his fist down on the seat next to him. "I will NOT allow that woman to ruin something else good in my life. She's already fucked up my career and I'm not going to let her fuck this up as well. I really enjoy spending time with you and I won't have her coming back from the grave like Carrie to haunt me."

"Well, that might be easier to arrange if you tell me about it,

Jasper," I said, keeping my voice low, to try to cool him down. His naked rage scared me a bit.

Jasper's whole face had become a scowling mask. It was hard to believe it was the same one that was so lovably open when it smiled.

"Come on, Jasper. Would you rather I just believed what everyone else has told me, or are you going to tell me your side of the story?"

"Fucking Liinda Vidovic was the worst thing I ever did," he said, suddenly. "I fucked her once and she fucked up my whole life in return."

"Wasn't the fact that it was only once the whole problem?"

"Yeah. She seemed to expect me to marry her, just because we'd had one root. I should never have done it, but we got really drunk and stoned one night, at least I did, and we just fell into bed. You know how that can happen . . . But we were really good friends and I thought she knew me well enough to know it was just a one-night stand."

No wonder he was such good friends with Plonker.

"So what happened after that?"

He lit a cigarette, and I felt so shaken I lit one too. Still horrible.

"Look," said Jasper, his face returning to its normal contours. "Liinda's been around, she's no country bumpkin, you know that, don't you?"

He looked at me questioningly, not sure how much I knew about her past. I nodded.

"Yes, I know about all that, Jasper." And the fact that he did too and he still thought she'd be game for a quick shag appalled me. He shrugged.

"OK. So I thought she could handle it. But she behaved like some kind of wronged virgin. I felt like a hunted animal. She used to follow me around Sydney. She was really good at it. I'd look round and there she'd be. I tell you, she should work for ASIO. Or the KGB."

I had to restrain a smile.

"She used to send me letters," he continued. "Every day. It was really creepy. And she knew everything about me. She managed to blab her way into every party I was invited to. There were endless silent phone calls and it made no difference if I changed the number, she still got hold of it." He shook his head at the memories.

"Did you ever consider getting a restraining order?" I asked him.

"I was just about to do that when Commandant Maxine Thane took matters into her own hands. Liinda had deliberately stuffed up a couple of really important jobs we were supposed to be doing together, and apparently she was being a psycho in the office as well. I think it was your friend Lady Muck—Debbie Brent—who told Maxine what was going on in the end. So Maxine told Liinda that if she carried on stalking me she would lose her job instantly, and she told me that I couldn't work for *Glow* anymore. Bye-bye career."

"But surely you didn't only work for *Glow*."

He looked a bit shifty.

"Liinda told my other clients a load of lies about me—the worst kind of lies, the ones that contain a grain of truth—and gradually they all stopped hiring me. And when you stop getting your *Vogue* covers it's amazing how fast your advertising work dries up."

"What kind of little half truths?"

"Oh, stupid shit about me fiddling expenses—when I'd just billed for a few more rolls of film than we'd actually used. I mean, all photographers do that. But when they looked into it, and found that there were a few rolls unaccounted for, they assumed everything she'd told them was true."

"Are you sure that's the only reason your career . . . slowed up? Did Liinda really have that kind of power?"

I was starting to feel like Angela Lansbury, collating all the facts and trying to work out who really dunnit.

"She's a total witch."

I wasn't sure I entirely believed him.

"Well, I'm going to have to tell her I've been seeing you," I said. "She's going to find out anyway—I think it would be better if it came from me."

"It's up to you. You're the one who has to work with her. I wish you luck."

He flicked his ciagrette end out of the window and reached for his little tin of grass and cigarette papers. He looked quite relieved it was all out in the open.

"Thanks for telling me all the gory details, Jasper," I said, standing up. "I'm going now."

"Don't you want to stick around and have a couple of Js with me?" He smiled his most winning smile.

"No, Jasper. I think you've been really sneaky with me and I don't want to stick around you at all."

"Well, fuck off then, you snotty English bitch."

"And a Happy Christmas to you, Jasper."

As I started down the stairs something crashed into the wall next to me. It was the plastic pineapple ice bucket.

"Grow up," I shouted back at him and he suddenly appeared at the top of the stairs.

"I don't know what makes you think you're so morally superior, Miss Manners," he said in a calm, measured voice. "You've been bad-mouthing my mate Nick Pollock all over town for not calling you after you screwed him once, and you haven't returned my last five phone calls after fucking me sense-less for the past two months. Men have feelings too you know, Georgia. Put that in your magazine."

And before I could say anything he went back up into the cupola and slammed the door.

I was shaking when I got home, but told myself it was a good thing I'd finally seen Jasper's true nature. I couldn't believe it was the same guy who'd taken me to a deserted beach and writ-ten my name in pink chalk on the pavements of Elizabeth Bay. I was upset by his nastiness, but I wasn't heartbroken. He never meant anything to me anyway, I told myself, and I went to bed to watch a video of *High Society* that he'd recorded for me in our better days. He'd known it was one of my all-time favourites and had stuck a photocopy of Grace Kelly and Bing Crosby round the video box, with our faces pasted over theirs. I threw it on the floor.

But as the familiar story unfolded and I watched my screen heroine, Tracy Lord, deluding herself that she wanted to marry a man she didn't love, I couldn't get Jasper's last words out of my mind. I realised with a sudden jolt that while he'd been leaving flowers on my doorstep and cooking me meals with only pink in-gredients, I'd been gadding around town, telling everyone I didn't have a boyfriend and that Jasper O'Connor was just my souce of anonymous sex.

Maybe the one with their pants on fire was really me.

Chapter Nineteen

That Monday morning I went into work full of new resolutions to be open and honest about everything, starting by telling all to Liinda. But somehow when she came back into the office, the first day after her Hawaiian trip, looking quite tanned (she never went near the beach in Sydney) and totally relaxed, I couldn't bring myself to dredge it all up. She was looking happier than I'd ever seen her—she was singing in the office—and I couldn't bear to bring her down.

As the weeks went by I missed Jasper much more than I'd expected to. I missed our spontaneous little jaunts. I missed his funny phone messages and the stupid cartoons he used to fax me at work. For the first time since our road trip I began to feel aware of how alone I was in Sydney.

One particularly homesick Sunday morning I rang Hamish to see when he was coming over and he told me—uncharacteristically bluntly for him—that he'd "cooled off" on the idea, which was very disappointing.

Spending weekends going round Kirribilli market and the Paddington art galleries on my own again, I started to wonder if there was something wrong with me. Why was every man I met in Sydney already hopelessly entangled with other people in my life? In London you could go to a party and bingo—you could just meet someone completely unconnected to the rest of your life. But it seemed impossible here.

I knew Antony would just tell me to stop being boring and have another drink if I broached the subject with him, Liinda would suggest I went to Co-dependents Anonymous and Debbie would just look at me blankly, so I decided to ask Zoe about it. Apart from her forays into binge eating, she seemed to be one of the saner people I knew, and certainly the one I had the fewest friends in common with.

"Is there something wrong with me?" I asked her one lunchtime, as we settled down with chicken laksas at our favourite grungy food court. "Or is it normal that the three men I've had flings with since arriving in Australia all have complex relationships with everyone else I know well?"

"It's pretty normal," Zoe said, ignoring her own food and spearing something out of my bowl with her fork. I smacked her hand. "Apart from blissful holiday romances in Europe, I've never gone out with a man who hasn't previously gone out with someone I know. I went to kindergarten with Ben. He came to my fourth birthday party. Now we are lovers."

"But how does that happen?" I asked her. "Sydney's a big place . . ."

"Yes, but it's divided up into very distinct sets. Take you— you've arrived here and moved straight into the Eastern Suburbs groovy A list. Fashion, art world, media, some stylish foodies and a few glamorous stockbrokers, that's pretty much it. They all live in Potts Point, Elizabeth Bay, Paddington, Woollahra and Bondi. Right?"

I ran through a mental Rolodex of my friends. "And Surry Hills."

"OK. And maybe the odd one in Point Piper, but that's it. Now I move partly in that set, because of my job, but I'm really one of the Eastern Suburbs young professionals B list. I've been part of it since I was born. Bellevue Hill, Vaucluse, Rose Bay, Double Bay. We went to school together, our parents all know each other. It's not as glam as your crowd, and it's certainly not as gay, but there's plenty of money in it. That's my scene. Remember how we went out on Mardi Gras night and bumped into a crowd of my friends?"

I nodded.

"You didn't really relate to them at all, did you? You can be honest."

I froze with my chopsticks halfway to my mouth.

"Well, no I didn't, but I adore you and I couldn't understand why I didn't love your friends."

"It's not your crowd. I bet you've liked every single friend of Debbie's you've met. Right?"

I nodded again.

"That's your tribe, you see? The different Sydney scenes don't mix much. So there are lots of people you could socialise with who wouldn't have heard of Jasper O'Connor, or Nick Pollock, or Antony Maybury, but they'd bore you to death . . . Like my friends did."

"I'm sorry, Zoe."

She sucked in a single piece of vermicelli with a theatrical slurp.

"Doesn't worry me a bit. I couldn't spend very long with your darling Antony and all his screaming bum chums, let me tell you."

We sat in silence for a few moments, trying to convey laksa from bowl to mouth without passing T-shirt. It wasn't easy, especially for Zoe who was also trying to avoid the coconut cream element and the deep-fried tofu.

"Maybe I could try another tribe then," I said eventually. "I seem to have really fucked up with this one. What else is there?"

Zoe abandoned her soup and snapped open her bottle of spring water.

"Well, you've got the alternative feral crowd—gay and straight—in Newtown, Erskineville and Enmore." She grinned at me. "Don't see you at the Metro listening to an indie band somehow. Then there are the groovier inner-city feral trendies—Darlinghurst, Surry Hills, Strawberry Hills, Redfern. They're cool, but a bit po-faced for you. No sense of humour. Then you've got your inner-west yuppies—young lawyers, professionals and journalists from the *Sydney Morning Herald*—they're a funny lot, they only seem to marry each other. Very amusing some of them, but not glam enough for you."

I could see she was enjoying herself. I was glued.

"Then there are the super-straight Mosman young mums and dads," she continued. "Nice people. You'd kill yourself. Then there's the Upper North Shore Liberal brahmins. You'd kill them. There's a well-off arty boho set in Balmain and Rozelle that you could possibly mingle with, but they don't wear good shoes." She shrugged. "I think you've landed where you belong. Is it really so different in London?"

"Well, there are cliques there too, of course, but it's not just one small gang of people going round and round holding on to each other's tails, and they certainly don't all live in one part of town—I had friends in every corner of London."

Zoe took a swig of spring water. "Well, here it's one crowd, one area. So don't blame yourself for your complicated private life. It's just the way Sydney is."

"I'll just have to get used to it then, won't I? But I must say, I do like the way I just bump into my friends here all the time. In London you have to plan your social life like a military campaign and you practically declare a national holiday if you see someone you know by chance on the street. Here it's an everyday occurrence."

. . .

And it happened again that Saturday, when Antony and I went to Randwick Races for the June Stakes. It was one of the biggest winter race days and we'd both been asked to judge the Fashions in the Field. I was thrilled to be at the track. Although I don't like riding myself, I love racing and I'd been studying the form in anticipation. Antony had been studying my outfit—nagging me endlessly, to make sure I had a felt hat and leather gloves, otherwise he said he'd refuse to be seen with me.

He came over to pick me up and declared himself happy with my light-grey wool shift-dress and matching coat, my black crocodile shoes, black bag, black suede gloves and mauve felt hat, with a pheasant feather. I had my good pearls on too.

"Perfect for a little Pussy," he said, eyeing the hat with satisfaction. Antony looked very dashing himself in a dark suit, blue shirt and bright Hermès tie with little cats all over it, which he said he'd bought in my honour. He had a silk handkerchief in his breast pocket and a Louis Vuitton cover for his race guide.

We had a few glasses of champers to get us in the mood (one of the big champagne houses was sponsoring the competition, which was the main reason Antony had agreed to do it), and then took our judges' seats to assess the thirty semi-finalists that had been selected by "spotters" in the crowd. At least half of them were wearing black, which struck them off my score chart straightaway.

"Save your little black dresses for after six, girlfriends," I whispered to Antony.

"Perhaps they're going to whip their pinnies back on afterwards and serve us our tea and scones," he replied. Loudly.

Most of them were wearing straw hats, which nearly brought Antony to tears, and another large proportion weren't wearing stockings. There were plastic handbags and a go-go. Gloves we could whistle for.

"Look at them," said Antony. Very loudly. "No fucking idea. How could they have got this far? The spotters should be shot. SHOT. Or given guide dogs. Look at her—open sandals, no stockings. She must be suffering from exposure for one thing, but I bet she thought, "These are my best shoes and I'm going to wear them even if it is sixteen degrees because they're so smaaart." Look—she's had a lovely pedicure specially."

I did look. I stared. It was Fiona Clarke. In a straw hat, the same red suit she'd had on at the party, and very high heels. She did have quite a pretty face, I conceded, and the bosoms were unmissable.

"Do you know her?" I asked Antony.

"Yes. She's a ghastly PR. Always trying to get me to go to hideous cocktail parties in appalling rabbit-hutch apartment buildings. She once rang up and asked me to make her a dress to wear to one of her 'events,' as she called it. I declined. Very particular about who wears my gowns, as you know. That girl in the chalkstripe suit looks less hideous than the rest. Nice bag. Nice teeth. Let's give her the prize and get back to the champagne tent."

"That's the girl Rory Stewart is knobbing," I said.

"What, that little thing in the chalkstripe? Bit *ordinaire* for a Stewart, isn't she?"

"No—Fiona Clarke."

"WHAT? You must be joking. She's appalling! He's a *Stewart*—one of the most eligible men in the whole country. Why is he rooting a little strumpet like that? I bet she'll get pregnant and trap him. Oh, this is too awful, it's Johnny Brent all over again. Come on, now I really do need a drink."

I did too. Antony was a terrible snob, but I couldn't really stand the thought of Rory with Fiona Clarke either. Though for rather different reasons.

"Drink . . . drink . . ." said Antony, walking like a man who was lost in the desert.

And drink he did. He drank himself senseless, to the point where I knew I had to get some food inside him or he'd fall over. They were only serving mimsy little hors d'oeuvres in the champagne tent, which Antony had already been extremely rude about—"What do you call that? A lump of snot on a cracker?"—while cramming them in with both fists. I thought I'd better get him out of there and look for something starchy in the main area behind the stand.

We found a pie counter and I pushed Antony onto a stool and ordered two pies and two Coca Colas, hoping it might have the same medicinal effect on him it had on me at the hat party.

He was just grumbling at me about being made to leave the lovely champagne tent and not wanting "this shit" when I looked up and saw Rory Stewart. He saw me, then Antony, and got the same look on his face he'd had when he saw me leaving Cordelia's party with Jasper.

"Hi!" I said, rather pathetically, and then the weirdest thing happened. I couldn't remember his name. I was so embarrassed to be seen with Antony in this state it just seemed to wipe my memory banks. I stood there gaping at Rory like a goldfish. I couldn't introduce him to Antony because a) I had forgotten his name and b) Antony was a gibbering drunk. At that moment he started to bang his head on the counter.

"Hi Georgia," said Rory. "Is your friend OK?"

"Oh yes, ha ha, I'm sure he'll sober up soon . . . too much champagne."

"Go and get fucked," said Antony distinctly. I knew he was talking to the pie, because I knew Antony, but anyone else might have thought it was aimed at them. I saw Rory sigh and I felt physically sick.

"Well, I'll see you then, Georgia. Have a good day."

"Bye," I said, feebly. Whatever your name is. I sat down next to Antony and put my head in my hands. Rory. Rory Stewart.

Gorgeous Rory Stewart. How could I possibly have forgotten his name? I groaned. Antony turned and looked at me.

"Who was that arsehole?" he asked and threw up all over his pie.

Great, I thought. Fiona Clarke is at the races with Rory Stewart. I'm at the races with a vomiting homosexual. Hello Sydney.

Antony rang me at work, full of excitement about something. I was still furious with him for humiliating me in front of Rory like that, but he couldn't understand why. The Vomity Pie Incident, as he'd named it, had taken place over a week ago. Ancient history to Antony.

"Pussy darling, you must come to dinner tonight. You must. Debbie's coming, and Betty and Trudy—it's just going to be the four of us."

"That's five, but sure Dolores, I'd love to. What's the special occasion?"

"Don't you know what the date is?"

"Well, I hadn't really thought about it—26 June, isn't it?"

"Exactly. It's five months today since we met."

"Crikey. Is it five months since that hat party? Good heavens. How nice of you to remember. I'm not sure five months is really a significant landmark, though. Is it our clingfilm anniversary or something?"

"Well, it's an excuse to open a few bottles of shampoo, isn't it?"

"I didn't think you ever needed an excuse, but it would be fun anyway."

"Actually, why I'm really calling is that we have to discuss our Cointreau Ball outfits. You got your invitation, didn't you?"

"Did I? I don't know—what does it look like?"

"You don't know if you got one or not? Are you mad? Anyway, I know you're getting one because I rang up and checked and you've made it onto the list. Five months in Sydney and you're on the Cointreau Ball list—good work, Pussy."

"What is it, anyway?"

"Oh, don't you know anything? It's the party of the year. There are only 400 invitations—for the whole of Australia, that is—and only the most In of the In crowd are asked. It's always a fabulous night.

"The location is a secret," he continued in a flutter. "They pick you up in a limo and you don't know where you're going till you get there, and then there's the most amazing decor, hot and cold running grog, great food *and* two first-class tickets to Paris for the best costumes, which we are going to win, darls."

"That does sound good. What does the invitation look like?"

"Go and ask Debbie, I've got to start cooking. Come straight from work. Bring costume ideas. Goodbye."

I ran round to Debbie's office. She was wearing a crown.

"I see your true status has finally been recognised," I said.

"Do you think it's *moi*?" she asked, twirling her chair around.

"Lovely, Your Highness. Is it for a shoot?"

"No, darling—it's my Cointreau Ball invitation. The theme's Royalty. Haven't you got yours? Antony said you were definitely invited. I'll ring Sera." She picked up the phone. "Sera darls, is there a crown on your desk for Georgie? Good. Bring it round, would you?"

So then we both sat in her office wearing crowns, coming up with ideas for our Royal costumes.

"Should be easy for you, Georgie. Antony says your grandparents live in a castle. Can't you just send home for the family jewels?"

"Well, it's more of a fortified house really. My grandmother does have a tiara, but I don't think she'd want to put in the post.

She says I can wear it on my wedding day. I've told her it might be a while . . ."

When we arrived at Antony's place the boys were already in a state of high excitement. They were all wearing their crowns. Betty had pinned on a few fake diamond brooches as well to get himself in the mood. Trudy was standing up very straight—practising being regal, he explained.

"You lot aren't going to need costumes," I said. "You can just go as a bunch of old queens." And from that point on the shrieking didn't stop.

As we sat down at the table (three candelabras for extra royal effect), Debbie made a formal announcement that she would not be going to the ball as Princess Diana.

"I know she had legs similar to mine, but it's just too obvious," she said.

"Well, that's a shame," said Antony. "Because I thought you could go in a swimwuit with wet hair and be Diana in her last few happy months with Dodi . . ."

She perked up visibly at the prospect of going out in public wearing practically nothing.

Betty said he was going as the Queen because he already had the right name. "I'm going to look up corgi breeders on the Internet," he announced.

Antony said that was fine—Betty could be frumpy Betty in her later years, perhaps in the lovely outfit she had worn at the Millennium Dome—but I would be going as the glamorous young Lizzy, because we were going as a themed pair and he wanted to be the young and beautiful Princess Margaret.

"Princess M. is perfect for me," he said. "We've got so much in common. We both love platform shoes, gin, smoking, camp queens . . ."

"So does the Queen Mother," I told him. "Maybe you should black your teeth out and go as her. You'd look lovely in mauve.

I definitely don't think you should go as the young Margaret. Those 50s dresses are so unflattering to the more mature figure. Go as Mustique Margaret. Much more glamour."

"Perfect! I've already got the kaftan . . ." and he disappeared off to the workroom, coming back moments later in a pale-blue swirly print mu mu, with matching turban, sunglasses and some badly applied coral lipstick. More shrieking. Trudy put Antony's crown on top of the turban.

"Bring me black men!" cried Antony. "Bring me gin! Off with their heads!"

The lights suddenly flickered.

"Hello Lee!" we all shouted together. They flickered again.

"I've got a more lateral idea," said Trudy, who I knew couldn't have borne to have gone to the ball as anyone unfashionable. "Let's go as a royal flush. The jack, queen, king and ace of hearts. You could have someone as Jack Nicholson for the jack . . ."

"Someone as Antony," I said. "For the quee—"

He threw a piece of bread at me.

"Someone as Martin Luther King," said Trudy. "And then . . . Martina Navratilova."

"Since when has there been a dyke card?" said Debbie, who was now wearing one of Antony's enormous hats.

"Tennis *ace*, stupid."

"Short skirt, Debbie . . ." said Antony.

"Antony, you could go as Prince Edward," I said. "Everyone says he's gay . . . Oh no! Scrap that, I'm not going as that awful Sophie Rhys Jones . . . Is she the Fiona Clarke of England?" I asked Debbie.

"Got it in one."

"Maybe I can borrow one of her polyester suits for my costume . . ."

"It would be too big in the tits," said Debbie. "Although come to think of it, she does look like a cheaper version of you."

"Oh, thanks a bunch," I said, realising it was true. Well, I could see there was some physical resemblance. We were both fair-skinned blondes.

"I suppose I could go as the Duke of Windsor," said Antony, now busy tying a headscarf under Betty's chin, "but I don't really see you as Wallis, darling," he said to me. "You're too obviously a woman."

Shriek. Shriek. Flicker. Flicker.

"I've got a good idea for you, Betts," said Debbie. "You can go as Zara Phillips because you've already got the pierced tongue."

"That's a great idea," said Antony. "And we'll get your father to come on a horse and ride around being rude to everyone. He'd be a marvellous Mark Phillips."

"Yeah, and you can be Princess Anne," said Debbie.

"It would almost be worth it, to be married to your father for a night," sighed Antony.

I was trying to think of something horrible enough to suggest for Plonker, but Antony beat me to it.

"Plonker Pollock could go as King Dong—after the porn star—from what all you girls have told me," he said gleefully. Then he put the Three Degrees on the stereo because they're Prince Charles's favourite singers, and that was the end of any remotely sensible conversation because we all started dancing.

"Just another quiet night in," said Antony, sashaying past with his crown on. And as he came back past me he gave me one of his disconcerting kisses right on the lips and whispered in my ear: "We're going to be the king and queen of the Cointreau Ball. My Pussy and I . . ."

Chapter Twenty

At last the big day arrived. The limo was picking us up at seven p.m., but Antony made me go to his place at ten in the morning, because he wanted us to spend the whole day together getting ready. He had his Polaroid camera set up, so that we could take pictures of ourselves to make sure we looked perfect, the way Bianca Jagger used to before going off to Studio 54. We were going to start with a Turkish bath in his steamroom and then he'd arrange for people to come and give us a massage, manicure and pedicure, followed by a light lunch, a nap and then hair and make-up. Trudy, Betty, Debbie and her date were coming over for drinks and we would all go on in our limos together.

Antony had finished our dresses at three in the morning. Mine was a long bias-cut oyster satin column with a low draped back. His was sleeveless white duchess satin, cut straight across the neck and slightly waisted. We'd decided to go as a tribute to Carolyn Besette Kennedy and Jackie Kennedy. My hair was the right length and colour and just needed to be straightened into perfect sleekness and then put loosely up.

"We're going as real royalty," said Antony, as he showed me the completed gowns. "People so gorgeous they had the status of royalty thrust upon them—so much smarter than just being born into it, don't you think?" He was purring with excitement.

I smiled at him. I did adore Antony, but he was so intelligent, so talented, so well-read, I found it hard to believe that this was really the sum of his endeavours. His knowledge of fashion history was encyclopaedic. He could date any garment to within five years—practically to the week, for anything later than 1920. And through his endless research into fashion and women of style, he was better versed in the social history of the twentieth century than anyone I knew. He might present himself as the silliest of fluff bunnies, but really he was an academic.

"You love all this, don't you Dolores?"

"Born to it, darling," he said. "I've been playing dress-ups since I was old enough to stand up by myself in front of a mirror. Nothing is more satisfying for me than the preparations for a grand costume ball."

We made ourselves comfortable on the hot rocks in the steamroom. I'd kept my knickers on, but Antony told me not to be such a prude and was marching around stark naked. I kept my eyes resolutely above his waist level and my towel to hand.

Every now and then he would spring up and turn on the shower—a huge thing the size of a dustbin lid in the middle of the ceiling—on cold. There was no escaping it, so the easiest thing was just to throw yourself underneath its full freezing blast, rather than being caught by chilly spray.

"Ooh, look at your nipples, Pussy," said Antony, tweaking them. "You could hang things off them."

"Stop it! Get off!" I shrieked, folding my arms across my breasts. "My nipples are private."

"Well, they won't be private for long in that dress I've made you. It's always freezing at the Cointreau Ball. And I don't suppose they're private to that hideous Jasper O'Connor either."

"They are now," I said.

"Really?" Antony's face lit up. "Have you given him the flick?" He turned the shower off and resumed his impression of a lizard lying on a hot rock.

"Yes, by mutual agreement." I really didn't want to talk about it. I didn't want to hear the glee in Antony's voice and I didn't want to think about Jasper. I still felt uncomfortable about it.

"That's excellent news. I told you your association with him was beginning to lower your stock in this town."

"Well, maybe my share price will go up again now," I said sarcastically.

"Yes, with rumours of a new merger . . ." Antony chuckled wickedly.

The rest of the day passed in a blur of pleasant physical sensations. The first champagne cork was popped at five, when the make-up artist and hairdresser arrived, which I thought showed remarkable restraint on Antony's part.

"Pacing is everything tonight," he said. "There will be unlimited amounts of grog from the moment we arrive, and it's essential not to peak too soon. First there's the early cocktails and milling, checking out what everyone's wearing and making sure the judges get a good look at us, then dinner, which is civilised jokey chat and lots of wine and table-hopping. Then a bit more milling and chatting, and you only want to be peaking when we hit the dance floor, which we will not leave until three a.m. when they throw us out. Then you can go on to an after party—they usually arrange one somewhere—but I warn you, they're always a let-down after the magical atmosphere of the venue. Much better to come back here with a select group of fashionable people."

After a whole day of preparations, suddenly we were ready.

Although I'd watched him have his nails and make-up done, I still hadn't really been able to picture Antony in a dress. He was as camp as they come, but there was something fundamentally masculine about him—maybe it was his Spanish blood. He had very black hair all over his arms, chest and legs and now I'd seen him stark bollock naked, I knew he had a nuggety male body too. Not a gym-pumped overdone pin-up boy body, but a man's body. Lived-in looking. Nice.

But when he put that wig on he was Jackie Kennedy.

"Wow!" was all I could say. "You look amazing."

He walked differently. All his movements were more delicate. In fact, he was being almost unbearably gracious. Antony was totally in character. I was still in my bathrobe and a tiny little G-string he'd provided for me (the only underwear he would permit under my House of Maybury gown).

"Come along, Pussy dear, go and get your dress on. The others will be here soon."

I went into his atelier (as he had taken to calling it) and stepped into the slippery silk. It felt like mercury next to my skin, so cool and smooth. I looked in the mirror. Even I was impressed. I actually looked quite like her.

Jackie swished in behind me.

"You look charming," he said. "Absolutely charming. Jack would have been so proud." He wiped a mock tear from the corner of his eye. "So sad, so terribly sad."

"Jack would have been hitting on her, Jackie darling, so get over yourself," said a voice behind us. It was Princess Grace of Monaco. A dazzling young Princess Grace, resplendent in a pale blue strapless satin gown, with long white gloves, rubies and diamonds at her neck and in a tiara.

"Oh, Your Highness," said Antony, dropping into a deep curtsey before Debbie. "You look so gorgeous, but oh those awful Grimaldi jewels. Rubies and diamonds, so unlucky. Blood on bandages, you know."

I just stared. Debbie was Princess Grace. She looked so like her. The same perfect nose, the blue eyes, the blonde hair.

"Are the rest of your benighted family, here, Your Highness?" asked Antony.

Debbie gestured back towards the main room with her head.

"You look wonderful, Georgie," she said. "Really beautiful. We're going to find a fabulous man for you tonight, now that you've finally seen the light and dumped that deadbeat . . . Antony rang and told me while you were having your nap," she added.

Debbie's date—some French guy she'd dredged up—made an excellent young Rainier. Trudy was an elegant Princess Caroline in a Chanel-style black evening dress and Betty was a hilarious, if somewhat overweight, Princess Stephanie. He was wearing a badge saying "I'm Stephie, fly me" on the shoulder of his electric blue dress.

We had champagne and toasted each other, then the buzzer rang to announce the limousines. We were off.

The journey took about thirty minutes and we got out at an old factory in the middle of some wasteland. Well, that's what it was on the outside. Inside it resembled Versailles. Or the Winter Palace. Or Marienberg. Or Sleeping Beauty's castle. There was a swagged ceiling festooned with enormous chandeliers. The walls were covered in huge gold mirrors and periwigged courtiers held candelabras to guide our way.

We entered on a red carpet where a page in silk stockings, a frock coat and a powdered wig asked our names, so we could be announced.

"Mrs. John F. Kennedy and Mrs. John Kennedy Junior," said the Master of Ceremonies.

"Their Royal Highnesses Prince Rainier and Princess Grace of Monaco."

"Her Royal Highness Princess Caroline of Monaco and Princess Stephanie of Potts Point."

"Oberon, King of the Fairies and his Queen, Titania." We were thrilled to see Michael and Cordelia. She was wearing the same outfit she'd worn to her party and looked glorious again.

"The King, Mr. Elvis Presley."

"Thank God I didn't do that," said Trudy. I've seen about five already."

"Her Royal Highness Princess Margaret." Antony nudged me when a kaftaned Princess walked in with a handsome black guy on her arm.

"His Majesty King Henry VIII and Queens Catherine, Anne, Jane, Anne, Catherine and Catherine." The wives were all men and they looked amazing.

"Her Majesty the Red Queen." It was Danny Green, taking photographs as he made his entrance.

"The Duchess of York."

"That's funny," said Betty. Fergie was a man in a perfect replica of the appalling blue and white check milkmaid outfit the Duchess had worn early in her royal career.

Antony rolled his eyes. He'd already told me he couldn't understand people who went to the party looking unattractive.

"Her Royal Highess the Princess of Wales."

"Part of a continuing series," groaned Antony. "People are *so* obvious."

"His Most Perfect Majesty, the Sun King."

Hello Plonker.

"His ego really is out of control, isn't it?" said Antony.

"The Duke and Duchess of Cornwall."

Antony roared. It was two of his friends, Joanna and Mary, as a very good post-abdication Charles and Camilla. Charles was in a gardening outfit talking to a trug of flowers, Camilla had her hunting coat on. They were followed by:

"His Majesty King William." Who was Ingrid.

"Hysterical," said Antony. "They wouldn't tell me what they were doing. Very good. Very good. Well, we can forget the prize, Pussy darling, the competition is just too tough this year, but at least we know we look beautiful."

"Her Majesty Queen Cleopatra of Egypt and Mr. Marc Antony." It was Maxine, with a rather attractive man.

"Who's that with Maxine, Debbie? Do you know?" I asked her.

"No idea. But she's been in a really good mood lately, don't you think? Let's go and find out."

We left our vantage point by the entrance and pushed our way into the crowd. It was like making the jump off the top of a slide—once you were on the ride there was no stopping it. The rest of the evening was a whirl, just as Antony had described it. Mingling and shrieking. Dinner and shrieking. Dancing and shrieking. And at three, as he had said, the music suddenly stopped and our carriages awaited us.

"We're all going to the after party at Rages," said Cordelia, wrapping a green velvet cloak around her shoulders.

"Forget that," said Antony. "Come back to my place. It's going to be an intimate gathering of glamorous crowned heads." He'd already sent Trudy and Betty off to pass this information on to a few highly select people and to find Debbie, who hadn't been seen since dinner.

"Great," said Cordelia. "See you there."

"We're all going to the after party at Rages," said Plonker, his arm around a busty young woman dressed as a rather short Princess Diana in a blue one-shoulder dress.

"Great," said Antony, nudging me hard in the ribs. "See you there," he said, followed by an aside of "not" to me.

Then I realised the girl with Plonker was Fiona Clarke—so much for Phoebe Trill—and I couldn't stop laughing as Sydney threw another of its hilarious coincidences at me. I wondered for a moment if Rory knew about Fiona and if he would mind if he did, and I was still laughing when Antony pushed me into the limo and said, "Take this," and popped a pill into my mouth followed by a swig from a champagne bottle.

"What was that?" I asked, swallowing.

"Just half an E. Won't do you any harm."

An hour later I knew no pain. I was sitting on the floor of Antony's apartment with my arms round Trudy telling him how much I really loved him. He felt the same, he said. Betty came and lay down beside me and put his beautiful head in my lap. Such a very beautiful head, why had I never realised that before? I sat and stroked it and told him how very much I loved him too. He stroked my knee in reply. I couldn't stop smiling. And when Antony came over holding out a silver bowl containing more of his little half pills, which we all took, he burst out laughing.

"Look at you. You people are pathetic. Are you all in love?"

We nodded and started giggling.

"Oh, shift over," said Antony. "I want to play too." And he wriggled his way in between so we were all lying, laughing, in a heap. Michael and Cordelia came over and joined us. So did Mary and Joanna and Ingrid and Norma, until we were all lying on top of each other like a litter of puppies in a basket, stroking each other's hair. Suddenly the lights started flickering madly.

"Hello Lee!" we all shouted.

Then Michael kissed Cordelia. Then Cordelia kissed me. Then Cordelia kissed Antony. And Antony kissed Michael. And Michael kissed me. And that was how the four of us ended up in bed together.

The others seemed to fade away somewhere and the next thing I knew a married couple, a gay man and myself were all naked in Antony's bed. At the time it seemed the most normal thing in the world. We all loved each other, didn't we? Why wouldn't we go to bed together?

We didn't actually have sex. As Antony made very clear at breakfast in Crown Street the next day, no actual penetration, orgasms or emissions of any kind had occurred, so you couldn't call it sex. Although it was everything but. A great deal of kissing and stroking, to be precise. Feeling like innocent creatures of a new dawn, we argued that there was nothing pervy or sordid about it. Was there?

"Oh no! It doesn't mean we're swingers, does it?" said Michael. He was wearing Antony's clothes—so was I. Cordelia was still in her Titania gown and cloak. Michael buried his head in Cordelia's shoulder and pretended to cry. "Cords, we've only been married two months, we can't be swingers already, can we?"

We all giggled. We were still in love. The pills hadn't worn off yet. Antony and I had held hands all the way to the café. Cordelia was holding my hand as we sat there.

"Am I a lesbian now?" I asked Antony.

"Only if you want to be," he said. "And if you're a lesbian I think I must be one too."

We laughed and laughed and we still couldn't stop smiling or bear to be apart, so after breakfast we all went back to Antony's and got back into his bed—all four of us, this time with undies and T-shirts on—and watched old movies on a huge telly that he kept secretly stashed away in a cupboard. I saw all of *My Fair Lady*, but fell asleep in the middle of *Rebecca*. When I woke up it was dark and Michael and Cordelia had slipped away, leaving a note written in lipstick on Antony's kitchen cupboards: "We will love you always."

Antony brought over some tea and Vegemite toast and got back into bed with me. We looked at each other and started laughing again.

"What are we doing?" I asked him. "They should give out those pills at the United Nations. They could solve all the problems in the world."

"Wait and see how you feel on Tuesday—you might not think so then. It's fun though, isn't it?"

I nodded.

"So who cares?" And he pressed the start button on *To Catch a Thief*. It wasn't until Grace Kelly's beautiful face loomed into view that Antony and I looked at each other and realised we didn't have a clue what had happened to Debbie. We hadn't seen her since dinner at the Ball, when she'd been in high spirits, but certainly not off her face.

"I'll just give her a quick call," said Antony. He put the phone straight down again. "Message bank." Then he rang back and left a message.

"Beds, it's me. Can you please ring me when you get in, it doesn't matter what the time is. I want to hear what you got up to."

Then he rang everyone he could think of who'd been at the ball to try to find out where she'd gone.

"Are you worried about her, Antony?" I asked him after the sixth call. "You're always so cavalier about her shocking behavior—why are you going to these lengths tonight?"

He frowned. "Because normally I keep enough of my brain together to make sure she gets home. I didn't do that last night— and I still feel bad about losing her at Mardi Gras."

"I don't mean to make you feel worse," I said, "but I'm worried about her too. That time I saw the two of you after Mardi Gras there was a really horrible man with her. I've tried to convince myself I was wrong, but I think he injected her. He told me to fuck off when he saw me looking."

"I did check her for track marks like I promised," said Antony. "And I didn't find anything, but I've a horrible feeling you might be right about that. I've been keeping an eye on her pupils."

"Her pupils?"

"Yes. Junkies have pin-prick pupils. Debbie doesn't have those, so I don't think she's using smack. But she has enormously dilated pupils a lot of the time now."

He turned and looked at me. "I think she might be injecting cocaine. Or speed."

I thought of Jenny. "We've got to find her, Antony."

We established that she'd been seen after dinner at the Ball—having an argument with Prince Rainier, who she'd been calling a bore and a party pooper. After about five more calls we managed to track him down, which was good work, because we didn't even know his real name.

The Sydney spider's web has its uses sometimes, I thought. We got him at home.

"Hi Thierry, this is Antony Maybury—you had drinks at my house last night with Debbie Brent . . . What? Oh yes, thank you, we had a lovely time. I was wondering if you knew where Debbie was this evening? Oh, OK. When did you last see her?"

He put the phone down looking significantly more worried.

"They left the Ball not long after dinner. Debbie wanted to find more drugs and Thierry told her he didn't think it was appropriate, so Debbie abused him, and they left."

"Did he take her home?"

"No, this is the part that worries me. She jumped out of the limo in Oxford Street and disappeared into Nightshade."

"Isn't that a horrible nightclub?"

"It's a really horrible nightclub. Full of really horrible drug dealers."

"Oh God." I felt sick.

"Pussy, I don't want to be a drama queen—she's probably just taken her phone off the hook, or she could be round at someone's house watching movies like we are—but I just have a bad feeling."

"Antony, so do I. And I made a promise to someone I'd look out for Debbie. Let's go round to her place and see if she's there."

Antony was already out of bed, pulling on his trousers.

He held my hand in the taxi all the way there. When we arrived outside Debbie's house our spirits lifted for a moment—all the lights were on—but when we knocked and rang, nobody came to the door. Luckily Antony knew where she hid the spare keys and we let ourselves in.

She was in the bedroom. She was blue.

Chapter Twenty-one

"Jenny, I'm so sorry. I should have said something sooner."

It was late Monday afternoon, the day after we'd found her. We were at the hospital.

"Georgia, Georgia, don't cry. You're the best friend Debbie could have. If you and Antony hadn't gone to check up on her she'd be dead now. You two saved her life, the ambulance man told you that. Another few minutes and it would have been too late."

"But Jenny, I suspected months ago that she might be injecting, I just wasn't sure enough . . . I thought I'd imagined it."

She put her arm around me. "It doesn't matter. You were there when it counted. And anyway, if she'd known you were on to her, she would have just got better at hiding it and you might not have saved her the way you did. Really, Johnny and I don't know how we'll ever thank you two."

Antony was getting his reward at that very moment. He was sitting in the hospital cafeteria with Johnny Brent. Although I knew he was desperately upset about Debbie's near-fatal cocktail of cocaine, ecstasy, ketamine and then more cocaine injected, I also knew he'd be storing up every second of Johnny's company for future swooning.

Jenny and I were sitting at Debbie's bedside—Maxine had told me not to come into work when she'd heard the news. Debbie was still unconscious but the doctors said she was going to be OK. Antony and I had stayed at the hospital until her parents made it down from Walton, and after two nights without sleep I was beginning to feel light-headed. I was very relieved when a glowing Antony came back from the canteen with Johnny and said he was taking me home.

He did take me home—his home. And it seemed the most natural thing in the world for us to get back into his bed and cling to each other all night.

I woke up late on Tuesday afternoon to the sound of Antony laughing.

"What? Uh? What is it?" I'm not at my best immediately on waking.

"HA HA HA. I'd forgotten you'd come home with me. I've just woken up to find a woman in my bed. Oh, this is hilarious. How do you feel, Pussy?"

I blinked a bit. "I don't know yet. Terrible, I think."

"Ecstasy Tuesday. I warned you. What we need is another steam bath. Sweat this expensive poison out of our pores."

He went off to the bathroom to switch it all on. I could hear him singing show tunes. Well, I'm glad he's happy, I thought, no doubt at the prospect of an imminent reunion with Johnny Brent. I was just feeling dazed and confused as I lay and reflected on the four men I'd been in bed with since I arrived in Australia nearly seven months before. Oh, five men, I suddenly realised, counting Michael. Impotent. Priapic. Deadbeat. Gay. Married. What a scorecard. If I'd thought my London love life was bad, this was baroque.

When the steam was ready I just sprawled naked on the bathroom floor. I couldn't summon the energy to drape myself over the rocks, as Antony had. He was positively perky.

"Why don't you feel as bad as I do?" I asked him.

"I have a constitution of steel. I can take anything. It will be the death of me." He peered at me through the steam. "You're not going to start crying, are you? I couldn't bear it. That's one of the reasons I'm gay. Less weeping."

"No, I'm not going to start blubbing, but explain this to me, Antony—you know everything. Why is my life so weird? I mean you know all about Rick . . ."

"And now he's in a gay monastery, even weirder."

"Yeah, er . . . anyway, then there was Billy the Unerect Willy and then there was the Priapic Plonker and then the charming chippy Jasper and then I was a free-love lesbian swinger for a night and now I've taken to spending the night with you, my gay best friend. This isn't normal. Why? Why do I attract such weirdos?"

"I guess underneath that Mary Poppins exterior you must be pretty weird yourself, Pussy. This might help."

And he turned the cold shower on—full.

When we got back to the hospital that afternoon, Jenny told us that Debbie had regained consciousness while we'd been away, that she'd cried a lot and asked over and over again for Drew. Heartbreaking. The doctor had put her back to sleep and said it was best for her to rest, to let her body get stronger.

He'd also suggested that it would be good to organise a rota so that there was somebody familiar sitting with Debbie whenever she woke up. Antony and I immediately volunteered to do a daily shift each, so that Jenny and Johnny could get regular meals and sleep. Antony valiantly said he'd take over straightaway and sent me home—my home—to get more rest.

After twelve hours' solid sleep, I felt well enough to go to work the next morning. At six, I returned to the hospital and

Johnny and Jenny went off to get some food. Debbie was sleeping peacefully. I sat and held her hand and talked to her, telling her how much people loved her, how she'd be able to get over Drew's death if only she would grieve for him properly, and how sure I was that eventually she'd fall in love with someone else. Maybe he'd never quite measure up to Drew, I told her sleeping face, because if Rory was anything to go by, the Stewart brothers would be hard to match, but he would be wonderful in his own way.

Then the door opened and Rory Stewart walked in. I desperately hoped he hadn't heard what I'd just been saying and did my usual impression of a recently cooked lobster. He was holding a beaten-up toy rabbit.

"Hi, Georgia." He smiled at me gently. "I've brought Bunny down from the country to keep Debs company." He nodded Bunny's head at me and waved his paw. Then he came over to the bed, kissed Debbie on the cheek and tucked the rabbit under the sheet next to her.

"Drew gave it to her. I thought it might help when she wakes up."

He kissed my cheek, and I felt a small and completely irrational pang of jealousy that he'd kissed Debbie first.

"Did you drive all the way over to the Brents' place to get that rabbit?" I asked him. "And then all the way down here to deliver it?"

He nodded. "But I'm staying down for a while to help you guys out with the roster. It's the least I can do."

We sat and looked at her sleeping peacefully. She was so pale and grey.

"Jenny told me you found her, Georgia. Said you saved her life."

"I don't feel like I deserve any credit—I wish I could have done something sooner, before this happened, but—"

"Come on, Georgia, we all know how impossible she was being. She was set to self-destruct—remember the rodeo? That wasn't rational behaviour. All that counts is that you were there when she needed you most. You knew she was close enough to the edge to go and look for her. That's what mattered."

"Well, it wasn't just me . . . Antony was there too."

"Oh, yeah—who exactly is this Antony? Jenny mentioned him."

"You met him at the races . . ."

Rory's eyes widened.

"I know, I know, he was appalling," I said quickly. "He'd had too much to drink—in fact, he vomited very shortly after you saw us."

"So was *that* Debbie's great friend the dressmaker—the one I've heard so much about?"

I nodded, smiling to myself at the thought of Antony hearing himself described as a dressmaker.

"I thought that guy was your boyfriend," said Rory, smiling his most attractive smile, most of it in the eyes. "I was beginning to wonder about your taste in men, Georgia. Are you still seeing the guy I saw you with at Cordelia's party?"

"No. It ended. No great drama. What about your love life? You looked very busy at the end of that party yourself . . . Has Fiona been up to the farm much?"

He looked uncomfortable. "Yes, she's been a couple of times . . ."

But before I could pursue the issue, Johnny and Jenny came back, closely followed by Antony, who was just arriving for his shift. Why were my conversations with Rory always interrupted, I wondered, as he kissed Jenny and was introduced to Antony, who I noticed gave him a very thorough once-over. And why did we always have to wait to meet by chance?

There wasn't really space for all of us in the room, so it was

284 Maggie Alderson

agreed Jenny and Rory should stay with Debbie, and Antony could go back to the canteen with Johnny. And I could go home. On my own. I know they weren't intentionally leaving me out, but I couldn't help feeling it. Antony practically dragged Johnny from the room so he could have him to himself. Then I went to kiss Jenny and Rory goodbye and as I was about to move away he held on to my arm and whispered: "You look very pretty when you blush, Georgia."

Which made me do it all over again.

Chapter Twenty-two

There was a very strange atmosphere in the *Glow* office. Although she wasn't in there much compared to the rest of us, there was a great gaping hole where Debbie should have been.

Everyone seemed to be talking in hushed voices, and every time I came out of my office there were huddles of people gathered round the photocopier, exchanging half-digested snippets of information about how they'd thought there was something wrong with Debbie, but they hadn't liked to say anything. I suspected they were enjoying the drama and that they felt a bit of malicious pleasure at seeing the spoiled princess cut down to size so publicly.

Finally I couldn't take it anymore. I marched into Maxine's office.

"Can you please do something about those whispering ghouls out there?" I said. "They're behaving like people who slow down to look at a car crash—and more to the point, none of them are doing any work." I knew that would make her sit up. Maxine was very keen on everyone doing as much work as possible.

"Good point, Georgie. I'd noticed a decline in productivity. SERA, COME IN HERE NOW—I WANT YOU TO ORGANISE A STAFF LUNCH . . . TODAY . . . EVERYONE . . . NO EXCUSES."

But the dramatic atmosphere did have its positive side. Maxine had taken charge of organising Debbie's rehab arrangements for the Brents (plenty of opportunities to talk to Johnny, I thought ungenerously) and it made me realise I had a duty to look after Liinda. She was wracked with guilt.

"I should have noticed the signs," she kept saying, rocking back and forwards in her chair. "If anyone could have saved her it was me." She was almost catatonic. "I had no idea she was injecting, George. I should have seen it coming . . ."

It was awful to see her like that, especially when she'd been so happy recently. As I had no intention of going to Maxine's free lunch for the rubberneckers, I insisted Liinda come to BBQ King with me.

"You couldn't have helped her," I said, lighting a cigarette for her and putting it into her mouth as our meals arrived. "To use your own parlance, she had to 'bottom out.' She had—and the great thing is that now you *can* help her—better than anyone. When she comes out of rehab and comes back to work and starts going to fragrance launches and all that crap again, it's going to be really hard for her not to drink, and you'll know exactly how to support her."

"I can take her to group," she said, brightening.

The thought of Debbie at an NA meeting full of "ghastly, ugly, ordinary people," as she would call them, was a bit hard to imagine, but I did have a strong feeling that now it was all out in the open, we were going to see a lot of big changes in Princess Debbie.

Liinda was already looking positively excited at the prospect of inducting another lost soul into the glories of the Twelve-Step programme. Now I had to take the first step towards my own little confession.

"Liinda, if you think you can take another small shock there's something I have to tell you. It's not easy. I feel bad about it."

"It's OK, Georgia," she said, snapping open a can of Diet Coke. "I already know what it is."

"You do?"

"Yeah. You've been seeing Jasper O'Connor since just before Easter." She lifted her can to me and smiled. "Cheers."

"You already know?"

"I've known since you went away with him."

"But you didn't say anything."

"No, I thought I'd wait and see if you wanted to tell me."

"Have I failed some kind of test?"

"Nope. In fact you've done me a huge favour." She took a big drag on her cigarette and blew the smoke straight up into the air. She was enjoying herself.

"I have?"

"Yes. But you obviously have reason to believe it would bother me. So tell me what you know about me and Jasper—or rather, what you've been told."

What should I say? Everyone in Sydney thinks you are a raving psychopath? Or should I give her a sanitised version that wouldn't really help either of us sort this out? I decided on the truth.

"Well, I've been told that you and Jasper were really good friends, until you slept with him once and then you turned into a raging psycho."

Liinda laughed an Antony-style laugh, that turned into a spluttering cough.

"Oh George, that's what I love about you. Total honesty. I'd love to hear you in a group therapy session—when someone was saying, 'I think you might be transferring the anger you feel towards your mother onto me,' you'd just say, 'You're a complete psycho—get back!' "

It was great to see her laughing again.

"And yes, that's exactly what happened. I went stark-raving mad. But, of course, there is more to it than that."

"I thought there might be."

"You see, I really loved Jasper. You know what I mean by that—I really *loved* him. You know how gorgeous he can be, right?"

I nodded. I did. And I didn't appreciate it at the time.

"Anyway, we were very close. We had one of those psychic friendships—he'd start singing a song that I had going round in my head, I'd always know when he was about to call, all that stuff. I really believed we'd get together eventually, but he was so tied up with the whole bullshit of fashion and models. A real woman like me just didn't figure for him."

She took another big drag and sighed.

"So when he slept with me I thought he'd taken a considered decision to move it on to the next stage. I never thought he'd just do it because he was drunk and horny and I was the only woman around. I didn't believe he could do that to me because Jasper knew everything about me." She looked at me. "Everything. All that stuff I told you—and a whole lot more, because you do some pretty stupid things to get your hands on drugs when you're a junkie. You go places you shouldn't go and do things you wish you hadn't. You sleep with people to get drugs, get my drift?"

I did.

"Anyway, all of that makes you very wary of having sex with anyone once you get yourself straight. It doesn't have many lovey-dovey romantic associations anymore. And Jasper knew that. He knew all that and he still thought I would be fine for a quick root, no strings attached."

"Ouch. I can see why you went round the bend."

"Thank you. It doesn't justify how I behaved, but I hope you'll think it explains it a bit."

I nodded. "And I'm sure you understand," I said. "That if I'd known all that I would never have gone near Jasper O'Connor. You did try to warn me off, I know, but just like you said, after all that business with Plonker Pollock, I wanted a nice, easy little affair with someone charming—and Jasper really is charming, as you know."

"He's bloody gorgeous . . ." said Liinda. "And he's a top root too, isn't he?"

Which made us both laugh like Antony.

"Sushi sisters!" I cried and we clinked our drinks.

"Double sushi sisters," said Liinda.

"Oh my god," I said. "So you were Plonkered and then Jaspered."

She nodded.

"No wonder you went insane."

"I'm over it now, but tell me, George—who told you about me stalking him in the first place?"

"A woman called Tania."

"Oh God, don't tell me she's still carrying a torch for him. Unbelievable. She's been chasing Jasper for years. Well, trying to get him back, anyway."

"Get him back?"

"It was worth telling you that to see your face," she said. "They lived together for ten years. Jasper met her when he first went to art school. She was the Older Woman. She's never got over him."

I had my head in my hands. It was all too much.

"Don't worry" said Liinda. "It's just Sydney. I'm glad you had a good time with him for five minutes and I'm also glad it's over. But don't think too badly of Jasper."

"Really? Sounds like he was a total bastard to you."

"No. He's just weak. We should both just remember the nice things about him and feel sorry for him that he keeps messing up his life by being so weak-willed. That's what I've come to realise, and it's all part of the big favour you've done me."

"Explain."

She took another long drag of her cigarette. "You've proved to me that I'm definitely over it. Like I said, I knew you and he had got together the moment it started and I was determined to handle it. I did. So this has been one of the most important proofs I've had that I'm truly well now."

"That's great."

"And that's not all. You know that press tip to Hawaii I went on? I met someone on it. Someone really nice."

"That's fantastic . . ." I think my voice sounded a little unsure.

"No, I'm not imagining it this time. I met him at an NA meeting in Honolulu. He's great. A session drummer. A Buddhist. A really interesting guy. We clicked immediately and he came on the rest of the trip to the other islands with me. He's a Cancerian. Scorpio rising too."

"That's the best news I've heard for ages."

"And you haven't heard it all yet. We've been emailing each other ever since and he's coming over here to see me in two weeks."

"Liinda," I said, grasping her hand. "You deserve this. I really hope it works out for you. What's his name?"

She laughed loudly again.

"Jasper."

My mouth gaped open.

"Honestly—his name is Jasper. But I'm going to make him change it to Jazzpa—the numerology is better."

.   .   .

Debbie was in hospital for a couple of weeks and then, on the expert advice of Maxine (who seemed to know an awful lot about it), she went into a long-term residential clinic for people overcoming drug and alcohol abuse.

As Maxine's army of specialists believed Debbie was likely to be in there for up to six months, Jenny had moved into the Brents' CBD apartment and Johnny came down every weekend to see them both. Debbie was allowed very few visitors and I felt honoured when they called to tell me I was on the list. Antony wasn't on it because he still used drugs, Jenny said, which was quite a reality shock for Mr. Party, although he pretended he was only pissed off because it cut down his opportunities of seeing Johnny.

"Don't you want to know who else is on the list?" Jenny asked, after I'd thanked her for including me.

"Now let me see, who do you know on here?" she said playfully. "There's Maxine, Liinda and Zoe, and a couple of very nice girls Debs went to school with, and my sister, Marie, oh yes—and someone called Rory Stewart. You know him, don't you, Georgia?"

What was that all about? I wondered as I put down the phone, but then I realised I was smiling at the thought of running into him. I shrugged it off. Rory was always charm personified when I saw him, but he'd never made any effort to get in touch with me apart from that, so sod him. And he was probably only coming down to Sydney to see that stupid Fiona Clarke anyway.

The fact was that after hearing the last convoluted revelations of my not-so-private life from Liinda, I'd decided to give sex and romance a big miss for a while and had deliberately downscaled my social life. With Debbie on extended leave, I took on her workload and made the magazine the main focus of my existence. I'd finally found a life-drawing class to go to and I'd joined a benefactors' programme at the Art Gallery. But although I met some nice people at both, Zoe was right, the spark of friendship just wasn't there with them.

I still saw a lot of Antony, but always in a relatively civilised context. I didn't want to be tempted by any more of his pharmaceutical adventures. There was a happy outcome of our free-love ecstasy experience, however—Michael and Cordelia had become good friends and their house became my new haven, replacing Caledonia.

I hadn't spoken to Jasper since the night I'd confronted him, but as we lived so close to each other I kept expecting to run into him on the street in Elizabeth Bay. In the end, inspired by curiosity as much as anything, I went round to Caledonia to see if he was still there. So much for the boutique hotel. They'd bulldozed the place.

Chapter Twenty-three

Far from being a boring duty, my Sunday afternoon visits to see Debbie quickly became one of the highlights of my week. The clinic was in an old house in a quiet suburb and if it was a nice day we'd walk around the gardens—which had beautiful harbour views—and talk.

At first it was hard. Debbie hated being there, hated all the other people in the place and really hated having to share a bedroom with "a stupid whinging drug addict," as she called her roommate. For a few weeks it seemed as though the whole experience was just making her more and more angry. Some afternoons when I visited she just sat in tight-lipped silence, while I told her jokey things that were going on with all her friends. But gradually, as the weeks passed, her attitude began to change, until she started to be excited about what she was doing there. She was even quite friendly to her roommate, Cheryl. There were still down days, but I could see steady progress to the point where Debbie was getting so much out of her therapy, she was starting to sound like Liinda.

"I can't believe I thought I was over Drew," she said one afternoon, as we sat in the watery sunshine. "I really thought that getting off my face was having a good time, and that was my logic—if I was having a good time, I must be over him. How could I have been so dumb?"

"You weren't dumb, Debs. You were in shock."

"You're right. Shock and denial."

I smiled to myself—that was one of Liinda's favourite terms.

"And do you know, Georgie, I really believed that no one would want to know me without him there. I thought it was Drew everyone loved being around—because I loved him so much, I suppose. I really believed I had to be the most beautiful and the most popular, or no one would want to know me. God, when I think of what I did at the Australia Club that time . . ."

She shuddered. I patted her arm.

"Anyway, enough about me—I talk about myself all bloody week in here. I'm sick of hearing about Debbie Brent. Whoever she is."

It was so good to hear her laugh again—a real laugh, not the hysterical drunken shrieks of before.

"Tell me about your life," she said. "I want to live vicariously. Got any pork on your fork?"

"No, I haven't," I said. "I don't want any boy germs in my life for a while."

"That bad, is it?"

"I just need a break from it. I've had such a run of dopes, I'm scared to risk anyone else."

"That's a shame," she said, looking mischievous. "I know someone who'll be very disappointed to her that."

"What are you talking about?"

"Nothing. Nothing. Just a little rumour . . ."

"Well, if the rumour's got a penis attached, I'm not interested, OK?" I think my tone was harsher than I'd meant it to be.

"OK, OK," said Debbie, looking a bit hurt. "I'm sorry, I was only teasing."

I felt ashamed. The last thing Debbie needed was someone snapping at her. She leaned over the garden table and looked closely at me.

"Are you OK, little George? Now that I'm a world expert on the subject, I'd say you were a bit depressed yourself."

I drove home wondering if she was right.

The following week Jenny called me at the office, to invite me up to Walton for the weekend.

"The doctors have said Debbie is well enough to have a weekend at home," she said. "And we'd love it if you would come up on the plane with her. It would save us having to do two return journeys."

Jenny made it sound like I'd be doing them a great favour, but I had a sneaking feeling Debbie had told her I was a bit low and she knew a trip to the homestead would cheer me up. She was right—I couldn't wait for some dog, horse and kangaroo therapy. Just the thing to put my head back on straight, because Debbie was right—I was miserable.

The country around Walton was just as beautiful in early spring as it had been in late summer, with the first tips of green coming through the gold. It was so good to be out of the city. On the way from the airport Debbie and I stuck our heads out the windows of Johnny's four-wheel drive and sucked in lungfuls of pure country air.

That night we had a quiet supper in the kitchen, with only mineral water to drink, to show solidarity with Debbie, who'd given up alcohol and cigarettes as well as drugs. The next morning she and Johnny went out riding and Jenny and I went for a long walk with Choccie and one of the cattle dogs. In the afternoon Debbie slept and I helped Jenny make a cake.

"We're going out for dinner tonight," Jenny told me as I weighed out the dried fruit and she sifted the flour. "The Stewarts have invited us over."

My heart did a high jump that would have impressed Scooby.

"Rory doesn't know you and Debbie are up here, so Margaret—that's his mother—and I thought it would be a nice surprise for him."

A nice surprise for me too, I thought, and unless I was mistaken, I saw Jenny's eyes twinkling.

"Does Debbie know?" I asked her. "Won't it stir things up rather a lot going over to their place?"

"Well, that's all part of the reason we're going," said Jenny, wiping her forehead on her arm. "We talked it through with her doctors and we reckon it's all part of the process."

We set off for the Stewarts' place at seven, as it took over half an hour to get there. I sat in the back with Debbie, who was looking a bit drawn. When we came to a pair of large gates with a sign saying "Welland Heights," the name of their property, I squeezed her hand.

"OK?" I asked her.

She turned her head and nodded quickly, squeezing my hand back and holding on to it.

When we got to the house—long and low like Bundaburra, with verandahs covered in purple wisteria—Mr. and Mrs. Stewart were waiting for us at the front door. Andrew, Rory's father, looked better than I'd expected. He was leaning on a stick and, although he had the slightly lopsided face that a stroke can leave in its wake, he could walk slowly.

Debbie sprang from the car before Johnny had finished parking it and ran over to them. They stood holding on to each other for a few moments, but far from being the tearful wreck I'd feared she would be, I could see that Debbie was excited.

"Oh, it's so good to see you," she was saying. "You look great, Andrew. You'll be back up on a horse any minute if you carry on getting better like that."

An old black Labrador padded round the corner and came straight up to Debbie.

"Blackie," she cried, falling to her knees and covering his grizzled head in kisses.

"That's Drew's dog," said Jenny, quietly. "He wasn't very original with names, God love him."

We went inside, with Johnny staying behind to help Andrew negotiate the steps. Debbie was like a little girl, running around to see if everything was the same and, to her great satisfaction, it was. She looked sad for a moment when she saw Drew's old polo boots on the back porch, but she just stroked them and sighed and gave Margaret another big hug.

"It's so good to see you," she told her. "I can't believe I've stayed away so long."

"That's all right," said Margaret Stewart, a silver-haired woman in her mid-sixties with a deeply lined, but very kind face. "You've come back at last, that's all that matters."

Margaret had made a special non-alcoholic punch in Debbie's honour and we went out onto the back verandah to drink it. The view was breathtaking, a much broader perspective than you got from Bundaburra. The vista looked strangely familiar to me and I suddenly realised where I'd seen it before—in Rory's drawing in the Art Gallery.

Where was Rory? I wondered.

"Rory will be along in a minute," said Andrew, in his slightly slurred voice, as though he'd heard my thoughts. "He's gone to pick his friend up at the airport."

What friend? I wondered and saw Jenny and Debbie exchange a quick glance.

Rory didn't appear until we were all seated at the long, shiny table in the dining room. He did a cartoon double-take when he saw Debbie and rushed over to kiss her.

"Debs!" he said. "How great to see you back at Welland. You look fantastic. Welcome back."

He did another double-take when he saw me, but didn't look quite so thrilled.

"Georgia!" he said, weakly. "You're here too. That's great. What a lovely surprise."

He was saying all the right things, but it didn't ring true, and I saw him glance nervously over my shoulder at the door. I turned round to see Fiona Clarke standing there.

"Hello everyone," she said, bustling over to give Andrew and Margaret showy kisses.

"Hello Fiona, dear," said Margaret. "Now, do you know all these people? This is Jenny Brent and her daughter, Debbie. You know Debbie, don't you, and do you know Geor—"

"Oh yes," said Fiona, brightly, not looking at me. "Hi Debs, great to see you. Are you out of hospital?"

Debbie looked at her as if she were a large pile of excrement and didn't even bother to reply.

"Hi, Jenny," continued Fiona, unabashed. "I've heard so much about you from Rory . . . and you . . ." she said, mincing around the table in her high heels and sticking out her hand, "must be the famous Johnny Brent. *Very* pleased to meet *you*."

I could see Debbie mouthing "*very* pleased to meet *you*" at her plate with her eyes crossed. Jenny nudged her hard. Rory came down and sat next to me, looking extremely uncomfortable, while Fiona wriggled in next to Johnny.

"Isn't this nice?" I could hear her saying. Not really, I thought. Not very nice at all. But at least Andrew and Margaret didn't seem to notice that Debbie was completely ignoring Rory and Fiona, or that Fiona was ignoring me and that Johnny Brent was clearly feeling no pain. Fiona had him enraptured as she prattled on, shrugging off her jacket to reveal the full magnificence of her mighty breasts beneath a tight white T-shirt.

As Fiona's giggles increased in volume, I saw Jenny starting to look a bit tense as she made determined conversation with the Stewarts. Eventually Debbie got up and whispered something to Margaret and left the room. I turned to Rory with the brightest smile I could muster.

"Sorry to spring myself upon you," I said. "I didn't know we were coming over here until this afternoon."

"No, yes, no," he said, his eyes glancing nervously from me to Fiona Clarke, who was now leaning with one elbow on the table, gazing up into Johnny Brent's eyes.

I wondered if it was jealousy or embarrassment that was making Rory behave so oddly and whether he knew that his girlfriend had been seen leaving the Cointreau Ball with Nick Pollock.

"The country here looks gorgeous at this time of year," I said, wanting to give him a break. He looked wretched. "It reminds me of a really beautiful pastel drawing I saw last time I was in the Art Gallery in New South Wales."

He looked surprised.

"Your drawing, Rory. You're so modest. I couldn't believe it when I saw it hanging there. I'd be handing out leaflets in George Street if I had a picture in the Gallery."

"Oh well, you know, I wouldn't want to big-note myself. Did you really like it?"

"I loved it—even before I saw your name on the plaque. It totally captures what's out there." I nodded to the back of the house.

Margaret and Jenny were clearing away the dessert plates and I sprang up to help. Jenny practically pushed me back into my seat.

"We'll do this," she said. "You carry on talking. Margaret is serving coffee on the verandah, when you're ready."

Fiona and Johnny were still locked in conversation—or rather he was talking, telling all his old polo stories that everyone else had heard a million times, while Fiona gazed at him adoringly. Rory glanced at them and then back at me.

"Do you want to see around the place?" he asked me.

"Won't it be dark?" I said.

"Not very. It's a full moon."

He took us out through the kitchen door and I looked straight up at the sky. The moon was a huge, plump disc with a butter-yellow glow. The night sky was vast and velvety and scattered with more stars than I'd ever seen. So many more than you could see anywhere in Sydney. The air had a wonderful smoothness to it, cool and caressing on my skin.

"Are you cold?" asked Rory, seeing me rub my arms, exposed in a short-sleeved cardigan.

"No, it feels nice. I think I'm having a moon bath."

"Do you feel like a little walk? I want to show you what's at the top of the ridge. What have you got on your feet?"

I lifted my long skirt to reveal my riding boots.

"You'll be right," he said, softly.

We walked through a formal garden with rose arbours and then went through a small wrought-iron gate. There was a dam off to the right, which Rory said was great for swimming in when it got really hot. Then we walked along a rough road, going steadily uphill.

Although it was dark and dead quiet, the country around us felt alive. I could tell there was a lot going on out there even though we couldn't see it. After a few hundred yards we turned off the road onto a path through the rough bush.

"You OK?" asked Rory. I just nodded. Words didn't seem necessary out there. As we walked the path got steeper and steeper and we fought our way through thick stands of trees and great knots of tangled bushes.

"Bloody blackberries," said Rory. "Introduced. Out of control."

The path was getting quite rough underfoot and I could see it was going to get even steeper near the top of the ridge. I lost my footing for a moment on a loose stone and it seemed like the most natural thing in the world for Rory to take my hand to steady me. He didn't let go of it.

When we got to the top of the ridge, I just stood and stared. The country rolled away on the other side—fold after fold of wooded land, as far as the eye could see, lit only by the full moon and the stars. There were no church spires, no pylons, no motorways and truck stops, no fast-food joints. Just endless miles of virgin earth.

"Oh Rory," I said. "This is amazing." I couldn't do it justice. "Look at it. It just goes on forever."

I turned and looked at him. He was smiling softly. Smiling at me in that fond, gentle way I'd grown to know and like so much over the past few months. He was looking at me and I was gazing back, and I could sense that we were imperceptibly moving closer together. My heart was pounding. I wondered if he could hear it as his head moved slowly towards mine. Without thinking I closed my eyes, but I could still sense him coming closer, as he turned his body towards me. And at the exact moment I thought I was going to feel his lips touch mine, he suddenly took a step backwards.

I opened my eyes in shock. We just stood there, swallowing and looking at each other. He had dropped my hand and I felt brutally cut off from him. We both took deep breaths, waiting for the other one to say something and then, of course, we spoke at the same time.

"They'll be wondering . . ." I said.

"We'd better get back," said Rory.

And without another word we turned and walked back the

way we'd come. He took my hand down the steep bit again, but dropped it as soon as possible, as if it was going to electrocute him. And we didn't say a word until we were about to step into the house.

Mustering all my dignity I looked up at him and said, politely, "Thank you for showing me that, Rory. It was really beautiful."

He didn't reply, and at that moment Fiona Clarke came bustling out.

"Where have you two been?" she asked in a piqued tone. "We've been looking everywhere for you."

"I was just showing Georgia—" Rory started to explain, but she came and grabbed his hand and pulled him inside.

"Come on, the Brents are leaving," she said, giving me a death stare over her shoulder.

"There you are," said Margaret Stewart, as we walked into the drawing room. "You're just in time, Georgia. You were about to miss your ride to Bundaburra."

Jenny and Debbie were sitting on the sofa looking tense. Debbie's eyes were a little red, but Johnny seemed to be his usual cheerful self. Fiona Clarke had both arms locked around Rory's waist and was holding on to him like he was about to take off.

"We'll be going, then," said Jenny, standing up. "Thank you so much, Margaret, Andrew. It's been a lovely evening."

Debbie got up too.

"Bye, you two," she said. "I'll come back again soon. I'm sorry I got so upset earlier, but seeing Drew's old bedroom . . . you know."

She went over to Andrew and knelt at his knees. He smoothed her hair and patted her back.

"That's alright, my pet," he said. "You just come and see us whenever you feel like it."

And we left, with the Stewarts standing on the verandah to wave us off, Fiona Clarke still clinging to Rory like he was a life raft.

"That Fiona's a nice girl," said Johnny before we were even halfway down the drive.

Debbie just groaned, and Jenny turned round in her seat to look at us and shake her head.

"Oh, Johnny Brent," she said, turning back and slapping him on the thigh. "You always were an easy lay."

I could see him grinning happily in the rear-view mirror.

After Debbie had been in the clinic for nearly four months, Maxine told me she'd heard from Johnny (how she loved casually telling me "Johnny just called"—she was as bad as Antony). Apparently Debbie was coming out of the clinic that weekend and would be going up to live with her parents on the farm until she felt ready to return to work.

I normally visited her on Sundays but I didn't want to miss saying goodbye, so I told Jenny I'd pop over on Saturday instead. It was a beautiful November day—my first Sydney spring—and the purple haze of the jacaranda trees all over the city was a revelation to me.

It was a relief to have my sense of joyful discovery return, because Debbie had been spot on, I had been feeling really low. I'd found the winter months so blank. Sydney in August just didn't seem to have much point. It was too cool to go to the beach, but not cold enough to rug up, eat crumpets and be cosy. It had been a dready winter, not a bracing one, and I felt an intense yearning for the crispness of a frosty morning.

And, while I hated to admit it, I had been affected by the unpleasant ending with Jasper. I certainly hadn't been in love with him, but our little affair had been a lot of fun. Those things he'd said to me that last time we met had really niggled away at me until I had to admit it—I'd been using him and I was just as bad as Plonker in my own way.

On top of that I couldn't shake off a sense of disappointment regarding Rory. He always seemed so pleased to see me, but something invariably got in the way. It had felt so right that night at his parents' place, but then he'd pulled away again. He clearly preferred Fiona Clarke to me, I decided, and I was just going to have to accept it. But on top of everything else, it felt like one romantic disappointment too many.

And now I had very mixed feelings about saying goodbye to Debbie. I was delighted she was so much better, and thrilled for her parents that she'd be spending some time with them, but I had something else on my mind that made me want to weep as I hugged her for the last time in that funny little room.

"I'm so proud of you, Debs," I said. "You've come so far. Keep on getting better."

"No worries about that," she said. "I'll soon be back at *Glow* to drive you all mad again—and thanks, George. You saved my life—literally—and you've been a wonderful friend. I'm going to make sure I find you the best bloody man on earth . . ." She had that cheeky look again. "Can I be your bridesmaid?"

"Oh, get out of here," I said and left quickly, before I really started crying.

By the time I hit the car park I was bawling and had no choice but to give in to it. I was leaning on the roof of my car, my body wracked with sobs, when I felt an arm go round my waist and someone stroke my hair. It was Rory. The last person I wanted to see me all frog-eyed and snotty.

"Hey, Georgia, what's wrong?" he said, turning me round and holding me the way I'd seen him holding Debbie at the rodeo that time. The way I expected him to hold me on that hill-top at Welland. It felt every bit as good as I thought it would.

His arms felt like a safe harbour. And that just made me sob even more. Lucky, lucky Fiona Clarke.

"Tell me what's wrong," he kept saying. "You know you can trust me."

"Oh Rory, it's just all kinds of stuff. I don't like saying goodbye."

"But surely you're going to come up and see Debs at the farm. It's not like you're saying goodbye to her forever."

That's what you think, I thought and started wailing some more. The nicer he was to me, the more I cried.

Just when it was starting to get really messy—I'd soaked his shoulder—I heard another pair of feet crunching on the gravel. I was too embarrassed to look up. Maybe it was one of the doctors from the clinic with a straitjacket for me.

"Jenny," said Rory. "Georgia is really upset and I don't seem to be making it any better. Perhaps you should take over?"

He lifted up my puffy red face and looked at me intently. How humiliating.

"I'll see you later, Georgia, OK?" he said. "Or up in Walton, very soon. Promise? Scooby's dying to see you."

Well, that just set me off some more. After kissing the side of my head—cue more hysterics, why did this man keep torturing me?—Rory let go of me and Jenny put her arm round my shoulder. Her motherly warmth calmed me down and once I'd stopped sobbing quite so violently she took me to the clinic's kitchen and made a cup of tea.

We sat outside and, as I tried to collect myself, we watched birds diving around in their mad mating dances.

"They remind me of my Sydney friends," I said to Jenny, still gulping a bit. "Totally wrapped up with flapping around in circles, getting nowhere with a great deal of fuss."

She smiled at me and then wisely changed the subject. "How do you think Debbie's doing?"

"I think she's doing brilliantly," I said, between sniffs. "She must be if they think she's OK to leave. Her shine seems to have come back. And she's got those pictures of Drew up everywhere now. I think she's come a long way. What about you?"

"Same. I think she's going to be able to get over Drew better than she ever could have without help. And in the end, she's going to be a much nicer person than she was. We did indulge her terribly, Georgia."

"Now don't you start blaming yourself," I said. "Debbie was always going to be the centre of attention, looking the way she does."

"I guess you're right. Like her father . . . Anyway, it will be great to have her at Bundaburra for a while and it's such a comfort to know that when she returns to work she has friends like you and Liinda to look after her."

And it was only because I'd cried so much already that I managed to keep it together when I told her.

"I don't think I'll be there, Jenny."

"Why not? Are you getting another job?"

I shook my head. "My year's contract with *Glow* is up in the middle of January . . ." I took a deep breath. "I'm going back to England."

Jenny looked amazed. "Do you have to?"

"No. Maxine's furious. She's offered me the world to stay, but . . . I want to go home."

"Really? I thought you were happy here—you seem to have made such a life for yourself. Everybody adores you."

That did start me off again.

"Oh, Jenny, I feel like I've stuffed everything up. Coming to Australia was such a wonderful opportunity and I've just thrown it all away."

Jenny knew exactly when to say nothing and let you vomit it

all up. So I did, between snivelling and blowing my nose and sniffing and generally being mucal.

"I can't tell you how thrilling it all was when I first arrived here," I told her. "I felt reborn. Sydney is so beautiful and everyone was so friendly—even going to buy a newspaper was fresh and new. Then I went to this great party and met all these fun people, who felt like family immediately, and I met loads of gorgeous men and everything was wonderful. Then it all seemed to fall apart. You know I came here after a five-year relationship broke up, don't you? We were engaged, actually."

Jenny nodded. "Debbie told me."

"I bet she did," I said with a teary smile. "Anyway, I had this opportunity for a whole new life and I feel I've made stupid choices all over again, like I did in London. It's just that I'm attracted to such excessive people."

"In my daughter's case, I'm very glad of that."

"I don't mean making friends with Debs was a mistake."

"I didn't take it that way. You meant men, didn't you?"

And then I started howling again. The full *wa wa wa*. Jenny put her arm round me.

"There seemed to be so many perfect ones when I got here," I sobbed. "And then they all turned out to be just as nuts and complicated as the men in London, only in different ways."

"So, let me get this straight—you're going back to England because you think you've wrecked your chances here by hanging out with the wrong people and no decent man is going to look at you now?"

I nodded miserably.

"And you don't think there are any decent straight single men in Sydney anyway. Right?"

I stared at her with my froggy eyes and nodded again.

"Well, I don't think you've made such terrible mistakes,"

Jenny continued. "And I know at least one very decent man who likes you a lot."

"Who?"

"Rory Stewart."

"Rory? But he's got a girlfriend."

"Fiona Clarke? That ended ages ago. He saw through her very quickly—he just needed to let off steam. And anyway, you were seeing that druggy guy at the time."

I put my head in my hands.

"That's what I mean about stupid choices."

"It doesn't matter—it hasn't affected Rory's feelings for you. He knows Fiona was a bit of a trashy girl, so why shouldn't you have had a fling with a bit of a trashy guy?"

"But what about when she was up at Welland that time?"

Jenny laughed. "You mean the time when she was practically having it off with my husband at the dinner table?"

"Yes." I laughed too.

"You know what happened that night? She had invited herself up. She rang Rory from Tamworth airport, just before we arrived for dinner, and told him to come and pick her up."

I looked at her stupidly.

"And of course Rory is too nice a guy to tell her to get back on the next flight. So he picked her up and was polite to her while we were there, like the gentleman that he is, and the next morning he put her back on a plane and told her he didn't ever want to see her again."

I sat absorbing this information. Such a gentleman that he couldn't kiss me while she was still there perhaps?

"But he's never even asked for my phone number. He's had so many opportunities. I just thought he didn't feel that way about me."

"Well, I think he does and there could be lots of reasons he hasn't asked for it. Maybe he's a bit scared of you. Look . . ."

She got out a pen and wrote a number on a paper napkin and put it in my bag.

"That's Rory's number. Why don't you do what you're always advising your readers to do and ring him? You've got nothing to lose—how does it go? If he doesn't like you ringing him he's not worth having anyway?"

"You really do read the magazine," I said. She'd made me smile again. "I'll think about it. Although I don't think any of us take the advice we give out so freely in *Glow*. I hope our readers are happier than we all are . . . Anyway, I am going to go back to England, Jenny. I've made my mind up. But thanks for listening."

"Well, you just make sure you come up and see us before you go. Oh and by the way—remember when we spoke to your brother about coming out to work for Johnny?"

"Yes, but he told me he wasn't coming . . ."

"That was all part of the surprise," said Jenny, grinning. "He is coming—next month.. We've been saving it as a thank-you for all you've done for Debs. So you'll have one of your family here for Christmas."

Hamish arrived in the middle of December and he was the best Christmas present I could have had. From the moment he landed I could tell he was going to love Australia as much as I did, and having him to share it with meant I could enjoy my last few weeks, rather than moping around feeling sad about leaving. I was determined to make the most of our time together before he went up to Walton after Christmas.

When I met him at the airport he was already wearing an Akubra hat. He'd bought it in advance so he could wear it in a bit before arriving at the farm.

"Didn't want to be the pink English git in a new hat," he said as I led him to the car. Suddenly he stopped and started sniffing deeply.

"The air smells different, Porgie. I can smell the gum trees. Does the water really go down the plughole the wrong way? I was trying to check it out as we crossed the equator in the plane—they have these really useful maps on Qantas that show you where you are—but it didn't work, and apparently there was a big queue forming."

It was a hot Sunday, so I took him straight to Bondi for breakfast. I had to physically restrain him from buying a surfboard there and then, he was so eager to try it.

"I don't think it's as easy as they make it look, Hame," I said.

"It can't be that hard." He was standing up, bending his knees and following the moves of the surfers out to sea. "It's just balance and I can stand up on a galloping horse . . . What are all these weird coffees?" He was looking at the menu. "I just want a white coffee, not a gospel choir. Long black, short black . . . flat white? Is that a honky who can't sing?" Then he went very quiet. Some Bondi babes were walking past in crop tops and tiny shorts.

"I say, Big Bum," he said. "Gorgeous girls here . . ."

Antony loved him. Hamish turned up at the apartment to meet him for the first time in a polo shirt bearing the legend C.R.A.C.—Cirencester Royal Agriculture College—and Antony was plum gone.

"Dolores—you are *fluttering*," I hissed cruelly in his ear as he fussed over long drinks in the kitchen. In the meantime Hamish was regaling Betty and Trudy with tall tales of his adventures in the Argentinian pampas. He really knew how to tell a story, and he loved an audience.

"Well, Pussy, you didn't warn me he was *totally* divine," said Antony, putting an extra shot of vodka in a drink I guessed was destined for Hamish.

"Hame? He's just a silly old horsehead," I said fondly. "And you'd seen pictures of him."

"Well, it didn't fully prepare me," said Antony. "He's a Scottish Johnny Brent." And he swept off to flutter around Horsehead some more.

We had a glorious Christmas. I took Hamish to the Fish Market at three a.m. on Christmas Eve and we bought a tray of mangoes, which we ate standing in the water at Camp Cove on Christmas morning, letting the juices run everywhere.

After a celebratory champagne breakfast with Michael and Cordelia, we went home and opened our presents—a pair of moleskins from me to him, an illegally imported haggis and a tin of my grandmother's shortbread for me, plus three issues of *The Beano*. Then I dressed him up like a country boy at the Easter Show in his moleskins, newly acquired RM Williams boots, striped shirt, his old school tie and his Akubra hat. After a few days on the beach he already had the pink cheeks and really looked the part. I thought Antony was going to pass out when he opened the door.

It was a very gay Christmas, and Hamish was perfectly happy. He didn't judge anyone, as long as they weren't boring, and none of Antony's pals could be accused of that. It was the usual shrieking and drinking affair, and with Hamish there I felt free to let myself go again like I used to. As always we ended up dancing.

And when I turned round to see Horsehead doing the bump with Dolly, I knew he was going to fit in perfectly.

Chapter Twenty-four

"How about 'How to Know When You've Found the One'?"

"That's a great idea, Zoe. We'll go with that. Any other ideas?"

"Ten Signs He's Perfect?"

"That's good too, Liinda. Perhaps we could use both of them, or we could save one for later in the year. Make a note of them, would you?"

"Or how about this . . . 'How You Know He's the One—Take Our Test' . . . or—hang on, I've got it—'You Know He's Perfect—Take Our Test and Prove It.'"

"Oh, that's great too, Liinda. I like all of them. What do you think, Georgie?"

What to Do When All Your Colleagues Have Gone Ga Ga? I was lost for words, I couldn't think of anything. They'd all gone nuts.

"Well, they're all . . . really . . . nice, Maxine," I said. "But they don't present much of a challenge to the reader. I mean it's a sweet problem to solve—Is He Mr. Right?—but does it make you want to grab the magazine?"

"Oh, it doesn't all have to be bad news, does it?" said Maxine, passing round the Tim Tams. "We can use an upbeat idea to sell a magazine too, you know. Some people do find happiness in love."

There was a collective sigh so intense it nearly blew me out of Maxine's office.

"I know," she said. "We're one person short with Debs not here—let's get Seraphima's input. Good to get some young energy. SERA DARLING, COULD YOU POP IN PLEASE?"

Seraphima came in. She was always such a pretty little thing, but these days she seemed to have added some ingredient X to the package. Corny as it sounded, in the twelve months I'd been working on *Glow* she'd turned from a girl into a woman.

"Got any ideas for coverlines, sweetie?" said Maxine, with her legs on her desk and her arms behind her head. "We're planning the next six months of issues and we need some real winners."

Sera narrowed her bright blue eyes.

"How about 'Taming the Monster—Getting the One Who Got Away from Everyone Else'?"

My jaw was in Tasmania. The line was a bit long, but we could easily polish it up—the point was it had so much punch.

"That's great, Seraphima," said Maxine, sitting up. "Did you get that down, Georgie? Got any other ideas?"

"The Fine Art of Pussy-Whipping—An Expert Tells All."

Maxine and I just looked at her in amazement. We both knew raw talent when we saw it—and we were seeing it.

"Or," she was enjoying herself now, "Girls on Top—Running a Relationship Your Way."

We clapped.

"This is fantastic, girls," said Maxine. "We've really moved things along. Isn't it amazing what a difference a day makes?"

She was serious.

"I'm seeing the dawn of a whole new age on *Glow*: positive

coverlines. Empowerment, not solidarity in misery. Go, girlfriends! Go and make these stories happen. You see what you'll be missing, Georgie? Are you sure we can't persuade you to stay?"

I shook my head sadly.

"OK, fuck off then. All of you. Except Seraphima." She was smiling. "Can you stay back, please?"

While Sera was occupied in Maxine's office negotiating a pay rise and a new job title, I took the opportunity to inspect the incredible number of bouquets and floral displays which were on her desk. I watched Zoe and Liinda disappear to their offices with exotic lilies and a flowering cactus respectively, and then had a good nosey at the others. There was a huge architectural display for Maxine (done by Cordelia, I noted) and, biggest of all, an enormous bunch of long-stemmed dark red roses for Sera. I looked at the card—I had to.

"To my angel—gloria in excelsis. N."

Mmm. Very interesting. Wonder who N was. Norman? Nigel? Neddy? There was one more bunch—they were for me. Hurray! They were from Nivea. "Thank you for the great writeup of the body range." You're welcome.

I couldn't believe it was my last week on *Glow*. A couple of days to finish packing up the unit and that would be it. My year in Australia would be over. Except for one thing—my leaving party.

One year later. Same room, same hat and a lot of the same faces. Except this time, I knew who most of them were. I was back at Danny Green's Australia Day party, which was also my official leaving celebration. When he'd heard I was going back to London, Danny had rung up and kindly offered to "lend" me his party to say goodbye to everyone. So here I was, back in his studio in Elizabeth Bay, wearing my pink feathery hat and my Pucci catsuit, which seemed the appropriate thing to do. That was how I'd looked when I met most of them for the first time; that was how I wanted them to remember me.

I'd also decided that I wanted to arrive at the party on my own as I had done the year before, to see how different it felt. The answer was: very. The second I put my big feathery head around the door a huge cheer went up and I was immediately surrounded by throngs of people wishing me well and asking for my address in London. Good job Antony had given me some beautifully engraved change-of-address cards as a leaving present. I remember with a smile how he'd bobbed up when I was standing by the drinks table a year ago, but now I couldn't even see him.

I could see Danny, who was wearing the Mad Hatter's teapot on his head, complete with dormouse. Betty and Trudy were resplendent in two of Antony's more lavish hats; Cordelia was wearing a big straw number swathed in ivy and Michael was wearing his barrister's wig.

Antony had done the guest list for me and, looking round the room, I could see all the people who had meant something to me over the past year—including Jasper, wearing a giant red and white spotted toadstool on his head. He came over and gave me a sloppy kiss on the cheek. I was really pleased to see him.

"Pinkie personified," he said. "As perfectly pink and perky as ever. I'm sorry I was so horrible to you that day. I felt like a rat in a trap and it made me shitty. Anyway, I enjoyed our kooky times together. You're still a babe, by the way. A babe with a brain, that's my Pinkie."

"Thanks, Jasper." I kissed him back. "I'll never forget our Blue Lagoon. It was very special. And you weren't that horrible to me—I deserved it. By the way, I'm sorry about Caledonia, I couldn't believe my eyes when I saw it."

"Bastards, aren't they? But that's OK, we're living in a boat shed on Scotland Island. It's pretty cool. See you later in the Persian room, Pinkus."

And off he went, while I wondered who the "we" was.

I looked around the room again. Maxine was there, wearing a man's fedora with a card saying "PRESS" tucked into the band, and at last I was able to meet the man who was making her so gooey at work. He turned out to be one of the therapists from Debbie's rehab clinic—which explained Maxine's expertise on the subject.

Zoe was there in a nurse's hat, holding hands with Dr. Ben, who was wearing a green theatre cap on his head. And there was Liinda, with her Jazzpa in tow—he'd moved to Sydney and they were living together in numerological, astrological, NA bliss. No need for him to put on a hat specially for the party. He was a Rastafarian and always wore an enormous knitted red, green and gold tea cosy affair to contain his dreadlocks. Liinda had put a red gerbera, a marigold and a big green leaf in her stack of hair to match.

Looking round the crowded studio, at all these people I adored, I knew I should have been having a fabulous time, but it was actually a bit of a blur. What do you say to people you've seen every other night for a year and suddenly may never see again? I felt like I was mouthing the same thing over and over again to everybody: "Yes, I'm really sad to be leaving. Yes, I'll come back and see you. Please come and stay with me in London. Yes, here's my address. Yes, I have email. Love you too."

I was starting to feel like a walking, talking Georgia doll. Pull the string and hear her talk. My face was aching from smiling and I was beginning to remember how much I'd hated my London leaving party. I was very glad when Liinda rushed over and grabbed me.

"Quick, come over here, I've got to tell you something before you see it and have a heart attack and die."

"What?"

"Sera's here, right?"

"Yes . . ."

"With her new boyfriend."

"Poor little pussy-whipped Nigel, or Norman, or whoever it is."

"It's Nick Pollock."

"Plonker Pants On Fire Pushead Priapic Pollock?"

"Yes, the very one."

"If he hurts that little girl I will personally have him killed . . ." I began.

"Georgia—it's not like that, he's ga-ga over her. He's her slave. She met him at a party and he tried the handwriting analysis bullshit on her and she told him to get lost. She said she'd heard all about what a fuckwit he was and she wanted nothing to do with him. He's had to pursue her relentlessly and she still only returns half of his phone calls."

"Well, I'll be buggered."

And there they were. Seraphima was wearing a very small white dress with a large pair of white feather wings and a gold halo. She looked completely angelic—until you noticed the fierce Gucci stilettos on her feet. Plonker was wearing devil's horns and was looking at her "like a monkey looks at a banana," as Liinda put it.

Grinning, I turned to see Jasper walk over to the bar with Tania on his arm, wearing a smaller version of his toadstool. She was holding on to him very tightly. Guess that explained who the "we" was. Suddenly I realised that everyone was in neat little pairs. Well, good on them, but I didn't even have Antony to play with. Where was he? I looked round the room again and saw another happy new couple: Billy Ryan, wearing exactly what he'd been wearing when I met him a year before, except that this time he had a new accessory—Lizzy Stewart, in a matching hat.

"Georgie, there you are," said Billy. "We can't believe you're going back to London before we've even had a chance to have you over for supper. When are you leaving? You will come back and see us, won't you? Can we have your address, in case we need somewhere free to stay in London? Just kidding. Have you got email?"

I answered all the standard questions and then Lizzy asked me one which surprised me.

"Is Rory here yet?"

"I haven't seen him," I said. "I . . . er . . . I didn't know he was coming."

"Oh, he's definitely coming," said Billy. "He's driving down with your brother and Deb—ow, why did you kick me, Lizzy?"

"Really? Hamish never told me. He said it was just him and Debs . . ."

"I think they just got here," said Lizzy, glaring at Billy as three more Akubras in various states of repair walked in.

"Porgie Pie!" said Hamish, rushing over, and then it all deteriorated into a mess of hellos and kisses and how-gorgeous-to-see-yous. When we'd all calmed down again Rory went off to get everyone drinks and Hamish was stolen by Trudy and Betty who wanted to hear all about his adventures on the farm. I had a good look at Debbie. She looked wonderful, and even more golden than before now that the strain had gone from her eyes.

"Debs, you look great," I said.

"Thank you, I feel great. No drink, no drugs, no men, no free facials—I haven't felt this good in years. It's fun at the farm with Hamish around. He's a great guy; Dad loves him. It's like having a brother of my own. Oh, by the way—he told me it's Georgia, not Georgie. Sorry about that."

"Doesn't matter, I'm used to it . . ." I started to say, until I realised that she wasn't listening to me. She was watching Hamish, his arms flailing around as he entertained Trudy and Betty with bogus bush adventures.

Rory returned with the drinks, but before he could hand them round Hamish had come back to grab Debbie to dance with him. It was "Disco Inferno"—one of his favourites.

"Would you like three glasses of champagne and a mineral water?" Rory asked me, as we watched them disappear.

"Thank you. Although I'm being a little bit more careful about my alcohol consumption than I was at this party last year . . ." We looked at each other.

I felt self-conscious, remembering Jenny's words and the night on the hilltop.

"Your brother's a good bloke, Georgia," he said. "The Brents love having him and he's been over to our place a few times too. My folks like him a lot too. He really fits in up there."

We turned from each other to see Hamish and Debbie on the dance floor. Interesting, I thought.

"I can't believe it's only a year since this party," I said.

"It's a year since we met, Georgia," said Rory.

"And look," I said, hurriedly, "there's Billy and Lizzy together. Who would have thought it, a year ago?"

"You're telling me!" He laughed and shook his head, fondly.

"And now you're going back home to London, so who knows where you'll be in a year's time, eh Georgia? When do you actually leave?"

"Tomorrow afternoon."

"Good old QF1, eh?" he said, raising his glass and clinking mine.

"Yes—how did you guess?"

"Afternoon flight to London, had to be QF1. All packed and ready?"

"Everything except this hat."

"What have you done with all your drawings?" he said, leaning against the wall. "Are you taking them home?"

"How did you know about them?"

"Lizzy gave me your cow sketch. It's really good. I draw cows too, you know."

"She told me. I can't believe she gave it to you—it was just for fun. I'm not a proper artist like you."

"Well, I like it. I've got it on the fridge door."

Suddenly I felt really shy again and was quite relieved when a big pack of Antony's friends arrived and swamped me with the usual hugs and questions. By the time I'd finished answering them, Rory had disappeared. Typical, I thought.

I stayed at the party until about one and then slipped away without telling anyone. I couldn't say goodbye to everyone again and I've never worked out how to do it so it has any meaning anyway. I did one last fruitless check around the rooms looking for Antony—and, if I was honest, for Rory—then I took off my hat to avoid notice and melted away.

I felt numb as I walked down the stairs. I'd done all my crying about leaving Sydney already, now I was just charged up to go. And it wasn't until I got out on to the street that I realised Rory Stewart was just about the only person at the party who hadn't asked for my new address in London. So much for him.

When I got home, I set about doing my last little bits of packing, but I was still too keyed up to go to sleep. I was also really furious with Antony for not coming to the party. It was after two a.m., but I was so cross I rang him anyway. I was surprised when he answered the phone. His voice was very slurred.

"Oh, Pussy darling, sorry I couldn't come to your little party. Ring me tomorrow," he said and put the phone down.

I did ring him the next morning. I rang his doorbell repeatedly for a very long time. Eventually a very croaky voice announced: "Whoever you are, fuck off."

"Antony—it's me. Let me in. I am not leaving without saying goodbye to you."

He pushed the buzzer and when I got up to his floor the front door was open but he was back in bed. With his eye mask on. The place was a mess—something I'd never seen before. There was a pizza box on the kitchen counter, full ashtrays, and empty wine and beer bottles everywhere. I jumped onto the bed as hard as I could and bounced up and down until I elicited some kind of reaction—sort of an *uueeueeerrgh* noise.

"Dolores. What's wrong with you? Why didn't you come to my party? Looks like you had a party of your own here . . . Don't you want to hear about it? There's lots of excellent gossip . . ."

He snorted.

"I'm going to tell you anyway. Guess who Plonker Pollock is madly, deeply, passionately in love with?"

"A mirror?"

"No. *Glow*'s editorial assistant, nineteen-year-old Seraphima. He follows her round like a lost puppy. It's pathetic."

He harrumphed in an unimpressed way.

"And Jasper O'Connor is back with Tania. And Liinda Vidovic's new man is a gorgeous Rasta. And Maxine's having a wild affair with one of the shrinks from Debbie's clinic."

He yawned theatrically.

"And there's another passionate love affair. My brother Hamish . . ."

A black eyebrow shot up above the mask.

"Is engaged to . . ."

Up went the other one.

"Debbie Brent!"

I know that would get his attention. He sat up in bed and ripped off the eye mask.

"What? How terrible. How fabulous. Oh my God—when

did that happen? Oh, imagine their children . . . Imagine them in bed together, aaaaaaaah . . ." He fell back onto the pillows. His eyes were all red. He looked terrible.

"Well, it hasn't actually happened yet, but it might, you never know. They look fabulous together." I laid it on with a trowel. "What happened to your eyes, Dolly?"

"Nothing. Tell me more about your brother and the future Mrs. Hamish Abbott. Lucky bitch."

"It's just wishful thinking at this stage, but when you see them together, it just looks right."

"I bet it does—and I suppose Johnny adores him."

"Yep."

"Imagine all of them together . . . It's too much. How divine. How completely sick-making."

"You look pretty sick right now, I must say. What did you get up to last night? Why did you have a party here instead of coming to mine?"

"I didn't have a party here. I spent the evening alone. I can't bear leaving parties. I hope you had a nice time . . ."

I glanced back at all the empty bottles. He'd wasted himself.

"Well, I did have an OK time," I said, slightly mollified. "But it would have been much better if you'd been there. So, are you at least going to come to the airport with me?"

"No. You must go to the airport on your own. Saying goodbye is always unsatisfactory and you'll find it much easier to be brave if you're by yourself. Trust me."

Now I was really pissed off with him and I think it showed. He paused and then continued down even more briskly.

"What you don't understand, Pussy, is that I have a pathological hatred of saying goodbye. I've said it too many times to people I love who will never come back. I can't bear it. It never works. That's why I didn't come last night—and I'm not going to say goodbye to you now either. I'm going to get up and go to the loo and when I come back you will be gone. OK?"

I could see he was serious. I knew there was no point in arguing with Antony once he'd made one of his proclamations, but I still couldn't believe he was behaving like this. Did a year of friendship mean nothing to him?

"OK," I said, with a big sigh. "But before I do my Captain Oates act—I may be gone some time, etc—I want to ask you to do one favour for me."

He raised one of those eloquent eyebrows.

"Rory Stewart came to the party, but he didn't ask for my number in London. Everybody else did. I know he could ask Billy, or Debbie, for it but I want him to know that I want him to have it. Would you ring him and give it to him? Here's his number."

I thrust a piece of paper at him. He ignored it.

"No," said Antony firmly, and then he got up and walked out the French window, across the roof garden and into the bathroom, slamming the door behind him.

And that was the last I saw of Antony Maybury. But as I turned to take one final look at his apartment before closing the door, I noticed a photograph in a silver frame on the bedside table that hadn't been there before. It was of him and me, at the Cointreau Ball.

Lots of people rang up offering to drive me to the airport, but I decided to take Antony's advice. It is easier to be brave when you're by yourself. So I told them all that he was taking me and we wanted to be alone and, to be on the safe side, I said I was leaving two hours later than I really was, in case any of them were planning a last-minute surprise farewell. Antony was right. Better to make a clean break.

Finally the time came to go. I said goodbye to my little flat, picked up my few bags—I'd given away all the homey stuff I'd acquired—and went downstairs to find a taxi. Every moment of that ride to the airport was impossibly charged with emotion and memories.

Up through Victoria Street, Darlinghurst, where I'd drunk so many lattes. Past the Albury, where Antony, Betty and Trudy had taken me to see a drag show. Past the Grand Pacific Blue Room, where I'd downed so many cocktails. Look—there was a gum tree. There was a frangipani. There was the clear blue sky. Oh Sydney. Oh Australia. When would I see it all again?

So much for being stronger on my own. By the time I reached International Departures I was weeping solidly. Fortunately I was so early for my flight there was no one there to see me, except for a kind man who materialised next to me at the counter and handed me a clean white cotton hanky.

It was Rory Stewart.

"I don't believe it," I said, grabbing the hanky. "I always bump into you by chance, when I'm making a total prat of myself."

"That's what you think. Chance can be carefully contrived you know, Georgia."

I looked at him, bewildered.

"We've only met by accident once," he continued. "The first time."

"But I've bumped into you loads of times—at the rodeo, at the hospital, at Michael and Cordelia's, at the races, at Debbie's clinic . . ."

He was shaking his head and smiling.

"All carefully staged, Georgia. I knew you were going to the rodeo. I just hung around until I found you. Billy told me you were going to be at Cordelia's party—except he told me you'd be alone—and Debbie told me you were going to the races. Then Jenny let me know when you'd be at the hospital—and the clinic—so that I could accidentally turn up at the same time. And Antony Maybury told me you were going to be at this check-in desk right now."

I stared at him like a halfwit. Antony. My dear darling Dolly.

"Is that how you knew I was on QF1?" I asked.

He nodded.

My mind was still racing. "But what about that time at your parents' house? You seemed pretty surprised to see me then."

He made a face. "Yes, you're right. That was a surprise. There were several surprises that night. Let's just say you were the pleasant one, OK?"

I stood there looking at him, trying to take it all in. I was expecting him to leave at any moment, based on his usual form.

"Well," I said eventually. "Lucky you're here, because now I can give you my bloody phone number, even though you've never asked me for it."

I scrabbled around in the bag at my feet for one of Antony's new address cards to give him. Rory bent down and stopped me, pulling me up.

"I don't need your address, Georgia."

What was wrong with this man? Did he have some kind of phobia about telephones?

"And I don't need your phone number—because I'm coming with you."

He kicked something and I looked down and saw he had two suitcases by his feet. He pulled a ticket out of his back pocket and slapped it onto the counter next to mine.

"Two seats—next to each other, please," he said to the girl behind the desk.

I just gawped at him.

"But what about the farm and your parents and Scooby and everything?"

"You've always said I do things for other people, so I've

finally decided to do something for myself. I've got a place at the Royal College of Art in London. And you don't have to worry about the farm—Dad's relieved I'm going." He laughed. "He says I'm the worst farmer he's ever come across and he'll be glad to have my sour puss off the place. They've hired your brother Hamish to manage it for them—and he's promised me he'll take good care of Scoobs."

I was still binking at him like a goldfish.

"Rory, I'm so happy for you, it's great that you can go back to your painting," I said.

He laughed again and put his hands on my shoulders.

"You still don't get it, do you, Georgia? I'm coming to London to be with you."

He was right. I couldn't take it in.

"But I still don't understand. Why didn't you tell me any of this before? You've never even asked me for my phone number, and you've had so many opportunities."

"Does it really matter?"

"Yes."

"OK. At first I couldn't because you were sort of Billy's squeeze, and then I wanted to but you'd seen me with, er, another woman and I didn't want you to think I was some kind of a playboy. Plus you were with that plonker fellow and I didn't think you were interested. And then I read an article in *Glow* called something like 'Phone Torture.' It was about women who give men their phone numbers and then wait in agony for the men to call them—and I decided I was never going to do that to you."

He stopped and held my face in his hands, looking at me the same way he had on that hilltop at Welland.

"Because I love you."

And then he did kiss me.